LESLIE WARDWELL

A Sumner falls affair

A Murder Mystery Novel

Book Cover and Interior Design Copyright © 2026 by Laura Boyle Designs.

Weston Heights Press.
westonheightspress@gmail.com.

Library of Congress Cataloging-in-Publication Data:
ISBN: 979-8-9927644-3-7 (ebook)
ISBN: 979-8-9927644-4-4 (paperback)
ISBN: 979-8-9927644-5-1 (hardcover)

First Edition

ALSO BY LESLIE WARDWELL

He Is Just Away

For Evelyn, who was always a gentle, introverted soul, who shared her memories through daily journaling. For over fifty years, her honest, heartfelt, and sometimes raw words revealed her deepest emotions and created a lasting legacy for generations to come.

To Matthew and Marie Kaspar, the sweetest, most caring souls who will always be true saints to our family.

Prologue

Officer Richard Poole—known as Dick to everyone in the bucolic, riverside Vermont town of Sumner Falls—drew his service weapon and kept it aimed at the floor near Charles Stanstead's feet. "Charlie, I need you to put down the rifle and relax… c'mon now, you know me."

Charles hesitated, flicking his eyes across the dimly lit bedroom toward his daughter, Cynthia. Chaotic dust drifted in the stale air as she rubbed her nose.

Richard didn't want to alarm the girl more than she already was, trembling at the sight of the dead man sprawled across her parents' bed, her wrists curled under her face in a self-protective pose. "Just set it down and let's see if we can sort this all out. What do you say, Charlie? I need you to think about your family. Haven't they seen enough for one night?"

Charles nodded once, looked away from his daughter, and focused on Richard's gun. "I thought you said we were friends?"

"We are, Charlie. I'm just here trying to figure out what happened tonight."

"Well, what do you think happened? I defended my family!"

Richard didn't flinch, his attention fixated on the small rifle held upright in Charles Stanstead's hand. He remained rigid as Charles stepped toward the bed, leaning in toward the dead man's face. An entry wound appeared to be through an eye socket, and blood had soaked an expanding area of the top sheet, leaving the pillowcase untouched. He stopped Charles before he placed the rifle near the victim. "Not there," he instructed. "Lean it in the corner behind you or lay it on the floor." Pressing his finger against the revolver's trigger guard, he added, "Slowly."

Richard Poole had never fired his service weapon while on duty. This was the first time he had unholstered it, and he wavered, trying to remember whether he had loaded it that morning before leaving home and running into Charles at the Ascutney Market for coffee.

Charles slowly squatted, his descent measured in inches. The tension was suffocating as his knees popped while he placed the bolt-action rifle on the hardwood floor—his eyes locked on the dead man's face, whom he would later admit to shooting in defense of his wife's honor.

"Next, I need you to step back, kneel, and put your hands on your head. I have to cuff you, Charlie, you know that. Let's not make this any worse than it already is."

Charles Stanstead dropped to his knees, obeying each of Richard's commands, his gaze never leaving the dead man they both recognized. After all, it was a rural town with fewer than a thousand residents. "I say again, Dick, I thought we were friends?"

Richard holstered his revolver and snapped the cuffs onto Charles's wrists behind his back. He then helped the man to his feet, whispering in his ear, "Yeah, we know each other, Charlie. Everyone in town knows each other—but we're not fishing buddies, that's for sure."

"Point taken. But we both know Ray," Charles said, nodding toward the body on the bed. He turned to his daughter. "Cindy, sweetheart, go to the kitchen and check on your mother." In French, he added, "Dis pas un mot—do you hear me? Pas un seul mot." *Don't say a word—not a single word.*

The young girl, with her thin, straight black hair damp with sweat at her temples, looked up at Richard, her eyes seeking his permission to leave the room.

"It's okay, Cynthia, go ahead. Just show me your hands first," he told her.

"For chrissakes, Dick, she's only twelve! And her hands are right in front of her face!"

Richard jostled the cuffs, silencing him.

Cynthia Stanstead lowered her hands, rubbing them against the folds of her nightshirt imprinted with tiny dinosaurs as she stood up from her crouched position by the far wood-paneled wall in her parents' modest, rented Cape Cod.

"What did you say to her?" Richard asked. "You said something to her in French."

"I told her not to worry… Don't worry."

Richard checked her shirt for any blood that the state police would need to identify. Satisfied, he motioned for her to leave the room. "Go ahead, but stay behind me and keep close to the wall."

After she slipped past him and out of the bedroom, Richard used his foot to slide the rifle along the floor, placing it behind Charles without losing his grip on the cuffs. "I have to place you under arrest, Charlie. We'll sort this all out in due time, but for now, you, Ginny, and Cindy will be taken upstreet and booked—if necessary. I'll have more questions for you there. The state boys will get here when they can, but we'll need everyone out of the house to process the scene and remove the bodies."

"C'mon, it was self-defense, Dick, I already told you that!" Charles half-heartedly shrugged, not putting much effort into his act of defiance. "Can't you just let Ginny go to her mother's with Cindy?"

"Not happening tonight, Charlie, and you know why," Richard said as he escorted him out of the bedroom, past the bathroom, and into the kitchen, where another officer was taking a statement from Charles's wife, Virginia—known to everyone in town as Ginny.

Cynthia clung tightly to her mother, wrapping her arms around Virginia's generous waist and pressing her face into her side.

Richard nudged Charles toward the sink, and they both stepped around the woman's body. Blood seeped from one of her ears, trickling under her chin and down her neck before pooling on the checkered linoleum.

"You see, Charlie, I'm having trouble understanding why Vera is lying here dead on the kitchen floor. Did you shoot her before you shot Ray?"

"I told you, it was self-defense." Charles stared at his wife, their eyes wide with shock, as their daughter, trying to crawl under her mother's blouse to hide her head, buckled at the knees.

There were two homicides in Vermont in 1964, both occurring inside the Stanstead household on a muggy late August evening. Ray Whittman was killed in the ground-floor back bedroom by a gunshot to the head, with the bullet entering through his orbital socket. His new bride, Vera, née Flynn, who owned the house the Stansteads were renting at the time, was found dead in the kitchen with a fatal head wound caused by a bullet entering her left ear canal. Autopsies confirmed that both victims were killed with a small-caliber weapon. The recovered cranial lead bullet fragments were too damaged for ballistic comparison with the rifle found in Charles Stanstead's possession. Officer Richard Poole testified under oath that he witnessed this and that no other weapons were found at the scene. Search warrants and witness statements turned up nothing conclusive. Fingerprints from all three Stanstead family members were found on the gun. Charles Stanstead later confessed to the killings and pleaded guilty by reason of insanity. He served a two-year sentence at the state mental hospital in Burlington, while the rustic New England town of Sumner Falls buried another secret.

PART I

The Family

Eva's Daily Reminder 1963: January 1, Tuesday

Got up 8:45 AM. ZERO.

Lots of snow. 8 to 12 inches of new snow fell yesterday.

Bright, sunny, cold day.

Took care of the rest of the Xmas things.

Cleaned the dining room. Did a load of washing and ironed two loads when I came home. Darn hose on the vacuum cleaner is on the fritz.

Sam absent—up to Ray Whittman's radioing.

Had dinner over at Al's—ham, scalloped potatoes, shrimp, cabbage salad, jellied salad, cornbread, grape nut pudding with whipped cream—Good!

Al did my hair.

Dad and I played cribbage—skunked but I won the rubber.

Connie and Warren out for the evening.

Connie all packed and ready to go back to college. Made her deviled food squares to take.

One Blue Jay.

1

Before heading into town on the first workday of her forty-sixth year, Eva Martin needed to toss a load of clothes into the laundry—whether they were dirty or not—and decide whether to wash her bedroom curtains or mop the kitchen floor, including behind the fridge. Tomorrow, she could start on the living room curtains, mop the bathroom floor, finish the living room on Friday, and then move to the dining room before sweeping the cellar over the weekend.

She reached a compromise: she washed only one bedroom curtain and mopped the kitchen floor, including the narrow space behind the fridge, before heading uptown to the shoe store, where she managed the window displays.

The two-and-a-half-mile drive north through the fertile Connecticut River Valley wasn't long enough to feel the heat from the floorboard vents in her Volkswagen Beetle. She reached down, feeling for the vent lever near her feet, and briefly took her eyes off the plow-scraped road, drifting toward the center double yellow line.

An approaching Sumner Falls police cruiser flashed its headlights at her.

She clenched the steering wheel and fought the urge to look in the rearview mirror, ignoring her cold feet and flexing her numb toes until she finally checked the road behind her. When the cruiser disappeared around the bend, she took a deep breath, hoping it was Richard Poole giving her some slack. He liked to park along the road, partway up McSwains' driveway, partly hidden, where he would sit and watch for morning speeders before heading south to grab a cup of coffee at the Ascutney Market.

The remaining drive was peaceful as she passed the McSwains' floodplain cornfields, cattle, and goats. She was eager for the snow to melt and the river ice to break up so she could get a head start on gathering spring fiddleheads and dandelion greens.

Parking was available on both sides of Main Street, with only a few vehicles in front of the Sumner Falls Diner. The fire station, which also housed the police offices, looked quiet, as did the fronts of the Congregational church, J.J. Newberry's, and the pharmacy.

Eva eased to the side of the street, stopping along the curb beyond the shoe store across from Western Auto. She released the turn signal, not wanting to risk being pinched by a younger, overzealous officer for an illegal lane change, then stepped out to check her footing on the road for black ice. Satisfied that the town had cleared the asphalt overnight, she smoothed her plaid skirt of wrinkles and closed the car door, leaving it unlocked as usual. (Small-town folks didn't bother locking their doors or vehicles.)

Inside Merrill's Shoe Store, her coworker Faye Stevens was already opening the boxes of new shoes that Merrill had brought up from downstairs. The store opened in two hours, and Eva still needed to make the coffee. "I see you two couldn't wait to get started," she said, walking behind the register to hang her coat and straighten her skirt again. She checked her saddle shoes for road salt or dirt, peeking over her shoulder at her soles.

"Good morning, you're fine, dear," Faye said. "I already made coffee. I couldn't sleep, knowing we had to swap out the Christmas stock for the new stuff. Can you believe it's 1963 already?" She looked toward the front door. "And I have no idea if today will be slow or busy, but a couple of hours should give us enough time, at least, to redo the windows."

Eva poured herself a mug of Folgers from the percolator Merrill kept on the nook table behind the register and sipped it black, without sugar. "We shall see, won't we? I'll arrange, and you keep opening boxes?" she suggested, knowing Faye understood that the front window arrangements were her domain and the interior shelving was Faye's area.

Merrill Martindale emerged from the basement, carrying two more containers boxes. Eva guessed these were the last, as Merrill usually carried three. He and his wife, Carolyn, bought the shoe store in 1957, transforming it from a telephone operator's hub—a job he was more suited for: being heard, not seen. His thinning gray hair was mussed atop his tall, lanky frame, with a loose necktie and Ben Franklin glasses balanced on a nose that looked almost feminine. "Good morning, Eva," he said, carrying the last boxes labeled 'Shoe Boots' toward the front. Before dropping them haphazardly on the stack, he added, "I have both of your paychecks from last week. We hit our numbers, so there's an extra $100 bonus for both of you."

Eva slipped past Faye, giving him a quick hug. "Thanks. You're the best boss ever," she told him before discreetly straightening the two boxes, aligning their corners with her fingers. She traced the label and looked at Merrill.

"Oh, let's mark those $14.99," he said.

Eva opened the top box and took out a pair of girls' leather shoe boots with square toes, thick soles, short chunky heels, and an inside zipper that closed at the ankle. "I guess these really are both a shoe and a boot, but oh my… $14.99? What these kids will pay for these days is beyond me."

Merrill faced Faye, patting her on the shoulder. "A new generation of kids. That's how we make our numbers." He pointed to the remaining boxes around Faye. "The rest of the usual new stuff, let's mark it as $2.99 and $4.99 and call it a New Year's Sale. I'll leave it up to you gals to decide what goes on the floor shelves and what goes on the wall."

Faye nodded and gave the remaining boxes another once-over before she said, "I think we have time for another coffee."

Eva took it as an announcement rather than a question and picked up her mug. "Still good. I haven't had a chance to take a sip yet. But, go right ahead," she said, gesturing toward the back.

She had known Faye for six years, working with her at the store since she first started. She also knew Faye's daughter, who was about Connie's age, but they moved in different circles. Now that Connie was attending Champlain College, Faye and her husband showed little interest in socializing with Eva and her husband, Sam. Faye wasn't a golfer, and neither she nor her husband hunted or fished. They lacked hobbies that involved drinking—what most folks around here would call teetotalers.

Eva worked on the front window display and finished before her coffee got cold. Since she was a few inches taller than Faye, she offered to help with the remaining wall of women's slippers, and they completed both tasks shortly after opening, before the first customer arrived.

Alice Fairbanks, Eva Martin's closest friend and neighbor, strolled into Merrill's, clutching her overcoat at the neck—its forest green wool matching well with her masculine black rubber galoshes. She owned and operated the town's beauty salon next door to the shoe store and was Eva's home hairdresser, as well as Connie's, when she was home from school. Her husband had passed away two years ago, leaving her with enough monthly dividend income that she didn't really need to run the salon, but staying at home as a widow and watching her flower gardens grow wasn't a fulfilling social routine. Besides, she needed someone else at her salon to keep her silver bouffant styled. "Are you and Sam stopping in for supper tonight?" she asked Eva.

Eva would have loved to say yes, but her parents wanted to see Connie before she went back to school. "I already promised my parents we'd have supper with them so they could see Connie off," she said, noticing Alice's pursed lips. "If Sam goes out radioing again with Ray, I'll stop by afterward for a Drambuie."

Alice's face twisted into a suspicious scowl. "Why's he spending so much time running around with Ray Whittman?"

"I dunno, to tell the truth. He's been doing this ham radio thing for twenty-five years. It's all about his buddies being on the air. They claim to talk all over the world, I guess. And about what?" Eva waved off her question.

Alice huffed, scowling deeper. "Seems a bit too much, don't you think?"

"What are you going to do?" Eva asked. It was her turn to purse her lips and furrow her brow, contemplating all the lost evenings since Sam had convinced one of his younger cronies to take his amateur radio test. With no yard work this winter besides snow blowing, Sam had been spending so much free time upstairs with his radio equipment that she finally told him to move his bed up there. At least then, he wasn't waking her up at night whenever he came home from Ray's—radioing or talking about all the gear they wanted to buy or trade for. This year marked their twenty-sixth anniversary, a milestone that seemed like a lifetime since they were inseparable, playing and winning local golf championships, with the radio hobby never interfering.

Alice, who was shorter than Eva, peered over the top of her silver-studded cat-eye glasses and glanced up at Eva's short, tousled black hair, then asked, "About due for a color and perm?"

"I suppose," Eva answered honestly. Her friend had been cutting, perming, and blowing out her hair for years since she and Sam bought their first house in a quiet neighborhood south of town, bringing Eva's aging parents from New Hampshire to live next door. Their friendship had grown so close that they took turns hosting dinners, evening drinks, and cribbage games, sandwiched between weekly hair days.

Alice fastened her coat at the collar with one gloved hand and hooked her bag in the crook of her other elbow. "Faye, nice to see you. And Merrill?" she asked, glancing toward the back of the store, unable to see past Eva and Faye in her heelless galoshes.

"Oh, he's probably gone downstairs for something," Eva said.

"I'll see you tonight then."

As Alice turned to leave the store, Eva slipped past her and pushed open the glass door, letting the scolding air rush in. When she let the door swing inward, she nearly shut it on Officer Poole as he stepped into view. He backed away, steadying his paper cup of coffee, and threw her a chastising glare before settling into a familiar Bing Crosby smile.

"Sorry, Dick—officer," she corrected herself. "Thank you," she added, maintaining eye contact until he nodded and turned away. Feeling guilty, she asked, "Refill your coffee?"

He glanced over his shoulder. "We're all good, Eva," he said, raising his cup. "You have a nice day," he added, then continued walking up the street, making his rounds.

"I can never tell if he's ornery or just looks mean," Faye said, sneaking up behind Eva and causing her to startle.

"I've seen him smile at town events. He's human, Faye. Just takes his job seriously. Though I think he doles out more warnings than tickets."

• • •

The store didn't meet its numbers for the day, but Eva was better when she came home to find not only her husband washing the road salt off his Chevrolet truck, but also her mother having ironed the laundry, including the bedroom curtains. It was so nice to have her folks living next door, always surprising her whenever a chore needed doing. Her dad had shoveled the back walkways and around the bird feeders, clearing a path for Sam to refill them before dinnertime—the grosbeaks and cardinals would be pleased.

"Dad cleared out the feeders. Maybe you can refill the suet before supper? Those darn squirrels keep cleaning us out," she said, standing firm and watching him dry his bucket of bolts with a lambskin chamois that had belonged to his father. She would do it, but she couldn't reach the standalone feeders.

Years ago, he jerry-rigged one T-shaped end of an old iron pipe clothesline into a standalone feeder pole, painted it black to stand out against the snow, and equipped it with hanging seed feeders and small cages filled with his unpatented mix of peanut butter, suet, and seed—most of which fed the gray squirrels and blue jays. (It would be a few more years before he learned to cover the poles with tin domes to prevent the squirrels from climbing.)

"We're having dinner at Mom and Dad's with Connie and Warren," she reminded him, dreading how soon the house would be empty. *Oh, how she would miss her so.* "I guess she's all packed and ready to go."

"I took the day off tomorrow, and I planned on taking her back," he said, twisting and squeezing the water out of the chamois. He used it to dry his hands before kicking over the rinse bucket and dumping it down the basement floor drain.

The house was built on an elevated bank facing the street, with a basement garage entrance between concrete retaining walls, where Sam Martin finished drying his pickup. "Fine." He snapped the chamois and shook it open. "I'll swap places with the cars so we can get an early start for Burlington. I'll wash yours, too, before cleaning up."

Eva stood and stared at her husband, not wanting to argue. He was turning fifty this March, and he was always cranky around his birthday—never failed. She loved him deeply and knew this mood would pass once he could get outside to weed the flowerbeds, mow the lawn, and tend to his vegetable garden. His gray hair was thinning, and he kept what was left combed straight over the top. But with his recent promotion from draftsman to blueprint manager and the 7 a.m. clock-ins, she wondered whether the $100 monthly raise was worth the added stress. Now, with late nights out and radioing, she was eating dinner alone more often and having drinks with Alice. "Can't it wait?" she asked him. "I'd like the feeders filled before it gets too dark, and then get washed up for supper. They'll be here any minute."

He threw the chamois into the rinse bucket, which was too light to make a sound, making him look childish. It was always his way or the highway, so she ignored him, climbed the cellar stairs, and let him fret. Her strength was never to argue or engage; instead, she let her emotions spill onto the pages of her daily journal, writing as she attended to her morning or bedtime ablutions.

• • •

Eva's parents, Henry and Ruby Fischer, were in their early seventies. They decided to leave their small farm on the Granite State side of the Connecticut River to move closer to their youngest daughter and granddaughter. Living next door, they enjoyed their retirement. Eva's two older brothers had joined the military—Benjamin in the Navy, settling near San Diego, and Donald in the Army, who moved to Alaska and lost touch. Eva was always closer to her big brother Benjamin, affectionately known as Big Ben because of his six-foot-six-inch stature. Neither of them got along with their middle brother, even as kids. Eva had written 'good riddance' in her journals.

When she and Sam entered through her parents' back mudroom, her father was sitting in his usual evening spot, reclining in his cushioned chair tucked under the stairwell leading to the upstairs bedrooms, which were used to store Ruby's knitting and sewing supplies or when Big Ben came to visit. Henry was reading the paper, lit by an accordion lamp mounted on the wall—his corncob pipe unlit inside the house. It only left his lips when he was eating or sleeping, and if it weren't for Ruby, he'd probably sleep with it, truth be told. Ruby, dressed in her daily uniform: a floral house dress, a deep-pocket apron, nylons, and wide black orthopedic shoes, busied herself preparing dinner. Her silver cat-eye glasses matched Eva's, which were black, and she took them off, letting them hang around her neck while she wiped her large hands on her apron. If she had arthritis, she didn't let it bother her while baking bread, hermit cookies, or cider doughnuts every day. Everyone shared the goods. Her hands resembled boxer Sonny Liston's from kneading dough every day.

Eva slipped through the kitchen and kissed her father on his cheek. "Howdy doody," she said, turning to look into the front room to see if Connie and Warren were already there, but they weren't, giving her stomach a butterfly dip. They would be there any minute because Connie wouldn't miss a game of cribbage with her grandfather.

The kitchen table, with its ends folded down, was set for two, but Sam was already pulling it apart to insert the leaf before Eva even asked. She grabbed the first of four extra chairs stored on the enclosed side porch. It wasn't wide enough to be a sunroom, only big enough to hold a few short bookcases for Ruby's cookbooks (all of which were now memorized), extra dishes, and a few token spider plants to add some greenery. As she lifted the last chair, there was a single knock on the front door, followed by the storm door being pulled open—its spring and metal hinges squealing against the frost.

Connie stepped inside, five feet ten inches tall, and hugged her mother. "Good to see you, Mummy," she said.

Eva loved that her nearly nineteen-year-old daughter kept calling her Mummy. Sometimes, she couldn't help but feel younger when she heard it. "Howdy doody, to you too," she said, noticing Connie's new look. "I'm so glad you finally picked up your new glasses before leaving. I hope they work out." Giving Connie an extra squeeze, she acknowledged her daughter's boyfriend. "Nice to see you too, Warren," she said, giving him a pat on the arm. "Got any more cuts or scars to show off?" she asked, scanning him from head to toe.

Warren Bradford and Connie were the same age, having graduated from high school last summer. It was only after graduation, when Connie entered and won the 1962 Miss Sumner Falls title, that Warren took notice of her. Whether he noticed her on the dance floor before or after Town

Representative Officer Richard Poole awarded her the trophy, he would never give a definitive answer.

Unlike Connie, who wanted to go to college, Warren stayed in town and took a job as an apprentice butcher at the local Super Duper. On his first day, he slipped and jabbed his thigh with a fillet knife that required three stitches. He limped for about a week, more embarrassed than injured.

"No, Mrs. Martin, not today. You're never going to let that one go, are you?" he asked. "As a matter of fact, I found out today I'm getting more hours and working full-time."

She was grateful that he occasionally visited her at the shoe store during his lunch breaks.

"Good for you. Now let's eat, time's a-wastin'."

In the kitchen, Henry, Ruby, and Sam were already seated, and the table-top was decorated with Hall serving bowls from Ruby's collection and modest Buffalo China place settings. Sam was the first to dig into his favorite dried codfish with white gravy, followed by baked potatoes, succotash, and Eva's apple diddle-de-dum-rum pudding dessert.

Connie rested her hands on her father's shoulders, giving a quick pat, then squeezed her grandfather's neck as she leaned over him with a fierce hug, inhaling the apple tobacco scent in his wool vest. "Gramps," she said. "You doing okay?"

"I was until you nearly choked me unconscious," he said, acting like he couldn't catch his breath. "Isn't it time for you to leave again?"

"Funny. We'll see who's laughing after Mummy and I skunk you later."

Connie and Henry shared a camaraderie that only she could inspire in him, reminiscent of the bond Eva once had when she was much younger. Overall, the apple did not fall far from the tree, and Eva Martin was her father's daughter—both introverted, with still waters running deep.

After Ruby and Connie cleared the dishes, only the sound of Henry's rhythmic puffing remained as he shot Connie and Eva a look that dared—not begged—either to challenge his cribbage skills at not only winning the rubber match but also skunking them to boot.

• • •

The short walk between the houses was crossed by a narrow dirt lane that provided vehicle access to the back of the property lots. Sam would fume if anyone strayed from the one-lane path and sank into his or Henry's grass, especially during the spring mud season when the topsoil was soft and squishy underfoot.

Eva and Sam climbed their back steps and entered the kitchen before any chill set in. Eva muttered to herself, knowing she had cleaned the floor that morning, and wondered why they didn't come in through the cellarway.

"I think I'll go downstairs and watch the Celtics," he told her. "It's Bob Cousy's last season, and they might win it all again this year."

Eva couldn't care less at this time of year. Watching the Red Sox tease during the dog days of late summer with a fan in the living room window was her quiet time, while Sam was too busy outside to pay attention to a Sox season that morphed into dour pessimism, crushing the hearts of all New Englanders.

Sitting downstairs beside the Magee cast iron cooking stove, nestled in his spindled rocking chair with peanut butter and crackers nearby, Sam was content on winter evenings to watch any Celtics or Bruins game. (He had always loved skating as a kid—unsteady if he wasn't holding a hockey stick.)

When Alice finally got her line and called to ask if it was too late to walk over for a Drambuie, Eva told her she had already watched Lawrence Welk and was heading to bed.

2

Sam drove Connie to school after lunch and didn't return until 9:15 p.m. He told Eva that the conditions were bad crossing Mendon Mountain, but Route 7 was clear all the way to Middlebury. He stopped in Rutland on the way home to check out radio receivers he was interested in, but by then she was ready for bed, writing in her journal that she already missed Connie.

She wished he would come clean if he wanted his freedom, instead of sneaking around. Still, she hoped he wouldn't cheat or lie.

When her alarm went off, the house was too quiet for Sam to still be there. He had already left for work. She didn't overthink it and grimaced at the pressure in her kidneys—a sign that the darn things were acting up again. She assumed she had a few pills left from when Dr. Read last refilled her prescription.

Even with a nagging throb in her lower back, she forced herself to stand and take down the other curtain and two loads that needed washing, while reminding herself to mop the bathroom floor before making breakfast. She paused at the top of the basement stairs, listening for any sounds that might prove her wrong, before settling onto the throne to journal the morning's weather. Still, the only sounds heard were the pine kindling crackling in the Magee firebox and the occasional floor joist shifting in the morning frost.

After breakfast, the pills seemed to lighten things up, so she took down the living room curtains, only to realize the windows needed cleaning again. The outside could wait until warmer weather, but she could tackle the inside this weekend after sweeping the cellar floor.

Sam had left a pot of coffee percolating on ole Magee, and she poured herself the black remnants into one of her Hall mugs, inhaling the smoky campfire aroma. The olfactory-triggered memories brought her back to dewy mornings, crawling out of their pup tent on weekend fishing trips to Silver Lake, where she would light the campfire while Sam cooked bacon and fried yellow perch. When a pine sap knot snapped in the firebox, she flinched, squeezing the mug tighter before relaxing her grip to examine its blue thistle pattern. She had been secretly collecting as many pieces as she could find with a similar blueberry pattern, which Alice had once commented on, planning to surprise her with them next Christmas. She and her late husband had been such good friends over the years, and with everything Alice had been doing these past two years since his passing, it was the least she could do to repay her for all she'd done.

Eva went upstairs to get dressed, pausing in the kitchen to finish her coffee. She looked out the double windows above the sink at her bird feeders and watched finches busy pecking at Sam's suet mix, while grosbeaks and blue jays gobbled up the ground feed, along with a lone male cardinal. She reached over the sink to rap her knuckle on the glass to scare off the jays, but stopped herself when she spotted the female cardinal perched in the barren lilac bushes between her and Vera Flynn's property next door.

Vera was standing in her kitchen, waving through the leafless bushes, her dirty blonde hair piled high in a rat's nest. It looked as unkempt as her gaudy, shaker-sided Cape Cod, painted lackluster green. The house had fallen into disrepair over the years since her husband's accident, who had dressed in his wool red-checkered hunting jacket, supposedly cleaning his deer rifle. Whether he tried to make his death look like an accident is anyone's guess, but the problem then was that he pulled the trigger a week before deer season, and it didn't fool anyone. *It takes a special kind of intellect to blow your own head off—accidentally.*

It had happened two years before Eva and Sam bought the house next door, and Vera had already gone back to her maiden name before she carried over and gifted a hefty half-gallon mason jar of mustard pickles to introduce herself. Like the pickles, she was a little tangy around the edges, and her yellow pallor matched her hair.

Eva lifted her coffee mug and smiled enough to be noticed if Vera had been bird watching. She lowered her gaze to where the female cardinal had been, but it was gone, and so was the male. After glancing up at Vera's kitchen window and seeing she was no longer there, Eva knocked on her own window, scattering the blue jays for now.

• • •

It had been a long week, including the holiday. Eva received a letter from Connie, who mentioned she had forgotten her pillow and bedspread. Of all the things to send, it would be a challenge to find a box large enough somewhere in the shoe store's basement, and the postage—*oh my Lordy.* Since she planned to go to the Post Office on Monday, she wrote a reminder note to pay the utility bills at Western Auto. She added groceries to the list and then headed for the stairs to start a load of laundry, dreading the shoe returns that would likely begin on Monday. It was a welcome sight to see that Ruby had already ironed and folded this morning's load.

She barely reached the top step when the phone rang, and Alice hollered for her to come over for a drink and listen to some Guy Lombardo records.

She hadn't even taken her coat off before Alice poured them each a shot of Crème de Menthe—one of their favorites—and then handed her the cutest hand lotion dispenser. What a thoughtful gift from her best friend as they sipped and listened to the sweetest music this side of heaven.

• • •

Sam was already home when she walked back, and he was puzzled by the lotion dispenser. At least, he didn't head downstairs to watch a game. Instead, he returned with a couple of trays of charbroiled cube steaks and offered her the first choice. She was impressed that he remembered the cloth napkins, which he had rolled up and tucked into the small red plastic chicken holders whose yellow-inked chicken decals had chipped and rubbed off years ago. They had bought them on an antiquing trip up in the Northeast Kingdom, when the foliage was at its peak in a riot of color.

She took the smaller portion and sat at the end of the couch near the television.

"They won't be as good as your Swiss steaks, but they'll do in a pinch," he said. "I assumed you were over at Al's, so I went ahead and got started. You want a Schaefer?"

"No, I'm good."

He sat across from her in her wingbacked reading chair, the farthest from the television, and looked out the window.

Eva didn't have much of an appetite. She drifted between cutting the thin, tough steak into smaller-than-bite-sized pieces while keeping one eye on the blank screen and the other on her husband of over twenty-five years, who was washing down his steak with a lager, wondering if he was stepping out on the QT.

"Connie said she forgot her pillow and spread," she told him, nudging pieces of meat around her plate as if she were slowly stirring an Irish stew. "I guess I'll have to mail it on Monday during my lunch hour." She pierced the smallest nugget of pounded beef and hesitated before raising it to her lips. "Unless you think we can drive it up in the morning?" she asked, hopeful.

"I can't," he answered. "I have to go into the shop early and start working half-day Saturdays."

"From now on?" she asked, trying to sound neutral, but her voice nearly broke. Her throat dry, she wished she'd accepted the Schaefer.

"No. 'Course not. We're behind on the new machine tool orders—more than three months behind."

After high school, where he excelled in drafting classes despite low grades in other subjects, Sam was hired by the Sumner Falls Machine Tool Company as a draftsman and Army Reservist. As a creative teenager, he doodled cartoon characters and painted watercolor nasturtiums for his mother. Connie had found these in disrepair, framed them behind glass, and brought them to college to brighten her room with their still-vibrant marigold hues against leafy backgrounds.

Sam turned his attention back to the window, staring. It was during his rise through the ranks of the local Freemasons that Eva knew he learned to keep secrets.

After finishing his steak, he swigged the last of his beer, walked across the living room, and turned on Jack Paar. Together, they sat and watched in silent incertitude before going to bed.

• • •

Warren Bradford stopped by the shoe store during his lunch break. Eva was always happy to see him when he visited while Connie was at school. She wondered if he had figured out her midday routine and was timing his visits to when she brewed a second pot of coffee. It didn't matter to her; he always shared news from Connie.

"Connie called me this morning," he said, greeting her with a light kiss on the cheek. His newly sprouted mustache was thickening, offsetting his nineteen-year-old, prematurely receding hairline, and it tickled her. He was a quiet young man with jet-black hair and dark skin, more olive-toned than red, despite his insistence that his mother told him he was part Native American. It was hard for her to argue after seeing a photo of his young father, who stood taller, with broad shoulders and fists the size of cannonballs, with the same dark hair and skin color. It was one of only two photos that existed; he had passed away at twenty-three, soon after Warren was born, collapsing where he stood from a brain aneurysm before his morning shift at the family lumber mill on this side of Mendon Mountain.

Warren, who lost his father at a young age, while her father was still alive next door and helping out so much, was a soft spot for Eva. She had bonded with him and couldn't wait for the day when he and Connie might marry. "You don't say," she said, embarrassed that she sounded funny, but she realized her quip fell short when he gaped like a caught fish gulping for air. For a moment, she wondered if he, too, was having a spell until he answered, "Yes… she called me this morning and wants to come home this weekend. Her last class on Friday is at eleven."

Eva knew Connie's classes and the marks she received on her first report, but realized she didn't know when her classes were—the days of the week or the times. Knowing how punctual Connie was, it was a darn good guess that she had scheduled all her classes for the morning as early as possible.

"We were going to surprise you," he said. "But if you wanted to ride up with me, then I could pick you up here?"

Not wanting to be a burden and indecisive about leaving her car parked on the street for so long, she stopped herself from making excuses.

"I already have you marked down on the timesheet," Faye shouted from behind the register, holding up a mug with steam tendrils swirling in front of her face that blended with her loose white hair. "Fresh coffee's ready!"

Warren perked up and headed straight for the back of the store, guided by the smell of Folgers. Eva waited until he passed, then shot Faye a fierce look that tried to hide her blush, which was as red as her signature socks peeking above her white-laced navy blue Keds.

Turning away from Faye and facing the front window, she caught a glimpse of Sam as he sped past, heading home from work. It struck her as odd, yet somehow fitting in these aimless times, that he didn't slow down or even glance toward the store to look for her and wave. Even with her quick steps to the door and the cold glass against her palm and cheek, he had already passed the diner and was out of sight. She hoped he had a good reason for rushing home.

• • •

Sam's Chevy wasn't at the house when Eva pulled into the cellar driveway. Her suspicions confirmed, she pushed open the double doors and found the inside parking spot empty. She nearly slipped and fell stepping out of her Beetle, probably spared a bruised tailbone because she left the driver's door open just enough to hold onto the frame with her right hand as she lost her footing. Inside, she cursed herself for not swapping her Keds for snow boots for the ride home.

She had an inkling where he was, but she decided to let the line settle and iron some clothes before calling Ray Whittman. Ever since Ray, who was ten years younger than Sam, joined Sam's radio group last year, it had been all radio, all the time. *Maybe it was infatuation—on both their parts?* One of Sam's many late-night excuses was that he was at Ray's helping him study CW (coded word, layman's term for Morse code). *Whatever the situation of it being, it was all midlife hokum.*

After ironing, folding, and putting away the two loads of laundry from this morning, she picked up the phone. Hearing the line clear, she dialed Ray Whittman's number from Sam's penciled list hanging on the wall next to the phone. She wanted to sound firm, but she took a breath to steady her nerves when a man's voice finally answered after several rings: "Hello?"

"Ray?"

"Speaking. May I ask who's calling?"

"It's Eva, calling." She paused for a few seconds, listening to dead air, then added, "Eva Martin. Is Sam there?"

"Oh… Eva… sure," he stuttered. "Sam's here. We were just—"

"Radioing," she interrupted. "Can I speak to him, please?"

"Actually, he's testing the tubes on my new stereo, but sure… hang on."

Sam constantly tested their television tubes whenever the picture went on the fritz.

Eva heard muffled noises, as if someone were trying to cover the mouthpiece but only halfheartedly.

"Hey, what's up?" Sam asked, taking up the line. At least he sounded sober.

"It's getting on towards suppertime, don't you think?" she asked him.

"I was just about to leave. We were working on his stereo. The tubes were all good, but the stylus needed a little adjustment."

She heard muffled noises again and expected to listen to another excuse when Sam came back on the line. "How about I meet you at the hotel for dinner? My treat."

She was pleasantly disarmed and couldn't recall the last time they went out for seafood.

"Been a long time since you had scallops," he added.

It was true. "Okay, I'll meet you there within the hour. I'll have to change into a nice dress."

"Alright. See you then."

After hanging up and heading to her closet, she changed her mind about wearing a dress and chose a plaid wool skirt and blouse instead, without needing an overcoat. The skirt was one of many she and Connie had made to fit her petite frame. (Dr. Read said her weight of 122 pounds was good during her last checkup.) Her hair would have to stay covered beneath a kerchief, but before tying it under her chin, she hung the other freshly ironed window curtain.

•••

The Sumner Falls Hotel was Eva and Sam's favorite local spot for enjoying fresh seafood during the colder months, when their usual summer hangouts closed for the season. Eva always ordered the broiled bay scallops and watched as Sam dug into the baked scrod. They sat at a cozy side table for two. A few dinner patrons were in the historic, ornately decorated room, and Eva wondered which table the Swedish Nightingale, Jenny Lind, might have sat at a century ago while passing through town by train.

"My treat," Sam said. "Does $14.95 sound about right?"

"That includes both drinks?"

He checked the receipt, scanning it with his trifocals. "Yes."

"Good deal, then," she said, wiping her mouth one last time. Before she stood to leave, she faced him and asked, "How come Ray has a stereo and we don't?" She waited until he left cash on the table and had his attention. "I enjoy listening to Al's records, but her stereo is old and sounds outdated to me. There must be something newer out there that sounds better?"

Sam blinked a few times, lines creasing his forehead. "I suppose I can stop in and take a look around Prescott's."

"It seems like we've bought enough TVs and radios from them over the years—along with the new washer—that they ought to cut us some slack on a new deal, don't you think?"

"Yes, I suppose so. It never hurts to ask, right?"

"I want to listen to music while I'm cleaning, instead of the records that Al plays while we're over at her place."

"Alright, I'll stop in after work tomorrow, then."

Eva wasn't used to getting her way in what seemed like an easy victory. Maybe it was the atmosphere, the good dinner, or perhaps the Manhattans that made this time different—Sam didn't get to make the decision alone, and she wasn't about to push her luck.

"I'll follow you home?" she asked, pressing, so he wouldn't have the gall to find an excuse to return to Ray's.

• • •

As soon as Prescott delivered the new Philco, with an optional reverb feature that Sam had paid an extra $60 for on top of the $395, Eva plugged it in and called Alice to bring over some records.

Alice went a step further and brought along a thermos of whiskey sours.

"I think we'll get enough enjoyment from the stereo to more than pay for itself, and I can't wait for Connie to see this," Eva said. "It's a good thing she's still in school, or else she'd probably take right over. Doesn't it sound lovely?"

"It does." Alice sipped from the thermos cup, refilled it, then handed it to Eva. "Now you'll have to start adding to your collection."

Eva accepted the chilled drink, embarrassed that they were sitting in the living room, sharing road whiskey while pretending to be younger than they were.

"No reason we can't listen and do your permanent now," Alice offered. "And I can do your brush out tomorrow after work."

3

Warren and Eva were making good time on a clear, dry Route 7 outside Pittsford when four white-tailed deer darted out from the right shoulder, barely missing his Corvair. It was Eva's sharp yelp that startled Warren into hitting the brakes after it was too late, and the last of the deer blurred past Detroit's finest in a rolling dash. His squirming in the driver's seat wasn't enough sleight of hand to hide checking his crotch and taking inventory before easing off the gas.

"I think the last one jumped over the hood?" he asked, glancing behind him before stealing a look at Eva.

"You shit your britches or something?" she asked him, catching him red-handed sniffing.

"Hardly." Returning his hands to ten and two, he added, "The last one must have been a buck… clearly bigger than the others."

Eva wasn't about to tease him about his near miss (in his britches) and slow braking, nor challenge his deer knowledge that it was impossible to tell this time of year when bucks hadn't yet started growing antlers. Instead, she said, "Well, it's a good thing, no matter what… We didn't hit any of them, and there's no need to call a wrecker… and *then* get ahold of Connie or Sam to come bail us out."

"Good thing. We're still too far away to walk."

"Ayutt," Eva said, a woman of few words.

The rest of the drive was quiet. Connie greeted them, rushing downstairs from her second-floor room after seeing their arrival through her dorm window. She first hugged Eva, wrapping her arms around her mother's neck and squeezing tightly enough for Eva to sense that something was wrong—more than just her daughter being happy to see them. When Connie's roommate, Catherine Anne, appeared behind them, standing silently with a familiar doe-eyed look, it only confirmed Eva's suspicions.

"What's wrong?" Eva asked Catherine over Connie's shoulder. In the few times Eva had met Catherine during their first semester at Champlain, Catherine was a friendly, well-mannered girl from Waitsfield who had been raised on her family's sheep farm. Her only shortcoming was being a full head shorter than Connie, which is why Eva could only see the top of Catherine's pixie cut as she pressed her chin lower to try to make eye contact.

"You should talk to Mrs. Hubbard, our dorm mother," Catherine said, moving closer and hooking Connie's arm at the elbow. "There's been an… incident."

Young men like Warren Bradford often struggle to understand contentment, anger, and jealousy. When he stepped forward, Eva broke free from Connie's grip. His fists clenched, and his face was tense, neither of which Eva wanted the girls to notice. She stopped him with an outstretched hand, then made room to embrace both girls. "Did anyone get hurt? Is everyone okay?" she asked.

"We are now, Mummy," Connie answered, finally reaching for Warren's hand and linking the four of them in a prayer circle. "I'm still coming back. We're staying in school," she said, gently pulling Catherine closer to her side. "It's over now, but you should still talk to—"

"What *exactly* is over now?" Eva interrupted. "I don't like the sound of this." She took a step back and inspected her daughter, searching for any signs of injury as if she were still a toddler who had fallen off her bike in the backyard and scraped her knee.

"There was an intruder," Catherine said. "A man came into the dorm during the night, but plenty of girls on the first floor were still awake and screamed. I guess all the doors opening and slamming must've scared him away."

Eva placed her hand over her heart, took a deep breath of the crisp Adirondack air blowing across the landlocked fjord that was now Lake Champlain. "Constance!" she coughed, trying to clear the dryness in her chest.

Warren moved to separate the girls and hugged Connie. "Why wasn't the front door locked?" he asked.

Eva examined the girls' faces, unsure of what to do next. "Where's Mrs. Hubbard now?"

Connie took the lead, answering, "She was in her room on the first floor near the kitchen earlier… she still looked pretty shook up the last time I saw her."

Warren placed his palm on Connie's cheek and gently tilted her face to make eye contact. "When did this happen?"

"Two nights ago."

"Did anyone call the police?"

"I saw a patrol car drive by yesterday afternoon," Catherine said, nodding toward Willard Street. "So I guess Mrs. Hubbard must've called someone."

"So it's been handled," Connie said. "Let's not say anything to Dad or pester Mrs. Hubbard tonight."

Eva wasn't convinced it had been handled, and she planned to discuss it with Sam. Somehow, she'd have to find a way to get past his temper. "Okie dokie," she said with a disingenuous smile. "Let's get a move on, shall we? We'll talk about this later when we're home."

"Can it at least wait until tomorrow?"

"Of course."

"Can Catherine come home with us? Please? It's just for the weekend."

No one noticed Warren huffing silently.

Eva predicted how Sam would react when she told him that a stranger had nearly assaulted his only daughter. It was too risky, and there would be other opportunities for Catherine to visit. "Maybe next time."

"That sounded more like a decision and not a question," Connie said.

Catherine eased the tension. "It's no problem, really. Next time." She gestured over her shoulder. "Lots of girls will still be here. Plenty of us have strong lungs… and we practice. No one's getting into the house again, that's for sure."

Eva itched to get home and do a load of laundry. She also wanted to start cleaning the inside of the kitchen cabinets. All of this anxiety made her doubt the young girl's facetiousness. "That's not funny, Catherine."

"Not funny, Catherine," Warren added.

Connie faced her new best friend and roommate, slipping both her hands and fingers into Catherine's rich, henna-colored hair. "I thought you were funny. It lightened the mood," she said, kissing the shorter girl's imperfect nose. "I'll see you Sunday night."

They made good time driving back to Sumner Falls, with Connie stretched out across the Corvair's backseat.

And no critter crossings either.

• • •

There was no further discussion about the dormitory intruder during the remaining drive south until Warren dropped them off at the cellar entrance and drove away. Once Eva was sure he had turned the corner and the Covair's rear-engine thrum had faded, she turned to Connie and said, "Let's go inside and start supper, and afterward we'll talk more about this with your father."

Eva followed Connie past the crackling warmth of the Magee, appreciating the coziness it brought to the cellar and how it warmed the floors in winter. Sam appreciated that it kept furnace oil costs down. However, it was a chore to keep the sawdust swept up and the alcove of bagged pine faggots stocked—gathering was Eva's responsibility.

Stepping on the bottom stair, she couldn't help but glance into the washroom. Where there had once been only a single GE washing machine, Sam had since expanded the space around it and added a large soapstone sink, allowing them to clean the dishes after eating downstairs without hauling everything up to the kitchen. Sam did all the plumbing himself without help (unless having Ray stand around and hover counted as help). He even installed a few clothes-drying lines strung between the floor joists and a simple open cubby beneath the sink to store a few pots and pans, which she had decorated with a lovely linen curtain. Coffee mugs hung on a pegboard beside the washing machine.

Even while climbing the steps, Eva couldn't help but think about the storage space under the staircase, with all its canning jars stacked haphazardly and loose containers of bird seed that attracted mice. She'd better ask Sam to dig out his traps and set a few. He'd probably pitch a fit about wasting some of his precious Skippy peanut butter to bait them.

Entering the upstairs kitchen, Eva expected to see him there noshing on his crackers, but he wasn't, and she didn't see him in the backyard either. "Sam?" she called out.

Connie stepped into the front living room. "Dad?" She moved to the upstairs doorway and peered up. "Dad?" she asked louder. "Are you up there on the radio? Come down now, it's time to make supper." In the kitchen, she told Eva, "He's not upstairs."

Eva saw his truck parked in its usual spot off the lane, behind the house. "Oh, he's probably over at Al's or your grandparents'. I'll call over there in a minute as soon as I light a fire."

Connie headed upstairs to her bedroom while Eva lit the edges of the kindling and watched as the yellow flames spread across the paper, turning blue as they reached the pine twigs and started to snap and spit. She closed the mesh curtain and stared at the smoke tendril wafting from the burnt match, wondering why Sam hadn't already lit the fire when he came home from work. She parted the screen, tossed the matchstick into the flames, and decided to call her parents.

When Eva picked up their only wall phone, hanging between the kitchen and bathroom, she saw Sam through the kitchen window across the yard and replaced the receiver—her grip not strong enough (though she tried) to pull it down and off the wall.

Sam was on a ladder next door, chopping ice off Vera's roof.

Eva shuffled to the sink, glancing past her empty feeders. The heavy hatchet pounding on the tin flashing kept the yard devoid of wildlife. When Vera entered her kitchen with a dish towel draped over her shoulder, Eva muttered, "What in the world?" She watched as Vera lifted a plate from the sink, dried it, and placed it on a rack off to the side. Eva lowered her chin. *Why isn't there a rug here in front of the sink? Too hard to clean. He wouldn't do this to her or Connie.* When she dared to look across the yards again, Vera was wringing her hands. Sam climbed down the ladder, his legs partially visible through her window. Vera waved, and Eva wasn't sure if Vera was waving to him or her.

"I see him," Connie said, popping into the kitchen and startling Eva. "He's next door up on a ladder…" She trailed off, noticing her mother standing at the window. "Want me to run over and get him?"

"No. That's fine. You'd better stay inside. No need to risk catching a cold." Eva turned her back to the window and smiled at her daughter. "How about chicken stew with biscuits and corn? You start peeling the potatoes downstairs while I toss a couple of logs on the fire."

"Green beans? Do you have any French-style in the freezer?"

"You betcha."

After Connie went downstairs, Eva glared straight toward Vera's house, expecting to see Sam in her kitchen, but he was crossing the yard with his ladder.

Vera's lights were out.

● ● ●

"I think we should involve the police," Eva told Sam between spoonfuls of stew. She had taken a second helping, smaller than Sam's, after sending Connie upstairs with her dessert. The two pieces of thigh meat needed to last through the rest of the conversation, so she pushed them around her bowl while waiting for his answer. "And I think we should call Mrs. Hubbard tomorrow morning… as soon as possible. I don't want to wait until we bring Connie back." Her tone was sharp. Connie's brush with danger stayed with her, along with wondering if Vera was having immoral sights on Sam.

"Oh, don't you worry," he said, dunking a biscuit in his broth and forking a piece of chicken onto it before slurping it into his mouth. "I mean to give her the business. There's no need for what happened… and it needs addressing."

The firebox popped, but neither of them was startled, as they were accustomed to having two fires burning in the house for nearly nine months of the year. April could be warm or cold; snow on green leaves during the first weekend of May was not unusual, and the humid dog days disappeared overnight in late August.

Eva watched Sam eat, switching between spoonfuls of stew and sips of Narragansett at their makeshift cellar dining table, built to seat three. It seemed like only yesterday he had made Connie's first scrambled egg and toast breakfast before sending her out to catch the school bus.

Under the warm glow of a small dome light, aided by a candle long since melted over the neck of an empty Chianti bottle they had shared somewhere in Boston's North End, she could see the crow's feet around his eyes and began to count them in time with her heartbeat. His birthday was two months away, but at only forty-nine and active all day, his thin frame, face, and receding hair made him look almost ten years older. *There was no way a woman as young as Vera would want to have anything to do with that.*

He looked down at her bowl, took his last sip of beer, and asked, "Full?"

"Pretty much," she said, forcing herself to finish the last piece of dark meat. "Game on tonight?"

"Not tonight… no. I think I'll try to work 80 meters. See how far I can reach out west." He shook his empty beer can, appearing indifferent, and set it down. "I've been helping Ray study for his general class operator's license, and I haven't decided yet if I want to go for my extra class. That would let me operate on the 160-meter band."

All this talk about radioing and Ray made her wonder if they'd ever find the time to go fishing again. She took a deep breath. "I suppose that means more wires strung between the houses?"

"Well, if I passed the extra class test, then yes. I'd have to string the 160 antenna on your parents' peak and run it diagonally across the yard… and anchor it somewhere up in the big oak behind Vera's." He looked distant.

Eva took another measured breath. Hearing her name made her guts churn.

When he came down to earth, he said, "I think I can keep it pretty much level across the entire span." He looked up, shifting his eyes left and right. "I think so. It shouldn't be too low." He stood and gathered their dishes.

"Never you mind. I'll do the dishes," she said and tapped his hand.

"At least let me help you carry them into the sink."

"I said, never mind. Run along now. Why don't you go check on Connie before you start radioing." She tried to sound playful, but her dwindling empathy came off as bossy.

Sam scowled as he trudged upstairs.

• • •

Warren returned after dinner and picked up Connie to go to the movies. Eva hoped they could enjoy themselves without being distracted by this intruder business. By this time tomorrow night, she aimed to have spoken her peace to Mrs. Hubbard and moved on from this terrible mess.

After she finished the dishes, she added a chunk of red oak to Magee's fire in hopes it would burn until morning. Then she turned off the light and climbed the stairs, forcing herself to ignore the voice inside her head shouting about the disheveled canning jars and their sprawling lids. There was no time to worry about mice either when the phone rang at the top of the stairs.

"You have time for a nightcap?" Alice asked.

Eva looked at the ceiling, forgetting Connie wasn't in her room. "Oh, I dunno."

"I have some Cherry Heering."

"Mmm," Eva moaned. That sounded delicious and fitting after everything that had happened today. She leaned into the living room and checked the time on the grandfather clock. "How's about you walk over with a flask, and I'll provide the ice? We'll turn on Lawrence Welk. Sam's upstairs radioing… we had a doozy of a day."

"Give me two shakes to throw on my rubbers… and I'll bring the whole bottle."

"Sounds good. See you then."

• • •

"Oh dear, that sounds terrible. Have you told your parents yet?" Alice asked. She was such a kind friend to walk over after dark on short notice to listen to Eva rehash the story of the intruder and how shaken up the girls in the dorm were.

"Sam will call Mrs. Hubbard tomorrow."

"Is Connie doing okay? Any of the other girls hurt?"

The warmth of the fireplace and the chill of the drinks created a perfect contrast, leaving Eva flushed and alert. The conversation was so engrossing that they missed The Lennon Sisters' cover of "Sad Movies (Make Me Cry)" and the encore of "Tonight You Belong To Me."

"She seems fine… doesn't feel the need to talk about it. I just hope Warren doesn't do anything foolish… or get his mother involved before Sam gets a chance to call tomorrow and clear the air." Eva smoothed the front of her skirt and crossed her ankles, prompting Alice to do the same, as if the act was contagious like a yawn. It gave Eva a moment before asking, "Has Sam been over to your place lately to take care of the ice on the roof?"

Alice held her Cherry Heering on her lap and glanced at the grandfather clock before turning to Eva and saying, "Not that I can recall. I haven't had any troubles… spring thaw hasn't come around yet. The kitchen ceiling has always been the first to see trouble, and I haven't had any issues so far." She tapped her knuckles on the sofa's wooden side handle. "Why do you ask?"

"Oh, probably nothing at all." Eva faced the television so Alice couldn't see her stony face. Even though she was watching the show's closing performer and Mr. Welk applauding, it didn't register. She drained the last of her drink and changed her mind. "When we came home, Sam was over at Vera's, up on her roof, chopping ice."

Alice swirled the last remnants of her drink with the remaining ice cube, watching it struggle in its final death throes. Eva hoped she could summon the strength to hear what Alice might have to say. She waited, scanning the room and glancing at all the curtains.

"As much as I don't really care for Vera's company, she's your neighbor, and Sam does so much work maintaining all the houses… I wouldn't put too much thought into it." She finished her drink and straightened her shoulders. "Now, I would give you a shampoo and blowout, but it's a little too late for that tonight." She glanced again at the clock. "And it's probably too late for another drink, so I'd better head out," she said, pushing herself up using the sofa handle. When Eva switched off the television, she noticed Alice wobble and misstep.

"I guess we were gabbing so much, I don't even remember who was on the show tonight," Eva said.

"Why don't we have supper at my place tomorrow? Invite your folks and Warren. Maybe afterward, while you're playing cribbage with your folks, I can teach the kids a little Bridge. We're always looking for new members to join the club."

"Good luck with that. Kids these days."

"I'll make a roast pork with boiled onions, cheese potato casserole, green salad, and lemon pie?"

"I'll see what they say. I don't know if Connie and Warren have plans again tomorrow, or what, but I'll be sure to ask. If everyone's free, then I'll make the rolls, unless, of course, mom beats me to 'em."

The grandfather clock's Westminster chime announced the ten o'clock hour. Last year, Eva and Sam drove to Springfield, Massachusetts, to the Eastern States Exposition (the Big E, as locals call it) and bought it. Sam agreed to pay extra for the *mellow-flower* pattern beneath a simple Roman numeral face. They chose a dark-cherry satin finish, left a $1 deposit, and it arrived a couple of months later on a truck from Michigan, cash on delivery. She kept a pair of white cotton gloves hidden behind the crown, out of sight but within reach on her tiptoes, and she used them every Monday morning to wind the brass weights before making coffee. It was a weekly task she would carry out, undaunted, for another forty-seven years before she would succumb to an aortic aneurysm—her last words to Sam: "Are we going fishing?"

Eva steadied her friend as Alice tugged her galoshes over her chunky heels, grunting audibly. "I don't know why I didn't wear my boots. They're so much easier to slip into without having to bend over so far." Alice straightened, buttoned her coat, then ran her hands over the side pockets, patting gently, then more firmly. "My flask?"

Eva extended both the flask and her hat to Alice, taking them from the old timber hutch that stood floor-to-ceiling against the enclosed stairwell. "Here," she said, handing Alice the flask while casually placing her hat atop her bouffant. "I'll toss the empty," she added, with a finger to her lips.

Alice snugged her hat over her ears. "Thanks."

"Get home safe."

"Will do."

Eva watched until Alice made it down the front stone steps without slipping and waved goodnight. She cracked open the upstairs door, feeling the warm air rush over her cheeks, and listened for Sam's telltale radio sounds, but only saw a faint bedroom light. Perhaps he was reading. She closed the door halfway and slipped into her front bedroom, knowing Sam would venture down and stoke the fire later.

• • •

Connie came home around midnight after Eva had fallen asleep. The next morning, Sam's raised voice in the kitchen woke her up. She slipped into a pair of sheepskin moccasins, which she kept beside the bed, and covered herself with a robe before shutting the upstairs door to avoid waking Connie.

She missed the conversation, arriving in the kitchen too late, and saw Sam hang up the phone, firm enough to startle her. He didn't slam it hard enough to break it. He had other things to fix and chores to do every day, so repairing a broken phone was unnecessary.

"Who was that?" she asked.

"I called Mrs. Hubbard at the school."

"What did she say?"

"Doesn't matter, but I gave her a stern talking to and threatened to call the police if she didn't get her act together and assure us this would never happen again."

Eva pointed toward the ceiling register and whispered, "Let's not wake Connie." She steadied herself, giving Sam time to cool off before suggesting, "Shall I make more coffee?"

He looked around the kitchen as if he'd misplaced his mug. "Sure." His demeanor cooled as if he'd never been hot to begin with. "I'll stir the stove… I wanted to get ahold of her early before she stepped out. I didn't wanna wait another day."

"Good. Then it's settled," she said, imagining the kitchen window pulling at her. "Al wants us to supper this afternoon. The entire crew." She fought the urge to look.

"I dunno. We'll see. I've got to get over to the Woodstock garage this morning. I think the truck needs new universal joints."

She gave in and looked. "Can you refill the feeders before you go?"

"Sure."

"And while you're at it, maybe dig out and set a few traps downstairs? I'm afraid we've been neglecting the seed bins. I'd hate to see the buggers get into them and make a mess."

Sam exhaled, part sigh, part moan. "I'll handle it." He stared into the woods behind the house for a moment before facing next door. "I dunno about supper. Maybe now's a good time to get the ice off your parents' house… get a jump on the spring thaw."

"What about Al's place?"

"Does she need it? Did she say anything? Is she having issues?"

Eva wanted to keep him busy with no rest for the wicked. "None that I'm aware of."

"I'll check both houses when I get back."

She wanted to keep him away from the chance of stopping at Ray's to radio on his way home from Woodstock. "What about taking the truck over to Chabot's across the river?"

He seemed to consider the question. "It might be cheaper."

"They're probably less busy today, too."

"Okay… sold." He moved toward the cellar stairs and led the way down. "If you make more coffee, I'll find those traps… and we'll see what time I get home from the garage."

Eva cleaned the inside of all the windows, starting with the kitchen, while he was gone.

Eva's Daily Reminder 1963: January 20, Sunday

About 4 inches of snow when I got up. Very wet, almost a rain. Good thing Sam got started on the ice.

Dad shoveled out everyone, including Al.

Did two loads of washing and cleaned the windows. Seems they shine now, how so!

Sam got back around 9. Seems to have a cold started.

Made cookies with Connie to send back with her. Chocolate chips, hope she likes them. Enough to share with the girls.

Connie got a kick out of popping off two Blue Jays out the kitchen window.

We ate dinner over at Al's house—roast pork, potatoes, casserole, salad, and lemon pie. Sure was good.

Al did Mom's hair while we played cribbage. Dad and I got the rubber.

Clear and cold when we came home.

4

Sam still hadn't shaken his cold. It had been nearly two weeks, and he was miserable the whole time, working only in the mornings and taking the afternoons off to nap on the couch in front of a roaring fire. He managed to struggle up and down the cellar stairs, barely keeping ole Magee stoked enough to keep the floors warm. Eva had urged him to see Dr. Read, but he refused, telling her he wouldn't take any more pills except aspirin.

"You're a stubborn old bastard sometimes, you know that?" she told him. She was reading "High Lonesome" from a stack of Louis L'Amour books, but lowered it to chide him when his snoring grew bothersome. When he didn't respond, she looked out at the grosbeaks, scanning the ground and bushes for the male cardinal. A flock of muted gray doves trampled the fresh snow, pecking at fallen seeds. She slipped a marker between the pages, letting the tassel brush her fingers before snapping the book shut enough to stir Sam. "When's the last time you had some Alka-Seltzer?" she asked as he pushed himself up into a half slouch.

"I think I'm doing better," he answered, sloughing off the afghan he'd earlier tossed over himself and pulled over his chest. It was one of many knitted by Ruby over the years as a winter tradition, keeping her hands busy while waiting for the next loaf of bread to finish baking.

He sat up, stretched, then placed his hands on his chest and took deep breaths. "Feels clearer."

Eva had seen this exaggerated routine before. It was tough for him to be down and out for more than a day. There was always a project in his wheelhouse that needed attention. If you weren't working, it meant you were dying, and there'd be none of that here. Her father had already sanded the walkways and brought in their mail, including a letter from Connie. She had done a load of laundry and wiped out the bottom kitchen cabinets.

"I'd better get a move on," he said. "I should throw some sand before things freeze over tonight."

"Already taken care of."

He pushed himself up with his fists, sinking into the couch cushions before slumping back down. "Say what now?"

"Dad already did that little chore this morning… and brought in the mail while you were sawing logs. Here's a letter from your daughter." She handed it to him. "You should read one now and then and be proud of her marks. Knock on wood, but so far so good, with no more of that intruder to report."

He skimmed both sides of the letter before refolding it. "Well, that's good."

He glanced at the letter, shifting his eyes between Eva, the fireplace, and the hutch. When he stood up and stretched, he handed it to her. She relaxed, relieved that he didn't toss it into the fire.

He stood in the middle of the room, staring at the dwindling flames, and after a moment, said, "I think we should get an actual woodstove for the room. Something the right size to funnel into the chimney flue. It would be a hell of a lot more efficient in the winter… and easy enough to lug out in the spring. Whaddya say?" he asked her.

They'd been married long enough that he could read her mind. She only wished she could do the same. "I've had my eye on a Jøtul that I bet they sell at the Lyme Country Store," she said, brightening her tone. She could sense he was imagining the right size and shape to fit the room. She stood, excited to go for a drive, before he said, "Let's think about it. Do some window shopping next weekend."

Eva sank into her chair, shifting her weight uncomfortably. There didn't seem to be any rhyme or reason to his actions.

"I gotta get going. Ray's taking the general test next month, and I should go and tutor him. It'd be foolish to drive all the way down to Boston and for him not to pass it." He rotated his waist and stretched, something Eva hadn't seen him do since their days stepping onto the first tee box. "I gotta do somethin' about this," he said, patting his non-existent belly. With a metabolism that could devour a diet of peanut butter and Ritz crackers, Wheaties and milk crackers doused in half and half, and vanilla ice cream at night drizzled with maple syrup, the man who couldn't sit still was practically a scarecrow. "Can't lie around all day gettin' fat."

When he came downstairs after getting dressed, he grabbed his truck keys and didn't bother to call Ray before leaving.

• • •

Eva was ironing when someone knocked on the front door. The only visitors who came to the front door were solicitors or trick-or-treaters; everyone else either went to the back door or was friendly enough to walk right in. She debated whether to answer, but decided her hair looked fine after checking it in the mirror beside the grandfather clock. She unlocked the door and was greeted by Vera, who stood on the bottom step holding a stack of records. Eva hesitated to see her neighbor. She pushed open the storm door; her tongue swollen as she decided on a salutation, but was spared the effort when Vera said, "I brought over some albums to share that I recently got from the Capitol Records Club. Do you have some time to listen? Catch up on gossip?"

"Sure. Come on in," Eva said, holding the door open for her.

When Vera placed the pile on the hutch, Eva counted too many to finish before starting supper. "Can I take your coat?" Eva asked.

"Sure thing. That would be great. Thanks."

Eva grabbed her coat, closed the upstairs door, and hurried into her bedroom to lay it on her bed before gesturing for Vera to sit on the couch. Vera smoothed her pencil skirt, and she wore a wool sweater that Eva hoped would become uncomfortable in front of the fire. She wanted to add another log but decided against it. There was no need to be petty right from the start.

"That looks like a nice stereo," Vera said after waiting for the short quarter-hour chime to fade. "I ran into Alice Fairbanks the other day, out walking her little whippy Terrier, and she mentioned you and Sam had bought a new one recently." She tugged her sweater and checked her updo. "Good thing I wore my hair up," she said, fanning her face.

Eva was happy with her close-cropped perm, which kept her natural curls and dark color. Still, she was a little envious of Vera's much longer, thicker blonde hair, even though it looked uncolored and dirtier, as if she'd used her head as a feather duster before leaving home. If her hair were a brighter strawberry blonde, Eva would've guessed it was Clairol. Either way, she wanted to ask her if blondes really do have more fun, though she really didn't want to hear the answer.

"Yes, it's a recent purchase," Eva said. "We're very pleased with how it sounds—plenty of enjoyment so far."

Vera lifted herself, smoothing the underside of her skirt again, then leaned forward, crossing her ankle boots. Looking down, she said, "Oh, I hope I didn't track in with these things." She uncrossed and bent her legs, checking whether any snow or sand still clung to her soles.

"No worries," Eva assured her, noticing Vera's boots weren't a brand she carried at Merril's.

Vera glanced at the vinyl on the hutch. "Oh, good… so I not too long ago joined that mail-order record club. I've been on a kick listening to The Supremes, Brenda Lee, The Springfields… I wish I could style my hair like Dusty's," she said, pushing her updo higher.

The fire was fading into glowing coals, and Eva turned on her reading lamp. Sam had repurposed an old wooden shoe tree into a sturdier base and wired it himself. (At least some good was coming from all his radio hobbies.) In the light, Vera's eyes were brown, the color of riverbank mud. Eva wasn't really in the mood to listen to music or gossip, but still asked, "So you wanted to listen to music… or perhaps talk about something else?"

"Well, to be honest, I didn't think you'd want to listen, but I wanted to drop them off and let you borrow them while I'm gone… that was the gossip I was hinting at. I just wanted to let you and Sam know I'll be heading to Florida this week. We're staying for a couple of weeks. I'm taking the Karmann Ghia and driving down with Phyllis. We both have a little cabin fever and can't wait to cruise around in the sun with the top down." Her subtle shoulder twitch couldn't be more obvious, and someone should tell her bullet bras had gone out of style.

Eva wished Vera and her friend would decide to stay down there longer, maybe even permanently, if she had her druthers. "Sounds lovely. I'll be sure to tell him," she said, standing up. She wouldn't waste time caring where in Florida they were headed, and she didn't care if Vera thought it was rude; she wasn't asking, choosing instead to avoid any prolonged conversation, and slipped into her bedroom to grab Vera's coat. Scooping the cumbersome overcoat into her arms brought a whiff of Vera's perfume to her nose, and she prayed to God the smell hadn't soaked into her quilt; nonetheless, she'd throw it in the laundry as soon as Vera was gone.

When Eva returned, holding the coat at arm's length, Vera was straightening the record pile on the hutch and said, "My only favor to ask is if there's a hard freeze… maybe Sam could check on my pipes? He…" She trailed off before continuing, "I'll drop off a key before we leave?" She took her coat and draped it over her shoulders, then glanced at the weather and slipped her arms into the sleeves. "Or I could leave it inside the garage. There's a nook shelf above eye level on the left side, as you face inward. I'll put it there."

"I'll be sure to let him know. When are you gals leaving?"

"Wednesday. We'll stop a few times on the way down before the weekend… maybe outside DC and Savannah? I've always wanted to see Savannah."

Not interested. Eva had never been *far* south and had no plans to go. Her silence seemed to encourage Vera to button up her coat, and she selected every other one to speed up the awkward process.

"I dunno what we'll do on the way back. Mix it up, I guess. Play it by ear."

"Sounds good. I hope you two have a good time. Get some rest before the long drive."

Vera nodded. "Eva, there's…" she trailed off before turning away.

Eva once again held the door as Vera stepped out, hoping like the dickens that Sam didn't happen to drive up the hill on his way home from Ray's, witnessing Vera leaving. That was a conversation she didn't want to have, yet what he had to say might be worth her while. "Try not to slip and fall," she said, watching Vera work her way down the stone steps. *Why was Henry always so faithful and prompt to lay sand on days like these?*

• • •

Sam visited Ray's house a couple of times a week after work while Vera was in Florida. When two weeks turned into three and stretched into March, Eva found it hard to read Sam's moodiness. Usually, his misery worsened in the weeks before his birthday, but this year, since he was turning fifty, she wouldn't be surprised if that was why he started sputtering early. Whether it was pride or vanity, she'd never understood why he would be happy one day and miserable, short, and ornery the next. If he wasn't keeping himself busy—which was much easier to do in the summer—he wasn't satisfied, and it showed. Often, he'd snap at her, being impatient rather than short-tempered, probably something he picked up from his father, even though his mother, who held onto life a few extra years, always gave it right back. Sam's mother was a talker who never knew when to shut up.

At least he was never short with Connie. She did things his way and always took it in stride, but Eva wouldn't know what she'd do without her sweet Connie. All she could do was be patient and hope Sam would snap out of it, whatever it was. She still believed they were meant to be together, and she still loved him, despite the exhaustion of coping with their on-again, off-again relationship.

• • •

Eva did two loads of laundry, wound the clock, dusted the front room lampshades, and mopped the kitchen floor before heading to the store.

Merrill and Faye were already there, getting a head start on unpacking the kids' spring line, and Eva, guilty, brushed past them. "Good morning, Merrill… Faye," she said, pouring herself coffee.

"Hey, good morning," Faye said. "Have a good weekend?"

"Ayutt," Eva replied. *It was a half-truth, but a truth nonetheless.* "You know how it goes. Another year older—"

"Another year wiser," Merrill interjected. "Isn't that what you tell Sam every year?"

Eva hid her disgruntled face behind her coffee mug. "Oh sure… that we do." She took a sip and swallowed the fib. She was about to turn to help Faye when she noticed Merrill's face looked thinner and asked tentatively, "Merrill? Are you losing weight?"

He scanned the room, then shifted his gaze between them, finally focusing on Eva. "Is it noticeable?" he asked. He brought a white-sleeved cuff to his face and nudged his wire-frame glasses askew.

For as long as Eva had known Merrill, he always wore a long-sleeve white Oxford shirt and a black tie under a V-neck sweater vest, even in the summertime and at every get-together outside store hours. His gray hair, whether brushed or not, she couldn't tell, was short and tussled, not yet ready for his spring flattop. "Your face does look a bit thinner," she said. "Is everything okay?"

Merrill took off his glasses, letting them hang at his side. He turned away from the women. "No… not really," he mumbled to no one.

"Beg pardon?" Eva asked Faye. She wanted to make sure she was loud enough for Merrill to hear before shrugging her shoulders.

He turned and faced them, his eyes shining. He seemed too proud to cry in front of his employees at his age. "It's Carolyn," he said. "She's been diagnosed with stage three breast cancer." He brought his hands to his face, his keening muffled, and sobbed once.

Eva and Faye moved closer, each grasping one of his elbows. "I'm so sorry, Merrill," Faye said, rubbing his back with her free hand. "Is there anything we can do?"

He shook his head.

Eva glanced at the store's clock, debating whether to shift their conversation further back. "How's Carolyn doing?"

Merrill flung his hands as if trying to shake the tears off his fingers. "She's already made up her mind. She's having it removed." He took a few deep breaths and shook his head. "The doctors in town said it would be best, and they've arranged everything for her to have the surgery at Mass General next week." He checked his wristwatch, noted the time, then moved toward the front door and unlocked it. "I don't know if I'm more worried about the surgery going well, or her being… well." He shuffled to the coffee area and refilled his mug. "You know what she's gone and done?" he asked them.

Eva looked at Faye, and together they waited for Merrill to break the silence, which he did after a moment, saying, "She's written a letter, or some story, to… not herself… but her breast. The *one*. She's saying goodbye to her own breast, and apologizing for anything she might have done wrong to cause this to happen."

Eva remembered her pain from when Dr. Read had removed small fiber cysts from her breasts more than twenty years ago. There wasn't much tissue to begin with, and after all the poking, prodding, and cuts, only a few marks remained—scars only Sam and Connie knew about. She planned to visit Carolyn this week, but right now, neither she nor Faye could get Merrill to understand.

A woman's business was entirely her own pain to bear.

"She'll be fine," Eva reassured him.

"We'll get through this," Faye said, her words catching Eva and Merrill's attention as they faced her. "She'll get through this."

Eva was pleased with Faye's correction and noticed Merrill had seemed to overlook it as he headed to open the door for the day's first customer with a forced smile.

• • •

There were four letters from Connie waiting in the box when Eva got home. Apparently, she had written one each day last week but waited to mail them all at once. Reading them would bring enough joy to outweigh Carolyn's news, so she hurried inside and upstairs to change her clothes. She read all of them before making supper.

When Sam came home, he bought her more time by washing the salt off his truck and her car, enough to warm a pot of fish stew and the rolls Ruby had left, along with the morning laundry, all of which was ironed.

She left Connie's letters on her side table, not wanting them to distract her during their meal.

"Chowdah's good," Sam said, dunking a butter-laden roll. "Is this the last of the frozen fish… or still more?"

"This might be the last of the perch, but there could be one or two more packages of bass." Eva enjoyed a spoonful of the sweet, dense white meat and closed her eyes, visualizing exactly where they had caught this mess—off a patch of cattails in a weedbed north of old Fort Number Four. "Can't wait to get back out on the water." She glanced across the two-person nook table, close enough that their bowls almost touched, and hoped he wanted the same.

"Maybe we'll do some trolling north of the bridge. See if we can hook into some walleye or largemouth," he said.

Eva wasn't fond of trolling, and she didn't have a strong preference for bass either. The walleye, usually caught in pairs, would strike at lures passing over their spawning nest and were tasty, but she preferred anchoring over a weedbed with a fat nightcrawler and catching as many yellow perch as their freezer could hold. "Meh," she quipped. "I enjoy walleye, from time to time, but I'll take a mess of perch any day of the week."

Sam wiped his mouth and turned, crossing his legs. He faced the kitchen window, but Eva knew they were sitting too low to see across the yard. She was about to change the subject to Carolyn's surgery when he took another roll, split it, and lathered on the butter. He hesitated before shoving it into his grocery hole, saying, "You remember that time I stood up in the boat and cast that godawful crayfish? I thought for sure it would land the biggest largemouth in the river."

She had been squatting at the front of the boat, doing her business in a coffee can, when suddenly she remembered a fishing line wrapped around her face multiple times before a crayfish the size of a chick lobster came to rest on her chin with its pincers tethered to the sides of her nose. It was only luck that saved her when the pincer, close enough to cause serious damage to her nose, grabbed a lead sinker on the line instead of her skin. It kept her safe—until the fort's noontime cannon burst overhead, spilling the coffee can into the bottom of the boat.

"How could I ever forget that little diddy?" she asked, trying to quell her embarrassment. She didn't want to know what other passing boats might have seen, but the river was wide down there, and hopefully no one witnessed her folly. "Good times."

When it was time to do the dishes, Sam carried everything downstairs. Eva didn't try to persuade him to rinse in the kitchen sink, knowing there was nothing for either of them to be distracted by on the other side of the feeders. *Let sleeping dogs lie until after his birthday was over.*

Returning to her reading chair, she unfolded each of Connie's letters on her lap. It warmed her heart more than the fire to read that her class marks were improving, and if she kept them up, she would finish her first year of college on the dean's list at the end of the semester. She and Catherine had strengthened their friendship and were already planning to apply to be roommates in the fall, but they would take their time deciding whether to stay in the same dorm as Mrs. Hubbard or move to another.

Eva had always encouraged her not to procrastinate, and she was proud to see her taking the initiative to plan. She hoped Connie would enjoy her summer vacation and stay around the house as long as possible. She'd probably find a part-time job, maybe even apply for one at the machine company. At least she'd be in her own bed for three months. Eva hadn't touched anything, including all her stuffed animals, which were still carefully arranged on her bed.

Connie had written and admitted that her fifth letter from last week, which she'd mailed to Warren, asked him not to drive up and get her this weekend or the next. She and Catherine needed time to study for their final exams. The only way she could prepare for her shorthand test was to have someone dictating to her who would be serious and not a distraction.

Eva was fond of Warren and would do her best this week to ask if it hurt his pride. She suspected he was planning to propose to Connie over the summer, even though she wished he'd hold his horses until after graduation. But it wasn't her place to meddle in their affairs, trusting that everything would work out the way it was meant to.

Sam came up the cellar stairs and, to Eva's confusion, sat on the couch across from her. Usually, he went upstairs to get on the radio for the evening, but she figured he was catching his breath before turning on a Celtics game when she noticed he'd seen the letters on her lap. She held them up and asked, "Can you see over there, or do you need to sit here under the light?"

He looked around the room and up before taking the letters from her. He again looked at the ceiling as he sat, appearing uninterested in reading. "What would you think about adding some kind of chandelier to the ceiling?" he asked, pointing to a spot above them and then to another area closer to the front of the room. "I think there's plenty of space as long as it's something broader and not too low. I wouldn't wanna put a single overhead light up there. It would look silly. The room's too big, don't you think?"

Eva hadn't considered it. Her reading lamp and the floor lamp beside the rocking chair, near the television, always seemed enough, and with the fireplace light, the long room was never dark. Still, if they installed a Jøtul, it would cut down the lighting.

They both stared at the ceiling and, without looking at each other, said simultaneously, "A wagon wheel."

Eva thought it was a wonderful idea, knowing it perfectly fit the farm theme she had curated in the dining room, with its horse-collar mirror and whippletree light; a wagon-wheel chandelier would be a perfect addition. "Sounds perfect," she concurred before he could change his mind.

The moment lingered in the room, warmed by the flickering flames, and Eva found it romantic; maybe her emotions lately had been stirred by her imagination. Sumner Falls was a small town, and she had to admit there was no hearsay; surely someone would have seen Sam and Vera palling around if it was true.

She took the stage confidently, realizing she had a chance to lift the March doldrums. "Why don't we go for a drive on Saturday morning? We can head up the New Hampshire side and stop in Lyme to see what they have for wood stoves. If they don't have anything we like, we can order what we want. We can take our time and hit some of the antique shops north of Haverhill. Grab some fancy grade on the way back… for my parents and Al too." When Sam appeared unconvinced, she added, "If we can't find anything we like up north, then we can hit antique alley along Route 4 on

Sunday—drive out to the seacoast. *Someone* will have a matching pair of wagon wheels you can rewire."

Sam's hesitation was frustrating, but at least he was still interested since he kept looking up at the ceiling. He wasn't listening to her—it wasn't the first time. "What do you think?" she asked. "Sound like a plan?"

Without looking down, he said, "I could probably make them on my bandsaw."

Always his way. He couldn't make a horse collar mirror on a bandsaw, so why would he say this now? He always had a way of taking the fun out of something she liked or wanted.

"I think I have some nice brass chain downstairs that I knew would come in handy someday. I'll make them out of rock maple. Come to think of it… I bet the mill on the Plainfield Road would have some leftover snath spindles thrown out on the slab pile. I can look the next time I pick up a load for downstairs."

Eva had seen this behavior from Sam before, again and again, always thinking about himself and not her. She kept a neutral face. "Did you read your daughter's good marks?" she asked, accepting her disappointment and moving on.

Sam riffled the pages, stopping at one randomly. "Looks good," he said, returning them to Eva. "Let's hope she keeps it up."

After his footsteps faded up the stairs, Eva got up and went to bed. She was too irritated to watch television, believing there was no one funny enough or a singer with a voice sultry enough on the airwaves to lift her mood.

5

Eva and Sam Martin met Sybil and Clark Hoisington for the first time around 1950 at a preseason dinner held at the Sumner Falls Coon Club on the outskirts of town. The hunting club was nestled among a stand of hardwoods, with rock and sugar maple, red oak, and hickory trees, all dressed in late-fall shades of burnt orange and red. It was built in a hollow on an unpaved stretch of the aptly named Coon Club Road, with one hillside serving as a backdrop for the shooting range.

It was before Eva began her diaries (when Connie first left for college), when she and Sam were full-time outdoorsmen, transitioning from a life of hunting and fishing to a more relaxed round of golf, where they could enjoy a twilight nine-hole game most evenings after work.

They were ready to put away their matching Marlins after that season because Sam had never had much luck hunting bucks. Only once, when they were out trying to rouse some partridge, did he manage to slip a slug into his single-shot 16-gauge and drop a four-pointer with a clean neck shot. But it was Eva who preferred bird hunting. As a young girl, she would often snipe ringtail pheasants in the cornfield next to her parents' farm using her father's single-shot bolt .22 that Sam had dropped once while trying to climb over a rock wall behind the farm and bent the front iron sight.

"What a surprise," Eva said. "I wasn't expecting you to stop by." She rejoiced in the reunion, hugging her friend. "Come in, Sybil… come on in."

"I'm not intruding, am I?"

"Not at all. I was just setting out some snacks. It's five o'clock somewhere, right?"

Sybil blushed. The flush on her cheeks contrasted with her resplendent blonde hair and pin curls, some of which Eva noticed she had left near her temples. She wore a Christmas-green wool coat and a matching pencil skirt, reminiscent of a Saturday Evening Post Rockwell cover. As she climbed the front steps, her part revealed gray roots—something Alice would be mortified to see on Eva.

"Where's Sam? Is he around?" Sybil asked.

"Oh, he's gone upstreet. Why don't we go sit in the kitchen?" Eva gestured with one hand while taking Sybil's coat with her other, and draped it over the couch. "So you left Clark out in the car?" she teased.

"So it's five o'clock, you say?"

"Oh dear." Eva raised a palm, unprepared to hear distressing news. "Why don't you head into the kitchen, and I'll pour us something stiff. We have a dry bar in the dining room now. It's nothing too fancy, just something Sam built." She struggled to recall what Sybil liked to drink. "Would you prefer a Manhattan or a whiskey sour?"

"Honestly? If I could have one of each, that would be fine, but for now, how about a whiskey sour?"

"Oh dear, do tell."

When Eva returned with their drinks, Sybil was eating a cube of cheddar cheese and looking at the backyard, scanning the treeline. "Did you and Sam ever take any deer from behind the house?"

"We did not, no," Eva said, handing her a tumbler, then grabbing an ice bucket from the freezer. "And especially not now. They've started clearing for the new interstate. That'll scare off anything that might've been there, up the mountain. You and Clark should hunt on the other side in Brownsville or Reading."

Eva couldn't help but notice Sybil wince at her husband's name, and as she sat down, she asked, "Is everything all right?"

Sybil drank half her whiskey sour, swirling the ice. She looked mesmerized. "I'm not sure, Eva… Clark had an affair last year." She didn't appear fazed, her eyes dry. "It was brief, and we talked." She finished her drink and set the glass on the table without paying attention to where it landed, partway off the cutting board and tilted toward Eva. "We've decided to move to Texas as soon as the weather lets up. I just wanted you and Sam to know before we leave."

Eva couldn't take her eyes off the foam at the bottom of the glass. She watched the bubbles burst like fireworks, their hypnotic effect leaving her speechless. *What could she say? Please stay?* The anguish was all too familiar. She settled on something halfway between introverted and empathetic, "I'm sorry for your grief."

Sybil noticed the mishandled glass and repositioned it. "What are you gonna do? These things happen." She closed her eyes and wrinkled her nose, her smile labored. When she opened them, they were shiny with tears. "It's not like I can accidentally shoot him—oops-a-daisy—deer hunting. We'll be gone by then."

Eva was stunned. "Now, Sybil… Don't even think about it. Let's not joke about it either. I'm sure you've straightened him out, and he's done with this foolishness? Do you know who she was?" Eva didn't want to know as much as she guessed Sybil didn't either.

"I dunno, and no. Just some floozie he ran into at the Howard Johnson's in White River after work, having drinks with coworkers, I guess. That's all I could get out of him." She reached for her empty glass. "I'll have a Manhattan if you're having one? But only if you have plenty of cherries."

Eva looked at her whiskey sour, untouched. "Sure," she said, taking a sip. Before returning to the dry bar, she slipped around the corner of the kitchen into the bathroom and poured the rest down the drain, careful not to clink the ice in the porcelain sink.

Adding a heaping spoonful of cherry juice to their new drinks, she overheard Sybil in the kitchen ask, "What would make a younger woman want to get her hands on an older man who's obviously wearing a wedding ring? Could it be his job? And if she assumed he was rich, I wish I could've been there to burst her bubble."

Eva hurried to the kitchen with the next round.

This time, Sybil placed the glass firmly on the table before eating another cube of cheddar. She dabbed at the corner of her lips, her eyes scanning the table.

"Oh, here," Eva said, grabbing some napkins from a cabinet.

"It's all right. Thanks. I did, after all, interrupt you in the middle of happy hour."

Eva sipped half her Manhattan while watching Sybil wipe her mouth and check her lap for crumbs, brushing at her skirt. "I honestly wouldn't know," Eva said, choosing to keep her cards close. She remembered mopping the kitchen floor that morning and bristled at the chore of doing it again.

"It must be the gray hair," Sybil said, dabbing at her part.

"Lordy, you must be loopy already."

"Hardly."

Eva wasn't interested in staying on this path. "What about the summer cabin on Amherst? Do you still have it? What if you get all the way down to Texas and change your mind?" she asked, switching subjects. "This is a huge change."

"We still have it. Clark doesn't want to sell it, and I agree. We could always sell it from down there… Would you and Sam want to take it over?"

Eva remembered all the summer Saturdays and fish fries they shared at the lake over the years. Clark had bought the lakeside lot with its old, rundown fishing shack before they first met at the Coon Club. He tore it down and rebuilt it, adding a cozy deck. He built a new dock where they first moored a canoe, and later added an inboard runabout that Sam enjoyed water skiing behind. (Not once did Eva try.) Mostly, they came for one reason: to fish for rainbow trout.

"Oh gosh, no. We couldn't afford the upkeep. It should stay with you. Clark's put so much work into it over the years." Eva took another sip of her drink, washing down a cracker. "Besides, I've been bugging Sam about getting back out on the river this spring."

"You were never crazy fond of trout, were you?"

"It was the company," Eva said with a smile that was returned in kind.

"So you and Sam are good? Still rolling along through life?"

Eva wasn't about to worsen the pensive mood. "Life's been good… so far. Knock on wood," she said, tapping her knuckle on the side of the table leaf. "But, it sure has been quiet without Connie around." Eva wished she hadn't said that, knowing Sybil and Clark never had children.

"I'm sure it would be."

"It's just that she's always been such a good little helper around the house, keeping me on my toes. I got so used to her helping with housework and spending so much time keeping company with my parents. But I'll take what I can get. It seems she's able to come home just about every other weekend."

Sybil took her time reaching for her coat, drifting as she struggled to fasten the toggle buttons with only one hand. Without making eye contact with Eva, she said, "I wish we were entertaining the men at the lake. Keeping them busy and…" She trailed off but brightened her face with a deep breath, glancing around the room, pausing as she seemed to linger on Eva's quintessential Vermont farm antiques. "I'll miss having another opportunity, but unfortunately… *we* won't be able to come and visit every other weekend. And I suppose there won't be any chance of getting you to come and visit us. We'll be far enough outside Dallas to still find deer, but I hear trout will be hard to come by."

Eva tried to keep her expression neutral, fully aware she would never leave home for more than a weekend, let alone all the way to Texas—a land and people unto itself—filled with tumbleweeds, scrub brush, and nothing taller than man-made oil wells as far as the eye could see. She was disheartened to see one of her friends leave, but she could tell how Sybil's lost face revealed how badly she wanted to distance herself from her home nestled in the prime state of changing seasons.

• • •

Henry and Ruby Fischer were in their kitchen playing cards when Eva walked in through the back porch. She had unexpectedly timed her entrance to see Henry place his cards face up on the table and announce, "Gin." Neither of them bothered to count Ruby's cards after she tossed them on the checkered cloth.

"We've got tea that's probably still warm enough, or I could put more water on to boil?" Ruby asked Eva, turning to stand.

"Oh, don't get up, Mom. Keep playing. I'll pour myself a cup."

The air in the kitchen swirled enough to lift the scents of cinnamon and cloves, prompting Eva to ask, "Got a pie in the oven?"

Ruby scowled, with one side of her lips turned up and her arched eyebrow mostly penciled in. A silver chain draped around her neck held her glasses, which she lifted to her face as she stood. Her orthopedic shoe heels added an extra inch, letting her peer down her nose at Eva. "With all that black strap and clove you're smellin'?"

Ruby eyed Eva's father, forcing out a guttural sound from deep within her bosom. "And we're finished. I think he cheats when I'm not lookin'."

Henry toyed with his corncob pipe between nimble fingers. "Me? You're the one always wearin' the apron." To Eva, he said, "Look at the size of your mother's apron pockets. I swear, she pulls a card or two she keeps stashed when I'm not payin' attention." He smiled at Eva and winked.

"Sometimes the man's insufferable," Ruby said dramatically, snatching the teakettle off the stovetop and pouring Eva a cup. "Do you smell apples? I don't."

Eva knew her mother was joking; she hated to lose, but she rubbed her shoulder while Ruby stood at the sink, grunting for good measure, and refilled the kettle. "Men," Eva said, smiling and winking behind her mother's back at her father, who was a quiet and introverted man. *So much for marrying a man like your father.*

"So, what brings you over?" Ruby asked. "Was I supposed to be makin' supper tonight? I don't remember whose turn it was, but I guess I've got enough food to feed everyone." She smoothed her apron, wiped her hands, then dropped her fake tantrum. "Is Al stoppin' in, too?" she asked, showing a hint of a smile.

"Oh, no… It's not that." Eva said, praising Henry's timing as he returned to the kitchen with an extra chair from the porch. "Sybil stopped by just now. Said she and Clark are gonna move down to Texas this spring."

"Oh dear," Henry said. "Sit down, and let's talk, shall we? Your mother made a batch of hermit cookies to last what's troublin' ya."

• • •

"I can't remember the last time we were at the lake, do you?" Sam asked. "It's probably a good thing we don't see them before they take off."

Eva found the remark strange. "Why do you say?" Besides Alice, they didn't have anyone outside their family who was close enough to call a friend. She didn't consider Ray a friend and often wondered why Sam wasn't closer to some of his Masonic brothers. She couldn't remember when he started slacking off from his lodge meetings.

"Oh… I'm too old to get behind Clark's boat again. Besides,"—he rubbed his rib cage—"I can still feel the pain in my ribs when I fell off my skates."

Eva couldn't decide whether she was more annoyed by Sam's lack of enthusiasm for saying goodbye to their friends with one last trip to the lake or his foolish, bruised ego from falling off his flimsy hockey skates last winter while trying to glide across a small patch of spring runoff ice in the backyard. He had tried to show off by stopping with a snow shower, but ended up toppling over after his momentum pivoted on an ice crack. He landed on his side with his arm tucked and broke three ribs. He sputtered for months like a peevish child every time she had to wrap an ace bandage around him.

"Wouldn't you at least want to go fishing one last time? And Clark might need help closing the place down. I definitely wouldn't mind a fish fry while watching her feeders. The ruby-throated hummers should return by the end of April." Eva paused briefly, hoping her subtle pleas were noticed. "Well, if you believe the Almanac this year," she added, looking out the window at the mottled ground around the feeder pole, where a crocus bulb moat was beginning to emerge.

Even though Sam hadn't mentioned anything about building the chandeliers since they last spoke, Eva hoped he hadn't forgotten about looking at wood stoves. "We're still on for Saturday?"

"We can drive up to Lyme on Friday, or else it'll have to wait until next weekend," he said. "Ray and I are gonna drive down to Deerfield to a ham radio flea market." He leaned on his elbows, knitted his fingers, and repeatedly nodded with puckered lips.

Eva didn't want to know what he might be plotting.

"Maybe we *should* aim for next weekend," he said. "I think the longer we wait, the more the prices might drop as the weather warms up... less demand." He nodded, declaring it the right choice.

"You still haven't decided about April," Eva said, once again trying to persuade him to see Sybil and Clark off to Texas. She wanted to remember them as they were. She and Sam would make the day a memorable foursome like old times, and not focus on the wedge—or wedges—splitting them apart. She wanted to ensure everyone parted on good terms, leaving the door open for Clark to realize what he'd done wasn't worth it, and for Sybil to trust him enough to return to what they all cherished most: the green mountains—monts verts, the invading French called them.

Eva held her ground. "I think we should commit to a weekend in April."

"Ray's test is gonna be sometime next month."

Sam's eyes were distant.

"You said that was sometime this month," Eva said.

"It is... I was gonna assume, like all of us, he'd fail it the first time—I did! And you're only allowed to retake the exam once a month for the first three times. After that, you can only try once a year to pass."

"Well, let's hope it doesn't come to that," she said, still worried his excuses were all hokum, yet she hid her lament from him. She couldn't wait for all this tutoring nonsense to be over. Sam needed friends—peers—not a younger protégé who took up all his free time. He had enough ham buddies across the region, and she was glad they all stayed at arm's length, remaining on the other end of the airwaves.

"I think I'm gonna make myself a bowl of milk and crackers," he said, rising off the couch. After a hiccup step, his gait as he ventured toward the kitchen wasn't as smooth as it had been early in their marriage.

Eva planned to see Carolyn after work tomorrow and would need to control her emotions to avoid upsetting Carolyn or Merrill until she had spoken her mind and said her peace. However, she would definitely go straight to Alice afterward to discuss why Sam was reluctant to see Sybil and Clark off.

• • •

Eva mopped the bathroom floor and dusted the crown molding above the living room, trying to ease the nagging distrust that crept down her spine in waves. She hoped that Sam would keep his promise to build a pair of chandeliers for the spacious front room, and maybe even repaint the ceiling with a brighter shade of mauve, since it looked like a faded dishcloth—something that couldn't be thrown in the washing machine.

The dining room had a connecting closet leading to Eva's front bedroom. When the block-style Cape Cod was built, it was intended to be a third bedroom. The two upstairs rooms were much smaller, with sloped ceilings, and only one had a tiny built-in closet; that one remained Connie's bedroom. Sam used the other south-facing room for all his radio equipment, leaving enough space for his twin bed tucked against the eaves. Since there was no closet in that room, he used the one in the dining room to hang his shirts and jackets, with a tie rack on the back of the door. He kept his bric-a-brac in a top drawer of the dining room hutch since it was the closest spot near the top of the cellar stairs where he could empty his pockets.

Eva paused at the top of the stairs and looked at Sam's tie collection hanging on the closet door before shifting her gaze to his shirts. She planned to rifle through them but instead forced herself to take down the room's two pairs of curtains, which she then washed before heading to work.

She was daydreaming about how she could comfort Carolyn when she passed Officer Poole parked on the McSwains' upslope. After checking her speed and glancing in the rearview, she was satisfied that he, too, was satisfied and would stay put.

Today, she was the first to open the store and fumbled at the bottom of the small, aging Nantucket basket she used as a purse, searching for the key. As soon as she found it, Merrill stepped up behind her, startling her.

"Allow me," he said. Before inserting his key, they both turned at the sight of Officer Poole's cruiser easing up Main Street—only Merrill waved in time for Richard to acknowledge. Eva's half-hearted wave came too late after she readjusted her basket between her arms.

Inside, Merrill didn't give Eva a chance to say 'Good morning' before telling her, "I'm heading next door to the diner. With Carolyn in the hospital,

I haven't been in the mood to eat at home alone, but I think I'm in the mood for poached eggs and hash. How about you? Can I bring you anything?"

Eva noticed he was wearing the same sweater vest as yesterday and couldn't help but catch a faint fusty odor that reminded her of Sam's parents in their later years. "I think I'm good, but thanks anyway," she said. "I was planning on stopping by the hospital after work to check on Carolyn—see how she's doing before they transfer her."

"That would be nice. I'm sure she'd appreciate that," he seemed to catch himself drifting, "Yes, they're transporting her to Mass General on Friday. Surgery's planned for Monday morning—early."

"Well, I'll be sure to be quick and just say hello. I wouldn't want her to get all worked up before Monday. Poor thing is probably worried about being carted all the way down there, too. I can't *possibly* imagine. And if it's food you need while all of this is going on, Faye and I can take turns bringing dishes over. We could start—"

Merrill interrupted, "Oh, there's no need. Really. I wouldn't want to be a burden. I'm fine. Honest. I could stand to lose a pound or two."

Eva saw this man nearly every day for years, and if anything, he needed to gain a few pounds. His face was as thin as she had ever seen it. His feminine nose looked almost witch-like. Reluctantly, she stepped back. "Alrighty then, if you say so."

"I do… but thanks for offering." He was almost to the door when Eva saw him take two big steps and push it open so Faye Stevens could walk right in. "I'm going next door to the diner. Do you need anything?"

"I'm all good, thanks, Merrill. Lovely day today, isn't it? This breeze should dry out the roads once and for all. I hope the town gets out and fills in the potholes before I find 'em, or there'll be hell to pay."

Eva had begun filling the coffee percolator but paused to say, "You tell 'em, Faye!"

"And that Dick Poole and his deputies should be out catching bad guys, not lining the town coffers with speeding tickets."

"You get pinched on the way in?" Eva asked her. "Dick runs a tight ship."

Eva finished filling the pot as Faye sidled up to her after hanging her coat. "Yeah, he stopped me upstreet, right along the straightaway. Nobody does thirty-five along there." Faye tore open a packet of Coffee-Mate non-dairy creamer, poured it into her mug, added a second packet, and then two sugars. "I swear… any time I've ever seen him, he's not smiling. No warning, either. There goes Merrill's springtime bonus—all spoken for, I guess." She filled her mug to the rim.

Eva chuckled inwardly, curious about who the so-called bad guys really were, according to Faye Stevens. As long as Richard Poole ran a tight ship, there shouldn't be any bad guys—maybe a few mischievous teenagers. Last year, there wasn't a single homicide in the state, and Eva remembered the last murder in Sumner Falls, committed nearly forty years ago—a jealous male coworker had bludgeoned a woman who worked at the machine shop. It was all over the national news when his murder conviction was overturned on appeal, thanks to the involvement of a defense lawyer who influenced the Lindbergh kidnapping case. "Easy come, easy go," she said.

Faye peered over the top of her mug. "Well, you're more fun than a barrel of monkeys this morning."

"Oh, pay no attention," Eva said. "I'm just upset over this Carolyn situation. I was planning to stop by and see her after work. Merrill said they're sending her down to Boston on Friday."

"After work?" Faye looked surprised. "Why don't you go after lunch? Take some time. I'll cover the floor. Besides, it's almost the end of mud season, and believe me, nobody is breaking down the front door to buy new sneakers and shoes that'll end up filthy as soon as they walk out."

Eva knew she was right and decided that was exactly what she would do before taking a deep breath and saying, "Thanks, Faye. I appreciate it. I'll return the favor tomorrow."

Faye waved her off. "Oh, I don't think that's necessary. Besides, you've known Carolyn and Merrill longer than I have. I wouldn't know what to say." She glanced over her shoulder toward the front of the store. "I think Merrill's losing weight. We should cook him a few meals for his freezer until Carolyn's back on her feet."

"Not gonna happen. I already asked, and he shot me down."

6

"Do you know if Carolyn had her surgery yet?" Alice Fairbanks asked. She had called last night to ask Eva if they had found the right Jøtul at the Lyme Country Store, and she was dismayed when Eva told her it was a no-go.

"No. I guess it's happening first thing Monday morning. We shall see, won't we?"

Eva reluctantly agreed to walk over to her friend's house for happy hour, aware that she had nothing better to do than clean an empty house while Sam was with Ray Whittman, supposedly hobnobbing at a ham radio flea market in Massachusetts. She braced herself for him to come home after spending money they should have saved for a new wood stove instead of more radio equipment he probably didn't need, which was of no benefit to her.

"I can't imagine," Alice said, refilling both their gimlets and the bowl of gorp between them. Her kitchen had the same layout as Eva's, but it was painted a solid baby blue. Unlike Eva, she wasn't a fan of wallpaper, and neither was her late husband, Reginald, who preferred a mid-century modern style.

"Me neither," Eva said as she scooped a small handful of raisins and peanuts. There was nothing she or Alice could do to help Carolyn or Merrill today, but she could ask for advice—something she had learned isn't necessary with Sam. He had a knack for offering opinions even when they weren't solicited.

"There's something I can't seem to shake," Eva said. "Vera Flynn." She turned away from the table and crossed her legs at the knee, her eyes instinctively drifting to the kitchen window where there was nothing to see but forest. Alice wrapped her gimlet with both hands. "I wish he'd just come out with it and be done. He's being so selfish. He gets me so excited one minute, telling me we'll go for a nice drive or that he wants to do something for me, but then he goes and breaks his promises. He has to make it all about him… And this Ray Whittman malarkey!" She reached across her body, fumbling for her glass until she finally grabbed it without spilling, taking more than a sip—draining it almost entirely. "I don't see the reason." She finished the drink, melting the last ice cube against the roof of her mouth to cool her temper. "And now they're supposedly off to Deerfield today, of all places, just to putter around and buy God knows what."

"Junk."

"Junk is right," Eva said, turning to lean on the table again. "I'll say." She glanced over Alice's shoulder at nothing but the field of blue paint. Even though they were as close as sisters, Eva was embarrassed to look her in the eye. "And to think… when we first got married, I bought him his first receiver. I sure hope I don't come to rue the day."

She made brief eye contact before glancing over Alice's other shoulder, remembering living with her parents on the farm across the river. She and Sam had taken in a beagle and named it Daisy, trying to train it as a bird dog, but they had no idea what they were doing. Daisy turned out to be nothing more than an overenergetic dog that ran through the cornfields willy-nilly. At least she had a cute face and stayed with them until a good dog's days came to an end. Between Daisy and their golfing, Sam's ham radio was a rainy day hobby, never an everyday obsession.

"So you haven't heard anything upstreet? No one's noticed anything that you know about?" Eva asked.

"I have not," Alice told her, seriously. "You know I don't care much for her, but to be honest, I never see her all that often in town. I know she pals around with her friend Phyillis, who I hear lives up in White River… so maybe that's how Vera met up with her? Working up there?"

"It galls me, seeing her tooling around in that sports car—imported no less, and going down to Florida… Where's the money coming from?"

Alice didn't have a ready answer, shrugging her shoulders. "Must still have life insurance money socked away."

Eva clucked and threw up her hands. It was nobody's guess—and nobody's business—where Vera got her money. She didn't care, but it still annoyed her. Why it did so wasn't entirely Sam's fault, nor his lack of candor. It was common sense to know that Vera's late husband had committed suicide, and his selfishness shouldn't have earned Vera the life of Riley. "We all know she never should have gotten that insurance payout… probably wouldn't be in this situation if she hadn't." *Perhaps wishful thinking.* "If Dick Poole had been on the job back then, he'd have straightened things out, but no, we had to have that halfwit fatso McCarthy, who was forced into retirement." She collected herself, almost getting up with the intention of opening the fridge to grab a Schlitz, but remembered she was in Alice's kitchen, not hers. "I guess I've said too much as it is. I'm sorry I got a little hot under the collar… My kidneys are acting up again, and that's the root of my irritation," she lied. "I'll have to go and get more water pills from Dr. Read—nip this in the bud."

Eva didn't really want a third gimlet, and Alice wasn't offering, but she wasn't ready to walk home and sit around waiting for Sam. It took everything she had not to want to wash and iron. Besides her love of bird watching, the next best thing that consumed her attention was her love of flowers. "I bet you can't wait for your gladiolus and peony to bloom."

• • •

Henry knocked on the door glass three times, startling Eva's private morning moment on the throne. The unexpected interruption caused her writing hand to jerk, splattering blue ink over the previous sentence as she jotted her thoughts and recollections from yesterday.

"Just a minute!" she yelled after opening the bathroom door, hoping her voice wasn't lost down the cellar stairs.

She placed the book in the bottom drawer, on top of last year's volume. She chose the hardcover journals because they felt timeless, like an old library book. She would fill them with steady penmanship, however many years she could, adding a narrative voice to their trays of 35mm slides. She would give the faces and places remembrance and hope that the years ahead wouldn't change—but they did—both her life and the journal's design, which she accepted.

"Dad?" Eva asked. She tugged on the doorknob, rattling the skeleton key before pulling the door inward, fighting the resistance of the felt weather stripping Sam had tacked on late that winter. "What's wrong? Is everything okay? Did mom have a spell?"

"No, no, nothin's wrong," he said, tapping and emptying his corncob pipe on his heel before climbing the steps into the kitchen.

Eva wondered how long he had been outside smoking between the houses before deciding it was time to knock. With the clement spring air, she guessed he had been out there for a while, probably watching and waiting for Sam to head off to work. He was wearing one of his long-sleeved wool shirts, a muted plum, under suspenders, without his bulky sweater vest, and she inhaled the scent of apple tobacco trapped in his collar as she hugged him. She couldn't help but think of Dina Shore singing "Shoo-Fly Pie and Apple Pan Dowdy." It was a good reminder to check the record club.

"I was wonderin' if you had time for a cup of coffee before work?" he asked.

"I don't. Faye usually has the morning pot ready by the time I get in, and Sam only makes enough for himself before taking off." She tried to read his eyes, looking for something to worry about. "Are you sure there's nothing wrong? Did *you* have a spell?"

"Lord no. I just had time to get outta the house 'cause your mother's a whirlin' dervish over there gettin' ready for Big Ben. He called last night, sayin' he was comin' for a week. Don't tell your mother I'm all excited to have 'em help me start scrapin' the house. It needs paintin'."

Eva missed her oldest brother and wished the weather was warmer so they could play a few rounds of golf while he was visiting. Swinging a club left-handed was a special bond they shared—something only they did naturally. Neither Henry, Ruby, Sam, nor Connie was left-handed.

"Don't you think it's still too cold outside to be painting?" she asked, her voice more interrogative than quizzical.

"Who said anythin' 'bout paintin'? I could use the help with scrapin'. That's the back breakin' part—the more help, the merrier. Paintin' is the easy part. That's when I get to relax," he winked.

"And which is more—cans of paint or cans of pipe tobacco?" she asked patronizingly.

Henry winked again.

Eva couldn't be late for work. It was only her and Faye holding down the fort while Merrill was in Boston for Carolyn's surgery. She didn't know when Merrill might call with any news or where he'd call first, but she tried to relax, knowing it was still early and he'd probably call the store sometime this afternoon or tomorrow. Hopefully, business would be slow, so she and Faye could share the earpiece and not make Merrill pay too much for the collect call.

"When's Ben coming?"

"Some time tomorrow afternoon. He's flyin' into Logan and takin' the bus to White River. We'll pick 'em up, and be home in time for supper." He started to move his pipe to his mouth, but hesitated, adding, "Be sure to invite Al, too. I'm sure she'd get a kick outta seein' him again."

Eva wanted to keep the conversation going, but she didn't have time to tell Henry that Sam hadn't come home from Deerfield on Saturday night. He called soon after she'd walked home from Alice's and told her he'd stopped by his brother's junkyard in Brattleboro. His truck wouldn't start, so he stayed overnight.

Sam's younger brother, Edwin, was a husky voice chain-smoker with a belly like a whiskey barrel and a matching nose—bulbous and capillary-ridged. He looked nothing like Sam, and Eva often wondered whether the milkman was to blame.

She didn't protest, having used up all her energy talking to Alice over gimlets, and instead skipped supper for a half-can of Schlitz. She had curled up on the floor in front of the stereo, listening to Connie Francis sing "Everybody's Somebody's Fool," until the last of the beer had turned warm and flat, before crawling into bed.

"Will do. Sure thing." She opened the door for her father and watched him take the three steps down to the walkway one at a time, childlike, not alternating his steps. It was only a matter of time, Eva thought, before someone took a spill. Sam rebuilt the back steps every few seasons, but no matter how many coats of gray paint he slathered on the wood planks, they'd wick up moisture and eventually rot out atop the mossy concrete pad.

Feeling guilty, she closed the door, watching him pack his pipe with a fresh pinch of ground tobacco, and wondered how long he'd stay outside, puffing and waiting for Ruby to finish tidying up. She paused and leaned her head out to get his attention. "Hey! Could you let Mom know I didn't have time to do any washing this morning? There's no need for her to come over looking for something to iron."

"Will do. Sure thing," he said.

Eva stuck out her tongue, chuckling under her breath, and shed all guilt as she closed the door without snicking the lock.

• • •

Connie and Warren tried to sneak into Merrill's store, with Warren doing his best not to disturb the decorative brass bell above the door with his outstretched hand, which tinkled once before falling silent—its patina now marked by his fingerprints.

Eva and Faye were in the backroom, finishing their coffee break, both energized by caffeine and the adrenaline rush from Merrill's good news, telling them that Carolyn's surgery had gone well—actually, better than expected. Her doctors credited her positive mindset before surgery, even telling Merrill she was cheerful and smiling when the anesthesiologist put her under.

The ring of the bell at the front of the store rang sharply in Eva's ear, as if it were right beside her, and she hurried over to greet them. "Oh my! What a surprise!" she exclaimed, hugging Connie warmly. "I wasn't expecting you until this weekend. Is everything good? Is everything going okay? No more Peeping Toms?" Eva turned to Warren, rubbing his upper arm like a genie's lamp—her eyes asking, hoping he'd give her an answer.

"Everything's fine, Mom. It's my spring break from school—the whole week. We just wanted to surprise you."

"Well, you certainly did," Eva assured her. Connie's infectious smile and bright laugh would bring her comfort, even if only for a few scant days. "The entire week, you say?"

Connie nodded.

"We can pick up some fabric for new skirts at Dewey's… or we can drive over to the new Dorr Woolen Mill that just opened and see what they have," Eva said, noticing Connie shift her eyes to Warren when she paused. Instead of a team of two, Eva realized she was now the third wheel. "Oh… plans already made? Movies? Bowling?" She hid her disappointment behind a quick, disingenuous smile that twinged her cheeks, and she dropped it before Connie could see her judgment.

"Yes… and no," Connie answered, her bright laugh seeming to highlight a secret in the air between her and Warren. "We had plans this week to go to the races in Claremont… but it's okay, really. Sewing by day, movies, bowling, and races at night. We can do it!"

There was Connie's youthful smile again, and Eva nearly gave in, saying, "Oh, don't be silly. You kids need to have your fun. Besides, you'll be exhausted by the time vacation is over, from the sounds of things." She was eager to steer the conversation away before tripping over herself and spoiling the day's energy, so she asked, "How's Catherine? Any special plans this week?"

"She's doing well. She went home to Waitsfield for the week. They were desperate for another pair of hands to help with sugaring." She looked at Warren, pursed her lips, and drew a deep breath. "Thank God we don't have that to deal with."

Warren shrugged, and Eva wondered if he was as quiet as his father, stopping herself from asking. He wouldn't remember.

"Speaking of manual labor," Connie said, scanning the store. "Why don't we help you around here until closing? We might as well drive up to Dewey's from here after work instead of going home first and then backtracking."

"Oh, there's no need to bother," Eva protested. "This isn't your burden to deal with," she said, turning to search for Faye, who caught her look and realized she'd been eavesdropping the whole time.

"Who are we to turn down free help?" Faye said. "If the four of us unbox these new tennis shoes and swap out the window display, we'll finish with an hour to spare. I can handle the last hour while you all head to Quechee and the mill—"

"You all?" Warren interjected. "Don't lump me into going shopping for sewing cloth."

"He speaks!" Faye shouted, pointing at him. She was about to say something, but couldn't get the words out before she slapped her knee and finally said, "Ha!"

Warren smoothed his mustache, either not understanding Faye's joke or staring her down, looking like Johnny Ringo—unimpressed—until Eva whispered, "She's teasing."

When Faye straightened up, looking dumbfounded, she said, "Why don't I start moving these last three boxes closer to the front?"

Eva nudged Warren, then lightly stepped on his toe, prompting him to offer Faye some assistance. To Connie, she said, "We should clear the window display first. It'll go faster as long as no one is in the store." She didn't want to sound gloomy, but she couldn't help but wonder if their sales were low this month because nobody wanted to face Merrill. If some people assumed the store was closed until Carolyn's cancer subsided, they'd stop by next month. "It's a good thing Merrill gave us a late Christmas bonus before Carolyn got sick, because our sales have been down since then. We might not hit our numbers this month."

Eva panicked, unable to remember if she had told Connie about her breast cancer. "Oh, gee willikers, did I not mention—"

"You did," Connie interjected, resting a hand on Eva's. "You wrote it in one of your letters. How's Carolyn doing?"

Eva took a deep breath. "She had her surgery this morning, and everything went splendidly." Eva tapped her temple with her knuckles. "I sure hope that's the end of it."

Connie climbed into the front window display, examining the dozen or so pairs of last-minute winter shoes and colorful children's rubber mud boots. "All of these, right?" she asked, picking up a pair of Chelsea boots and inspecting them more closely. "Are these men's or women's?" she asked, handing them to her mother.

"Does it really matter now?" Eva laughed.

"Good point!"

Connie faced the store's window and squatted, trying to handle too many pairs of boots at once, when Richard Poole stepped into full view. She startled and dropped what she was holding when he knocked on the glass.

Eva jumped at Connie's sharp inhale, but she didn't notice anything concerning until Richard opened the door and rang the bell.

"Good afternoon, Constance Martin, or should I say Miss Sumner Falls 1962?" He tipped his cap. "Eva Martin," he said, then spotted Faye in the shadows, kneeling with Warren and opening boxes of tennis shoes. "Faye Stevens. Take it slower next time?" He squinted, appearing indifferent and unsure of who Warren was. "Are you ladies working hard or hardly working?" he asked, smiling at his own wit. He extended his left hand and helped Connie step down from the window display before Warren could get there first, then shook his hand with his right, briefly connecting them like a priest, presenting them as a newly married couple.

Officer Poole removed his uniform hat, revealing a high forehead and thinning black hair slicked with Brylcreem. Without his uniform and wearing a Panama hat, he could easily pass as a mid-life Bing Crosby look-alike—if only he smiled more often.

"Thanks," Eva and Connie said.

"Mr. Poole—" Connie interrupted herself, "Officer Poole, good to see you again. Yes. Last year's ceremony. You remembered." She motioned, introducing, "And this is my boyfriend, Warren Bradford."

"That's quite a mustache for a teenager you've got going on there," Richard said, squinting.

When the police officer's squint lingered, Warren glanced at Connie, signaling between them, and said, "Same class of '62. I was her date... then... also..." If there was any flush to his face, it was obfuscated by his reddish-brown skin tone as he took an awkward, small step backward.

Officer Poole offered a smile that was neither warm nor trusting, as if he foresaw some ugly truth about a future young ne'er-do-well coming true, and he'd be there to catch him in the act. "Well, I'll let you all get back to it," he said, scanning the entire store, appearing to memorize every inch of it, and noting the time on his watch. "Where's Merrill today? I don't hear anyone in the back."

Eva was glad to keep things moving along, offering up, "He's in Boston with his wife, Carolyn. She had surgery this morning—cancer."

The expression on Richard's face shifted to genuine empathy. "I'm sorry to hear that. I hope everything's okay. I'm not all that familiar with them… which is a good thing—in my line of…" he trailed off, looking somewhat uncomfortable with his attempt at comedic relief.

"Everything turned out hunky-dory," Eva assured him.

"Well, give 'em my well wishes."

When he turned to leave the store, Eva noticed his thinning crown before he put his hat back on. Losing his hair at his age, it occurred to her that she didn't really know his age or anything else about him beyond his town duties.

Eva's Daily Reminder 1963: May 5, Sunday

Sunny and warm. Had the heat off and doors open. Sam put the screens in the doors and a few in the windows.

Saw the indigo bunting. Darn blue jays pestered but put an end to that.

Music festival in Burlington. Connie and Catherine went and took a carload of girls.

Mom's birthday. Gave her note paper and money for a new pocketbook.

Sam dug dandelions. Mom bought lobsters and we had supper here. I made biscuits and how we did eat. Al hated to watch the lobsters go into the pot. Made caramel pudding and I goofed the ingredients up. How we all laughed!

Did 4 loads of washing and Mom got them in for me.

Did all the ironing and mopped the floor. Two good jobs done!

Al gave me a perm and it came out tony regular.

Played 5 games of cribbage and Mom and I lost them all!

Sam went out after supper. Took a bag of dandelions down to Brattleboro. Home late and has to work in the morning.

7

Eva couldn't help but realize that her life with Sam was now like two ships passing in the night. He appeared to come and go as he pleased, and his moods shifted unpredictably.

He finished installing the two living room chandeliers, and although they weren't old farmer's, season-dried, weathered antique wagon wheels, they were modern, clear-coated, and symmetrical with brass lamps and a matching tire band. Adjusting their hanging height tested his nerves, and he sputtered a few times before finally positioning them so they didn't look out of place or garish in the room.

When he was satisfied that the new lights were hung at the right height, she asked if he wouldn't mind taking a drive to pick out a new Jøtul. He complained that he was too tired and suggested waiting until later in the summer, around the Fourth of July sales.

After complaining about sweating, he took a bath and said he was going to Ray's to work the radio bands. She accepted the day's victory and didn't protest the battle.

Eva poured herself some iced tea and stepped outside into the backyard. She grabbed a lawn chair from the toolshed and unfolded it in the shade of a butternut tree beneath a few fluffy clouds drifting along the jet stream. The air was fresh with a hint of humidity, and high above the treeline, the sound of a single-engine plane was no louder than a bumblebee. She sat and watched her feeders, hoping the indigo bunting would return. Sometimes a purple finch appeared alongside the bunting, and a few times, the rose-breasted grosbeak fed on the ground with a male cardinal. She appreciated the coordinated visits by color.

The yellow evening grosbeaks were gone now, leaving only the red cardinal, finches, and those pesky blue jays as the only colorful birds of summer. A bright orange-and-black Baltimore oriole was often heard high in the treetop canopy but rarely seen.

A hummingbird darted into the red plastic feeder hanging from the door canopy. It grabbed her attention, causing her to miss a small flock of blue jays that landed beneath the pole feeders. After the lone ruby-throated hummingbird zipped off, she shouted, stomping her foot, "Go on! Git!" When that didn't scare them away, she added louder, "Go on now!" Again, they ignored her warning. "Don't make me get up! If I make it back into the kitchen, you'll be sorry!" It infuriated her that only one would look at her while the rest kept gobbling up the fallen seed, even ignoring a chipmunk that appeared from her yellow primroses and zig-zagged among the jays. Mad at herself for giving in to them, she stood and clapped her hands, which scared everyone away, including the chipmunk.

She was so distracted by the blue jay bully robbers that she initially missed Henry, who now stood by the corner of his house, holding a gallon of paint and a brush. His pipe drooped from the corner of his mouth, and the brush dripped into the open can, which he wiped before setting both down on the ground. The long-billed cap he used for fly-fishing had been repurposed as a painter's hat, and Eva thought it looked silly, extending so far over his face that it hid the length of his pipe in its shadow.

Heny withdrew his pipe from his mouth and called across the yard, "What in hell is all your yammerin' for?" He took two steps toward her, then turned back, kneeled, covered the can, and dropped the paint-soaked brush into another coffee can that Eva guessed was filled with turpentine.

She waited for him to stroll across the yard before telling him to get another chair from the toolshed, which he did. His spontaneous attempt to unfold the webbed chair, switching between holding his pipe in one hand

and shaking the aluminum frame with the other, made him look like he was acting in a Three Stooges sketch. Even as a middle-aged woman, he could still embarrass her beyond measure, but she ignored him until he settled with a huff. If his bottom had fallen through the brittle nylon straps, she would have laughed hysterically instead of asking, "What's Mom up to?"

"Last I saw, she was elbow deep kneadin' bread dough," he said, crossing his legs and leaning off to the side. He tugged a tobacco pouch from his Dickies back pocket and packed his pipe, checking the draft without lighting. "She'll be bakin' and knittin' all afternoon. If I don't keep movin' around the house, findin' things to keep busy with, I'd end up as fat as a Miller's horse."

Eva couldn't imagine any of them being fat, except Edwin, who probably spends more time sitting in his junkyard office, buying more junk than selling it.

"Sam around?" he asked.

"Gone upstreet."

All she wanted was to sit and enjoy the birds. That was the reason she first stepped outside. Late spring was her favorite time of year, when she could appreciate the perennial blooms and birds before the June rains arrived. During the dog days of summer, she would find herself climbing onto the Simplicity riding mower every other day to cut the grass across both backyards while Sam used a push mower on the retaining wall banks. After a quick beer break and cracker snack, Sam would detach the mower, and they'd head into the forest with the matching trailer to cut wood for the upcoming winter. Wearing long sleeves in the heat and humidity to protect herself from mosquitoes and black flies was the worst part of living in rural New England—something flatlanders never saw in Vermont Life Magazine.

"Can I get you something to drink?" Eva asked.

"Oh, I'm fine… The shade's nice and does the trick."

The ground around the feeders stayed empty, except for the brave little chipmunk that reemerged from the flower bed to gather winter seeds. Eva never took umbrage at the cute creatures, which appeared so innocent—unlike others that acted as if they owned the space around her feeders. On rare occasions, it saddened her to see a hawk swoop down and catch one, and she tried not to think whether it was a mother or a father as the hawk carried the tiny, back-striped creature away to its death. She looked toward her parents' house, unable to watch if it happened again, and asked, "I thought you were done painting the house?"

"Gosh, no. That's all primer. Ben worked like hell helpin' me scrape."

"Tell me about it. I barely got to see him before he was gone."

"We were workin' the whole time you were," he said, shrugging his shoulders. "It really needed it, though… too many layers. Ben ended up buying a couple of those fancy electric paint strippers. Saved us some time, or else we wouldn't have finished before he had to leave." He mimed with his hands, holding something up in front of himself for a moment, then lowering and motioning side-to-side with his other hand. "Damndest thing. Hold it up against the siding for about a minute. Let the heat blister the old paint—then scrape it off like butter. Your mother was mad as hell, seein' the mess in her flower beds. We got so excited, we forgot to put down drop cloths." He snapped his fingers. "That reminds me, I came over and bor-rowed one of Sam's extension cords. I've still got it."

Eva wasn't worried he'd forget. "No worries. Sam probably hasn't even noticed it's missing yet. He doesn't spend much time downstairs these days," she said, glancing at her feeders, pleased to see several finches and chickadees clinging to the suet. She sensed her father's eyes on her, watching her, waiting patiently for her to continue, so she did, saying, "This whole Ray Whittman business has got me all shook up. Sam's been spending so much time with him, obsessed with radioing. I thought it was all supposed to be over after he'd passed his test, but Sam said he'd failed the first time he took it and had to go to Boston last month for a retake. He never did tell me the outcome, and I didn't bother asking." She lifted her iced tea, noticed it was mostly melted ice, and flung the contents in an arc over the grass. "He's only driven Connie to school once this semester—took her up one time and called from Rutland on the way home. I don't remember if it was some excuse about the weather, the roads, or something else. At least Warren's been a blessing, bringing her home as often as he does."

"Speaking of Connie, she should be home for the summer any day now?"

The pain in Eva's derrière moved up her spine and settled on her shoulders—another heavy burden. "She said she's staying up there over the summer, found a good job in Brandon, and thinks she might be able to stay on permanently after graduation. As much as I miss her dearly, I'm hopeful she'll get to keep it. Good jobs are hard to come by these days, but hopefully Kennedy can do something about that."

"You think those kids will end up gettin' married?"

"Your guess is as good as mine. I wish she'd wait until after graduation next year, but if I'm reading Warren right, he's bound to propose this summer. He's been a big help, dropping by the store almost every day. I think he wants to find out what Connie writes to me in her letters. It makes me so happy that she writes so often, keeping me updated on all her news. I think she's made some lifelong friends up there, too."

The late afternoon sun was fading behind the treeline, and neither of them knew or cared what time it was. As long as at least one hummingbird kept returning to her sugar and water elixir, Eva was in no rush to leave the day behind. Her row of white lilac bushes that separated her house from Vera's was sprouting green leaves but had not yet started to bud. Once their bloom clusters were in full display later in the month, Eva would keep all the windows on that side of the house open to let their sweet, powdery scent drift inside.

She had been avoiding Vera's house, telling herself there was no need to worry. As she relaxed her shoulders and shed the weight, she noticed the driveway behind the house was empty. There was no sign of Vera's car. If she lingered too long, looking away, she was sure Henry would notice and mention it, but when he snicked the flint wheel of his Zippo, she was grateful he was a man of few words. "About time," she said.

"I had a feelin' you were missin' the smell of apples. I need another few minutes before havin' to deal with cleanin' my brush. Back at it again bright and early."

Eva struggled to see her father's bright eyes beneath the long brim of his cap, but his smile was visible between his pipe puffs, which he subtly directed her way. Occasionally, he tried to huff an O, puckering his lips like a fish gulping for air. It was all to no avail, and she dismissed his antics and residual smoke with a wave of her hand.

They both turned toward the squeaky, protesting sounds of Henry's screen door. Eva winced, recalling distant schoolhouse memories of fingernails on a chalkboard. Henry must have noticed her flinch, prompting him to say, "I know. I know. I gotta put some oil on those hinges." He crossed his leg, knocked the burnt tobacco out on his boot heel, and then waved to Ruby, who pushed through the door's screeching without wincing.

"Scrape the house, prime the house, paint the house, tie up the blackberry bushes, weed the iris beds, and now oil the door," he said. "If I were you, I'd keep workin' as long as you can, because let me tell you, bein' retired is more work than there are hours in a day." He waved again.

Ruby turned around, looking up and down at the door.

"I know. We all heard it," Henry whispered.

"You think she'll hear you all the way up here?" Eva asked, teasing him. "You two have been married since you were nineteen. How do you two keep up with it?"

"I was nineteen, your mother was still eighteen," he said, waving down to Ruby, married fifty-three years. "How do *we* do it? *We* don't do anything… I keep my mouth shut, and she's the boss, that's how *I* do it. Look at her. She's happiest when she's wearing an apron. Whether she's stirrin', cuttin', choppin', kneadin', bakin', fryin', roastin'… makes no difference, that's when she's smilin'." He faced Eva. "At least you inherited your mother's cookin' skills. I don't suppose you got much from me."

"You taught me to hunt and fish," Eva admitted.

"Oh, hell. You didn't want nothin' to do with castin' a fly."

Eva knew she was her father's daughter in every way—minus the pipe.

"Henry!" Ruby shouted. "Time to come in and wash up—supper's almost ready." She appeared to tilt her head, looking at Eva, then glanced at the empty parking spot behind the toolshed where Sam always parked his truck. "How's about you, Eva? If you haven't started anythin' yet, there's plenty to eat. I've got a chicken in the oven, and the last of your father's pole beans. You can finish talkin' to him over cards while I clean up."

"I knew I should've taken you up on that offer for a beer," he winked.

They stood, stretched, and Eva shooed him away before insisting it was no trouble for her to refold the chairs and latch the toolshed.

• • •

Eva and Henry finished their cribbage rubber game. Her double run of eight left her final peg a few holes short of winning, while Henry lowered his cards and counted off a double-double run with fifteens, scoring twenty-four, enough to peg out.

"Show off," she said, scooping his cards off the table and ending his shoulder waggle celebration. "You sure got help on the cut."

Heny pulled the four green and red plastic pegs, flipped the board over, and used the pad of his thumb to push the tin plate out of the recessed bottom, dropping them into the peg holder. He was careful not to cut his thumb on the sharp corners of the thin strip of sheet metal.

He was teasing her—smirking—as he waited, palm up, to accept the card deck from her.

When her mother mumbled at the sink, she turned in her chair to see what the fuss was about and saw Ruby looking out the kitchen window to her right, toward the dirt lane that separated the two houses.

"Looks like you're a day late and a dollar short," Ruby said as she placed the last china plate in the rack and dried her hands on her apron. "Fool thinks he's gonna wash his truck now? It's almost dark."

As soon as Eva heard the last part, she realized Sam was finally home and joined her mother at the sink, watching Sam struggle to unwind the garden hose from the side of the house.

"By the time he gets all the kinks out, it'll be too dark to see a thing," Ruby said. "I've already put away the leftovers, so he's outta luck, but I *guess* I can make up a plate for you to take home."

"That's all right," Eva assured her. "He doesn't need any excuses to settle for a bowl of milk and crackers."

"Are you interested in any excuses?" Henry said from behind them.

Ruby faced Eva, her scowl almost masculine. "What's goin' on? Something I should know?" she asked, focusing on Eva, not Henry.

"Oh, it's nothing. Nothing to worry about. I expected him to be home earlier and not miss supper."

Ruby checked on Henry to see if he'd offer anything more, and her expression made it clear that he better not lie. She seemed indifferent when he shrugged and held out his hands. "Well, I'll make a small plate anyway, just in case. If he doesn't eat it tonight, he can always take it tomorrow for his lunch."

Eva thanked her mother for the delicious meal, commenting on how moist the chicken was, and gave a sarcastic nod when Ruby said her recipe called for nothing more than simple butter basting. (Probably equal parts whole chicken and butter by weight.) Then she thanked Henry for a well-played game, and he offered to bring out the bocce ball set if she wanted a change of pace.

Outside, Eva rubbed her arms, chilled by the late evening air, which had grown noticeably cooler since she had been sitting and bird-watching. Sam had managed to stretch the hose far enough to reach his truck, parked on level ground in the roadway, and she could hear the water trickling down the dirt-sloped lane, likely causing a mess in the street. She hesitated, unsure if she should ask him why he's been gone so long, and if it was a shame he had to miss supper, or why he seemed compelled to wash his truck so late. She chose the less confrontational approach and asked, "How can you see in the dark?"

Sam didn't startle at the sound of her voice. "It'll only take a minute. I wanna rinse all the dust off before work tomorrow. I didn't even bother with the soap bucket. I'll be in in a minute."

Eva clung to the leftover plate. The warm chicken radiated through it to her palm and through the plastic wrap, keeping everything in place. It took all her strength not to toss the plate into the truck bed, but she couldn't disrespect her mother's unconditional effort. "Mom made you a leftover plate. I'll bring it inside."

Sam jogged past her and turned off the hose, the handle squeaking softly with each turn, like a child's tricycle wheel compared to the screech of the screen door hinges. "Thanks. I'm not… Ray and I ended up stopping by the Masonic lodge and got to yapping with some of the guys. You remember Red? And Dick Taft? Retired from the machine shop? I was surprised they weren't interested in shop talk—just wanted to brag all afternoon about how good life's been since they retired. Everyone's getting ready for deer camp. Can you believe that? So soon? Red even asked if I wanted to go up for"—he wrung his hands, air drying them—"opening weekend. I'd have to dust off my Marlin." He looped the hose several times over the hanger, brushed his hands once more, holding them closer to his face, and inspected them in the dark. "Anyway, we ended up helping ourselves to too many doughnuts and coffee, and lost track of the time. Tell Ruby thanks again. And instead of packing a lunch, I'll come home for lunch tomorrow."

It was well past sunset before the waxing moonlight illuminated the stars. Eva had stopped listening to Sam's hogwash around the time he mentioned stopping at the Masonic lodge, and now she was a little dizzy from standing so long. She took a step, tried to steady herself, and nearly stepped into a silty dust puddle that hadn't soaked into the dirt tire path yet. If her tennis shoes had found their way into the dirty water, there would be absolute hell to pay.

She jumped over the tire path, first onto the grass median, then across the far side, before finally reaching her walkway safely. Leaving Sam behind, she approached the door and reached for the handle. She fell and lost her tenuous grip on the plate, letting it slip from her hand, and it broke on the concrete. Saran Wrap kept the pieces from shattering.

After Sam helped her into the kitchen and sat her down, she told him she was fine, just a little dizzy from standing and holding out the plate for too long. She asked him to clean up the mess and keep quiet about her having a spell, warning him not to blab to Connie or her parents.

What she wasn't about to tell him was that as she reached to open the back door, the light across the yard was enough for her to notice Vera staring at her from her kitchen. When Vera waved, Eva was sure she was smiling.

• • •

Eva woke up the next morning, her kidneys throbbing and pounding like a bass tuba. She wasn't sure if the pain was from falling last night or if this was another one of her recurring kidney episodes. She also couldn't remember whether she fell down the stairs and bruised herself or if she only fell to one knee, unscathed. Either way, she had no water pills left, so she'd have to call in sick to the store and hoped Faye would understand. Hopefully, she'd be able to see Dr. Read as soon as she could pull herself together. Getting out of bed was a chore, but she wasn't falling back asleep at this point. The ache in her kidneys radiated up into her shoulders, questioning why she had given Sam such a hard time when he fell and broke his ribs. Maybe she should have been more empathetic when tightening the ace bandage in haste.

To her surprise, Sam hadn't left for work yet; instead, he made her breakfast of sunny-side-up eggs and toast, which he covered with a lid from one of her frying pans to keep warm. "I wasn't sure if you'd be up so soon," he said. "Are you feelin' okay or all lamed up?"

Eva pressed her hands against her kidneys and went into the bathroom, closing the door behind her without answering the question. She sat on the toilet, unable to urinate, and suddenly remembered seeing Vera through her kitchen window the night before. *Had Vera waved and smiled before or after she started slipping?* She couldn't recall; either the memory was fuzzy, or her view across the yards and through the lilacs was unclear.

A quick peek in the medicine cabinet confirmed her memory that she had used the last of the water pills. She considered calling Whitey at the pharmacy to see if he would refill her prescription without contacting Dr. Read. She could ask Sam to pick them up while she tried to eat her eggs. The sensation of dry toast or cold butter in her mouth made her apathetic. She wished Connie were home so they could snuggle under the covers.

"Your eggs are gettin' cold out here," Sam said from the kitchen.

Eva looked at herself in the mirror and saw that her hair was a tangle of gray, loose snarls, even though Alice had given her a color and perm last week. Perhaps maintaining her natural black hair was a losing battle against gray roots, and she should consider a more brownish shade sooner rather than later. Alice wouldn't steer her wrong.

Hopefully, she'll feel better before Wednesday, confident she'll beat this since the pills usually start working within a day or two.

Reaching for the doorknob, she glanced down at her bottom drawer, aware that her recent journal was half-full with all the morning temperatures, weather, dinners, store business, bird sightings, the start of her curse, and whether or not she had lit a fire in the fireplace. But what about yesterday? It would all have to wait until she called Whitey or was forced to drive up and see Dr. Read, something she dreaded, bouncing in the Beetle's stiff seat.

Sam was still sitting at the kitchen table when she shuffled out of the bathroom on slippered feet to join him. He removed the lid from her eggs and buttered toast, and the air that wafted toward her face was neither warm nor smelled like a country breakfast, but for a faint hint of black pepper that Sam had generously sprinkled over the eggs.

The instant the toast met her lips, it was cold and dry, and she dropped it on the plate. "I think I'll just have tea this morning," she said, grimacing more than smiling.

Sam didn't look pleased with her rejection and carried the plate to the sink. The food was cold, and neither of them said a word as he sputtered incoherently, then filled the teakettle and set it to boil. "I'm gonna be late," he said. "I guess you'll have to fend for yourself when it's done." He gestured toward the kettle with his chin and looked at her, waiting for a reaction, but she didn't give him one; she only sighed softly with a look she hoped he'd recognize as a face only their beloved beagle, Daisy, could make. It seemed to work, and he returned the same soft sigh before bringing her basket of tea bags—an assortment of Earl Grey, green, black, and mint varieties—and a mug to the table. Even though she preferred Earl Grey, she made a mental note to add lemon and chamomile to the grocery list, hoping she wouldn't forget after calling Faye.

Eva arched her back, grimacing—both genuine and for effect. "I think I'd better give it a rest today. I'll call Faye. It feels like my kidneys are acting up again, and I'm out of my usual pills. I'm debating whether to call Whitey or wait until nine and then call Dr. Read's office. See when he can fit me in today—as early as possible."

Sam stood with his fists on his hips, swaying from side to side, and like her, struggled with the situation being six of one and half a dozen of the other. As she waited patiently, she asked, "Were you still planning on coming home for lunch? Probably not now…"

His swaying stopped, and his face lit up, revealing the rarely seen, tight-lipped, youthful smile she remembered from last summer. It was the face of the old Sam, and she sensed that he still loved her—he was her soulmate.

"I'll call in sick too," he said. "I'll take you up to Dr. Read's… just in case there's something else going on. See if we can nip this in the bud." He turned at the sound of the first tea kettle whistling. "Earl Grey?"

"Please. Same old, same old, I guess."

"Want me to make new toast? I might as well have one myself."

"Sure."

After their quiet tea, Eva surprised herself and wrote something different in her diary—something hopeful.

Eva's Daily Reminder 1963: July 4, Thursday

Windy, chilly, sunny. Curse.

Heat on. Golly's sake is this summer? Unusual!

Woke up feeling lousy and went back to bed for a while. Hemorrhoids are a little better. Got some Pazo cream.

Got Connie's washing and ironing done.

Sam cut off the bottom of a plastic bleach bottle to make me a scoop for the bird seed.

Al came over and we cooked some goodies for Connie. She and Warren went on a picnic and then surprised us all by coming home with a new diamond ring!

We ate out in the backyard with sweaters on. I made ham macaroni and cheese, corn casserole, cabbage salad, biscuits, and pecan pie.

Sam worked on the fan in the kitchen. Has the hole all cut. Ran into all kinds of trouble, wires, etc. Gave up and took a basket of raspberries down to Brattleboro with still no promise to go shopping for a new stove.

Connie and Warren got started early for Brandon so they could see the fireworks when they got there.

Not looking forward to cleaning the downstairs tomorrow.

Behind for the week at the store.

8

Henry tried to finish painting before the Fourth of July, but he never seemed to get much done after priming. Without Benjamin's help and amid the endless days of weeding flower beds, mowing, and tending his abundant raspberry and blackberry bushes, he rarely had a minute to himself.

Eva criticized him for wasting valuable daylight, using an old push mower with a wobbly wheel that he struggled to keep straight. "Why do you insist on using that old thing? It came over on the Mayflower, didn't it? I said I'd mow your lawn with the tractor."

She stared at him, exasperated by his stubbornness, and worried that one day his heart might give out. Unlike a worn spring in a pocket watch, his heart couldn't be replaced with a new one under a jeweler's loupe.

Her closest support was already a widow, and if anything happened to her parents, she would only have Connie to rely on, which wouldn't be fair to her. Benjamin was on the West Coast, and God only knows where Donald was these days. It wasn't the first time she had considered leaning on Connie before Sam.

Henry didn't blink. He stood in the middle of the yard where she had interrupted him, leaning on the mower's handle, and moved his pipe up and down in his mouth like a cow chewing cud.

Eva had seen this look before, and it instantly brought her back to her childhood, making her feel like she was five years old. It had nothing to do with his pride in her or her accomplishments, such as raising an intelligent and independent daughter or keeping a tidy house. A parent always sees their own children as just that—children, regardless of their age, because long-term memories outlast the passing moments.

"You wouldn't give Big Ben that look," she said, causing Henry to step back and drop the handle. Her father didn't favor Benjamin or Donald, and he wasn't patronizing her—he was disappointed that his sons weren't there helping him. Plus, he was too proud to ask Sam—stubbornness wrapped in frustration. "I take it that Ben's not able to break away from whatever it is he's doing out in California?" she asked. "When's the last time you and Mom heard from Donald?"

"Ben's busy with some promotion. He called the other night, or maybe it was a week or so ago—I can't keep track of it all. Your mother probably doesn't remember either if you asked her… somethin' about a promotion in rank." He nodded, looking confident. "Now, Donald… your guess is as good as mine. Who knows what the hell he's got goin' on up in Alaska, but I'd assume the army would get in touch with us if he were dead in a ditch somewhere." He shook his head, then shrugged. "Whatcha gonna do?"

"Why the hell don't you ask Sam?" she said, noticing that Henry's wincing and flinching looked like he'd been slapped in the face with a rotten fish.

"Oh, I don't want to bother him. He works all day. Besides…"

"Besides, you're both stubborn? Afraid he'll tell you how to do it?"

Another slap and flinch.

"Nah… I was gonna save him for the real job this year. I could use his help redoin' the shingles."

Eva imagined the two men falling off a ladder while painting, hauling shingles, or even falling off the roof altogether. *Why did life have to be so complicated with these two?* "Well, I'll ask him," she said. "Maybe it would do Sam some good to spend more time with you, working outside while the weather stays nice." She hoped Sam might learn a thing or two about how a marriage can last fifty years through hard work at home. That's why she told him the kitchen needed an exhaust fan and set him up for success. "I'd think you'd be happy to get it done. Having only the primer coat on there doesn't look nice. You don't want the neighborhood to start making a fuss. Even Al might not want to come for supper anymore if she assumes everyone's watching her going in and out of a riffraff house with its shutters removed." She hoped her words would light a fire under him, and he'd give up the mowing for painting. When he only looked toward the house without moving, she pressed him, "I'll finish the lawn. Why don't you go back to work?"

"That detailed trimwork takes forever," he said, pausing, then adding, "Are you all excited about Connie's engagement? Has she started askin' you about helpin' to plan for the weddin'?"

Damn, he knew exactly how to press her buttons. "Very pleased," Eva said. "He's a nice boy. Helps her a lot. There's no date set. Nothing's been planned... Next summer, after graduation, seems to make the most sense, don't you agree?"

He nodded, but added, "Although a lot can happen between now and then."

• • •

Late July in Vermont marked a crossing, demarcating nature's line between mosquito season and the appearance of the first firefly, whose flickering, iridescent green patterns danced against the rising moonlight, trying to attract a suitable mate.

Eva had agreed to Alice's offer to walk over for a Drambuie and settle in before the dusk showtime began against the backdrop of her forested cul-de-sac. Eva also invited Ruby to come along and see the flower beds, and she did, offering to sit in one of Alice's lawn chairs while the other two sat at her iron outdoor table. A single tube bent into a U-shape allowed them to rock gently as they sipped the honey-and-anise liqueur. Ruby sat upright; the webbed nylon straps kept her posture stiff—her feet were planted apart, and her hands were folded neatly on her lap, which was covered by her apron. Like Henry's pipe, she only removed it at bedtime.

"I wish my gladiolus looked as good as yours," Ruby said. "Mine should be gettin' just as much sun." Ruby unfolded her hands and drummed her knuckles on the aluminum armrest, the sound of which made Eva flinch. It was loud enough to scare off any fireflies before the show even got started. "You waterin' your garden every mornin' or every other day?"

Alice pushed an ice cube out of her mouth with her tongue and into her glass hard enough for Eva to hear the clink. "Oh, Ruby! That's too much. A good, deep watering once a *week* is all you need to do." She looked at Eva, eyes wide enough to see more white than iris, and Eva shrugged, mouthing the words, "What are you gonna do?" so Ruby wouldn't hear and start a fuss.

"So, Ruby… Henry didn't want to come over and watch with us?" Alice asked.

Ruby stopped drumming and crossed her legs. "He's all tuckered out from paintin' all day. Seems he's got a new boss that's been crackin' the whip," she said, eyeing Eva out of the corner of her eye before scanning the treeline again. "He's probably readin' his paper in his chair by now and already watched all fifteen minutes of Cronkite." She propped herself forward, arching her back. "I haven't seen a single flicker yet, have you? I guess it's not dark enough yet… And what about fertilizer? Isn't Sam buying the same stuff for all of us at Agway?"

"He does," Eva said. "It's probably because you're overwatering, as Al said. Why don't you forget about it? I'll remind Sam to do it when he's washing the cars—one less thing on your plate to worry about." She reached over and patted her mother's hand, her arthritic knuckles as big and round as schoolyard marbles.

"Speaking of Sam, what's he up to tonight?" Alice whispered.

Eva caught her mother's slight head tilt and knew there was nothing wrong with her hearing. There was no need to tell any white lies, as he had spent all day in the forest behind their house cutting wood. "He bought himself a new toy and spent all day sawing wood. He was taking his bath when I left. He wants to get everything down, split, and piled before he starts helping Dad with the new roofing shingles. And… he wants to get all *that* done *before* we have to move Connie into her new room at school, ideally before Labor Day. She wrote in her last letter that she's been elected hall president."

"The wedding will be here before you know it," Alice said.

"Ha!" Eva laughed. "She *just* got engaged! I don't need any more gray hairs."

"Don't you worry about that, I've got you covered. Speaking of which, you're about due for another shampoo and blowout. Ruby, why don't I do your perm this week, too? Wednesday after work or after supper?"

Ruby tilted her head back. No stars were visible; the evening sky was thick with clouds, and there was no breeze, making the air feel lukewarm and humid. "Hmm," she moaned, exhaling, before sucking on her lips.

"What are you doing?" Eva asked her.

"I'm ruminatin'."

"What is there to think about? You know you're not going anywhere—anytime soon."

Alice chuckled and finished her Drambuie along with the remaining ice chips.

"All right, fine," Ruby said. "I guess I'm free after all, accordin' to my boss."

Eva realized her mother's sarcasm meant she was bored while waiting. She and Henry usually played cards before bed, and they weren't drinkers, preferring Folgers at sunrise over Earl Grey. Henry would stock only a six-pack of beer when Benjamin came to visit, buying a whole case if he stayed longer to help Henry with projects around the house.

"I ain't seen a one. Have you?" Ruby asked. "I'm calling this performance a bust and goin' home."

"Are you sure? Can't you wait a little longer?" Alice asked. "We can walk you home if not."

"I'll be fine. Ever since they put in all these streetlights, the whole neighborhood is lit up like a city. When I was born, and the sun went down… the night was as dark as the inside of a black cow."

"Mom."

"'twas so, I tell ya."

"All right… If you say so. Ring once when you get home."

Eva watched as her mother stood, walked around to the front of the house, and made her way down the street. Even with orthopedic shoes, swollen knees and ankles, her seventy-three-year-old gait was steady enough not to need a cane. "I don't know how she does it. She's on her feet all day in either the kitchen or bending over in the flower beds or picking berries. She sits for supper and then plays gin rummy… that's it. She even bends over when we go and pick strawberries on the River Road. Tough old bird, I guess."

"All those years of growing up on the farm. Can't imagine being a kid and having no electricity, pumping well water with a hand pump—"

"I still have their old hand pump," Eva interjected. "It's downstairs. Been sitting on Sam's workbench, waiting for him to turn it into a lamp. I've got a spot all picked out—in the front window on the north side—if he ever gets around to doing it." She wasn't trying to sound aggravated, but maybe she did. "He's been busier than usual, cutting wood, but he broke his promise about getting a new stove for the living room." She told Alice about wanting a Jøtul. "At least he seems to have cut back on his Ray Whittman get-togethers, but spends more time driving to Brattleboro to see his brother. There's always something he needs, or else he takes something down there."

"And Vera? You still think something's going on there?"

Eva had her doubts. Sam was moody—he was always running hot or cold—and worked extra hours at the shop, still going in for half-days on Saturday mornings. With Ray less and less in the picture, he hadn't been staying out late anymore, unless he was spending the night at his brother's. "I don't think so," she said. "If something was going on or if he wanted his freedom, then I hope he would just ask and be done with it."

"One more Drambuie? Let's give the firefly show a bit longer to start."

Eva assumed Sam was watching the Red Sox, or else he was upstairs on his radio. "Sure, why not. Who cares if it's a school night," she said sarcastically.

When Alice returned with fresh pours, they clinked glasses, and Eva said, "I wasn't going to bother saying anything, but I had to laugh this afternoon. Vera was outside mowing her lawn, and I don't know who she was trying to impress, but her getup?" Eva let out a short laugh, wondering if Vera saw herself as a schoolgirl. "She had her hair all tied up in a bandana, sleeveless shirt with too many buttons undone... short shorts, and oh my... bare feet! Can you imagine that? Mowing the lawn barefoot. What on earth was she thinking?" After a brief pause, she added for good measure, "Red, white, and blue colors, nonetheless."

"You think she was showing off?"

"Well, Sam was up behind the house when I got home. From the sound of his chainsaw, he must have been quite a ways up there, out of sight. Either she runs overheated, or I can't imagine she was showing off to Henry, who might've still been painting."

They both shared a good laugh over that last thought.

• • •

Eva paused at the bottom of the stairs. The door was ajar with the amber light from Sam's room spilling down the stairwell. He was awake and still on the radio. She could hear his finger taps, sending out Morse code dits and dahs—that's how Sam had described the short and long sounds in the radio-coded alphabet to her.

She closed the door, pushing it shut without turning the knob. She wasn't trying to be loud or as quiet as a church mouse until Sam's footfalls broke the silence. She stepped past the doorway into her bedroom, not bothering to wait for him to appear.

He slipped around the door into the tight space and faced her as she turned on her bedside lamp. He was dressed in faded sweatpants, soft and stretched from repeated washings, along with a collared white T-shirt and his after-dinner moccasin slippers—at least more comfortable for her to see than a sleeveless undershirt and boxers, which he'd wear on sticky, stifling nights. She could smell that he was freshly bathed, catching a hint of Zest soap that she inhaled without sniffing, and for a brief moment couldn't breathe again, thinking maybe he was in her room to make love.

"I guess you've been over at Al's," he said. "Ruby rapped on the back door and said not to bother walking over because it was too early to see the show."

"Seems so."

"Hey… whaddya say we take off for Lyme first thing this weekend?"

It was too late for Eva to get excited about shopping now, but that was okay; things would work themselves out. "If you think so," she said, realizing this conversation was all about him.

"I got a $100 bonus at work, and time off, so it seems right to take advantage? No?"

The Drambuies were smoothing over the rough edges, and Eva had to work in the morning, getting up early to make sure she had enough time to pull some curtains and start a load of laundry. "Sounds good," she said, turning down her bedsheet. "If you've already done your business, then I guess I'll brush my teeth now, unless that's why you came downstairs." She waited to see if he would move or reply—her tepid amorousness vanished like a firefly in the forest canopy.

"All right. I guess I'll have some milk and crackers and finish the paper."

Eva hesitated, letting Sam get a head start to the kitchen before she followed to the bathroom. He was still fussing around in the kitchen when she stepped out of the bathroom, and she couldn't help herself—she looked through the kitchen window and across the yard to see if any of Vera's lights were still on, but the house was dark.

•••

After work, Eva was excited to find a letter from Connie in the mailbox. It was hefty in her hand, and she couldn't wait to bring it inside before tearing it open. The two pages, written in cursive on thick stock paper, were still light enough that the envelope didn't require extra postage beyond the standard five-cent stamp. She always enjoyed walking to the post office when she got the chance, taking advantage of her lunch break on slow days at the store to buy sheets of special stamps for Christmas or anything artistic enough to catch her eye, which she'd tuck away in an ever-growing philatelic binder. She had recently bought some 100th anniversary Gettysburg battle stamps, which she was using to correspond with Sybil down in Texas.

The entire first page—front and back—featured enthusiastic testimonies from every girl in Connie's dorm, and the second page seemed to be a written account from Catherine about how Connie was managing her duties as hall president. It said that Connie was using all of her 5'10" to intimidate the freshman girls into behaving, ending with, "Just kidding!"

Eva entered the kitchen and found a fresh stack of pressed curtains on the table, next to a pile of her work shirts and blouses, all neatly ironed. *What in the world was she going to do with her mother? How did she always manage to find the hours in a day?*

Eva gently gathered her tops and tucked them into her dresser. On her way to the kitchen, she caught a flash of red through the window next to her reading chair and couldn't tell if it was the male cardinal, but she'd get a better look at the whole yard from the kitchen window, so she didn't stop to peek.

To her amazement, it was a scarlet tanager—a rare sight—Eva couldn't remember the last time she'd seen one at the feeders. They were as scarce as the oriole in summer, usually heard high in the butternut trees behind the house, and not on the ground. They were clever to stay far from the neighborhood's roaming cats. She didn't mind the occasional feline sighting as long as they kept the darn blue jays away. Sam wished someone's kitty would stay busy and patrol the yard for shrews and moles—those little buggers that dig tunnels beneath the surface and wreak havoc on the grass. Sam was never quick enough to get them with a shovel, instead using it to flatten the dirt hills so they wouldn't ruin the mower blades.

A rap on the aluminum screen door nearly made Eva lose control of her bladder, her fear turning into frustration as she watched the tanager fly away, probably the only time she'd see it this year.

Peering through the glass, there was no mistaking Vera's outfit for anything Ruby or Alice might wear outside in public. She had dyed her burnt-cornsilk hair a brighter blonde. The Hollywood shade wouldn't fool anyone into thinking she was Jayne Mansfield, even though she tried with her eyebrows colored to match and plucked thinner. At least she wasn't wearing a bullet bra.

Eva reluctantly opened the door to see what Vera was selling after noticing she was holding something under her arm. As she pushed the door fully open, Eva was pleased to see that Vera's white shorts were a more appropriate length over her thighs, along with matching tennis shoes that looked new, though not a style Eva recognized. Not knowing where Vera worked gnawed at her like reflux. Aggravating, because it was none of her business.

"Hello Eva, I was out taking a stroll, enjoying the last of this summer weather, and saw you pull in." Vera held out at arm's length a small, lunch-sized paper bag, her face twitching, and her lips moving as if she were self-conscious about her teeth. "I was out mowing the other day and realized that either you or Sam must have hit these plastic golf balls into my yard by mistake." She pulled a handful out of the bag as if to prove they were real. "I'm sorry that I hit one with the lawn mower before I stopped to look around."

Eva hadn't picked up a golf club in years, even though Benjamin always asked her to play whenever he visited, weather permitting. "Don't make me the only leftie out on the course. C'mon, I'll let you teach me a thing or two," were a couple of things he'd often say. She was so out of practice and a decade removed from being a three-time local women's champion. *So why was Sam practicing in the yard? Was he trying to improve his swing and surprise her with an invitation to play again?*

She took the bag from Vera and peeked inside, saying, "That seems like a lot of balls. Are you sure, Sam, hit all of those onto your property?" Eva was aware of Sam's hook and glanced past Vera at the yard, wondering why he was hitting toward the house instead of away from it and into the woods. It seemed strange to Eva that he would set himself up that way, and as she reached into the bag, rolling the thin plastic balls with their dimples over her fingertips, it reminded her of times spent on the putting greens. She gently stirred them, then held a handful close to her face, confused when she swore she caught a whiff of a familiar fragrance, Wind Song—the Prince Matchabelli perfume she used to wear years ago.

Vera shrugged her shoulders, acting clueless. Maybe her new bottle blonde look suited her after all. "I dunno what to tell you. They look brand new. I didn't want to run over them and chop them into pieces. They must have cost a pretty penny, so I didn't want to waste them. Hopefully, Sam isn't embarrassed he lost 'em, but I guess it was my fault for having such deep rough," she winked.

Eva didn't want to appear ungrateful or look a gift horse in the mouth. "Well, thank you, Vera. Much appreciated. I'll give these to Sam when he gets home from work." She was about to let the door swing shut, but decided it would be neighborly to have a happy hour instead. "Would you like to share a beer? It must be almost five o'clock. The chairs are in the shed if you want to pick a spot while I change. Narragansett okay?"

"How about Miller High Life? It's the champagne of beers."

Eva dismissed the hint of ingratitude as Vera headed toward the tool-shed. "Sorry, no can do." Louder, she asked, "Would you prefer Schaefer instead?"

Vera thrust an arm and finger straight into the air. "Sold," she said, putting a little extra twist in her hips.

Eva's Daily Reminder 1963: October 26, Saturday

Warm and sunny in the 80s.

Sam took off early for Brattleboro to help Edwin wash and put on his storm windows.

Connie called and we chatted for half an hour.

Mopped the kitchen floor and waxed the bathroom floor.

Mom and Dad went over to Rutland in the morning to do some shopping. I gave Mom all my green stamp books. Hope they use them on something nice. Told them not to buy any Halloween candy.

Refilled bird baths. Three Blue Jays.

Took down drapes and aired them out.

Had supper and bathed, then went over to Mom and Dad's to watch "hootenanny".

Al popped in with a crème de menthe.

Sam still gone when I came home. Guess he's lost all love for me. He is very interested in Vera but can't imagine him being untrue unless he came to me and told me. I really don't think I trust Vera though.

Set clocks back an hour.

9

Eva bought Halloween candy for herself and her parents, stacking bags filled with an assortment of Mars bars and Curtis Candy's new junior-size Babe Ruth and Butterfingers. The cellar pantry cabinet was the place she trusted to keep them safe from the heat and mice, having kept the loaves of Wonder Bread safe from those little pests so far.

Henry was furious when Ruth was traded to the Yankees in 1920, and Red Sox owner Hank Frazee used the money to finance and produce his Broadway play "My Lady Friends." The Red Sox were baseball royalty, winning the World Series five times in the fifteen years before the trade and none since—over four decades and counting—a curse Babe took to his grave. At least this year, the Dodgers beat the Yankees earlier in the month.

Eva was trying to remember whether the 1920 baseball season was the impetus for Henry to start smoking a pipe when the phone rang upstairs. She double-checked that the cabinet was shut tight before climbing the stairs, muttering, "Hold your horses, I'm coming."

It was comforting to hear Connie's voice on the other end of the line. "Mummy? Is that you?" she asked, sounding hesitant and distant, with a hint of forlornness in her tone. Eva was still trying to catch her breath.

"Who'd you think would answer?" Eva asked, followed by Connie's defeated sigh in her ear as if she were standing there in the kitchen and not clear across the state.

"I didn't like the sound of your voice this morning, and I knew something was wrong. You've been rather quiet lately. It's been bothering me ever since you and Dad didn't help bring my stuff to school. Warren had to make three trips!"

Eva didn't recall anything she might have said during their morning conversation that would make Connie think there was something wrong. She had shared the facts and nothing more. *Did she mention something she couldn't remember? Was her tone morose?* There was no need to upset Connie. "Not that I can think of… oh, I wanted you to know that I saved our copy of the Eagle Times that had your engagement announcement in it," she said, changing the subject. "It took some doing, getting it back from your grandparents, but I have it tucked away. Your picture was so nice and lovely."

"Thanks, but I don't want to talk about that now. I need to tell you something."

Eva didn't want to admit that Connie somehow knew. She had tried her best to hide her depression. Connie deserved to graduate with the highest honors, and she didn't need any distractions. This situation with Sam would hurt her deeply, even though she and her father didn't share the closest bond. Most of Connie's childhood as an only child was spent with her by her side in the kitchen or around the dining room table, sewing or swapping seats when Alice was giving them both perms. She was kind to her grandparents, always making time to talk to them, and occasionally letting them drive her to and from school last year. If it weren't for Henry's patience, Connie might never have learned to play cribbage. She didn't care to learn how to fish, play golf, or decipher Morse Code from her father.

"What is it?" Eva asked, leaning against the refrigerator. *Would Connie tell her if she were breaking things off with Warren?*

"After we hung up this morning, I called Edwin."

"Why in the world…" Eva couldn't handle confrontation—she could only express her reality in her private words, sometimes finding acceptance after a year had passed.

"What's going on, Mom? I called Edwin. He said Dad wasn't down there… and hadn't been there. He said he never mentioned anything to Dad about helping with the storm windows, and in fact, he wasn't even planning to do that until after deer season. If he needed any help, he always had local buddies who owed him favors—he wouldn't ask Dad to drive all the way down there."

Eva pushed away from the refrigerator and sat down. *Why did he lie to her this morning?* She stood and shuffled over to the kitchen sink. Turning on the faucet, she prepared to be sick.

"Mom?"

"Just getting a drink of water, hon. I'm still here." Eva looked across the backyard, where Vera's Karmann Ghia sat in its usual place. Her queasiness ballooned, then subsided. "I'm fine."

"Are you sure? You're losing weight!"

"Everything's hunky-dory. No need to get upset. I'll track him down— make a few more phone calls." Eva knew precisely who to call first: Ray Whittman. This skulking around needed to stop. "He'll turn up."

"What if he's dead in a ditch somewhere?"

"Don't think like that. I'm sure he's off radioing. You'd better get back to your schoolwork, and I'll be sure to call you when I hear something, okay?"

"Promise?"

Eva would not make any promises, at least not when it came to her husband, who might not be long for this world. "You'll be the first to know."

• • •

"Ray? It's Eva Martin. Is Sam around—with *you*—by chance?" She aimed to sound confident, not accusatory, and definitely not scared. She believed she sounded spot on, yet braced herself to hear Ray chuckle.

"He is not, Eva. I haven't seen him in some time."

Eva wasn't expecting this; she had only hoped to scold Ray for keeping Sam tied up with radioing. A tendril of worry crept up her spine.

"I take it he's AWOL?" Ray asked.

"Seems to be, yes."

She was about to thank him for his time and trouble when he said, "If he's out and about, he probably has his two-meter rig in the truck. I'm licensed now, thanks to Sam, by the way, but I don't have a two-meter rig yet." After a brief pause, he added, "But let me give Charlie Doe a call; he certainly does, and maybe he can reach Sam. Let's hope he's not… sorry… I'll give you a ring if I hear anything."

An hour later, the phone rang while Eva was fretfully trying to read. She closed the library book, realizing she wouldn't remember much, if any at all. "Hello," she answered.

"Eva? It's Charlie Doe down in Claremont—a ham buddy of Sam's. I got a call from Ray Whittman this morning, saying you needed to get ahold of Sam. Hope everything's okay. I wanted to let you know that I finally reached him down in Keene. He was at a small hamfest I didn't really feel like going to."

"Gosh, thank you for doing that, Charlie."

"And I told him you were looking for him."

Inside, Eva was a roiling wasp nest. Outside, she stayed calm, saying, "Okey-dokey. Much appreciated."

When Sam called later that afternoon, he sounded embarrassed, offering excuse after excuse. "I didn't think you'd let me go if I came right out and asked you if I could take off and go to another ham festival, but these all shut down over the winter, and I figured I might find a season-ending deal."

"We could have gone to Keene together. There are several spots down there where we've enjoyed some nice meals. Don't you think I want to get out of the house once in a while, too? Is that why you lied about seeing your brother? You knew there was a darn good chance I'd say no to that, so that's why, right? Are you in Keene? Not that I want you to spend our money, but you'd better bring home something that looks like a damn radio… or radio parts."

"No…" he trailed off, sounding defeated.

"No? You're not in Keene?" Eva caught herself and frantically tried to stuff all the wasps back into the nest. She disliked the sound of her voice, embarrassed by her weakness in lashing out, but she was no milquetoast. It was the first time in twenty-six years of marriage that she'd raised her voice to Sam, and she could feel the anger melting her insides, the heat radiating to her skin. Practice what she preached when facing confrontation—remain steadfast—but this was far worse than any snide remark Sam had ever made, including ridiculing her with a masticating crayfish wrapped around her face. "No?" she asked again.

"No. I mean, I didn't think you'd want to come."

Eva's Daily Reminder 1963: November 22, Friday

Foggy, mild. President shot.

Finally feeling better. What a siege I've had of it.

Started out doing a bit of dusting etc ended up doing a little ironing after Sam left.

While ironing got a terrible shock to hear on the radio that President Kennedy had been shot down in a motorcade in Texas. Died in the hospital. The Texas governor was also shot but not fatally.

Connie called in the evening. Sam was out.

Everything on TV canceled. All the president's life etc.

Merrill and Faye came down after store hours. Brought me a full weeks pay. Nice people!

Eva's Daily Reminder 1963: December 21, Saturday

15 Below.

You might say there was frost on the pumpkin this morning! Really cold!

Business very slow! We are way behind! Where is everyone buying their shoes!

Came home for supper and Connie and Sam here. Connie was getting ready to go to the Super Duper banquet with Warren and afterwards bowling. They had a nice evening.

I went over to Al's and had a coffee liqueur with her and watched the Lawrence Welk Xmas show.

Sam out and not in when I came home.

Connie said he got in at 2:30 and now I know something's amiss. I smelled perfume on his clothes and lipstick on his shirt! Oh! My! God!

PART II

The Affair

Eva's Daily Reminder 1964: January 5, Sunday

Beautiful day. Curse.

Got up early. Felt lousy but made a meatloaf for Connie and a pumpkin pie. Got dinner started early.

Al stopped in after church and gave me a shampoo.

Sam left for Burlington at 3 with Connie. Had a carload.

I waited up until 11:15 for him. He got in at 11:30 and Vera right behind him. They both signaled with their headlights and I called him on it. Also told him about them being seen together recently.

Well there goes a marriage. Asked him to be a gentleman and go.

Stayed up all night. A lot of words said but nothing accomplished. This is why people start their cars up in the garage and pfft it's over.

He's not worth it though—I tell myself.

10

Despite Sam staying home from work and wanting to talk, Eva headed to Alice's house. Her thin deerskin gloves were barely more than windbreakers in the hostile January snow, offering little protection for her hands as she tried to keep her coat fastened under her chin. Cross breezes attacked her legs, pushing her coat above her knees, the draft biting her like a hound's teeth through her rayon slacks. The thin cotton socks she wore indoors did little to insulate her toes inside rubber boots meant for mud season, and without a hat—she worried it would blow off and disappear over a snow drift—leaving her ears exposed to the same windchill. Alice's house at the end of the street was only six houses away, hardly more than the length of a football field, but she was shivering uncontrollably after passing the first—Vera's.

Eva refused to look to see if she was home and instead wished the woman's heat was turned off or that she had her head inside the propane stove—one could only hope.

Alice must have seen her approaching and leaning into the wind, tiring herself out, because she was waiting with the door open, and Eva walked right in, stomping her boots more for circulation than manners.

"What would I do if I didn't have you for a dear friend?" Eva asked. "You've certainly helped me over some bad spots in the past, but this one—"

"You should have known about Vera ages ago," Alice interrupted. "I did… but I *trusted* Sam." She stood firm, her fists on the hips of her floral house dress as she waited for Eva to unbutton her coat and step out of her boots. "Let me take that. I'd normally offer something stronger, because we—*you*—sure as heck deserve it, but today you look like you need hot tea."

When Alice took Eva's coat, she nearly tripped over her aptly named Boston Terrier, Impy, who darted under the kitchen table on knitted red booties and curled up in her bed. Her tongue flicked rapidly between her fangs and against her nose, appearing more obsessive-compulsive than testing the air.

The phone rang, and it seemed to push Alice even further over the edge, more than she already was. "Oh, for God's sake," Alice said, reaching for the receiver. "Now what?"

Eva had a good guess who was calling on the other end of the line.

Alice answered, "Hello? Sam? What do you need? Yes, she's here; she made it." She looked at Eva, apoplectic. "He wants to know if you'll come home because he's called Henry and Ruby over to your place to have a talk."

Eva returned the livid look. "For Chrissakes, I just got here! Tell him I barely got my boots off and I'll come home when I'm good and ready… And I'll talk to my mother and father in due time, not on his schedule!"

"Did you catch that? Well, I hope so. Sam, listen… I know, I know, I hear you, but I'm not jumping into the middle of this right now. She just got here, leave her be." Alice switched the telephone receiver between her ears and Eva's coat between her arms. "No! Don't be silly!"

"What's he want now?"

"He wants to come over and get you in the truck so you don't have to walk back in the snow."

Eva stood and took the phone from Alice. "Sam—hush up now and listen—don't call my parents over to the house; don't bring the truck over here; and under no circumstances are you to go next door. Do you hear me? Are you listening?" Whether he was or wasn't listening to her, she resisted arguing and didn't repeat any of his banter to Alice. "Why don't you go downstairs and watch the Celtics, or go upstairs and get on your rig? Tell your buddy Ray all about it!"

Alice returned from depositing Eva's coat over a chair in the living room in time for Eva to read her lips as she mouthed, "Really? Are you sure about that?"

"Do as I say, and I'll walk home when I'm done here." Eva hung up. "It's all about his pride and embarrassment."

"Oh, I'm sure. It always is."

Eva's face slackened. "Did Reg ever stray?" When Alice looked confused, Eva asked, "You?" which brought a look of surprised defeat to Alice's face.

"No," she answered. "But it's not uncommon. I hear things at the salon from time to time—speaking of which, have you heard from Sybil?"

"No," Eva told her. "I've written her a few letters, but she hasn't written back yet. I hope everything's okay… I guess we've got something to write about now, don't we?"

Alice didn't seem fazed either way; her shoulders eased as she sighed until Impy yipped from under the table, startling her. "Oh, it's not time yet. You'll have to wait another hour before lunchtime." She tilted her head to check the time on the overhead clock and then added, "And no walk today, either. It's too cold outside."

Eva heard the dog whimpering. "She's no dummy," she said, taking her turn to look at the clock. "Well…"

"Well, what? I haven't even had a chance to put water on to boil yet."

"I know, and I appreciate you asking me over, but I can't focus here, knowing what kind of mess he's getting into at home. Who knows what he's up to… so I guess I'd better head back." Eva moved closer to her boots, grateful that at least the circulation had returned to her fingers and toes, and that her blood was no longer reptilian-cold. "I'll take a rain check on the tea, and thank you kindly for the warm-up."

Alice snapped her fingers. "Almost forgot your coat." When she offered to help Eva slip it over her arms, Eva flinched as if her hand was caught in a mousetrap. "Sorry," she said and pulled the coat off, reaching into the sleeves. "Forgot I stashed your gloves in here."

Eva was disappointed that the insides of her gloves were still chilly, the air unable to circulate while they were cramped. She did her best to flex her fingers and then blew into them until she was sure she could make it home before frostbite set in. It would be bad luck to lose to Vera over the elements before that bitch had the chance to choke herself on propane.

•••

Eva made it home, no worse for wear and no colder than when she had arrived at Alice's back door. She paused to warm her hands and legs by the Magee's firebox before heading upstairs, where she found Henry and Ruby sitting in front of the Jøtul.

Sam was sitting in her chair by the window when he suddenly jumped up as if he'd been shocked with a cattle prod, and hurried across the room to the rocking chair near the television. Without Brylcreem in his hair, it was unkempt, dry, and thin, with a shock hanging over his temple, flung there by his frantic dash. His sweatpants no longer smelled fresh in the stale, static air of the room.

"How long have you been here?" Eva asked her parents, still hesitating to sit in her chair.

Ruby rose off the couch and hugged her. "Oh, not too long," she said, then whispered in her ear, "I'm so sorry you're going through this." After a hug that felt like Ruby was a deep breath away from squeezing water from a stone, she sat back down.

Henry sat hunched forward with his legs spread, twiddling with one of his well-worn winter toques in his hands, and appeared focused on the flickering flames through the wood stove's air damper. His face was sullen; his lips drooped, and his eyes lost.

Eva gave up waiting for Henry to speak and sat in her chair. "Well, I suppose he's already fed you a pack of lies," she told her parents, avoiding direct eye contact with Sam, who said, "I told them that I admit being out with her."

Eva couldn't face him and turned to look out the window before realizing that was the last place she wanted to see. Luckily for her, the backyard was a powdery white landscape, and the falling snow obscured her view enough that she couldn't tell if Vera's house was lit or not. The low barometric pressure kept the feeders empty of wildlife, but there was enough filtered light to see what appeared to be a medium-sized, oblong rock under one of the densest branch-packed lilacs. It wasn't supposed to be there, and she couldn't imagine how or who had dumped it there.

"I bet you're glad to get that off your chest," she said, fixated on the stone for a moment longer before turning to face Sam.

"We think you should stick it out," Henry said. "Even *with* all the goin's on."

Eva moved to her father, then to her mother, who sat quietly, hands clasped. "I will until Connie graduates… if she wants."

It's funny how something inside you dies when you see unfaithfulness.

She turned her attention to the window, where she noticed the stone was gone.

• • •

Eva went to work and left early, driving to Burlington to see Connie. She had never done a harder thing in her life, telling Connie that her father had broken his marriage vows. It wasn't shocking to her, but she told Eva that she could never come home again with him there, and that he should move out.

Connie seemed unable to say goodbye, even though Eva stayed long enough to enjoy a nice pasta dinner with all the girls in the dorm. She glanced around her room, searching for something, pausing briefly on a framed photo of herself and Eva, before focusing on the watercolor of nasturtiums that Sam had painted when he was a teenager—the only thing in her room that reminded her of him—and lifted it off the wall. "Can you take this home and give it back to him for me? I don't want it anymore."

Eva nodded and took the glass frame with her, driving home alone, slow and hesitant over a snow-covered Mendon Mountain.

Whether Sam was upstairs on the radio or watching the Celtics, it didn't matter to Eva, who found him sitting on the couch. As much as it itched, she refused to wash his sweatpants. He should take care of himself, which he'd be forced to do sooner or later.

"I called the shoe store. Faye said you left early and drove up to Burlington? By yourself? I wish I'd known. I would've added some weight to the VW. It must have been touch and go."

His tone was genuine, and Eva realized he wasn't a complete monster.

"I had to tell Connie," she said.

Sam covered his face with his hands and broke down as best he could, unable to cry or show emotional pain. Over the years of their marriage, she came to believe that his father might have been the real monster. Sam couldn't shed tears because he didn't know how. He sat with his elbows on his knees, keening and hyperventilating, and Eva knew the shame was real—it wasn't an act. The only other time she'd seen him like this was when he cut down a dead tree, and a branch fell on his head, lacerating his scalp as cleanly as an Apache hatchet might have done. In the Sumner Falls emergency room, while getting stitches, he was so embarrassed and scared at how close he had come to dying. Holding her hand, all he said was, "I'm so sorry… I'm so sorry," with the same dry keening he was showing now.

Did she feel sorry or *pity*? Maybe she needed to focus more on self-defense. "Was it worth it?" she asked. "The sex, I mean." When he didn't answer, she pushed on, "To think what that hot bitch has done to all of us. Please give us the strength to carry on… I guess there won't be much sleeping tonight for either of us."

After Sam went to bed, Eva quietly crept downstairs and, over the garbage can, put a hatchet to the watercolor, including its glass frame.

• • •

Sam begged and pleaded to stay, even threatening to kill himself.

"Oh, so that's your answer?" Eva asked him. "Don't you find it kind of ironic?" She bit her tongue and changed mid-thought, "Vera's husband? The one who committed suicide? Stop and think about that for a minute, why don't you?" She wouldn't give in to his immature ramblings, but her eardrums needed a rest, so she relented and said, "For God's sake, stay… I don't know what Connie will say. She wants you out! I don't think she can even look at you right now, so we need to agree on a timeframe for you to move out. I'll give you two weeks."

Eva fought to move forward, her body only able to handle so much, but Merrill, Carolyn, and Faye were wonderful and supportive throughout it all—such kind people to have in her corner.

She came home, pulled out a package of deer steaks from the freezer—courtesy of Ray's buck last fall—and cooked them right away, adding some frozen asparagus directly into the buttered frying pan. She didn't feel like making dessert.

Sam would need to learn how to do his own laundry before moving out. When it came to feeding himself, she figured he'd probably eat out on his own dime since his cooking skills only included grilling hot dogs and hamburgers over a fire, boiling corn on the cob, pouring milk over crackers, spreading peanut butter, and dishing out ice cream.

When he came home from work, he didn't go out radioing; instead, he ate only after asking Eva if it was okay to sit in the kitchen with her. After supper, he wrote a long letter to Connie, and Eva knew it was tough for him. When he finished, he fixed a headlight on her VW and then sat next to Magee to watch the Celtics, who were the only thing keeping him grounded.

• • •

It started snowing in the late morning and continued all day, with sleet in the evening, making Eva's drive home exhausting. She was taking off her coat when everything whirled and spun around like Dorothy's bedroom in a Kansas tornado. She was half on the bed and half on the floor when Sam found her. Alarmed, he called Dr. Read, who arrived at the house in no time, sleet be damned.

She guessed it was due to a lack of sleep and a phone call from Alice at work, who told her that someone at the salon had seen Sam and Vera talking in the machine shop parking lot. Dr. Read gave her two shots, which calmed her shaking. He was also worried about her weight.

Connie surprised her by coming in after supper. She had called Warren to come and pick her up, and she and Sam talked. *It sure has taken a lot out of her—poor sweetie.*

• • •

Sam had already left for work when Eva woke up, and when Connie came downstairs, they busied themselves, changing the beds, washing the sheets and linens, and ironing everything. Eva was content to have Connie home with her—a sense of secure calm.

Connie gathered all of Vera's records and took them to her house, dumping them on the porch without clearing the snow first. She believed the only solution was for Sam to leave. If he wanted a new life with Vera, that was his business.

It was painful to watch him keep looking over there, checking on her.

Eva couldn't tell if it was pity or sorrow. She couldn't seem to swallow much food and hadn't had a drink since smelling that bitch's perfume and seeing her lipstick. One thing she wouldn't be, coming out of this, was an alcoholic.

Alice called to ask if she could give Connie a perm before heading to Middlebury, where Connie would meet Catherine and her parents, who would then drive the girls the rest of the way to Burlington. She was upset about this mess and found it hard to face Sam, but managed to finish Connie's hair before leaving for church.

Eva made brownies, and Ruby baked a banana loaf and filled cookies for Connie to take to school, calling her "Grammy's pet." They rode together in the backseat, with Connie's head resting in Eva's lap for most of the trip.

• • •

It was a merciful morning, signaling the start of a January thaw, with the temperature rising to thirty degrees above zero. Rain was forecast overnight, making it a bleak day for skiers who would once again face icy slopes on the inevitable backside of the thaw—a black diamond trail nightmare.

Eva woke early and decided to clean her bedroom windows, inside and out, then mop the kitchen floor to stay busy. She was down to 118 pounds and regretted the two-week trial period she had given in to Sam, wondering when her bad dreams would finally go away. Waking up at 4:30 a.m. in winter, in the dark, knowing she had to feed the wood stove, was something she used to take for granted, and now it might leave her overextended and unable to follow her morning routine.

She finished mopping and hadn't yet had a chance to sit and write in her diary when Alice called, saying she was on her way over.

"I guess it's too early for whiskey sours?" Eva asked deadpan, before Alice could cross the front threshold.

After giving Eva a chagrin, she stepped inside and said, "In your condition? I'd say very. How're you doing? By the looks of you, I'd say you've had better days, and judging by the time and your robe, I assume Merrill's giving you some time off."

Eva took Alice's coat and draped it over the back of the couch, wishing there was something else that could fill the space between the front door and the end of the sofa. "You betcha, two weeks," she said, trying to sound normal. She broke eye contact, unable to mask her face from her best friend. At least the time off wasn't a lie. "Merrill said my full back pay would be waiting whenever I decided to come back. He'll make his numbers. There's always a big run on skates when the spring thaw comes to an end."

Alice headed toward the kitchen, prompting Eva to follow. It was a damned-if-you-do, damned-if-you-don't situation—either sit still and avoid cleaning or move around the house. Whether she sat in her chair, unable to enjoy the birds flocking to the feeders, or sat in the kitchen, Vera's house was visible from both windows. Even if she chose to work in the store, she couldn't concentrate, unable to keep her eyes away from the storefront window to see whose car might pass or who might be following.

"Can I get you a cup of coffee?" Eva asked, desperately needing an excuse to move into the cellar sitting area. "I think I might've left the percolator in the washroom—take but a second or two to get it going."

When she began to stand, Alice said, "Sit. I know where it is," and found the percolator in its usual spot in a lower kitchen cabinet. She also knew where Eva kept the coffee grounds, in the second-largest container of the matching set, tucked against the backstop between the flour and sugar. "I'm surprised you don't switch the coffee and sugar tubs."

"It's a toss-up, that's for sure, but between us"—her voice catching in her windpipe—"and Henry and Ruby, we drink more coffee than I use sugar for pies. I can't wait for rhubarb this summer."

"Don't you have some frozen?"

"I used the last of it at Christmas and gave plenty to Mom. She keeps all the blackberries. I don't usually make those pies or jams—the seeds bother our bridgework, but she and Dad don't seem to mind either way."

"Speaking of which… what's the latest with Sam? Do I dare ask?"

Eva could hear the percolator and focused on the rhythmic burps, trying to drown out the voices and advice from everyone who only wanted what was best for her. Connie was at odds with Henry, and she couldn't help feeling caught in the middle. "Connie's dead set on wanting him to move out, and Dad thinks I should stick it out—hope for the best."

"And Ruby?"

"She keeps her mouth shut, but I know she's on my side—as are you."

"Aren't Connie and Warren planning a summer wedding? She must be beside herself—poor thing. I can't imagine Warren wanting her to go through this. What does he have to say? Anything?"

Eva got up, unplugged the percolator, and brought it to the table instead of standing at the counter to pour their mugs. She chastised herself because it didn't help, since she still needed another trip for the sugar. The view out the kitchen window showed an empty driveway, but that didn't mean Vera wasn't in a clandestine meeting with Sam somewhere in the machine shop parking lot. *Is this how Charity Barnum felt—bewildered—while her husband, Phineas Taylor, and Jenny Lind traveled the country?* The mix of not knowing and the need to know, along with the fear of knowing, created a monster that scared Eva. "I honestly have no idea what she's told him," she said. "But I know he adores Connie, and he's been such a gracious boy around me that he'd probably do anything we ask."

"Well, let's hope he doesn't up and shoot 'em."

"Oh dear. Well, as mad as I am at him, I'm trying to be madder at *her*. You know, I called Sybil the other night, and she said the same thing, 'Want me to come up there and tear him to shreds?' That's all I need right now. He's no good to me dead. We agreed that when he finds a place and moves out, he'll pay me $25 a week. I spoke to the lawyer upstreet, Carl, and he advised me to talk Sam out of cashing in his life insurance, which I tried to do, but he's like a different person now. Connie says he's like a caged animal."

"Oh dear… is right."

"He said I was being lenient on him, only asking for $25 a week." Eva sipped her coffee. "I should have told Sybil if she wanted to tear anyone into sheds, then by all means, have at it with Vera—no skin off my nose."

"So I take it, Sam's at work?"

"Nope. He also put in for time off and took the VW over to Woodstock for an oil change. Said it needed new wiper blades. He told me he was looking for a room in Claremont. I assumed for a minute he might go and stay with Ray, but I guess he wants his freedom—so you know what that means."

Eva crossed her leg over her knee and bounced her slippered foot. They sat quietly sipping their coffee while it was still hot until, finally, feeling a cramp coming on, she said, "I wasn't going to tell you, and thank God Connie wasn't here either, but the other night he came home all upset and woke me up in bed. It was after eleven—scared the bejesus out of me. I was pretty sure he'd been drinking somewhere… I guess at the lodge. He wanted to know what stories I had been spreading. Said he'd stick to our agreement if I didn't throw a suit against Vera. I'd like to throw something at her." She finished her coffee, adding, "Dad will help me get the locks changed as soon as he's out."

• • •

If the mild rain had been snow, the neighborhood would have had a conniption. It was a fitting day with alternating bouts of drizzle and buckets as Eva and Sam said their goodbyes before heading off to work.

"If it stops raining, I'll either come home at lunch or as soon as I can get off work, to pick up my radio stuff and the rest of my clothes," he said. "I can't put anything in the back of the truck now while it's raining."

Two things cleared from Eva's mind: his radio clutter and half the household laundry—along with half the ironing.

"I finished Connie's taxes last night and left them in a folder on the dining room hutch," he said, taking a deep breath as if he were about to deliver bad news. "I said I'd stick to the agreement of the $25 a week, and deed the house over to you and Connie, but only if you sign your name stating you won't sue Vera or involve her in anything—she's moving away. You can either leave it at the Hotel Wimmer in Claremont, where I'm renting a room, or I can pick it up from you at the store. Whatever's easiest."

"Is that what it's come down to? Whatever's easiest? That bitch really has you buffaloed, doesn't she?" Eva swallowed hard. She could cry and wanted to, but wouldn't until he was long gone. "I'm not signing anything, but… I will keep her out of it if you stick to the money and insurance. And Dad will help me file my taxes separately." That would put a bee in his bonnet.

When Eva came home from work at five, all of his stuff was gone, and the house didn't feel lonely. She called Alice and Ruby, inviting them over for drinks and conversation, but no card playing. The two Drambuies tasted good—the first since the mess started.

Connie called to say she would be staying with Catherine over the weekend. She took the news of her father's departure well, reiterating that it was for the best. It gnawed at Eva that Connie didn't sound emotional—not sad, nor angry, somewhat unempathetic.

Eva hoped Vera was proud of the disaster she had created, not knowing when she would sleep again.

Eva's Daily Reminder 1964: February 1, Saturday

Rain. Sleet. Snow. Curse.

A real lousy day. Sam called and wanted to know if he could come and get some stuff he left on his side of the dining room closet. Asked if Connie would be there. He came at lunch time and started right in raving about the locks on the doors. I finally told him it was none of his business. He left the $25.

Catherine came down to see Connie. They have a week off and went with Warren to Woodstock to visit his grandmother, then came home with steaks to broil. Also French fries, onion rings, green salad, jello and whipped cream.

Connie and Catherine went skiing on the hill behind the house. They had a ball. I gave Warren the mahogany wood I had given to Sam years ago to make something he never got around to. I hope Warren can use it to build a nice shadow box for Connie.

The kids went bowling and then to the movies.

Walked over to Al's and had a triple sec with her. Watched Jimmy Dean.

Was really feeling low when I got home. I must get over this. There will be plenty of low days. I still think I've been dreaming it all!

Had a cramp in my leg and had to get up at 4. Still sore.

11

There were enough snowflakes to dust the walkways, and Henry had swept everything off before Eva left for work. She'd had a lousy night, tossing and turning, and didn't feel like doing much cleaning, except for a small load of her underwear. Her daily diary pages were filling up completely, with her cursive writing getting smaller, and the pen colors changing more often. Her words were dour, not out of pity, sad about this whole mess, and how that bitch got away scot-free. She hoped better days were ahead.

With only a partial load of light laundry, she paused to enjoy her coffee after adding two small pieces of rock maple to the Jøtul, hoping it would be enough to keep the coal embers simmering until she returned. She wasn't planning to come home for lunch; her appetite could hardly handle even the smallest of meals—much to Ruby and Henry's disappointment.

There was activity outside Vera's house: three men were hauling trunks and boxes. Eva recognized Ray Whittman but not his other two helpers, whose faces were hidden by their cupped hands as they tried to stay warm in their barnyard frocks at four below. They looked young, probably teenagers. This was perhaps the last place they wanted to be, having to move some woman out of her house in subzero weather.

There was no sign of Sam—he wouldn't risk being seen by the other neighbors, and if Henry saw him, he might try to kill him with a snow shovel. Eva couldn't imagine Vera shacking up with him at the hotel. It would be a blessing if she packed everything and took her little fancy sports car down to Florida for good.

Eva tapped her knuckle on the wooden side table, hoping tonight would be the first of a better night's sleep. She decided not to finish her coffee before Ray had a chance to show interest next door and come knocking. That wasn't a fracas Eva wanted to deal with before leaving for work.

Merrill convinced Eva to go home for lunch, then went to the store's basement and grabbed a spare lock he remembered. It was still in its original dust-covered packaging—an extra he said he needed for the bulkhead door after some high school kids tried breaking in. (They told Officer Poole they wanted the new Converse sneakers and had no intention of damaging anything.) She called Henry to come over and help Merrill install it on the outside cellar door, and he seemed tickled that she asked. However, Merrill said Henry ended up getting in the way more than helping, so Henry decided to rinse the salt off her car instead.

Eva found two letters in the mailbox: one from Connie and one from Benjamin, who definitely made it clear he was her brother and Connie's uncle. It made her feel good to know her family was protective.

After work, Eva hadn't even reached the top of the cellar stairs when Ruby buzzed and asked her to come over for dinner. That woman knew precisely how long it would take her to park and climb the stairs, having had years of practice.

Henry got a kick out of the three of them eating together. "Feels like it was just yesterday," he said, holding his hand level to the floor at his knee. "Always the quiet one. I never had to do much to keep you in line, and your brothers looked out for you."

"You can't possibly remember," Eva said. "You're confusing me with Connie." She almost winked, but it didn't come naturally to her.

"'Cause you're both so quiet is why I still got my hearing," Ruby said. "Although your father decided now was a good time to start paintin' the kitchen cabinets. You should've heard him carryin' on. I don't know why he couldn't wait until the weather warms up, but I wasn't gonna argue with him."

Eva looked at her father, who shrugged and snuck a peek at Ruby, sticking out his tongue before she caught him, and said, "Can't sit around all day cooped up."

"Oh, are you still here?" Ruby asked sarcastically. "I assumed you'd gone off to read the paper, bein' so quiet and all."

Being forced to laugh at her mother was almost painful for Eva, as she briefly choked, trying to clear her throat. It was the perfect excuse to say, "I knew I smelled something, but didn't want to ask… why don't I help you clean up?"

"No need to bother," Ruby told her. "I barely had time to dirty any dishes as it is. Unless you want to stay a bit longer and have a drink, I could have Henry wash the dishes since he's complainin' about nothin' to do around here."

Eva wished she were in a better mood to enjoy her parents' vaudeville act, with Ruby playing Jimmy Dean and Henry as Rowlf the Dog.

• • •

While Alice was at church, Eva decided to wake up early and start cleaning Sam's room, beginning with all the dust he had left behind after removing his radio equipment from the oversized cherry executive desk. She remembered he had to disassemble it to get it upstairs—a project for Henry to reverse. Tangled coils of coaxial cables alone filled several boxes. She had no idea where Sam had taken everything, but assumed he had probably asked Ray Whittman to store it at his house. The long antenna wires remained strung between the houses and trees on the hill, but she planned to wait until spring to have Benjamin take them all down. She didn't want Henry to risk falling off any ladders. Last summer, it was stressful enough worrying about him as he painted from a ladder halfway up the side of the house. (Big Ben broke a wooden rung that nobody had noticed was rotted.) For now, wet, heavy snow clinging to the wires looked pretty in her winter wonderland, and she smiled every time a gray squirrel ran along the span, performing a high-wire act with its fluffy tail for balance.

Sam had left a framed, colorful drawing that Connie made when she was nine. It was dated 1953 in Sam's printed handwriting and showed a small radio shack with his call sign beside a large, barren tree, a black cat between them. Eva realized that the tree was so big because it was meant to be in the foreground, with the cat walking from the crude building toward it. Connie used black, brown, and red crayons to create the scene, and Eva couldn't bring herself to take it down from the wall, remembering how Connie looked up to her father at that age. Now, she hated him, and Eva had no idea how to temper her daughter's spite. She began to cry, losing the joy she had cultivated while cleaning.

Alice stopped by after church and gave Ruby a perm, shampooing Eva's hair while the perm set. Ruby brought a sweater pattern with her, thinking it would be good for Eva to start knitting again, but that was a hobby Ruby shared more with Connie. Eva preferred sewing with Connie, making braided rugs, quilts, and skirts.

They had a few drinks and talked little about Sam, except for where he was staying and whether he was still paying Eva $25 a week, which he was, slipping the money into the side pocket of her car while Eva was at the shoe store.

She didn't feel like making dinner for everyone, so she chose to do a little ironing—nothing too much—and took a bath before turning on the television.

It was strange to look at Vera's house. From the outside, it didn't look vacant, and Eva wondered how many trips Ray and his helpers would need to clear out all her junk. She didn't care to know where Vera was going and wouldn't ask Ray if she ran into him. If he, or anyone from the Masonic lodge, or the machine shop called here looking for Sam, she was ready to tell them to call the Hotel Wimmer and hang up.

As Eva was about to look away from Vera's and toward the television, her eyes caught sight of what appeared to be the same dark gray stone tucked beneath one of her lilacs. This time, it moved, and there was still enough light to see that it had perked, triangular ears—it was a cat.

Instead of knocking on the window to scare the cat away from her feeders, she went to the back door, watching it through the kitchen window. She opened the door and called, "Here, kitty, kitty..." She saw the cat stretch and called again. The feline bounded across the yard and approached the steps, sniffing the air cautiously. "Aren't you a pretty boy?" she asked. "I don't see a collar. Who might you belong to?" The unfamiliar cat, with fur that looked clean and healthy, stepped onto the cement pad and sat on its haunches. He was handsome, even though she didn't know if it was male or female—it certainly seemed aloof and unafraid. "Well, make up your mind, will you? I'm not holding the door open all night, heating the outside."

The cat bounded up the stairs and into the kitchen.

• • •

Eva sat at the kitchen table, sipping coffee, and watched the solid gray mouser (visibly male in the morning light) as he hunched over the two small ceramic bowls she had set out. The only food she had on hand that she assumed all cats loved was tuna fish, but after opening a can and dousing a forkful of flakes with juices, the big boy only sat at attention after dismissing the dish with a single sniff. Her only other meat option that she was willing to part with was a small container of chicken livers. After slicing one into several bite-sized chunks, it was apparent this fellow was a meat-eater who gobbled it up, cleaned the bowl, and politely asked for more.

The color of his fur reminded her of the dark gray smoke that billowed from the end of Magee's stove pipe when Sam disconnected it, took it out back, and burned off the creosote buildup. Sam was responsible for this and wondered if Henry could do it next time. *How did Sam know when the time was right?* She remembered seeing him tap the pipe with his fingertips now and then.

Eva sipped her coffee, inhaling the last of the aromatic steam rising under her nose, and said, "Smokey. It sounds about right to me that I call you Smokey."

With his back turned to her, he paid her no mind as he cleaned his paws. He sprinted down the cellar stairs into the darkness when a loud knock came at the door.

Eva unlocked the door and welcomed Ruby inside, who was carrying a wrapped offering. "I brought you over some bannock bread. Your grandmother's old recipe," she said, handing the plate to Eva. "It's still warm outta the oven this mornin' and don't worry, I left some for your father—brings him right back to his childhood. Thought I'd catch you early before work to see how you were doin'." She didn't bother waiting for Eva to bring out the butter from the refrigerator; instead, she presented a small mason jar of her homemade raspberry jam, which she slipped from her apron pocket with a magician's sleight of hand. "Seein' as it's Valentine's Day, I'll give your father the day off too. He did such a nice job on those cabinets… I'll make him a batch of hermit cookies this afternoon that'll stick to his ribs—probably spoil his supper."

It had escaped Eva's mind that today was Valentine's Day as each day blurred into the next, but she would see it marked across the top of her daily reminder page later when she opened it to jot ten degrees on the first line and document Smokey's first meal.

"Sit yourself down," Ruby said. "I'll make us a little spread. And don't bother makin' anymore coffee, Henry and I have already loaded up this mornin'."

Eva obliged and sat down, holding her tepid, almost empty mug. "Sam called," she said. "He said the insurance I paid for didn't include collision, and he'd call Wright to get it sorted out."

"Well, good for him," Ruby said, joining her at the table with the plate of bread and open jam. She pulled a butter knife from the other pocket of her apron, always prepared. "Maybe you'll be able to save some money once he takes over payments on his own truck and gets your name off the paperwork."

"One can only hope so."

Ruby spread a heaping tablespoon of jam and handed it to Eva. She savored the light texture combined with the sweet, bright berries. She closed her eyes, trying to summon her own early teenage years, when her parents made lengthy drives along provincial highways to visit Henry's family in Nova Scotia. "What's the secret?" she asked Ruby.

"Don't over-knead the dough, and heat it low and slow so it doesn't burn on the outside, but long enough so it's not too raw in the middle. You have to watch it like a hawk."

Eva loved the flavors of berry jam, but still, she had to rinse the tiny seeds with a mouthful of cool coffee before swallowing the treat. "Yummy," she said. "You've outdone yourself this time."

The look on Ruby's face saw right through the tease.

• • •

Henry had shoveled all the walkways and the driveway before Eva left for work. It was a rare morning when the urge to wash or clean was a dull ache somewhere in the back of her mind. She credited this to a good night's sleep, made possible by Smokey, who slept in bed with her all night, finding the right spots to keep her warm. The cat seemed to sense when and where she grew cold during the night, shifting from her feet to her shoulders and neck—a warmth that lasted longer than any hot water bottle. She liked it best when he curled up on her pillow, and she could feel the soothing rhythm of his purring as it lulled her to sleep. The impenetrable barrier kept her nightmares at bay.

After feeding him his breakfast of raw chicken livers, he would sit alert by the door, waiting for Eva to let him outside. He would perch on the bottom step, licking his face and whiskers until he deemed himself ready for adventure. She watched as he zig-zagged across the yard, disappearing beyond the fieldstone wall and into the woods behind the house. She hated to see him go and hoped he'd stay away from catching the chipmunks that constantly inhabited her stone wall, as well as from becoming a meal himself to any wild fisher cat that might be roaming and hunting in the forest. Smokey knew where his bread was buttered, and she was confident he'd be waiting on the steps for his dinner when she came home from work.

Connie's birthday was approaching fast, and Eva had her eye on a stunning amethyst pendant that had recently appeared in the jewelry case at J.J. Newberry's, nestled on a gold rope chain that looked the right thickness. She decided today was the perfect day to buy it before someone else grabbed it. Hopefully, it would be something Connie would always cherish—a happy memory of her twentieth birthday.

Eva had already purchased a set of six matching glass tumblers and a silver maple leaf pin as gifts, which she had hidden deep within her bedroom closet. Henry and Ruby were driving to Middlebury to pick up Connie, and they would be home before she was. Eva knew her daughter well and understood that she would give the house a cursory once-over, snooping for birthday presents left in plain sight.

It was always pleasant to have Connie home from school; this time, Eva hoped the house looked nice and couldn't wait for her to meet Smokey.

• • •

Eva couldn't have imagined a more beautiful winter day—sunny, warm, and thawing. She wanted to start dinner before the birthday girl woke up, so she had everything ready by early afternoon.

Everyone sat around the dining room table, with Henry and Ruby on one side, Connie and Warren across from them, and Alice and Eva at opposite ends. It was a comfortable fit, with only Sam as the odd one out. He had shown up while Connie was still asleep, leaving her a nice card and $10.

Dinner included roasted pork, mashed potatoes, peas, a shrimp and cabbage salad with ranch dressing, blueberry muffins, and chocolate cake with whipped cream, enough for everyone to take home in doggie bags.

Connie received a variety of gifts, including sheets from Alice, as well as extra sheets and a butter dish from Henry and Ruby. Warren gave her the mahogany shadow box, which she loved, along with a small knick-knack shelf he made from leftover wood. Eva gave her the amethyst pendant—which she loved and asked Warren to put around her neck—plus pajamas, jeans, shorts, two summer blouses, the tumbler set, and a few ashtrays for Warren to use, along with a special thank you gift to Henry for handling all the snow shoveling—a one-pound can of apple tobacco.

After a cribbage round robin that Henry and Ruby won—probably because Eva and Alice enjoyed a couple of cherry brandies, and Connie and Warren indulged in too much dessert—it was time for everyone to say good night.

Connie decided to take the bus to Burlington rather than risk someone driving her there late on a Sunday night, so Warren took her to the station in White River Junction, leaving behind all her gifts except the amethyst.

Smokey didn't show up, even though Eva checked the steps regularly throughout dinner and after everyone had left. Maybe the cat had sharp hearing and watched the house, staying out of sight until the noise died down.

Since she had skipped writing in her diary that morning to make dinner, she recorded the day's events before bedtime and decided to call Smokey one last time. He leaped out of the shadows above the stone wall and bounded across the yard, making a beeline for the open door. Once inside, he made figure eights, weaving between Eva's legs as she tried to cut his chicken livers without tripping between steps to the refrigerator and filling his bowls. He gobbled his food as if he hadn't eaten in a month. *Thank God.* At least she could sleep tonight without worrying.

Smokey woke Eva an hour before sunrise, scratching along the sides of the firebox at the end of the hearth as if to let her know he was hungry or that the house needed warming with another log in the Jøtul. She started with the latter, dismissing either his protests or attempts to help, both of which only delayed his breakfast. This time, at least, he ate less ravenously before she let him out and watched him retrace his steps in the loosely packed snow. As he disappeared once again into the pre-dawn shadows and below-freezing temperatures, she shut the door and, under her breath, said, "It's a good thing you have a fur coat 'cause it's colder than a well digger's ass out there."

After her coffee, she waited until there was enough light to clean the inside of the kitchen windows. Once satisfied that all of yesterday's cooking had been wiped away, she put Connie's room to rights. She stowed the silverware set in the drawers built into the eave kneewall and placed all of Connie's gifts into the recessed closet opposite the slender oak cabinet that held her, Sam's, and Henry's guns.

Peering down from Connie's bedroom window at the bird feeders, she reminded herself to ask Henry to fill them before heading into town to open the store—Merrill was scheduled to have the day off—then glanced at Vera's lifeless house, an eyesore that needed upkeep against the other winter-white houses in the neighborhood.

Good riddance.

• • •

Faye was already inside the store, packing up the men's rubbers and all the felt and inner sheepskin-lined boots, but she stopped nonetheless to unlock the door before Eva had to dig around inside her purse to find the key. "Come in quick," she told Eva. "It's freezing out there." After relocking the door, she added, "I didn't make the coffee yet. I wanted to wait and make it fresh when you came."

"Good to know… thanks much," Eva said, taking off her coat. "I see you've gotten a head start."

"I'm better at tearing down the displays, and you're better at putting them up. That's your job." Faye closed a box that was full of heavy men's boots, then asked, "Is it too early to bring up the boys' and girls' patent leathers?"

"I should think so. Who's wanting to dirty those up? Unless the Almanac's predicting a drier spring?"

Faye laughed. "I don't know anyone who believes all those wives' tales."

Eva noticed the light fade from Faye's smile and wondered if Faye regretted mentioning the word 'wife'.

"How are you doing?" Faye asked, lifting the boot box.

"Oh, pretty good. We all had a nice time on Connie's birthday. She was pleased to be home." There was no need to retell the whole Smokey, the newly adopted cat, story. "Sam was somehow compelled to call me as I was about to leave this morning, letting me know that he had a flat on his way to Claremont after work. I couldn't care less is what I told him. When he said he was alone and had listened to the Liston Clay fight on the radio, I didn't want to hear about it and hung up."

"You don't think he and—"

"As I said, I couldn't care less… as long as he pays me a stipend. I'm not flush with cash these days, but I hope to pay off the bank note on the house soon. Then I'll be okay."

Faye nodded and carried the box of boots downstairs while Eva made coffee. When Faye returned, Eva suggested, "What would you say if we were to take down all the older heavy boots and replace them with newer Williams' heeled boots? Business will probably be slow next month either way."

"Okay, let's do it."

Eva's Daily Reminder 1964: February 29, Saturday

15 Below.

Was surprised to see the thermometer so low when I got up. Smokey stuck his nose out the door and turned right around and went down cellar. I hope he doesn't do his business down there somewhere. Better go to Claremont and pick up a kitty litter box just in case.

Well this is the end of February. A hard month! Have made a hole in the note at the bank and one more dorm payment left for Connie. I'll make it!

Still have trouble sleeping off and on. Am wondering if I'll ever get over this! I try not to think about them, but find it tough not to.

Ralph Weiss came into the store. He surprised me when Merrill went downstairs and asked me for a date. Had heard I was living alone. Put him in his place. Old whoremaster. Merrill would have a fit!

Did two loads of washing and got them dried. I did my ironing—not too much.

Got groceries. One Blue Jay.

Had supper at mom's. Al there. Shepard's pie, lima beans, green salad, walnut cake and ice cream.

Al came over afterwards and we had a crème de cacao.

12

The rain fell in torrents throughout the day and the night before. Eva appreciated Warren's excellent driving, which got Connie home safely late in the afternoon. It wasn't the heavy rain that made driving difficult; it was the fog that cloaked the Champlain Valley, as thick as sheep's wool.

Warren stayed for supper but left before cribbage to check on his parents' flood-prone house, leaving Eva and Connie to face Henry and Ruby, who once again proved that the wiser elders made the better team.

The relentless sound of rain sheeting off the roof, overflowing the gutter spouts, and splashing onto the front steps and stone flower boxes outside Eva's bedroom window woke her. Smokey was oblivious, curled in a ball near her feet. Eva had wondered before going to bed if he would be curious enough to venture upstairs and sleep with Connie. Instead of disturbing the cat, she reached over and turned on the bedside radio, keeping the volume low enough to avoid waking her bed partner or Connie.

The White River bridge was washed out overnight, according to WRLM AM. Water covered the roads north and south of Sumner Falls, with traffic being rerouted around the mountain. The newscaster said the northern parts of the state were still experiencing heavy rainfall.

Smokey jumped off the bed before the first phone ring stopped, forcing Eva to bail out from under the covers and rush to the kitchen to answer it before waking Connie. She needed her rest.

"Hello," Eva said, finally able to cinch the front of her robe.

"This is Percy Bliss, chief of the Ascutney fire department. I'm trying to get ahold of Sam Martin. Is he there? I'm calling on all civil defense volunteers in the area, and we need radio operators."

"I'm sorry. I can't help you." Eva didn't want to hesitate any longer than necessary before Percy would ask more questions, adding, "He's not here, is what I'm trying to tell you. Try the Wimmer, he's apt to be there."

"Hotel Wimmer? Claremont?" he asked, confused.

"You betcha." Eva hung up.

"Who was that?" Connie asked from behind.

Eva startled and readjusted her grip on the collar of her robe. "Just somebody looking for your father. They need people with radios to help coordinate flood crews, I guess," she said. Eva glanced around her feet, into the kitchen, and then into the living room. "Did Smokey sleep with you at all last night?"

Connie followed Eva's eyes around the house before finally rechecking her mother's bedroom. "He's still in your room on the bed. I guess it's still too early for him, or else he likes the radio." She straightened the front of her flannel birthday pajamas. "These feel nice, but I guess I should have washed them first." She hesitated before adding, "No, he didn't sleep with me, but he sure was a curious little bugger. He sniffed all around my whole room, tracing along the baseboards. Checked out the window, scratched on the gun cabinet glass, and even went inside my closet"—she sniffed—"I hope he didn't do any funny business in there."

"Speaking of the radio, they said the roads were all flooded north and south of town. You'd better call Warren and check on his parents' house. That whole section north of town makes me so nervous this time of year. It makes for good farming, but the river always floods north of the covered bridge."

While Connie called Warren, Eva went to her bedroom, got dressed, and turned off the radio, which woke Smokey. "Oh Lordy, look at you," she said. "I come in and get dressed, making a heck of a racket. You don't even flinch, not even an ear twitch, but I turn off the radio, and *that* wakes you up? You're one odd duck. Let's go eat."

Smokey followed Eva into the kitchen, where she could hear a hint of distress in Connie's voice before she hung up the phone. "Everything all right?"

"Actually, no," Connie huffed. "Seldon and Pearl's house got flooded. The entire basement is flooded, with water over the cellar windows—almost above the foundation. He said he doesn't know what they're doing in the meantime, other than staying with cousins in Woodstock." Connie gave Eva puppy dog eyes. "Can Warren stay here with us?"

Eva was good with math, having balanced their checkbook throughout their marriage. Still, she hesitated as she counted bedrooms and the potential days until the river might recede. *Connie doesn't ask for much.*

"I can see the wheels turning behind those beady little eyes of yours," Connie said. "The wedding's in only a few months, so it's—"

"Beg pardon," Eva interrupted. "This is news to me. The timing—"

"I know, it's not good. That's what you were about to say. The plan all along, before this"—she flailed her arms—"fiasco, was to get married in the summer after graduation. The way I see it… We can all crawl into a hole, or we can move on." She planted her fists on her hips, then moved toward the door to glance into the yard. "We were thinking of something small anyway… just us, really. And I'd like to have the ceremony in the backyard—there's no need for a church." She faced Eva. "And you said"—she hooked a thumb over her shoulder toward the kitchen window, stabbing twice—"she's gone now? Out of the picture?"

Smokey interrupted them by meowing at the door. Eva sidestepped Connie and cracked the door enough for him to squeeze through. He looked both ways before rushing into the woods.

"Who knows," Eva said. "But yes, apparently she's moved out of her house. Where to? Anybody's guess. Is your father still seeing her? Who knows," she said again. "I thought we were soulmates."

Eva sounded robotic. It was too early in the day to show emotion. She wouldn't have tears cascading down her face like today's falling rain.

"I think he'll come around. I think we can be a family again," Connie said.

"Oh, I don't know about that, Connie. I honestly don't think I can do it." Eva found herself slipping down from the walls she had been fortifying. "It's been so hard to take."

Connie wrapped her reassuringly and said, "I have a plan. I've been thinking about what I want to tell him. And I'll put it all in writing. That'll give him a chance to hear what I have to say, and I'll make him read it over more than once until it sinks in."

Eva slipped a hand between them and pushed away enough to see the resolve on Connie's face as she stood resolutely. "I don't want to see you do something so difficult—to put yourself through it. We've got your grand-parents right next door. It'll be okay."

"Mummy, they won't be around forever. Then what?"

Eva had no idea how many winters of being responsible for multiple houses Henry had left in him. Between shoveling, roofing, painting, and raking, it was all too much to worry about now. "That's very sweet of you, but why don't we focus on all of us getting past this flooding first? Go ahead and call Warren back. Let him know he's welcome to stay here as long as he needs to. He can even offer to drive me to and from work. I wouldn't mind a little chauffeuring. Now, why don't you start on the coffee and scrambled eggs while I feed the grosbeaks."

• • •

It was a beautiful, sunny Palm Sunday, and with no snow in sight or on the ground to shovel, Henry caught Eva in the middle of her general cleaning. He offered to pull out the stove and refrigerator, and both of them were surprised to find so many dust bunnies lodged along the baseboard. Eva made quick work with her mop, removing them before Henry could ask why there were so many or why she had been so lax. Her biggest concern was hoping he wouldn't notice the abundance of dark gray cat hair.

"Slackin' off, I see," he said, pointing.

Eva leaned on the mop handle. The tip jabbed into her armpit, making her wince. She felt around with her fingers. She was losing muscle along with the twelve pounds she'd shed since Sam moved out. "Well, it's not like I can yank these appliances out myself without Sam here to do it for me. And I'm definitely not going to risk Connie hurting herself either."

"Sorry. I *was* gonna make a joke about Al and puttin' her hips into it, but—"

"Sounds like you just did."

"Sorry," he said again. Henry looked at the empty floor where the stove used to be and asked, "What's that?" He pointed to something small on the checkered linoleum. "Is that an empty .22? Evie, have you been—"

Eva snatched it up, cupping it in her palm, and then slipped it into the back pocket of her jeans. "Oh, it's nothing," she said. "It's a brass charm from my bracelet, or Connie's. Either way, no harm done. It must've fallen off while we were cooking." She finished mopping the two sections of flooring. "I'll look at it later. Warren can reattach it with a pair of needlenose pliers."

Henry looked skeptical and was about to say something, so Eva told him he could push the appliances back into place.

"What's Mom up to this morning?" she asked.

"Well, usually I'd say she's in the kitchen, but not today. She's fussin' around with that sweater pattern you gave her. At the rate she's goin', she'll be lucky to finish before snow flies again."

Eva chuckled a little too much, annoyed with herself for not keeping her emotional boundaries in check. "Be careful of what you wish for. You know damn well it can snow all the way up to the first weekend in May." After regaining her composure, she asked, "So, will you be able to tear Mom away from her knitting to bring Connie back to school? Al's stopping in after church to give me a tint, and I told Connie I'd make her some cream puffs to take back. I've also got some baked beans simmering downstairs, and some brown bread that'll make a few nice dinners for her and her housemates."

If Eva couldn't shoo her father away before Connie came downstairs, he'd probably never leave until it was time to pack the car.

"Are you sure you don't need me to help take down any curtains? Pull the screen windows out from under the eaves? I bet they need paintin'."

He wasn't asking; he was practically begging for a project to work on.

"I'm all done today, but sure, that sounds like a good plan for you to get started on tomorrow while I'm at work. Let me know how much paint money you need if you go to Claremont and…" Eva almost asked him to pick up a kitty litter box but caught herself. "Sam left $40 on Friday, so that little extra will come in handy."

She was proud of her quick thinking, recalling the hockey term Sam had used right before he fell while skating in the backyard. He had said, "Watch me deke the defenseman," right before he stopped short and toppled. Hopefully, not all deking and dancing with little white lies would come back to haunt her.

• • •

Alice Fairbanks kept her nose to the grindstone and her ear to the ground. Juggling running the town's beauty salon, organizing the Unitarian church dinners, and hosting a rotation of bridge games, she couldn't avoid hearing the gossip around town. Yesterday, she acquiesced to the younger women on her staff, who wanted to hold an open house to attract more spring customers. Once the word spread that there were complimentary mimosas, a steady stream of both new and loyal customers came in for the extra treat.

Eva sat with her back turned to the kitchen sink, in a straight-backed rush chair she had brought in from the dining room. "You look a little rough around the edges," she told Alice. "You're sure you're okay?"

"You can always wear a hat in the store tomorrow if something goes wrong. Yes, I did end up tying one on yesterday, but I've been doing this a *long* time, and I could do it with my eyes closed, maybe even with one hand tied behind my back. Besides, it was worth it to hear loose lips sink ships. Luckily, it wasn't so much that I couldn't keep my wits about me."

"You're lucky Poole didn't pinch you."

"Oh, it wasn't that bad, c'mon now. So, do you want to hear the bad news or the good news first?" Alice asked, squeezing a line of color tint along Eva's part line, using rubber gloves to keep the dye off her fingers.

Eva wanted to end on some good news for a change, so she said, "Might as well start with the bad."

"Well, the bad news shouldn't come as any surprise, but… *everyone* knows Sam's been messing around with Vera Flynn. Those who didn't know he had moved out… do now. Pretty much everyone whose husband works at the machine shop knew already."

"Water under the bridge. Let's get on with it."

"Well… the *good* news—maybe *better* news is a better word, no pun intended—around all of this is that it seems little Miss Flynn has been seen coming into the church during the week with Ray Whittman."

It was as if Smokey had a grip on Eva's tongue. Unreacting, she tried to weigh her options, distracted by the fumes. She assumed Vera was two-timing Sam behind his back. His only friendship—destroyed. It was what she had wanted to happen last year. Maybe it was the best news; maybe Sam confided in Ray, who took advantage, and now Sam knows, and he's moved on—straightened himself out—two birds with one stone. *Why was she even considering this?*

"Okay, all finished. It needs to sit for a while." Alice checked the towel around Eva's shoulders, using both hands to tuck it snugly into Eva's shirt collar and against her neck. "Not much to say. Cat got your tongue?"

Eva returned the chair to its spot in the dining room, keeping her shoulders and neck straight and the towel securely in place. "Any word on her selling the house?"

Alice paused, gazing across the yard. Whether she was looking at Vera's house or the bird feeders, Eva wasn't sure. "Jan Chabot said Vera asked her to rent it out. I suppose this must have happened pretty recently. I don't see a sign over there yet. Jan didn't mention what Vera was asking for or why she wasn't selling it, but who knows? And no—before you ask—Jan didn't offer, and I didn't ask either, where Vera was living these days."

"Janice graduated a couple of years before Connie," Eva said. "I guess she decided to stick around for the money once she got a taste of her uncle's real estate business."

"I see her at the salon for a trim every couple of months. She reminds me of Doris Day with her natural blonde hair and blue eyes. Add to that an outgoing personality, and I'd say she made a wise career choice."

Eva snorted. *Blondes. The last thing she ever wanted to be.* "Well, I'll believe it when I see it," she said.

•••

Daybreak on Maundy Thursday greeted Eva with a gamut of northeast weather: wind, drizzle, snow, thunder, and lightning. The wet snow, with flakes the size of quarters, was melting almost as fast as it was sticking to the ground—poor man's manure, as Ruby called it. The trees were full of protesting grosbeaks. Eva had never witnessed such a racket for as long as she could remember.

It seemed like nature was in an uproar over Sam's fiftieth birthday, and he called before Eva even finished her coffee, asking who was taking Connie to school tomorrow. "I already spoke to Warren earlier in the week. Who'd you think was taking her?" she asked, the acidic black coffee rising in her gorge at the tone of his voice. He had a way of pushing her buttons.

"I wasn't sure about the condition of the roads north of Rutland. The forecast calls for high winds through Friday. It would be wiser to use the truck. I didn't think… or want you or Henry to take any chances."

Since when did he start caring lately? It made Eva paranoid that something was up, and she didn't have time to hear him out. She needed to pull some curtains before work and give herself extra time for the drive into town. Easter weekend marked the start of spring and white tennis shoe season, which kept her busy for the next two days as she organized the displays. The last thing she wanted was to fall behind and have to finish on Good Friday.

"I'm sure she wanted to spend the extra alone time with Warren so they could discuss their wedding plans," she said. "I don't know if she's told you or not, but—"

"She told me. She wrote me a pretty long letter. Said they wanted a small backyard ceremony this summer. That'll save them some money."

He sounded less than enthusiastic, and she remained silent, waiting for him to drop the next shoe, until she finally asked, "And?" She counted to three before giving up. "That's all you have to say?"

"She wants me to stop seeing Vera, whether we stay together or not."

"Who's… *we*?" Eva asked him point-blank.

"Us… You and me. I'm thinking about it."

"Samuel!" Eva shouted, tasting the coffee and bile in her throat. "Do you have any idea what this is doing to me? And to Connie? Can you imagine what this would do to her—and Warren—if we divorced?" She swallowed, pushing everything down, unsteady on her feet. "She'd have nothing to do with you—ever! And I betcha they'd call the whole thing off! I wouldn't blame her. Who would? Do you want that on your conscience?" She almost spit in the sink as she moved closer to the window. "That bitch really has you bamboozled, doesn't she? So much so, you don't know which way is up anymore."

Sensing a spell coming on, Eva said, "Hold on," and hung the phone's receiver on the edge of the base before she managed to open the fridge and lift a pitcher of iced tea with both hands. After pouring herself a glass and taking a sip, the coldness dispelled enough of the dizziness for her to feel capable of staying the course, but she mishandled the phone, unable to catch it before it clanked onto the floor. Reaching for the unmoored handset, she was about to apologize for the noise but decided he deserved to hear it. Make him worry that something bad had happened to her instead.

"Sam, if they end up not going through with the wedding… because of this stunt of yours… it'll crush Connie's heart. Whatever she took the time to say to you *and* write it all down, I suggest you read it again, and ask yourself if it's all worth it. To you. To Connie. To us."

"I have. I will."

"Warren's already bought them a new maple bedroom set. They're already looking at new apartments. It would be a shame to screw that all up, don't you think?"

Eva was unsure if guilt would influence him. She definitely knew he had never apologized for anything in his life, except for that one time when it was all about himself. If he ever felt disrespected or wronged, he would give the cold shoulder until, begrudgingly, whoever his narcissism was directed at would cave in and apologize first, then life would move on as if nothing had ever happened.

Did she have the strength to do it again this time? She would if Connie asked, but it seemed an insurmountable life dilemma.

After taking down the curtains in the front room and filling the washing machine, and before leaving for work, Eva used two blank greeting cards from the extras she kept in her desk to leave in the car for his birthday, writing her name on one and Connie's on the other. She had no idea if he'd recognize the difference. It was odd not to wish him a happy birthday.

The cards were gone, and Sam had replaced them with $30 sometime during the workday.

Ruby broke down and mailed him a card and a handkerchief.

Eva's Daily Reminder 1964: April 2, Thursday

Connie and Warren off for the day went bowling. Not here when Sam came at 5:15.

We had a talk. He admitted still seeing Vera. Blamed me for "kicking" him out and throwing him at her. I reminded him that he was already sleeping with her when he left. Nothing was gained by talking. I told him Connie and I had hoped he would give Vera up by now and straighten out. No hopes for a reconciliation and can see that now very clearly.

Sam changed VW oil and greased it.

I was emotionally exhausted and went to bed at 10.

Connie slept with me. She sure tries to comfort me and does. Lulls me to sleep when she rubs my back and traces our initials with her finger on my neck. Sure love her dearly.

13

Eva woke up dizzy and dehydrated. She staggered into the bathroom and vomited, struggling to maneuver around the inward door and the tight squeeze before kneeling. Cleaning the bathroom wasn't on her list of chores for today. After rinsing her mouth with cold mountain tap water, her head steadied. However, something passed, a small blood clot in the toilet after urinating. Luckily, there were still kidney pills leftover from her last visit to Dr. Read, and after taking a couple, she felt better by the time she made herself a small breakfast of bacon and toast.

She missed having Connie sleeping with her but was glad she wasn't there to worry, seeing—hearing—her in distress.

Graduation was only a couple of months away. Connie's last letter home included her marks, showing only one transcription class as satisfactory, with all the others above average. She was a smart cookie. Eva had no doubt she'd land a secretarial job before summer ended—she and Warren had a new bedroom and living room set to pay for.

Eva couldn't remember the exact day of Warren's birthday, but it was this week, and she had no idea what to get him. It would be funny and practical to wrap up the rest of her S&H Green Stamp books in a big box and let him choose something for their new apartment. Hopefully, he'd exchange them for something practical at Montgomery Wards instead of a bunch of ribeye steaks at Super Duper. Even as she donned a pair of rubber gloves to scrub the bathroom floor, she had to stifle a laugh at hearing Henry's voice inside her head, always calling it Monkey Wards.

By the time she was satisfied that the linoleum was clean and the toast had settled her stomach, Eva only had a minute to plug in the coffee percolator and spot a rose-breasted grosbeak at the feeder before Ruby knocked. She stood off the steps, wearing a house dress without her usual apron. Her purse, which matched her black orthopedics, was securely clasped in both hands. She was dressed more for a trip than a day of cooking in her kitchen.

"C'mon in," Eva told her. "You're early. Al isn't here yet. Why'd you bring your pocketbook?"

"Your father isn't home to watch the house. I didn't want any damn kids breakin' in and stealin' my money."

A doleful expression spread over Eva's face. It was a look her mother wouldn't recognize. "Mom…" she trailed off, not wanting to think about her mother's senility. As long as Ruby could score her cribbage hands and knew who everyone was, Eva wouldn't worry for now. "Come inside. Where's Dad?"

Ruby climbed the steps into the kitchen, where Eva took her purse and leaned it in plain sight against a large ceramic bean pot that Ruby had used for years as a doughnut jar. "He's outside, rakin' your banks." She pointed over the sink and said, "Have a look for yourself."

Eva craned her neck, twisting to see if her father was outside on her front lawn, and he was. Only a small patch of snow remained in the shadow of the multi-trunk white paper birch tree that Eva hoped to light up at night—someday, if Sam ever got his act together and came home. "Hopefully, he can thin out the periwinkle around the birch tree… but not *too* much," she said. "I don't want the bank above the retaining wall left too sparse."

"Oh, you can't kill that stuff," Ruby scoffed. "It always comes back."

Eva didn't want to argue with her and was spared from doing so when she noticed Alice walking down the road with her oversized bag. Alice stopped to say hello to Henry, at least as far as Eva could tell. Eva watched as she sneered when Henry probably asked her what was in the bag, then peered inside and seemed to mock her by pointing to her knee before he let her pass.

"What was that all about?" Eva asked when Alice finally made it up the front steps.

Alice's bouffant was always neat and styled, never cut too short or too long, and Eva never asked her how she styled her hair in the morning by herself, but today it looked somewhat tussled. "Oh… he knew there was a jar in my salon bag and wanted to know what was in it," Alice said, her cheeks flushed as she nudged past Eva.

Once in the kitchen, it was Ruby who noticed the ragged knee hole in Alice's slacks. "What the hell did you do to yourself?"

If Alice's cheeks were flushed after being poked by Henry, her face was now entirely red, and she stammered with embarrassment, turning her back on Ruby and Eva as she set her canvas tote on the countertop. When she turned around again, she showed them a scuff mark on her palm and pointed at her knee. "If you must know, I tripped over my own damn feet, walking out of the driveway, and fell." She stood firm, letting the moment sink in, and took her ridicule in stride. "You can both laugh at my expense, but you know what?" she asked, reaching into her bag. "At least I didn't break the jar of whiskey sours." She laughed, and Eva laughed. Ruby snickered and rolled her eyes. "So who's going first?"

Ruby volunteered for her shampoo and perm first. She didn't want to go outside until her hair had dried, and Alice could comb it out. They suspected she didn't want to miss any gossip.

While Eva leaned her head over the sink, she said, "The rose-breasted grosbeak was at the feeder this morning. It's always such a treat to see him."

"I bet it is," Alice said.

Eva considered herself patient and always hopeful, with spring her favorite time of year, as she enjoyed the colorful blooms before the summer green canvas. "I've been having Dad keep the feeders filled with black sunflower seeds, and I know it's still a bit early, but I asked him to hang the thistle feeder. I don't want to miss the indigo bunting's first appearance."

"Did you check last year's journal?" Alice asked.

Eva didn't want to tell them why she couldn't write in her diary this morning. "I'll have to start looking through last April and May this afternoon—good idea. If memory serves, he'll show up early next month."

"Better make sure your bifocals are up to date," Ruby interjected. "You wouldn't wanna shoot it by mistake when you're poppin' off those blue jays."

Eva gasped, trying to lift her head to glare at her mother. "Mom!" she shouted. To Alice, she said, "Pay no attention to her. I guess she can't handle her drink anymore." She managed to make eye contact with Ruby and shot her a glare. Before her mother had a chance to quip about Annie Oakley, she said, "Zip it," and hoped Alice had taken her advice not to pay any attention.

Ruby clutched at her purse and swallowed a guffaw.

The last thing Eva wanted was to offend Alice, but if she had to plant the seed of senility, she would.

Whether Alice knew it or not, she changed the subject, saying, "So the word upstreet is that Vera's house has been rented."

• • •

By week's end, a moving van was parked behind Vera's house. It must have arrived overnight while Eva was asleep because she never heard a thing; however, it sat quietly in the driveway, its Mayflower-green-and-gold colors unmistakable. There didn't appear to be any movement, and all the doors were shut. Eva didn't know whether everything had been unloaded overnight or if any action would start that morning. Either way, she wasn't about to distract herself with cleaning while waiting. She sipped her coffee, waiting patiently to catch a glimpse of the new renters before heading to work.

She debated whether to call Connie and risk waking her or wait and call from the store with the news. Meanwhile, Smokey jumped onto the console table from behind her reading chair and sniffed the shoe tree lamp before turning his attention to the activity around the bird feeders. "Oh, you little bugger," Eva said, startled. "Hadn't I already let you out?" She stroked the cat's neck and scratched behind its ears while taking notice of exactly what the little scamp's eyes were focused on. "Don't you even dare think about it, mister," she chided him. "You'd better stay away from my birdies. You've got plenty of room to roam and play up back."

Eva finished her coffee and shooed Smokey out the door, making sure he was on his way to the wall before closing the door behind him.

• • •

Connie called the store before Eva had a chance to decide whether to call first. She didn't sound well; her voice was raspy, and Eva suddenly wondered if this was what her daughter might sound like if Warren kept smoking his unfiltered Camels around her.

"Goodness, you sound so froggy," Eva said. She couldn't believe Warren was smoking inside their new apartment, which was filled with their brand-new furniture, or how to get the smell out of the upholstery and curtains. God forbid they decide to have a baby soon after the wedding. "Think it's a bug going around?"

"I think it's a cold. I'm all stuffed up. Ears ache."

"Let's hope it's not pneumonia. I'm so sorry you're not feeling well, hon. Will you miss any of your classes? We don't want that to happen. You're so close to finishing."

Eva heard Connie exhale.

"It's not a big deal," Connie said. "I'd rather come home and rest before taking final exams. It won't make a difference and won't affect my marks. Everything is class review now, then I'll have four finals, and turn in all my books."

Eva tried once more, asking, "Does Mrs. Hubbard have any Buckley's to give you?" And again, Connie sighed more forcefully.

"Mummy, hearing the name makes me want to throw up. I have no idea how you and Dad can stand that stuff. It doesn't work."

"Well, your grandparents swear by it."

Connie coughed into the phone, and Eva could hear her sniffle. "All right. Have you called Warren?"

"He can't get off work. He's working a new shift."

Connie had trouble asking for anything directly. "Do you want me to call your grandparents? Or do you want to?" Eva barely hesitated before continuing, "Never mind, sit tight, and I'll come home for lunch and ask them—no need to spend another nickel on calling again. The weather looks good today, so I'm sure your grandfather won't mind going for a drive, but I don't want them to get sick and catch whatever bug you've got."

"Don't worry, I'll stay curled up in the backseat, buried under a blanket."

• • •

The first thing Eva did when she got home from work was force a heaping spoonful of Buckley's down Connie's throat, who half-pleaded but didn't throw up. She slept with Eva, and by midday, she sounded much better, much to her chagrin—especially after Eva said, "I told you so."

• • •

The bird baths were covered with a thin sheet of ice, still frostier than the morning sun. The lilacs were beginning to show signs of budding, and the same was true for the white birch. The purple, yellow, and white crocuses were the only colors to decorate late spring.

Eva decided to let Connie sleep in. Although Smokey enjoyed his chicken liver breakfast, he seemed to sense that Connie needed his company more than the local wildlife, so he retreated into the bedroom, where he circled the pillow three times before curling around her neck.

Eva agreed to give Faye the day off so she and her husband could drive to Boston and help their daughter move out of Emerson College into an apartment in the Back Bay. She had secured a job with the Globe during her final internship, making it a better use of her journalism degree than returning to rural Sumner Falls to work on the weekly town Chronicle.

Eva's only job was to hold down the fort behind the register. All the shoe displays remained in place; all the heavy lifting was done until early fall. It was a slow sales day, and she was grateful for the lack of stress, even though revenue was down.

However, on the drive home, everything changed when a rear tire blew. She could steer and brake, hoping she could make it home, but decided to pull over as far as she dared at the halfway point. She didn't want to walk a mile. The shoulders were clear, but the poison ivy along this sunny stretch of the road was always present unless buried in snowdrifts.

She checked the rearview and driver-side mirror before exiting the VW.

The passenger-side rear tire appeared to be in poor shape, with visible strands of rubber and white fibers in the torn sidewall. Her first instinct was to blame Sam. *Why wasn't he here to swap out the spare?* When she paused to scan the McSwains' barren cornfields and the hills of New Hampshire across the river, she relaxed, recognizing her location and the situation. Sam wouldn't have been with her to change the flat anyway.

She leaned against the rear hood, facing town, and hoped the next car would swerve around her. Her robin's egg blue Beetle was easy to spot against the shoulder. Her navy sweater and matching Keds blended in somewhat, but her fire-engine red slacks stood out, making her visible from quite a distance. What she didn't expect was a car slowing as it headed into town from the opposite direction, catching sight of its flashing lights before hearing its engine.

Officer Poole extended an arm, pointed at her, and waved before slowly making a U-turn. He pulled his cruiser to the side and parked behind Eva, leaving his lights flashing. The fuss embarrassed her as she waited for him to get out of his car and approach, his hands on his utility belt.

He tilted his head, appearing to notice her car's flat tire, before acknowledging her. "Eva," he said, pointing, "looks like that tire has seen better days. How about I help get you out of this mess?" He looked at her for confirmation and never once seemed inclined to look inside Eva's car.

"Sounds good to me," she said, and waited for him to either move toward the passenger side or ask where the spare tire was. She had no idea if he knew it was under the front hood. When he started to return to his car, she said, "Officer? Richard?"

He paused, turned, and raised a hand, palm out. When on duty, he commanded respect, never smiled, and, regardless of anyone's age—even if they were older—he was all business and efficient. "I'm not bothering to change your tire. I'll call Bud and have him or one of his guys come and tow you to the Gulf station. That tire will need replacing. There's no fixing it. I'll take you home as soon as I'm off the radio."

Oh goodness—all this fuss. It would be a good time for Alice to swing by and pick her up, but she'd probably miss seeing her and drive right on past.

After radioing in the tow, he stepped out with one foot and motioned for Eva to get into the passenger side of the cruiser. "Make sure you have everything you need and leave the key in the ignition," he said. "Nobody will steal it in this condition at this time of the day." He waited for her to grab her purse. Once inside, he added, "And if anyone did… I'd catch 'em." He winked without smiling.

The mile-long trip home and drop-off only took a few minutes. Eva's stomach twisted at the sight of Sam's truck parked in front of the house. Officer Poole, an expert at making U-turns, pulled alongside and said, "Be sure to have Sam call Bud later today. I imagine he'll have you all taken care of, probably by tomorrow morning, though you never know. Depends on how busy he is this afternoon."

"Will do. Thanks. Have a good day," Eva told him. She didn't wave, nor did she watch him leave; instead, she turned to the garage door. She didn't even think to wipe her Keds on the rug at the foot of the stairs.

Eva found Sam and Connie in the kitchen. Connie, who was sobbing, cradled Smokey in her arms.

Eva's Daily Reminder 1964: April 18, Saturday

Sunny. Chilly.

Worked in the morning. Slow day. Flat tire on the way home. Got towed.

Sam here with Connie when I came home. It was pretty rough. One of the most heartbreaking moments was seeing Connie break down and cry.

I don't see why there was any doubt in my mind that I couldn't do it for her. I'd do anything! Sam said he'd like to come back and promised, after tomorrow, not to see, talk to, or in any way have anything to do with her. It's hard on him. I am so much at fault also. Should have fixed her hot little red wagon years ago! Maybe somehow we can salvage something.

I still think Sam's and my names are written in the book of destiny and they should stay there but we both have to want it that way to make it work.

14

Eva's vacation week started sunny and cool. The air was dry and breezy, with cotton-candy clouds drifting east over Mount Ascutney. Her daffodils and azaleas were in full bloom, and the scent of crabapple blossoms—a bumblebee bonanza—drifted from several old trees in the neighborhood through the open windows.

She considered calling Alice to check on her peonies, but decided to wait until she cleaned the oven, washed, and ironed two loads of laundry.

Her hand was on the receiver when someone knocked at the front door. Whoever it was didn't hesitate; they walked in and called out, "Anybody home?"

Eva recognized Alice Fairbank's voice. "Come on in. I was about to call you," she said, wiping her hands on a kitchen towel. "I was all set to walk over and treat myself to a flower show." She hadn't seen or heard Alice's terrier, Impy, until her little toenails clicked on the hardwood floor. "Oh my, isn't she dressed up today?" she asked rhetorically, noticing the dog's knitted red coat.

Whenever Alice walked through the neighborhood, Impy was always right beside her, dressed in weather-appropriate attire, whether it was a yellow raincoat with matching booties or one of many knitted or vinyl coats.

"Again, come on in, both of you," Eva said, gesturing toward the kitchen. "I just finished cleaning. It's almost happy hour, right?"

"Somewhere, that's for sure," Alice answered.

In the kitchen, Sam was drinking a beer. He had washed his truck and Eva's while she was busy. He noticed the different tire and asked Eva how much Bud had soaked her for it. When she showed him the receipt, he nodded, but she was sure he wanted to find fault with something. (Bud never mentioned if the tire was new or used, and she hadn't asked.)

Impy wouldn't even look at Sam. She bounced on her restless paws as if standing on hot pavement, her tongue lapping while her face was buried between Alice's shins. The petite terrier never barked, choosing instead to communicate with excited grunts, pug-nose snorts, and sniffles.

Alice darted her eyes between Sam and Eva. "We don't need to interrupt. I can always stop by later," she said, gauging the room's mood.

Alice's eyes shifted from Sam's beer to Eva's side of the kitchen table.

"Are you having supper amongst yourselves tonight?" Alice asked tentatively. "If everyone's gathering at your folks', I could bring the diddle-de-dum dessert. Ruby gave me a copy of her recipe."

"Did she now?" Eva teased, drawing out each word, hoping she sounded offended. *Alice could be gullible.* The joke failed to hide the conundrum of letting Sam come home, and whether she could do it for Connie. Luckily, she could put her feelings aside for another day. "I'm teasing. You'll have to take a rain check. We're bringing Connie back to school this afternoon."

"Oh, isn't that nice? That sounds like fun. Is she here? Can I say hello and goodbye?"

Eva touched Alice's elbow, proudly saying, "No, she's in town with Warren's sister, trying to pick out a wedding dress. Well, not actually, they're looking through a catalog. I'm sure once she's in Burlington, she'll find something nice up there. And Catherine will help her. No doubt Connie'll ask her to be her maid of honor. I hope she gives us enough leeway to get her the money."

Alice returned the touch. "I do not doubt both fronts." She acknowledged Sam with barely a glance. "C'mon, Imp, let's get going."

The dog didn't need to be told twice, as it tugged on her leash—if one could even call it a tug based on her weight and spindly legs.

Before she left, Alice whispered to Eva that she hoped she was doing the right thing, and when Eva returned to the kitchen, she said, "You're going to have to get over it, you know. We have friends and family." She gestured north and south with her hands and arms. "We trusted—"

"I know," Sam interjected. "I know."

"Well, today's as good a day as any to start. We should call Connie and let her know we'll pick her up on the way. Let's put our good faces on, for her sake."

• • •

Sam seemed like his old self during the drive to Champlain—Connie even whispered this to Eva when saying goodbye, hopefully for the last time before finals.

The turnaround was swift, and with daylight to spare, they decided to cross the river to pick up the rest of Sam's clothes from the Hotel Wimmer.

Eva hadn't seen Sam pack a paper grocery bag before leaving, so she said, "I thought we were bringing bags home, not there."

"A little surprise."

She was skeptical, but after retrieving the rest of his clothes, Sam paid his final bill, returned the room key, and she sat quietly as he took a detour around the mountain. He had made a jug of daiquiris and brought along a pair of field glasses. They shared both, stopping and nipping along the way to spot and watch deer, around forty in total.

It was a lovely and enjoyable evening, so much so that, as the adage goes, 'if you fall off a horse, you get right back on,' and she did.

Unable to sleep, Eva woke up at an early hour. Not wanting Sam to lose sleep, she quietly slipped out into the living room, which felt much larger without the Jøtul. Sam had taken it apart as soon as he got home, and she stayed out of his way until he finished using the lawn tractor and trailer to haul it downstairs. He had chosen a corner of the basement to winterize it, and she was okay with that spot since it was outside her usual cleaning areas.

It was so strange sleeping with him—someone different. She had gotten used to sleeping with Smokey and on the weekends, Connie.

They swapped places between the bedroom and the sofa when Sam realized she was missing.

Eva's Daily Reminder 1964: April 22, Wednesday

Rain. Miserable. Cold rainy day, all day long. Kids aren't having a very good vacation week.

A long day for me. Felt low when I came home and then Vera comes down to her house just before 5. Didn't get a good look at the new renters. Had their backs to me the whole time. Hung around till Sam came home and was just leaving when he came. It bothered me quite a bit.

After supper he held me in his arms and we started our married life anew. I think it meant a lot to him. I hope so. He went radioing around 7:30 and home at 11:30. I waited up for him. I've got to trust him and he me. He put my ring on again and told me the magic words.

15

If Eva wanted to wash any curtains, she would have to look at the house next door. Although Vera no longer lived there, her house still stood, taunting, because Vera and Sam had communicated at night with light signals. Those flashes stung like yellow jackets and carried the scent of Vera's perfume.

The sky resembled a black-and-blue bruise, and the morning rain's damp chill seeped deep into the house so thoroughly that even a fire couldn't dry or warm the rooms. Downstairs, a dehumidifier struggled to provide even a little relief as it kept pace with her laundry and ironing.

Eva was conflicted. She should introduce herself and bring a dish to welcome the neighbors. Maybe they could persuade their bitch of a landlord to repaint it in a more appealing white rather than the lackluster green. At least she had finally seen the new family but hadn't spoken to them yet. There seemed to be only three members, including a young girl who looked to be in elementary or high school. The wife appeared rounded from the side—not as jolly as Mrs. Claus, like Alice—with shiny hair the color of a black bear. The husband resembled how Eva imagined Warren would look at twice his age, with fairer skin and no mustache.

A practical family wagon, the color of wheat flour, now replaced

Vera's Karmann Ghia. The dark green license plate was unmistakably from Vermont.

Sam came home for lunch, carrying groceries up the stairs, and Eva could tell he was morose, hiding his face behind the paper bag. She watched him pace back and forth in front of the kitchen sink like a zoo lion. She wasn't playing his cat-and-mouse game, waiting for her to ask him what was wrong—she refused.

When he finally stopped and pulled an envelope out of the grocery bag, he faced her. "Someone left this under my truck's wiper at the shop," he said.

It had already been opened.

He removed the single sheet, which was folded once, and waved it half-heartedly, pretending to reread it. "Whoever wrote it is calling me a rat—what I did to Vera. They said she's been threatening to commit suicide!"

Eva grabbed the note from him and read it twice. The cursive handwriting was unmistakably a woman's. "Obviously, Phyillis wrote this," she said, shaking the paper at him. "Vera has gotten her to do her dirty work. She wouldn't do anything that drastic. Did you not read the part where Phyllis says she's going to start dating Ray—and whoever else asks her out? It'll be a Fourth of July in December when someone's dumb enough to get involved with her again. You still don't realize the kind of person she is, do you? Maybe someday you will."

"I'll talk to her tomorrow, then. I'll put a *stop* to this."

The last thing Eva wanted was for him to have contact with that woman ever again. "I don't like it," she told him, bluntly. "I don't know why she can't show an ounce of grace and bow out. Leave us alone."

The only way Eva could salvage the afternoon was to ask Sam for a drive, which took them near Keene and led to a late lunch at the Ox-Yoke. She wanted the broiled swordfish but couldn't pass up the seafood casserole in Newburg sauce, while Sam had the broiled haddock. Even with their iced teas, he paid with a crisp $5 bill he kept tucked away in his wallet for emergencies. The last time he used one was to pay for dinner at the A&W in Springfield after a long day of fishing on the river.

Her spirits were high, and she teased Sam about whether he was in a good mood because the Celtics had recently won the championship when they stopped in Brattleboro to see Edwin. He gave her the impression that he knew nothing about his brother's affair, and it irritated her to wonder what stories, if any, Sam had shared with him.

Pulling into the cellar driveway, they both startled at seeing the lights on in the living room visible above the garage doors.

"I didn't lock the cellar door," Sam said. "I didn't see a need anymore."

Not panicking and knowing Henry had a key, Eva said, "Maybe my father came over to stoke the fires and left a light on for us. We didn't tell them we were going out—and I should've."

"I can see shadows, that's for sure. Someone's moving around up there."

Inside, someone turned on the stairwell light. Eva noticed that chivalry wasn't dead when Sam smoothly stepped around her and took the first step up, then hesitated. "Oh," he said. It was too little to judge the tone of his voice, but she was relieved when she recognized Connie by her shoes, standing at the top of the stairs.

"Oh my goodness, what a surprise," Eva said, pushing on Sam's backside to hurry up. "What brings you home? We weren't expecting you. You didn't mention anything in your last letter." Eva could hear another girl's giggle. "I take it you're not alone? Is that Catherine's voice I hear?"

"Yes, Mrs. Martin," Catherine said, reaching to shake Sam's hand when Connie stepped back. *She wasn't ready to hug him yet.*

"Did you gals take the bus down?" Sam asked.

"No," Connie answered. "Grandma and Grandpa came and got us."

"You called your grandparents?" Eva asked her, trying to ignore Catherine's beaming smile and antsy tip-toeing.

"That she did," Henry said from the living room, peering around the wing of her reading chair.

Eva should have noticed his pipe sticking out. "You and Mom drove all the way up there and back… *again*? Spending all your money on gas and oil?"

"Oh, that's not the least of it," Henry said, disappearing again into the wingback chair. He stretched his legs and crossed them at the ankles, resting them on the edge of the hearth. He appeared content to watch the fire. "But I'll let them tell the rest of the story."

Eva wasn't done with her father yet, asking him, "And I suppose you dragged Mom along too?"

"Of course, she's never the one to miss out on an adventure. She might've had a little accident on the way home, but she's fine now."

In her periphery, Eva noticed that Catherine had stopped bouncing, and both girls stood rigid.

"Grandpa," Connie said. "You promised it would be our secret. Everything's fine."

"She asked," Henry said.

"No… she didn't," Connie retorted. "Can we get *on* with the surprise?" Eva heard the change in Connie's voice before she added, "Thank you again for driving us down to Manchester. Everything worked out perfectly."

Sam slipped past Eva into the kitchen. It was the sound of him twisting off a beer cap that made her glance at his Miller High Life bottle. Experiencing déjà vu, she asked Henry, "So, you and Mom drove all the way up to Burlington, picked them up, *then* drove all the way down to Manchester?"

"Ayutt."

"What on earth ever for? And *what* accident did Mom have?" Eva asked the girls, exasperated.

Catherine looked at Connie and nodded. "Everyone, calm down," Connie said. To Eva, she added, "Do you want to *see* the great news or *hear* about the *not*-so-bad news? Which, in hindsight, isn't really anything to worry about."

Eva recognized when Connie was stalling, and this was one of those moments. "Does this, by any chance, have anything to do with why your grandmother isn't here?"

"Maybe," Connie said, rolling her eyes.

Catherine buried her face in Connie's armpit. Eva guessed she was blushing. Maybe this wasn't something to worry about after all.

"I'll show you why we went to Manchester in a minute, but first… When we got there, Grandpa took us to the 88 for lunch, and Grandma had the buffet chicken, which none of us did. We went shopping—I'll show you—and we lost track of Grandma."

"Lost track?" Sam asked.

Eva shot him a look for interrupting, irritated that he was drinking a Miller High Life instead of their usual.

"When we were all finished and ready to leave the store, Grandpa couldn't find Grandma. We searched everywhere, and finally, Grandpa went out to the car and found her sitting in the backseat. She was all embarrassed because, apparently, she had a little… accident… inside the store."

Catherine clutched her mouth, desperately trying to hold herself together. She turned away from Eva and faced the grandfather clock.

Connie at least looked more empathetic. "She had… you know…"

"She shit her britches," Henry interjected. "We figured it was the buffet chicken. Good luck ever gettin' her down there again. She might not ever eat at the Chinese buffet in Claremont, either."

"Oh dear," Eva said. She clutched her ribs and stomach, her own gurgling with sympathetic cramps. "She's okay now?"

"She's fine," Henry said. "Got her dress and underwear all washed. Poor thing couldn't find a bathroom. Said it all came on too fast, so she high-tailed it outta there." He leaned forward, faced them, and pointed at his chest with the pipe stem. "Me? I suffered 'bout as much havin' to clean the damn seat. I don't think I'll ever get those tiny dimples in the vinyl clean. I guess I'm gonna have to find a cover that fits the Biscayne as soon as it's all dried out." He waved a hand in front of his nose.

Both girls faced the clock, trying in vain to smother the giggles—a futile attempt at best.

"Shouldn't you be getting home?" Eva asked him.

"I've been waitin' for you to get home so we can get on with the weddin' dress show and tell!"

•••

"You were awfully quiet," Eva said. "I don't think you even cracked a smile at Connie's dress. She had the wherewithal to find exactly what she wanted. It looks so pretty with the sequins and the fingertip veil she picked out to go with it." Recalling her mother, embarrassed and trapped in the long ride home, almost made her lose her train of thought, but she continued, "Mom's pearls will look so fitting—something old, something borrowed, something new…" she said, trailing off. "The least you could've done was tell her how beautiful she looked."

Eva rolled over, wishing Sam hadn't spoiled her evening, and didn't blame Smokey for sleeping out on her chair instead of curled around her neck or feet.

"I didn't know what to say," he said, facing away, his voice a whisper off the wall. "I didn't know *how* to say something… She probably hates me."

"She doesn't hate *you*… She hates what you *did*… I hate what you did."

Eva was keenly aware of Sam's inability to express his emotions. She blamed his parents, who were complete opposites: his father, silent and controlling; his mother, outwardly expressive, who thought she was socially gregarious but was, in fact, plagued by diarrhea of the mouth.

When she and Sam first started dating, he was more outgoing, like his mother, fitting in well and always goofing around with her brothers. But as the decades passed, he grew moody, like his father. She never knew which version of Sam she'd see in the morning—it depended on which side of the bed he rolled out of.

"You didn't know what to say because you had your head all twisted around that letter. It wasn't enough for you that we had such a wonderful drive and lunch? Didn't we have a nice afternoon?" she asked him, twisting her shoulder to direct her words closer to his ear.

"Yes… We did."

"I say, good riddance. And on top of that, I say it's a good thing that you got all of your radio equipment from Ray *before* you read that letter. I guess we know where she's been staying." She rolled onto her side. "She dropped you like a hot potato. Like I said, maybe someday," she whispered.

"Something blue."

Eva rolled onto her shoulder. "What?"

"You said something old, something borrowed, something new, and I said something blue."

Eva had no idea what he was trying to say. "Yes."

"I think we should give Connie your VW."

"Because it's blue?" Eva asked him, stunned at his left-field suggestion. "Typically, a bride wears something blue—not a car. Where's this coming from? How would I get to work?"

Sam rolled onto his shoulder. "I'm not trying to be funny or an instigator, but there's something I didn't tell you earlier—because of the whole distraction with your mother… and yes, I'll help Henry clean the seat in the Biscayne. I've got some spray cleaners down cellar."

Eva gritted her teeth before asking the obvious question, "Why didn't you bring up—whatever this is—during lunch?"

"I didn't think of it until you said she didn't hate me. That's when the whole blue thing popped into my head and…"

"Samuel Coburne Martin! Out with it! I'm tired. I want to go to sleep." Eva grew more irritated; something about the evening still itched under her scalp in a way she couldn't scratch or wash away. She'd be exhausted on her feet tomorrow at the store, and snapping at Faye or Merrill was the last thing she needed.

She was about to ask him to go sleep upstairs when he said, "I got a raise at the shop. A big one. They told me this morning. Not only is it hefty, but I don't have to work Saturday mornings anymore, either." He placed a hand on her shoulder. "I think we should go look at these new Ford Mustangs. What do you think?"

"I've always wanted a little red MG… a convertible."

Eva's Daily Reminder 1964: May 2, Saturday

Sunny. Warm.

Sam mowed the lawn. Put down 100# of lime.

Worked till 12:30, then headed off to Holyoke with Connie. Had a wonderful lunch at Yankee Pedlar. Such a day. A nice place to eat.

Sam gave me a good talking to after Connie and Warren left to work on painting their new apartment. Said I was knocking myself out for Connie and for what? Also about the wedding. He said to let them go off and get married that a big one was foolish and I was wrecking myself physically. Guess he's right but I do enjoy doing things for someone else.

Made Sam an apple pie and a raspberry for Connie. Sam changed the oil in his truck and put on the screen doors.

Warren stayed for dinner and we had a talk with them about the wedding. Neither one of them said much. He took Connie back to Burlington.

We were both awfully tired and popped into bed.

16

When Sybil Hoisington called to say she and Clark were returning to Sumner Falls, Eva was more relieved than shocked, taking any sense of vindication to her grave. "It's been a helluva mess, let me tell you. I'm down to 110 pounds. I weigh less than Connie now," she said, desperately wanting only good news from her friend. "But enough about me and my troubles. You said you've moved back into the camp? Is that temporary until you find a new place in town? It would tickle me to no end if I could tell you the house next door was for sale, but—"

"She who shall not be named, and my God, Eva! Your letters!" Sybil interrupted.

"Yeah, the floosey has already put it up for rent. A couple with a young daughter moved in. They seem nice, but I haven't had much of a chance to get to know them all that well. I suppose it's a bit too late to bring over a pie—guess the time has passed. Henry probably knows more about them than I do at this point."

"Give it some time… so yes, to answer your question. We're staying at the lake for now. Trout are biting, so it's not like we're going hungry. We'll have plenty of time before snow flies to find a house in town."

"I should think so." Mentioning her name would make her face flush, and Eva said, "Let's hope she goes off with Ray, and they both skedaddle outta town. One can only hope,"—she rapped her knuckles on the kitchen table—"for everyone's sake. Maybe we can get some folks to put a bug in Janice's ear. Put her to work."

"We'll find something, don't worry."

"And don't you worry, either. I'm feeling like my old self. I've been eating and sleeping pretty good, but this crazy mixed-up guy of mine has a new diddy—says I'm *pretending* my love for him. What's next? How can anyone pretend? He should know how much I adore him and how much I want to make him happy. I wish he would make me a little bit happy." Eva could hear Sybil sigh, drawing it out until her lungs sounded empty. "I hope he at least keeps his promise to buy me the car I've always wanted, but there's no telling once we get it, if it's mine, his, or ours."

"I remember you wanted an MG—red to match your socks."

"You've got a pretty good memory."

"Don't all of us gals. Speaking of which, what's he up to today? I brought back something special from Texas. Thought Clark and I might stop by later."

"Oh my, sure thing." Eva couldn't wait. "Sam's next door, helping my father and Olie shingle the roof. It's not enough that I have to worry about Henry falling off a ladder while painting; now they're on the roof! And there's no snow to break anyone's fall." She knocked louder on the table. "Sybil, I swear, I can't even sit out back and watch 'em. If one of 'em falls off the roof, my mother and I would tell the other to dig a hole right there in the iris beds."

"Well, try not to let anything happen before we show up with a case of Texas Pearl."

"I'll trust you that it's good." As soon as Eva heard herself say, 'trust', she scratched her scalp and uttered a grunt.

"Beg your pardon?" Sybil asked.

"Oh, it's nothing. I just thought of something I need to do—something I forgot to throw out."

"Alright, I'll let you get to it. I wouldn't want to be responsible for making you forget again. I'll round up Clark, and we'll stop by around five to shoot the breeze—catch everyone up."

"Why don't you make it four? I bet the boys will be done for the day by then. I'll make us a spread. Everyone will be thrilled."

"Sounds good, the more the merrier. And besides, it's 5 o'clock in the Maritimes, so we're still good on the happy hour front. See ya then."

"Buh-bye."

Eva wasn't about to forget. After hanging up the phone, she headed down to the cellar, opening cabinets until she found the remaining Miller High Life tucked away under the stairs. She poured each bottle into the sink, rinsed the suds down the drain, and tossed the empty clear glass bottles into the trash, finding it a satisfying cleaning.

• • •

Clark Hoisington was a slender man, taller than Sam, who slouched in the lawn chair, keeping his knees level with his hips. He wore a two-tone camp shirt that accentuated his height, and a pork pie hat that covered his still-youthful hair. The one he wore today from his collection was a faded olive felt adorned with a partridge feather. (Rabbit fur-lined blaze orange and red and black checkered wool ones worn during deer season were tucked away in a cedar chest, while several with trout flies hung on a rack above the bed at the lake camp.) He regaled Sam and Henry with tall tales about stringers full of Texas lake bass. With each can of Pearl beer, the size and number of fish grew until Henry called his bluff.

Everyone's attention shifted to Sybil, who crossed her legs, gently bouncing her knee, and rested her cheek in her palm. A navy bandana covered her salt-and-pepper hair, and her long legs had a Southern glow, highlighted by polka-dot short shorts that accentuated her slim frame. She was a few pounds heavier than Eva, especially when she was soaking wet and wearing dungarees.

All the women—Ruby, Eva, Alice, and Sybil—wore cat-eye glasses hanging on chains around their necks that sparkled in the setting sun.

Sybil removed hers and pointed an earpiece at her husband. "He's exaggerating," she told everyone. "Tell 'em about how you'd always get into disagreements about largemouth versus smallmouth versus black spotted whatever," she told Clark, then to everyone, "And after he'd get nowhere with that, he'd bitch and moan about how much he missed fishing for trout."

Clark popped the tab on another can of beer and asked Sam and Henry if they wanted a refill, too. He started to raise the can to his lips when they shook their heads.

Ruby cleared her throat, interjecting, "Aren't ya gonna ask me?" She eyed the can before glancing at the ground between Alice and Eva's chairs, then over to the folding table that Sam had set up as a buffet and dry bar. "If you can't spare another, I understand," she said, sounding facetious. "Otherwise, I'll have what they're havin' in the thermos."

Everyone laughed except Henry as Clark surrendered the beer and opened another for himself before toasting the group, "Here's to having good friends... and good fishing." He gulped his beer, then added, "Brookies, brownies, and rainbows. Anyone who isn't blind can tell 'em apart, right? And they're the best eating too. But, bass? C'mon. They *all* look alike... and, especially in warm water, they don't taste good at all. No matter how you cook 'em. I don't care that they're white meat. And don't get me started on the bones!" He gulped his beer again. "So, yeah, no stringers of bass—catch and release. The only thing I'll confess—the big ones can put up a good fight." He finished his beer and looked around the Martins' backyard. "This place needs a fire pit."

Eva listened to Clark's stories and had intended to keep her opinions to herself. "Oh, nonsense," she said. "If you broil them, you can peel the bones out in one piece. Break up all the meat in your fingers when you're done to see if you missed any, then dump it all into a pot of corn chowder."

"And don't skimp on the butter and cream," Sybil said, toasting with her can.

Ruby, who hadn't cooked fresh fish since she and Henry visited Nova Scotia early in their marriage, cleared her throat again and looked at Alice, who said, "I'm with you. I don't see what all the fuss is about. And all the trouble. Shrimp and cocktail sauce is where I draw the line."

"I'm with you, too," Sybil said, who winked at Clark. "Anyhow... we missed you all, and we're glad to be back. One Texas summer was enough. We need our changing seasons."

"And trout, it seems," Henry interrupted before lighting his pipe. "I only smoke this to keep the damn bugs away."

Eva smiled at Sybil, glancing to see if she was doing okay, then nodded discreetly. She hoped Sybil caught the hint, reached out to squeeze her hand, and then Alice's, who asked, "So what's the latest on the wedding plans?"

"Hard tellin', not knowin'," Ruby said.

Henry plucked his pipe from his mouth. "Ruby," he said firmly, "leave the kids alone. Let 'em do what they want, what makes 'em happy."

"It's alright," Eva said. "We've talked about it. Sam and I didn't want those kids to have to spend so much money so soon. Money's not growing on any of these trees." Her stomach turned, guilty about whatever sarcasm her mother might say when a little red convertible drove up between the houses. "Warren's parents don't have a pot to piss in, especially after they had all that flood damage. Lord knows how much that set them back. And now we have to worry about the same thing happening again, seeing as they're renting the place next door to them… but at least they're on the second floor. He's been spending money left and right on all new furniture—bedroom and living room. They've been re-painting and papering the place, too. At least Connie let me give her some dishes and enough cookware to get them started."

"Did you give her any of my mother's dishes?" Ruby asked. "I don't mind you givin' 'em to Connie, but I'd like to keep track so everythin' stays in the family. I don't want to drive by someday and see my mother's stuff in a yard sale they're havin'."

It wasn't often that Eva gave her mother dirty looks, but she did. "Mom…"

"Ruby," Alice said. "You've got some memory—"

"Like a steel trap," Ruby said, pointing to her temple. She asked Henry to fetch her another paper plate of cheese cubes and crackers, and when he got up, she discreetly slipped a beer out of her apron pocket, popping the tab under the cloth. Nobody bothered asking how or when, but when Henry turned around, plate in hand, he took a cheese and cracker for himself. He paused before downing it in one bite, as if daring her to complain.

Everyone laughed, and Sybil asked Clark for another.

"For your information, I didn't part with any of your dishes or your mother's. I knew I'd never hear the end of it."

Eva turned to Alice. "I did get a letter from her yesterday. Apparently, they had plenty of time to talk on the way back and weren't none too happy with our suggestions, so I called her, and we hashed it out." To the group, she said, "We're having a small private ceremony here in the yard with his parents and us, and then afterward we'll have a little cookout reception."

"Any talk of honeymoon plans?" Clark asked. "Seems unlikely by the sounds of it."

"Clark, that's none of your beeswax," Sybil said, scornfully.

Eva grabbed a few more pieces of cheddar, passing on the crackers for herself but giving Sam two, with a spoonful of Skippy in between. "If my intuition is correct," she said, "I think I overheard them mentioning that Warren has relatives in California, and he wants to drive cross-country. If that's the case, I sure hope it's somewhere near the Redwood trees—something Connie has always wanted to see."

"California's a big state," Sybil said.

"Like Texas," Clark said, rubbing his hands together. To Sam, he asked, "You sure you don't want me to help you build a fire pit out here?"

"Nothing like Texas," Sybil said, poking him, then finger shooting, and smiling.

"You said you were glad—"

"I am!" Sybil interrupted her husband. "Eva, when's Connie's graduation? Gotta be soon, right?"

"A couple of weeks, coming right up—June 13th, actually."

"Why don't we plan a fishing trip on Champlain that weekend? It'll save you an extra drive. We'll bring the pup tents, poles, and a bag of charcoal. Sam, you're in charge of finding enough night crawlers before then. Let's hope it rains in the meantime."

Henry spoke up. "Weddin's, receptions, fishin' trips… When the hell are we gonna make time to put a new roof on Al's place?"

"Oh, Henry, no need to bother. It can always wait another year," Alice said dismissively. "I was thinking of having one of those new standing seam metal roofs put on."

Both Sam and Henry scoffed, with Henry offering his two cents first. "Oh, Christ almighty, that'll cost a fortune, Al. If this one here"—he hooked a thumb at Sam—"can't find the time this summer, then I can get Olie Buchanan to help me."

Eva didn't want any of them to help, especially not her father working side by side with one of his retired shop buddies two stories up. One major house project a year was enough. Reginald had invested wisely, providing Alice with enough monthly dividends to afford a new, fancy roof. "We'll talk about this later," she told him. The best way to throw him off his game was to ask, "Care to tell us about our new neighbors?"

Henry shrugged and looked at Ruby, who either didn't know or refused to indulge him. "Why would I know?" he asked, clearly feigning. "Al probably knows more than I do. She's the one who walks every day."

Alice Fairbanks took a defensive breath and stood up. "Don't try and drag me into this, Henry." Her tone sounded more like a teacher scolding a misbehaving student. "And that's my cue. I should be getting home to let Impy out to do her business. Sybil, Clark, Ruby… 'twas a pleasure. Supper tomorrow?"

"You betcha. I'll keep you posted," Eva told her.

"Shall I leave the thermos? I can always grab it tomorrow." She leaned in closer to Eva's ear and lowered her voice. "Let me know if you and Ruby want your hair done tomorrow. I can stop by anytime. The other girls are covering the shop."

"Sounds good to me. And watch your step out front. Better yet, why don't you walk down between the houses? There's no light on the front porch."

"Oh, I'll be fine. I don't want to get my shoes dirty."

"I think I'll call it a night myself," Ruby said, standing up. She was empty-handed, and Eva couldn't remember seeing her finish the last beer. "Don't be too late, Henry. Lord knows you need a good night's sleep before climbing up there."

"Mom, I just got him off the subject." Eva waved goodnight and watched Ruby amble across the verdant lawn, shuffling through the grass that needed mowing. She'd get Sam to pull out the tractor before he went to work—fill the thistle feeder too—and mow both yards after breakfast. If she happened to see the renters, she'd stop and chit-chat. After Ruby went inside, she extended her hands, palms up, toward Henry and told him, "Alright, spill. But keep your voice down in case their windows are open."

"Name's Stanstead."

"His name?" Sybil asked.

"No, family name is Stanstead. He's Charles, his wife is Virginia, and they have a young daughter. I forgot her name—Suzy, maybe. Said they wanted to move out of Springfield, even though he works at Smith and Lamson. I guess the Precision Valley was getting a little too built up for their likes."

"That company's been around a while," Clark said. "Wasn't it built initially in Sumner Falls in the 1800s, and *then* relocated to Springfield?" he asked.

"Ayutt," both Henry and Sam said together. "They still make machine-turned lathes similar to what we do in the shop," Sam added.

Eva wondered if they were about the same age as she and Sam. "One can never tell these days, but since I'm guessing their daughter looks younger than Connie, they're a few years younger than us?"

Henry looked confused. "Well, I wasn't planning to interrogate the poor guy right away. He seemed clean-cut enough, I suppose. Give it some time." He shielded his face from Sam with a hand. "Maybe I should ask him the next time I'm out and about, if he's any good with a paintbrush or laying shingles."

"As long as he's not into radioing," Eva said.

"Hey, now," Sam grimaced.

Henry stood. "I think I'll call it a night. You kids try and keep it down." He started to turn away, then hesitated. "The wife's not as big as the state, but she could probably use a few laps around the neighborhood loop. Maybe she and Al can buddy up."

"Henry!" Sybil yelled. "Just because Ruby isn't here to smack you, doesn't mean I won't! Now vamoose before I do!"

Henry squinted at her, pursed his lips, and bobbed his pipe.

"Skedaddle," Eva clarified for him before he rapped his pipe on the heel of his boot and sauntered off toward his house. "He tries to be funny, but sometimes…" she trailed off, shaking her head in disappointment. Perhaps he was funnier in his younger years, but not tonight. Looking at Sam, she was unsure if she would ever be able to laugh again, outright. "We should introduce ourselves formally. Let them know there'll be a wedding and reception here in the backyard. Don't you think? We wouldn't want to get off on the wrong foot with them. It would be just our luck to have them call the police, thinking it was too much commotion."

"I don't imagine there'd be much hootin' and hollerin' going on with something so small," Sybil said. "Is that Dick Poole still around town? Hasn't he moved on to bigger and better places?"

"Unfortunately not," Eva said. "Just keep your nose clean, and he'll stay out of your way."

"Are we invited to the reception?"

"Of course. The ceremony should be pretty quick. I think Connie will only have Catherine as her maid of honor. Otherwise, she'd have to invite all the girls from her dorm, and that would be too many. I don't even know who Warren's planning on having as his best man—probably one of his brothers. I can't keep 'em all straight."

"Well, just so you know, we might be a hoot and a holler when we show up," Sybil said, poking Clark, who looked like he was dozing.

"Speak for yourself," he said, coming awake. "Time to go."

After hugs and kisses between Eva and Sybil, and handshakes among the guys who made bets on who would catch the biggest fish out of Lake Champlain, everyone went their separate ways.

Eva followed Sam, carrying the leftover snack plates and the thermos with the rest of the whiskey sour mix under her arm. She paused at the door, calling out to Smokey, who emerged from under the folding table, then sprinted across the lawn. He stopped at her heels, eyes bright, patiently waiting for her to open the screen door.

Eva's Daily Reminder 1964: May 12, Tuesday

Sunny. Warm.

Such weather. Just like summer.

When Sam came home we decided to take off and go to Woodstock to look at MGs. We made an offer but didn't like the trade for the VW so we left. Hopefully they'll call back.

Stopped in to eat at the White Cottage. Had lobster rolls. It was a beautiful ride and we took drinks. We were very tender and close.

Met Vera heading north on our way home and damned if she didn't turn around and come back. She followed us back to her house and flashed her headlights.

I sure was upset but we went to bed and she left around 11.

What maliciousness she has doing that. Didn't sleep.

Olie and Dad finished the roof.

I think Sam saw what a fool Vera made of herself coming down here.

17

Eva was thrilled when Sam called the shoe store at noon. The news that the credit union approved the final loan after the Woodstock garage lowered its offer made her beg Merrill for the afternoon off. Sales had been brisk all morning, and she wouldn't be able to concentrate, knowing something could go wrong if they waited too long. Having Sam wash the tar off after work blocked her urge to clean it again, so why was she hesitating? She'd convinced Sam, after a brief back and forth, not to bother giving the aging Beetle to Connie as a wedding gift. With the mileage and rust, it wasn't worth it, and it was a project too much for Warren to take on. The garage had already accepted the trade, and the bank note was approved. She waved goodbye, skipping out the door like a schoolgirl, her Nantucket basket jangling in the crook of her arm.

She picked up Sam at the shop; the nearest exit to his desk was by the loading dock, and for once, his timing was perfect. She barely slowed the Beetle as he opened the passenger door and slipped inside. She sped over the train tracks, jarring the suspension and rusted frame, then turned north out of town.

Driving past the Frosty Whip along Route 5, Eva said, "Let's stop at Mattie's on the way back for seafood baskets. I'm in the mood for scallops and whole belly clams." She briefly turned to Sam and smiled, hoping he noticed her appreciation without words, but she added, "My treat," for good measure.

"You should take Skunk Hollow. It'll pop us out by Taft's."

Skunk Hollow Road was a tunnel of green, funneling the warm, dry afternoon air. The open windows blew Sam's thinning combover more wildly than Eva's short perm.

There was no time to stop at Taftsville General for cheese and maple syrup for Sam's evening bowl of vanilla ice cream. When they arrived at the Woodstock garage, there she was, sitting pretty—Little Miss Riding Hood. "Oh, my," Eva said, her hands turning the rusty Beetle's wheel for the last time as she admired her new little bomber beauty, patiently waiting outside the dealership's front door.

Sam leaned toward her and sputtered. "I guess it was foolish to fill up the tank yesterday."

"Knock it off, you didn't know. What's done is done." Eva parked next to the shiny MG Midget with its bold frog-eye headlights. She hesitated, feathering her fingers around the steering wheel once more, and noted the rolled-over odometer. Looking one last time in the rearview mirror, Connie popped her head up from the nook and smiled, playing peek-a-boo, her short brown curls framing her impish cheeks. Eva could hear her angelic voice asking, "Are we there yet, Mummy?" A montage of their road trips flashed behind her eyes—driving up the Maine coast to Nova Scotia, stopping at lobster pots along the roadside, getting lost in the Back Bay while searching for a parking spot near Fenway, visiting the Granby Zoo in Quebec, where three-year-old Connie once got way too close to a grumpy warthog who lifted its leg to let loose. Eva chuckled before turning off the ignition. She handed the key to Sam, laughing even harder.

"What's so funny?" he asked, taking the key from her.

"I was thinking of crayfish and cannons."

Sam, confused, clearly missed her joke. "Nothing," she assured him. "I was reminiscing about all the trips we've taken in this old girl. She never let us down, did she?"

They both rubbed and patted the dashboard, then stepped out.

Eva's old car blended with the sky's hue as she turned and caressed the MG's fender and supple black leather seats. The top was down, and its two bucket seats sat lower to the ground than the Volkswagen's—and there was no space behind the seats—only enough room for a single suitcase.

A sandy-haired man with cattle-farmer looks, dressed in a paisley jacket over mud-colored slacks, emerged from the showroom. "Afternoon," he said, shaking Sam's hand but not reaching for Eva's, which she found irritating since Sam had assured her the new car would be hers. "I'm Nathan Fitzpatrick. I'm the sales manager at this dealership. You can call me Nate or Fitz; either one gets my attention around here. You must be the Martins?" Nathan Fitzpatrick gestured toward both the Beetle and the MG before extending his hand to each of them this time, shaking them more cordially. "Wonderful to finally meet you, Mrs. Martin. I know you've been regular customers for many years now, and it's my pleasure to start you on a new adventure." Again, he gestured toward the freshly waxed sports car.

"Can't wait," Eva said, doing her best to stay sharp.

Nathan Fitzpatrick held the door for them, gesturing inside. "This shouldn't take too long at all. We received all the paperwork from the credit union, and I have all the trade-in approvals signed off by my buyer and in hand. The MG's tank is full, and we'll get you on your way shortly." He waited for Eva to enter first, then extended a hand. "Oh, I almost forgot," he said, pointing toward the convertible. "We only had the one red vehicle on the lot with the optional wire wheels and white sidewalls, but since you agreed to the full base price and are existing customers, my regional manager decided to let it go. We hope you'll be back."

Eva bent a knee and examined the spoked wheels, running her fingertips over the chrome wires. "Spiffy," she said. "Very…" she trailed off, hesitant to tell the men it looked like a James Bond car. She didn't want to give Sam any ideas. *If it made anyone else jealous, well, that was their problem.*

After two signatures and two handshakes, Eva and Sam Martin received the keys to their new British coupe. Eva sped out of the lot and headed home, unaware that the Beetle and its hideaway nook filled with memories had already been moved and loaded for scrap. She looked like Grace Kelly, with her hair tied up in a floral kerchief that rippled in the airflow; her black cat-eye sunglasses and freshly applied, matching red lipstick made her look like a movie star.

• • •

Eva was eager to park *her* new vehicle in the front driveway. "Connie's gonna be tickled pink when she sees this," she said, trying to contain her enthusiasm.

"And you know what that means, right?" Sam asked, gently closing the passenger door. He ran his finger along the joint between the door and the frame. "Pretty tight tolerances."

Eva didn't understand what he meant, nor did she care, but Connie would commandeer the coupe if she weren't careful. All that mattered was that her new car was a joy to drive—peppy.

Henry appeared alongside the front retaining wall. "What do you expect from the Brits? I should hope so."

Eva sighed. "Of course you'd be the first to come nosin' around. Can't keep a secret from anyone around here for very long."

Henry tipped his pipe up the road as Eva turned to see Alice and Impy strutting their way along, flaunting bright, beaming smiles. When they reached the house next door, a young girl on a bike darted out of the driveway, skidded to a stop, and startled the jumpy terrier. It wasn't so much the sight of the girl as it was the bluster of tassels on her handlebars and the off-key blaring of her bicycle's bell.

"Sorry," she said, reaching down and rubbing her fingers together, as if trying to coax Alice's dog closer. "Is it a he or a she?"

"She's a she," Alice told her. "And her name is Impy. If you let her lick the back of your hand, you'll have a friend for life. Go on, Imp, it's okay." Alice gently nudged the leash with her finger, guiding the dog toward the girl. "And I assume you must be our new neighbor, Cynthia, is it?"

Cynthia Stanstead got off her bike and crouched down to Impy's level. Her white sneakers and socks were covered in dust—thanks to the unusually dry early June weather and Vera's unpaved driveway. The short-sleeve shirt she wore under a corduroy romper remained bright white, its wide collar contrasting against her black hair. Impy appeared grateful as she licked her hand—salty sweat, dust, dirt, and all. "Yes, ma'am… Why's she so excited?"

Alice was uncomfortable around small children, having never had any of her own, so Eva felt compelled to rescue her. Although Connie had grown up under her feet, she was still set in her ways. Answering a child's curious questions was easier for her than asking her own questions. "I guess she likes you," Eva said. "Do your parents know that you're riding around in the street?"

"Oh, sure." Cynthia hopped on her bike and circled Alice and Impy.

Eva could tell the girl was precocious and unabashed. "I suppose you ought to see my new toy," she told Alice.

"I love new toys!" Cynthia shouted, pedaling toward Eva, who glanced at Sam, furious if the girl lost control and bumped her bicycle into her new car and scratched it.

Another fleeting memory of Connie flashed before her eyes: Connie learning to ride a bike, Sam letting go of the seat. She coasted down the sloping street and hit the Houghtons' aging wooden mailbox dead center, snapping it clean off. Sam had stayed up all night, making repairs to make sure the next day's mail wouldn't be interrupted.

Sam stepped in front of the car, guiding Cynthia safely out of the way. "Run along now." When she stopped and pouted, he added, "Just be careful."

"Cynthia!" shouted a woman who suddenly appeared on the street, unbeknownst to the group. She was a tad shorter and rounder than Alice. Her flipped bob dark hair matched her proportions, with curls bouncing atop a floral sundress. She clutched a black vinyl purse that would have matched the shine on her shoes if they hadn't been covered in dust. As she faced everyone, she brushed the front of her dress, seeming to gather herself. She waved and called out less enthusiastically, "Cynthia."

Eva noticed the woman's pallor and wondered whether she was perhaps sickly or merely an indoor homemaker—her pear-shaped figure as she moved closer suggested the latter. Eva glanced toward Henry and silently mouthed, "Virginia?" When he nodded, she turned and said, "You must be Virginia, our newest neighbor. Nice to finally meet you."

"Yes, likewise," Virginia Stanstead said, shaking everyone's hands demurely. When she seemed to recognize Henry, she said, "I think we've met already."

Henry smiled, removed his pipe, and tipped his Panama hat.

"I see you've all met my daughter, Cynthia."

"Hi," Cynthia waved again.

Virginia placed a hand on her daughter's shoulder. "We're the Stansteads. My husband, Charles—he goes by Charlie—isn't home right now. He's working the second shift down at J&L." When she looked at Henry, she said, "But I guess you all already knew that." She nodded at Henry, who nodded back. "And I assume Henry here already told you we moved up from Springfield. We wanted to slow things down a bit—find a house away from town and a school for Cindy that's smaller before she's ready for high school." She tilted her head, gesturing toward Henry. "I don't believe you mentioned how you fit in with everyone here?"

Henry pointed at Eva, who said, "He's my father."

"Makes sense." Virginia nodded in turn to each before stopping on Alice.

"Alice Fairbanks. My house is that way,"—she pointed—"at the end of the street. I've been friends with Eva and Sam for years." When Henry smirked, she added, "And yes, Henry and Ruby, too."

"Ruby?" Virginia asked.

"My wife," Henry told her. "Her mother," he gestured.

"I got that."

Everyone collectively took a breath once all the formal introductions were over. Ruby emerged from her and Henry's front door and now stood at the top of their wooden-railed steps. "I knew I could feel my ears burnin'," she hollered.

Ruby carefully stepped down one at a time, gripping the rail with one hand while clutching her purse with the other. Her chunky heels pressed firmly on each tread as she moved steadily down the stairs. She glanced at Virginia's purse and seemed to inspect her house dress. "I like her already," she declared.

"You must be Ruby," Virginia said, extending her hand.

"The one and only… I used to proudly wear my hair like yours, back in the day. Not as big, mind you, but still. Now look at me." Ruby waved her free hand over her head. "All I've got is this short perm, thanks to that one," she said, looking away as she dismissed Alice with a curt wave.

"Mom," Eva said, reaching out to grab Ruby's elbow, embarrassed. Virginia had never experienced her mother's dry humor, and Eva didn't want to give the little girl an excuse to sass her mother.

"I've never gotten any complaints from you," Alice shot back, grinning.

When Virginia looked confused, Eva explained that her mother was joking and that her obstinacy was only an act. "She does this sometimes."

"I like her," Virginia said. She told Ruby, "You've got spunk. And speaking of spunk, I like your style," she added, gesturing toward Eva's new car. "It looks brand new."

"It most certainly is," Eva beamed. "I've always wanted one, and it was time. My old bucket of bolts was on its last legs."

Virginia peered closer at the car's interior. "Gosh, I could never…"

Eva shot Ruby a disdainful look, silently begging her to stay quiet. One joke was enough for the day; Eva couldn't handle hearing anything else that might embarrass her. "Not much room for a family of three," she said. "Our daughter, Connie, is all grown up—about to graduate college next weekend, as a matter of fact." She stepped past Sam, waved to Alice, who'd resumed her walk around the neighborhood loop, and touched Virginia's arm. "I know it's getting somewhat late, and you probably have supper to make, but I wanted to let you know—and we can talk about this some more later—but we're having a small backyard wedding next month. There'll probably be a few extra cars parked out here on the street. Hopefully, the noise won't be too much of a burden. We'll be sure to wrap things up before dark. If anything were to become too much, by all means, give us a shout through the lilacs. Probably be a dozen or so folks at the most."

"Well, we appreciate you letting us know," Virginia replied, returning the arm touch. "We wouldn't want to have to call that officer who looks like a handsome Bing Crosby to come and break up the party." When Virginia saw that Ruby's stone face wasn't changing, she added, "Just kidding."

"You know Officer Poole?" Eva asked.

"Oh sure," Virginia said. "He and Charlie are well acquainted. Whether he's late for work or thinks the road's empty after work at 11 o'clock, that police officer always seems to be in two places at once, or else he never sleeps. Charlie says he flashed his lights at him just about every other day or night by the turnoff near the Ascutney market. Charlie gave up guessing and now has a routine. He meets Officer Poole at the same time every afternoon at the market register on the way to work. The first time he tried offering doughnuts, that went over like a lead balloon. Man's got no sense of humor. Then, he offered to buy him his daily second cup of coffee, which went over better for a few days until Charlie finally caught the guy dropping the money into the tip jar."

"He'll pinch anyone," Eva said. "Lord knows we've all had our encounters."

Henry lit his pipe, puffing smoke in an attempt to flush away the gnats. "Dick's bark is far worse than his bite. Don't get me wrong, he bites, but only if you poke 'em with a stick. Man's good at his job."

Eva's Daily Reminder 1964: June 13, Saturday

Showers. Warm.

Got up early. Had the day off. Made lasagna for supper.

Mopped the floor and we were on the way to Burlington at 10:45.

Connie drove her grandfather's car with them. Would have loved to take the MG but drove Sam's truck instead in case Connie had more than a trunkful to bring home.

The graduation was lovely and guess I was the proudest mother there!

Black gowns. We didn't go to the reception after. Connie anxious to get back with Warren.

Supper went off a-okay and everyone ate like pigs. They left around 10:30.

Heard from Sybil and Clark. They missed us fishing on Champlain. Clark landed a big sheepshead and Sybil hooked into an eel! How he screamed she said but it was good eating over the fire. The rain cut their trip short. Glad we didn't end up going.

18

June weekends in Sumner Falls and throughout Vermont are consistently disrupted by rain, year after year, as if decreed by the gods, regardless of who compiles the current year's Farmer's Almanac. It almost never varies; a workweek of clear sunshine followed by two days of heavy downpour—wash, rinse, repeat four times until the 4th of July.

Saturday, June 20th, 1964, broke the usual pattern. The sky was clear and robin's egg blue—a sign perhaps—with a high-pressure system over the northeast that caused temperatures to rise.

After work on Friday, Sam decided to add more color to the backyard by digging a circular flowerbed about a yard in diameter in the lawn, halfway between the back door and the toolshed. He filled it with annual Johnny-jump-ups and petunias in white, deep purple, and pink. In the center, he placed a decorative rain gauge. The walkway iris beds had few weeds, but he gave the entire circumference of the house a thorough hand cultivation.

Eva hoped the piece of cardboard he used under his knees as he moved along the flowerbed would be enough to keep him from being lame. He seemed fine this morning, taking his coffee outside to set up the folding tables while it was still cool. Luckily, they didn't need to call on anyone else after deciding that three tables would be enough, but she still thanked Merrill Martindale and Clark Hoisington. Even with a few more guests added because they called and hinted, the three folding tables should still have enough room for appetizers, Warren's steaks, and desserts—guaranteed to be the most crowded table with enough pies to fill a farmstand. Hopefully, there'd be space for the cake.

She scrubbed the stone birdbath with a wire brush, refilled it, then checked the feeders for the tenth time. The lime had worked wonders for the grass, filling the yard with a lush Irish hue, and she had mowed it the day before yesterday. Henry helped rake the clippings, hauling, tugging, and sliding them into the woods using an old bedspread. At least he seemed to enjoy himself, calling out "Ho-ho-ho," which drew no laughs from Eva.

Before returning to the kitchen, she paused and checked on her special perennials near the corner of the back steps—Stinking Benjamins and Jacks-and-Jills-in-the-pulpit. These hidden gems, nestled around the base of the propane tanks, were always a delight to see emerge each new season.

Eva was about to climb the steps, worried she might have forgotten some last-minute food prep or another check on the bathroom and kitchen floors, when Warren appeared around the corner of the house carrying a small Hibachi grill. Although he held it by its two wooden handles, he still managed to grip the top of a bag of charcoal briquettes with his fingers. What looked like wrapped packages of steaks were stacked atop the grill plates.

"Morning, Eva," he said, scanning for a good spot to park the grill. "I come bearing fruit… just kidding, it's ribeyes. Hopefully, there's enough." He placed the handheld grill on the walkway and struggled to lift the package of steaks, as if it were a forty-pound bag of cement. "I hope there's room in your fridge."

"You ain't kiddin'." Eva paused, mentally checking her refrigerator to see whether all the meat would fit in one of the two bins. She needed to save a spot for the cake, but maybe it would be fine on the kitchen counter. Worst-case scenario, she'd ask Henry to find space in their fridge. "Why don't you set it down and let me take a look inside first?" When he complied and stepped back, she was sure she would see leaked blood on the waist of his khakis or across the front of his polo shirt, striped black and white horizontally. If it weren't for his saddle shoes, all he needed was the matching skull cap to complete the prisoner look.

After combining the cucumbers and summer squash from one bin into the other and bagging the few corn husks, she cracked the screen door and gave him a thumbs-up to bring the meat inside. "See if it all fits in there," she said, pointing. "And I guess this corn will be all right if I bring it down cellar." The sudden shift in temperature and humidity between the cellar and kitchen made her shake once, like a dog wringing its wet fur. It felt good to be back in the heat.

"You gonna make it?" he asked.

"Ayutt. It's an… A-number one day!"

"Where's Sam? Is he around? I didn't know if he wanted the grill put somewhere in particular."

"Just leave it where it is. He's gone over to Al's to help her pick flowers for the arrangements. How are the girls getting down here? I can't imagine your parents can fit them all?"

"Oh, no. I'll head back. I left my tux at my parents' house, too. Between my brothers and me, we'll find a way to get everyone here."

"And?"

"Don't worry, Connie will ride with my parents and leave after me. Catherine will probably go with them. I'll bring Polly and Suzy… and the cake."

"I can't wait to see their orchid and yellow dresses. I hear they match the two layers of the cake?"

Warren didn't get a chance to answer when Henry knocked on the screen door. "Hey. We can't leave this grill right on the corner of the walkway. Someone's bound to trip over it."

The sounds of hummingbird and honeybee wings tickled Eva's ears and neck, and her legs and feet were restless. It was the middle of summer, and all the windows were open, yet a sense of claustrophobia settled over her like a dense fog. Moving to the door and pushing it open, she said, "Of course, it's not staying there, Dad. What did you think? That we were gonna light a fire on the ground and grill steaks right by the corner of the house?"

"How's I supposed to know? I damn near tripped over it. Why's it so small?"

"Cook to order," Warren said. "As a matter of fact, I brought a roll of numbers from the meat counter. The guests at the reception will take a tag, and I'll call it out every time a steak is done."

"Son, are you kiddin' me? I could've built a fire pit up behind the shed."

Eva had heard enough of their jibber-jabber. "Dad… now listen. Warren has to head upstreet, get his parents, and bring the girls down. Why don't you take charge of where the Habachi goes?"

"Well, where's Sam?"

"Never you mind."

"He's over at Al's picking flowers," Warren told him. "I gotta go. I'll see you in a few hours." He kissed Eva on the cheek. "Take good care of my grill, Henry. I don't expect to find any scratches on it tomorrow," he said, hitting the middle step before dashing past him.

Eva followed Warren outside, took a deep breath, and said, "I think I'll walk up to the pump house. I need to work a little something off—clear my head. Why don't you put the grill next to the shed and find something to set it on? Don't worry about cooking anything. Sam will take care of that when the time comes."

Henry smiled and patted her shoulder. "Alright, ol' girl. Take a breather, and if you're not back within the hour, don't think you're too big for your old dad to come lookin' for you like I used to. You remember that time you were knee-high to a grasshopper, and I had to go traipsing all over hell and creation looking for you up on the hill, cryin' over some schoolboy who'd done you wrong?"

"Ayutt. Lyscom Grant. I remember. A girl never forgets her first rejection!"

"I always wondered whatever happened to that boy."

"Don't know, don't care." Eva wasn't ashamed to admit that she might have prayed once or twice that he drown in the river. After baiting her with smiles when no one else was looking and walking her home from school—not just once, but three times—he turned belligerent when in the company of his friends. He pulled her braid in class and flicked pebbles at her in the schoolyard. It had been the Fischers' farm protector, an obstinate, oversized male goose that hissed, nipped, and chased Lyscom away after pushing her onto the dirt. Her dress was soiled and scuffed, and she'd never forget that Ruby washed it several times to get it white again.

•••

The pump house on the hill in the woods behind the Martin and Fischer houses was used to gravity-feed spring water to the neighborhood homes before town water lines were installed decades later. All that was left was the exterior pine shiplap shell over a concrete foundation. The interior workings had long been stripped out, leaving only a dirt-filled concrete trough that once held the wellhead. After being abandoned, it turned into the neighborhood *fort* where kids played. Crushed RC and Moxie cans were tossed into the corners and the bottom of the waist-deep trench. Eva used the toe of her tennis shoe to push sand aside in a few spots, and it didn't take her long to uncover a few cigarette butts as well. She made a mental note to come back later with a bag to gather as many as she could, knowing it was a lost cause.

She stepped over the foundation wall where a door once stood and scanned the forest floor. It was late June, the peak season for her secret garden. Legally, it wasn't her property since the McSwains owned all the land and logging rights behind the neighborhood, down to her stone wall, including Henry's berry bushes. The wild lady slipper orchids were a rare treat, blooming only in June and sparse under the right soil conditions. They were so rare that state law protected them from being picked.

Eva was grateful to see dozens of blooms scattered among the pine needles on the forest floor. Before the pink flowers appeared, only their twin oval leaves were visible, blending into the typical fauna and out of sight of the kids, who only wanted to hide inside the pump house.

It was still about an hour before the ceremony, and she had set aside extra time before the reception for Sam and Warren to heat the charcoal. All she needed to do was slip into her dress and give Alice a moment to brush out her and Ruby's hair. She never wore makeup, nor did she learn, as her mother did not either. Connie would be on her own today with Catherine's help.

In the fall, she could see the backyards through the leafless trees, but now, Eva could only listen. She tilted her head and stared through the treetop canopy, praying. Not expecting a reply, she hoped the day would pass without incident and shook her head in disbelief at how the past two years had flown by. If the house had felt like an empty nest before, it would definitely feel even emptier after today. She was thinking about a first road trip with Sam and the MG when something rubbed against her pant leg, startling her. Smokey ran his chin up and down her shin before sitting at her feet, his tail sweeping an arc through the pine needles and last year's fallen leaves.

"Well, hello there. Where'd you come from? Been hunting? Any luck?" Eva asked the cat, who half meowed and half squeaked, then resumed rubbing his chin and whiskers on her legs. "Would you like to come inside?" she asked, bending over and scooping him up. After a few neck scritches, Smokey settled across her shoulder, and the two walked out of the woods.

• • •

Connie looked stunning in her tiara and veil, complemented by Warren's elegant black and white tuxedo. The ceremony started on time, and Warren couldn't wait to be back in his khakis and striped shirt after kissing his bride, ready to light the grill, where his brothers would undoubtedly corner him with a list of dos and don'ts for a happy marriage. Even though Connie wanted only family present for the ceremony, Eva convinced her to let Merrill and Carolyn arrive early, since they weren't planning to stay for the reception. Carolyn's recovery was progressing more slowly than expected, and they didn't think she'd have enough energy to wait for a big meal and post-ceremony frolicking.

Bridesmaids Suzy Hughes and Polly Shoreham, along with maid of honor Catherine Anne, looked adorable in their canary yellow and orchid dresses that matched the two-tiered cake, courtesy of Suzy's mom's bakery. Both Suzy and Polly had frosted their hair, styling themselves in updos, while Catherine chose a more amber henna, pulling her pixie cut straight back and holding it in place with gel, giving her an almost wet look. They mingled with the guests, serving food for everyone else, while Sam tried in vain to preserve the day on 8mm film. The girls seemed to have a sixth sense when he focused on them; their smiles gave way to crossed eyes and protruding tongues. Even Eva hated having her picture taken.

Henry and Ruby sat with Edwin and his wife, while Sybil and Clark chatted with Alice, who had nothing in common with the outdoorsy couple but whose eyes widened and brightened when Eva pulled up a chair next to her. "I must say, it turned out to be a beautiful day, don't you think?" Eva asked, handing Alice a refill of her whiskey sour and clinking her tumbler with her own. Eva had already shared a beer with Warren and his brothers, pretending to be captivated by their fly-fishing conversation while secretly watching them to make sure they didn't overcook the meat. A well-done steak only applies to a cobbler, turning it into a pair of boots for Merrill's store.

"It certainly has," Alice said, accepting the chilled tumbler. "I love the new flowerbed and rain gauge. The bees have already found it, I see."

Eva grunted. "And so have the Japanese beetles, I'm afraid. Darn buggers. Now I'll have to add a trap. It'll be such an eyesore."

"I'd hoped the birds would take care of 'em?" Sybil asked.

Clark made a face, looking like he'd almost lost his appetite for ribeye.

"Oh, they do, alright," Eva said. "But unfortunately, it's the darn grackles and blue jays. The songbirds don't want anything to do with them. Clark, are you sure you don't want to take any home with you to use as trout flies?"

Eva was joking but delivered the deadpan line perfectly. She was rewarded when Clark's reaction was somewhere between nauseous and irritated. "Well, on that cue, I think it might be time for more potato salad, steak, or cake. I can't decide… so I *might* be a while."

"There's always more of Ruby's green jello salad," Sybil said.

"It's always been Connie's favorite of hers," Eva added. "Special request. The marshmallows are the secret that makes it stand out."

Eva winked at Sybil, who kept the ruse going. "I had some, dear. It's a Rutland State Fair blue ribbon winner. Try some. It'll make you a winner too."

Alice, who could never tell a white lie, said, "Oh, don't listen to them, Clark. I've had Ruby's green jello surprise, and it's not a world changer."

Eva playfully swatted Alice's forearm, not wanting the fun or the day to end. The whiskey sour, on an empty stomach after the beer, was making her lightheaded and uninhibited, so much so that she didn't balk when Suzy, Polly, and Catherine ran past them barefoot, carrying lawn darts from the toolshed. They proceeded to set the opposing rings parallel to her lilac bushes.

"Mr. Hoisington! C'mon. We need a fourth!" Catherine shouted.

Eva watched the exchange between Clark and Sybil. He shrugged while she squinted and pursed her lips—a mental tug-of-war—seeing who'd blink first. "I wasn't all *that* excited for green jello," he said, a schoolboy whine to his voice. "It's fine," she said, still squinting. "Go play. Enjoy yourself, but not *too* much."

After Clark joined the girls, Eva reassured Sybil. "He'll behave. Those girls are half his age… and besides, they'll want to head back as soon as Connie and Warren decide enough is enough."

The girls and Clark threw a few darts high into the air, back and forth, with the girls squealing and hopping whenever one of them hit the inside of a ring, falling to the ground with overexcitement.

"Oh dear… It's a shame to get those pretty dresses all grass-stained." Eva couldn't bear witness, waiting for the inevitable. Grass stains on that colored silk fabric would be a nightmare to get out. They'd most likely left their change of clothes at Connie and Warren's apartment, and without presoaking, she had no idea how long they'd have to stay into the evening while she washed and ironed all three.

"I'm more worried about their toes," Alice interjected. "Those girls should have shoes on, shouldn't they? Makes me so nervous throwing those things up in the air."

Eva was about to stand up and say something to the girls when Charles Stanstead appeared, stepping around the last lilac bush with Cynthia beside him. He wore a white sleeveless undershirt tucked into khaki shorts that would be more suited for a wedding reception if paired with a button-down Oxford shirt. Dark penny loafers over socks that matched the tank top made him look like a rube, not someone trying to make a good first impression with the new neighbors.

Cynthia made a bold beeline for the girls, running her excited fingers over their silk dresses, then pulled them down to their knees for a closer look at their hair.

Clark, seeming like the obvious fifth wheel, headed toward the three women his age and announced he was having more of Warren's ribeye and another beer.

Charles Stanstead followed Clark slowly and motioned to Eva, Sybil, and Alice. "Afternoon, ladies," he said. "Please sit. I didn't mean to intrude. My wife, Ginny, had mentioned that you were all having a family wedding." He tilted skyward. "It looks like the weather gods came through. It usually rains this time of year, right? Lucky us."

He wasn't a tall man; he had a soft middle, which Eva noticed from the snug fit of his tank top. His face was round and on the small side, and with his dark hair, he would have seemed more distrustful if he had any facial hair.

Eva introduced Charles to Alice and Sybil before asking, "Stanstead? Are you—"

"Quebec, yes," he interrupted. "Long line of French Canadians… Québécois," he added with an accent. "No maple syrup jokes, please. I hear enough of those at the shop."

Eva pointed to the lawn chair where Clark had been sitting. "Sit, please. Would you like a beer? We've got plenty of food. Don't be shy. I don't want to have to put away leftovers."

"I'm fine, really, but thanks. I honestly didn't want to interrupt, but Cindy noticed the girls playing. Once she saw their dresses, she was determined to introduce herself. She doesn't have a shy bone in her body."

"More like *heard* the girls playing," Alice said.

"Oui."

Eva noticed Sybil in her peripheral vision, lips covered, and decided to run interference. "We met your wife and daughter the other day—Ginny, is it? Or does she prefer to go by Virginia?"

"Yes, she's fine with Ginny… and I'm good with Charlie. She's not Canadian, by the way. She was born in Newport. Vermont, not New Hampshire. Actually, she claims her parents, who lived in Derby Line, wanted her to be born on the other side of the border, in Stanstead. Cindy was born in Bellows Falls after we moved down, and we eventually bought a house in Springfield. That's where we've been the past dozen years, but it was getting too crowded. Sumner Falls was still close enough for me to commute in the evening, and it has the more rural setting we were looking for."

"Glad to hear," Eva said.

"I'm not sure how much Ginny told you the other day, but the contract we signed with Vera Flynn has a rent-to-buy clause if we decide to stay after a year."

Eva looked at Alice, then shifted her gaze to Sybil before checking on the girls and Cindy, who were all sitting cross-legged on the grass. The sight of Connie in her white wedding dress, who had somehow joined them unnoticed, made her scalp itch. She forced herself to look away, convincing herself that the girls and their dry cleaning were their own responsibility.

"We signed the rental contract with the realtor. She's the only person we've met. Janice Chabot. Nice lady. Assumed perhaps she was French, but turns out she's Polish."

"Well, let's say we're not sorry to see her go," Eva said.

"I'm sorry to hear that. I guess that's good news for us?"

Eva couldn't miss Connie walking toward them, hand in hand with Cynthia, whose smile shone as brightly as Connie's dress. "Dad! I'm gonna frost my hair! And cut it short. I want a…" Cynthia looked up at Connie and tugged on her dress.

"Pixie cut," Connie told her.

"That's right, a pixie cut. I'm telling mom now!" Cynthia Stanstead spun on her heel and hurried home, turning to shout over her shoulder, "You look beautiful, Connie!"

"Well, we should probably get going," Sybil said. "Hopefully, I can tear Clark away from the grill and cooler."

"Me too, Eva." Alice hugged her. "It was a fabulous day. I'm so proud of you, Connie. When are you leaving on your honeymoon? Do you know yet?"

Eva interjected, glaring at Connie. "Haven't a clue. I hope she gives us a heads up."

"You'll be the first to know. I *just* graduated… geez. We'd like some time to get the apartment situated first."

Eva looked at Charles. "They're always painting and papering something."

"Don't I know that to be the truth. I'll be busy doing that next door." Taking a step back, Charles excused himself. "Well, it was nice to meet all of you. Eva, I'll take a rain check on that beer. Perhaps one night the four of us can sit out and catch up. I'm sure we can set Cindy up with something to watch on TV while the adults get to know each other, but until then, I'll bid you all adieu."

His attempt at a curtsy was a bit much, but Eva and Sybil took it in stride and kept smiling.

After Charles followed Cynthia, Eva told Connie she should thank her grandparents for a good day and start hinting around Warren, or he, his brothers, and Sam would never put out the charcoal until all the meat was gone.

"No leftovers!" Eva shouted to everyone still hovering around the tables. "The only thing to save and freeze is the top layer of the cake.

"Sybil, make sure Clark takes the last of my mother's green jello surprise.

"Warren, why don't you have your brothers take the coolers and the rest of the beer—bring 'em back tomorrow.

"Sam, why don't you fold up these tables and set them against the shed? Deal with 'em tomorrow. It's not supposed to rain tonight.

"Catherine, always a pleasure to see you. We'll have to meet up someday for lunch at the Dog Team Tavern.

"Polly, Suzy, thanks for coming. I know Connie really values your friendship. The dresses turned out so beautiful. Tell your mother thank you again for making the cake. I can't believe she got the fondant colors to match your dresses."

Eva finally took a deep breath, thanked the Lord for a blessed day, and looked forward to nothing more than a hot bath followed by Jack Paar with Smokey curled and purring on her lap.

Eva's Daily Reminder 1964: June 20, Saturday

Hot! Hot! Hot!

We had a perfect hot day. Got the floor done and last minute things and tables all set.

Catherine and Polly came dressed in yellow. Suzy dressed in orchid. Polly came with the flowers and cake—orchid and yellow.

We started on the dot and were finished by 2:15. A perfect ceremony. Connie just beautiful. A lot of guests and everyone ok.

They decorated Warren's car and crossed the wires. He ended up calling Sam from upstreet—teed off!

Sybil and Clark stayed after everyone gone. Charlie and Cindy popped in for a visit.

Perfect wedding!

19

Connie and Warren were traveling across the country, with plans to stop at the Grand Canyon and Redwood National Forest. They wanted to spend a week near Mount Shasta with one of Warren's relatives, who had promised him some excellent trout fishing. A week went by, and Eva hadn't heard from them.

The legal name on her birth certificate was Constance Isabel, named after both of Sam's grandmothers. They called her Connie the first time the nurse wheeled her into the delivery room, and it was the only name they shared with Henry and Ruby. Eva couldn't remember whether they'd ever asked or guessed, but she assumed Alice knew, too. Sam called her "Izzie" once, before they brought her home, claiming it was the name his parents called his grandmother, but Eva nipped it in the bud—it sounded too much like "Lizzie" as in Borden.

Mrs. Constance Bradford was a name too mature for Eva to fathom, even though bringing her swaddled bundle home from the hospital seemed like only yesterday.

Hopefully, she'd call once they reached Shasta.

Eva had never been this far from her daughter in twenty years, but instead of staying home and worrying about their long trip, she convinced Sam that they deserved a vacation. It was a long Fourth of July weekend, and as much as Eva would have loved to be out on the river fishing, they'd still be home at night. She had plenty of future weekend plans, including driving up the coast of Maine, crossing the Kancamagus Highway later in the fall, and heading to the Outer Cape as far as Provincetown. She couldn't wait to put some miles on Little Red Riding Hood; break her in, Sam had said. There wasn't a single mile of New England roads they hadn't explored, and wanted to retrace. But this time, she longed for the bright city lights of the Big Apple. It was a place neither of them had ever visited—Boston, hundreds of times; Canada, dozens; but New York City, zero.

Eva finished all their packing before work. Sam stayed home, mowed the lawns, washed his truck, and swept it clean inside and out. Little Red Riding Hood stayed home, safe in the garage.

Henry and Ruby drove them to Springfield airport. Ruby found an old wool cloche hat that had belonged to her mother and wore it despite the summer heat, but left her apron in the kitchen. Eva wore a new yellow jersey dress and hat, along with comfortable walking shoes, while Sam wore a light navy blazer over Levi's and loafers. (He didn't want it to take up extra luggage space, and Eva hoped he hadn't forgotten to put on deodorant this morning.) When he started sniffing, it looked like he was testing his armpits, but Eva eventually realized he was sniffing the backseat for something else, and she slapped his thigh.

Together, they looked stylish and confident as they boarded and departed on time.

• • •

It took two buses and a cab to reach the Taft Hotel on Seventh Avenue in midtown Manhattan. They grabbed a quick drink after checking in; Eva ordered a Manhattan, and Sam ordered a fancy Löwenbräu on tap. Then they walked a few blocks south into the theatre district to dine at Le Champlain, where they shared a steak for two. It was cooked perfectly and paired nicely with a bottle of French wine that Sam ordered after Eva picked it out from the menu—Gloria was the only wine name she could pronounce.

After dinner, they returned to the hotel lounge and enjoyed a lively performance by pianist Charley Drew, who sang "Songs Your Grandma Never Knew."

"What did you think? Pretty good?" Eva asked. "I know it wasn't your favorite. The world can't always be about Boston sports and organ music." She waited for him to finish his frosted pint.

"Well, this guy was no John Kiley, but he was entertaining. I'll give 'em that."

The last time Eva and Sam stayed up until 2 a.m. was probably when Connie was born.

• • •

It was hot and breezy in the city the next day, the fourth, and they slept in. The room was comfortable and air-conditioned with a small TV and a radio, though they didn't think they'd use them, preferring to walk as much of Midtown as possible.

They had breakfast at Calico Kitchen—a meal and service not worth re-membering—before joining a mile-long line outside the 46th Street Theatre to buy tickets for the day's first showing of "How to Succeed in Business Without Really Trying," starring Rudy Vallée and Darrell Hickman. The show was breathtaking and well worth the wait, the likes of which they'd never seen locally at the New London Barn Playhouse.

After the play, they headed to the hotel for a quick drink before an early bird dinner at Pearl's Chinese on 48th Street. Eva had never experienced a meal quite like that. Everything was perfect, but not as perfect as the end of the day, which wrapped up on Broadway with Carol Burnett on stage at the 51st Street Theatre, singing and dancing in "Fade Out-Fade In," after which they were exhausted.

"I can't believe this vacation is already half over," Eva said, crawling under the sheets and kicking the duvet cover onto the floor with her feet. "It's gone by so fast." She wasn't fooling herself; the blanket on the floor wouldn't let her sleep, so she got up, folded it, and draped it over the back of one of two small chairs in the room. She checked the curtains, pulling them tight. She wanted to vacuum, but shivered and shook it off, pulling her nightgown over her shoulders and slipping between the sheets. She needed to scratch the itch.

• • •

Sunday was clear and cooler, or maybe it was the stronger breezes blowing through the midtown canyons. Eva woke about an hour before Sam, but stayed still on her back, with the sheets pulled snug to her chin in the artificially cooled room, until he stirred. The 2 a.m. high-water mark was broken last night (this morning) when their lovemaking ran out of steam at 3 a.m. While Sam showered, she took a whore's bath at the sink and brushed her hair. Looking in the mirror, she hoped it would last a couple more days until Alice could work her magic.

There was no time to waste as they hurried down Seventh Avenue, eager for a big breakfast at The Californian, where they both filled their grocery holes with hickory-smoked Irish bacon and eggs sunny side up, after waiting an unusually long time for service.

Eva wanted to remember this hearty meal. "Let's not forget and try to remember to ask Warren if he has any connections to anyone who might sell this kind of bacon. I've been thinking about adding a second freezer down cellar. One for garden vegetables, maybe fish, and a new one for meat. It might be cheaper to buy half a cow. Though I might feel funny asking Warren to process it."

"It's his job. Add a pig, and give them enough to fill their own freezer. I'm sure he wouldn't mind."

"If they make it back."

Sam scowled, then patted his stomach, paid the check, and found the nearest bus stop before hopping on and getting off at the Museum of Natural History, where they waited until opening. The time spent inside was entertaining for both of them, and by early afternoon, they were exhausted from all the walking and head-turning that had burned off the Irish bacon.

At the hotel, they changed clothes, had a beer, and headed to Rockefeller Plaza for a cocktail before finally feeling rested and empty enough to mosey over to Davey Jones, across from Radio City Music Hall, for a seafood dinner. Eva let Sam talk her into trying the Alaskan King Crab special. They both chose melted butter and a hot biscuit instead of the Russian dressing, which must've been a New York thing, like tomato clam chowder. Eva enjoyed having another French waiter—not the same one who served them at Le Champlain—who suggested pairing the crab with an Alsatian Riesling, which he brought in a silver bucket and placed in a tableside stand. She was embarrassed as she stopped him from leaving, but then changed her mind and pointed to the appetizers on the menu. "May I please have a cup of the chowder?" she asked, enunciating her accent away. "White?" she added for good measure.

"But of course, madam," he said. "A cup of New England clam chowder." The waiter looked at Sam. "And you, sir? As well?"

"Sure. Why not… sounds good."

Eva waited until the waiter was out of earshot. "I thought for sure you were gonna say something uncouth like, 'Does a bear shit in the woods?', so I'm glad you didn't."

"We still hate the Yankees."

"Samuel. Shh." Once Eva was sure no one was paying attention, she added, "You have a *Ruth* signed baseball in the hutch."

"I'm well aware. Lou Gehrig, too. My grandfather knew the Red Sox clubhouse manager. It'll be worth some money someday. Changes nothing. My grandfather, my father, your father… still hate the Yankees."

Eva did too, with a passion, but she kept it to herself.

After dinner, still buzzing from adrenaline, Sam wanted to hit a few nearby bars for nightcaps—Astor's and Edison's. But he was done after two, refusing to pay 85 cents for a pint of beer.

• • •

Eva woke up early on the last day to a bright, clear morning. Sam had forgotten to close the curtains completely, and the rising sun split the room in half. She wanted to get out early before checkout, so she nudged him awake with her elbow. "Let's go, we're burnin' daylight," she said. She'd wanted to do a little window shopping yesterday around Rockefeller Plaza, but they had dilly-dallied too long while people-watching and nursing their happy hour drinks. "Time's a-wastin'. I'd like to look for some new clothes before we have to head out."

Sam grunted like a black bear awakening from hibernation, and continued to grumble while Eva got a head start on packing their suitcase. Eventually, she got him into the shower without bothering to shave.

They took a cab into the shopping district, where Eva enjoyed darting in and out of stores, looking for new things that caught her eye. She limited herself to two pairs of shoes, both with heels—one in a light blue patina and the other in black. She also found a skirt and three overblouses: two in silk and one in a red-and-black polka-dot cotton.

They made it to the hotel by noon, killed their bottle while packing their shoes, then checked out and grabbed a cab. "Idlewild," Sam told the driver, who sat unflinching and eyed them in the rearview mirror. "Idlewild, the airport," Sam told him again.

Eva elbowed him, embarrassed. She sighed and turned toward the side window, taking in one last look at Midtown.

"Airport. Gotcha." After pulling onto Seventh Avenue and coming to the first light, the taxi driver caught their attention in the rearview mirror. "It's JFK now," he said. "They changed the name last year."

Eva shot Sam another look, slapping his forearm this time. "Shame on you," she whispered.

At JFK, the baggage check receptionist informed them that an earlier flight was available, so they took it and arrived back in Springfield ahead of schedule.

After calling Henry to explain that they arrived two hours early and that nothing was wrong, Eva managed to convince him to pick them up. It was too short notice for Ruby to leave three loaves of bread in the oven, so she stayed home, still worried there was trouble.

"Has Connie called you yet?" Eva asked Henry as he pulled onto Route 5 heading north. "It's been over a week, and she still hasn't called me. With us being gone over the long weekend and all, I was really hoping she'd call you to say they'd arrived."

"Nope."

"I guess I'll have to call Warren's mother as soon as we get home. I don't think it'll be too late. Maybe he's called her already."

When Henry brought the Biscayne up the hill and around the corner, Eva spotted Smokey sitting proudly on the stone wall. *It was good to be home again, back in our little house.* "There's my little trouper. I hope he doesn't give me the cold shoulder tonight."

After calling Warren's mother and hearing she hadn't heard from them either, Eva's happiness while away, living vicariously, vanished. Too tired to cook, she called Alice to see if she wanted to go into town for a bite at the A&W, and she readily agreed, offering to drive and pay.

• • •

"Well, it sure sounds like you two were off living the life of Riley," Alice said. "But now it's time to come back to reality. What are you thinking? Give it a few more days? What if they decided to take it slow? I bet they ended up stopping and staying in more places than they'd originally planned. My money is on giving them ten days. I bet as soon as they crossed the Mississippi and then got a look at the Rocky Mountains, all their plans went out the window. Heck, even Reg and I stayed several days at the Grand Canyon." She closed her eyes, drew a breath, and smiled inwardly. "I remember he didn't want to leave El Tovar until he spotted some big horn sheep along the walls of the canyon. I was fine watching the mules. Though Patton's whole army couldn't get me on one of those."

"I bet he wanted a trophy," Sam interjected. "I don't know who would wanna go on that hunt more: Reg, Clark, or… Sybil, for that matter."

Eva ate a forkful of fried bay scallops, pushed her fries around the basket, and sipped her root beer. *You're my most empathetic friend and listener, but this is all about being a mother.* "Maybe you're right. I bet they just lost track of time." She looked at Sam while he took two big bites from his burger and chased them down with milk. "I'll give 'em the rest of the week before I *really* start to worry." She wanted to say 'we,' but his lack of focus changed her mind. "How's your hamburg?" she asked him.

"It's okay. I always have the fish and chips, but I think I'm still digesting those king crab legs."

Eva and Alice exchanged eye rolls. "Widowed life isn't half bad," Alice whispered, pointing at Sam, who was enjoying finishing his burger and chasing it with a couple of fries. "So… I ran into Carolyn recently at the Congregational church. She was inquiring about coordinating potluck schedules, and then she—"

"Oh, how's she doing?" Eva interrupted. "I try not to pester Merrill about their business, but she seemed like she was coming along okay at the wedding. She looked pretty darn good for what she's been through."

"She does, yes, good for her… so… anyhow, as I was…" Alice smiled, looking between Eva and Sam, apparently conflicted. "What you said… it makes me think it's not my place…"

Eva could see that her best friend was struggling; a dull shadow had replaced her usually jovial glow. She reached across the table with a comforting hand. "Are you sure Carolyn's doing okay?" *Alice wouldn't lie to her.*

"Yes. That's not it." Alice glared at Sam and waited for him to finish his milk and wipe his face with a handful of napkins. "Carolyn heard from Faye, who overheard Father William talking to Ray. Apparently, he's been petitioning to allow Vera to join the Catholic Church. And… well, you don't need anyone else to help you with those puzzle pieces."

Eva bit her tongue and tilted her head toward Sam. She waited for his reaction, wondering if he would spoil the fun they'd had in the city. *Would he say nothing? Ask about Ray?* She was patient. It boded well that he stayed silent, wiping his face again. *Or was he hiding?* When he reached for his wallet, Alice waved him off, reminding him it was her treat.

Eva put on a smile. "I'm sure Faye will tell me all about it tomorrow."

"Be interesting to hear if she misheard. Who knows? Probably not so lucky. I'm glad you had fun this weekend and made it back okay. No troubles?"

"No troubles at all," Eva assured her.

• • •

Almost no trouble at all was the truth. Connie called later that evening. She and Warren had arrived, taking a few extra days to stop in the Colorado Rockies and then through the Navajo Nation to the Hoover Dam. By the time they reached the Redwood National Forest, she was feeling under the weather with a stomachache. They decided to stay in Shasta for another week, and she promised to rest up.

Eva's Daily Reminder 1964: July 25, Saturday

Hot! Kidneys.

Got up feeling lousy. Got going on the pills and liquids and felt better.

Got our stuff packed away and did some washing.

Guess Vera is really joining the Catholic Church to marry Ray. What extremes will she go to next! Sam was quite disgusted.

Al was home sick yesterday Mom said but better.

Clark away in Canada fishing.

Had Sybil and Al for supper. Sybil brought deer steaks. Too chilly at 7 to eat outside so we ate inside. Had Swiss chard and fresh cukes Al gave us.

Connie down and wanted to stay for a perm but Warren was getting out of work.

20

After dicing a good-sized portion of Cabot cheddar, Eva stood at the sink, rinsing the tacky residue off her fingers. She hoped to have cheese-and-cracker snacks ready around the same time Sam finished mowing the banks, finishing what she had started earlier on the flatter sections. She'd asked him to refill the feeders before he started, and after a moment of joy watching the purple finch at the thistle tube, he flew away when Sam killed the mower engine, and it backfired.

Her eyes drifted past the hanging feeders toward the neighbor's house, now rented by the Stansteads. It was midday, but dark ocular shadows clouded her peripheral vision as she tried to focus on their kitchen window. She remembered the night she saw Vera, whom she imagined was contemplating her in return. An increasing sense of static electricity prickled at the roots of her hair as she fought the urge of an inner monster that demanded to know where she and Sam had been intimate. *Was it merely infatuation, burning the candle at both ends? Or had they planned a future together?* She couldn't help but wonder, desperately trying to suppress the anger. She closed her eyes, exerting an inner strength capable of snapping shut the wire handle on a mason jar lid.

Smokey startled her by jumping onto the counter, then climbed into the window above the sink before she scolded him. "You little dickens," she said, watching him bristle at the sight of grazing blue jays on the lawn. She didn't want him to develop bad habits, so she rapped on the glass, scaring them away. He slipped through her hands, trying to focus on the cheese cubes on the cutting board. "You've been fed already this morning." She nudged him off the counter, opened the door, and he wasted no time, bounding down the steps and stopping briefly to check beneath the feeders out of curiosity. "Go on. Find some mice. Leave my chippies alone," she told him, as if the cat understood.

She made an executive decision and grabbed a couple of bottles of Schlitz from the refrigerator, holding them snugly between her fingers as she picked up the cutting board. She managed to press the door latch with her knuckle and push it open with her knee.

Outside, Sam grabbed a pair of lawn chairs from the toolshed when he must have seen her balancing gingerly down the stairs. He unfolded them and started toward her to help. He hadn't taken more than two steps before she said, "I'm all right. Go wash up." He obeyed, jogging toward the garden hose. "Grab a folding end table from the shed before you sit down," she called after him.

After setting the table between them, he took both beers, and she placed the cheeseboard. "Looks good," he said. "Perfect timing."

Eva scanned the stone wall, searching for Smokey one last time before settling down and taking another sip of beer. She wasn't able to enjoy watching the action at the hummingbird feeder or the ground feeders without being drawn to the Stansteads' house—Vera's house. "We should plan to take Little Red Riding Hood somewhere… don't you think? I bet this time of year would be perfect to drive along the Cape with the top down. Let's go all the way to P'Town. What do you say?" She interjected, adding, "And no, I don't want to park her on the street or pay for some garage, stopping at Fenway. I don't want to risk her getting scratched. Let's drive straight through."

"C'mon, I can get extra tickets from one of the guys at the shop."

She gave him his one shot. "In the three hours it takes to watch one game out of 162, we could already be at the end of the Cape, having a nice dinner. I say we don't think too hard."

"I think I've gone and created a monster."

I'm not the monster. "How about I'll treat you to a bonus. We'll go deep-sea fishing for a day. I'm sure we'd run into a mess of cod, haddock, cusk… maybe bluefish."

"We won't have room in the car for a cooler."

"We'll keep whatever's the best catch and bring it back to the cabin. Give the rest to the boat captain. Fourth of July crowds are gone. I bet we can find a vacancy in one of those shoreline cabins in Truro." She watched his wheels turning.

"I can't remember the last time I had grilled bluefish."

"Grab some farmer's market vegetables, wrap it in foil over charcoal. I'm sure those cabins have their own little outdoor grills."

Eva ate a piece of cheese, and it tasted strange after all the talk about grilled fresh fish and vegetables. She followed it with a gulp of Schlitz, then saw Ginny carrying a basket of laundry toward the clothesline, who waved after setting it down. "Hello. Good afternoon," she said, after Eva waved back.

"Afternoon to you, too," Eva said. "How're things going?"

"Not too bad, yourself?"

"Doin' good. Why don't you come join us when you're finished," Eva said, deliberately sounding non-optional. "I've got plenty of snacks and cold beer, unless you'd like a cocktail. Is Charlie home? Send him over. The more the merrier."

"Alright, thanks. Give me a minute, then."

Eva lifted her beer bottle to the light, checking the level. Satisfied, she shielded the side of her face closest to Virginia. "It'll do us good to have a moment of peace to get to know them a little better, don't you think?" There was no hesitation on Eva's part or defensiveness toward Virginia. The woman wasn't unattractive, nor was she particularly attractive. Carrying a laundry basket across the backyard was the only exercise Eva had seen her do, and it made Eva wonder how she kept house. "Do you have enough clothespins?" she shouted across the yard, loud enough to be heard without repeating.

"Yes, thanks for offering." Virginia Stanstead finished up, giving her arms a workout as she spun the square clothesline without moving her feet. She was dressed in men's white tennis shorts, matching sneakers, and a sleeveless blouse. Her hair was held back with a bandana and pulled into a high pony.

Eva turned toward Sam, setting a trap, but he was looking at her parents' house, dropping cheese cubes one by one into his mouth from his fist. "What are you looking at?"

"Oh, you know me. Never satisfied. I'm eyeballing all the little mistakes we made shingling the roof."

"Don't be silly. Nobody's gonna notice but you. Why don't you go and grab some more beers before they come over? There's still half of the Cabot in the fridge. Bring it out, too, with the knife on the counter. Hopefully, that's enough for now. If not, well, we'll have to find something else unless you want to switch over to peanut butter and crackers and let them have the cheese."

After Sam went inside and before the Stansteads arrived, Eva enjoyed a brief moment alone. She envied the hummingbirds' freedom to come and go as they pleased, flitting off and reappearing whenever they wanted. They had no worries about paying taxes, utility bills, maintaining vehicles, dealing with politics, or sinking into a deep depression when the Red Sox began to slide in the standings.

Charles Stanstead arrived first, followed by Virginia. Eva didn't see any sign of Cynthia, whom she had expected to tag along. "Cindy not wanting to bother?" Eva asked.

Virginia laughed. She'd removed the ponytail and had brushed her hair out. "Oh, believe me, she'd be the first one out here. That one hates to miss a thing. Luckily, for us, she's in Springfield having a sleepover tonight with one of her old friends. Well, I shouldn't say *old* friend—a friend."

Charles wore off-white Bermuda shorts. Eva couldn't picture him in dungarees. Khakis or Dickies were probably his usual work pants, with shorts his weekend uniform. Today, he must have read her mind, sporting a well-worn Sox cap covered in white sweat stains and creases. She pointed, "I like your hat, but be careful, they'll break your heart. It's getting to be that time of year."

Eva didn't know why Sam was taking so long to bring their beer and a refilled board, but she went ahead and pulled out two more chairs from the toolshed.

"Allow me," Charles said, taking them from Eva.

Sam swung open the door, and Eva was sure he would sprain an ankle falling down the steps, as he seemed to be trying to do too many things with too few hands. "Hey, hello. I was gonna do that," he said.

"Too late," Eva chastised him. "Just don't fall and dump the snacks."

"Or spill the beer," Charles chimed in.

Sam righted the ship, regaining his balance. "No need to worry about that." He briskly crossed the yard, handing out choices of beer that he held between his fingers, and some that he pulled from his pockets like an amateur magician. "I didn't know what you liked. I've got Schlitz, Schaefer, and Narragansett. I had some Miller, but I guess we drank 'em all."

Charles reached first. "Ah, no worries. Narragansett is fine. Ginny?"

"I'll have what Eva's having."

Sam handed her a Schaefer. "Hey, I can show you something special. I've got another bottle of Schaefer in the house." He started back.

"Sam, sit down." Eva didn't want to be embarrassed by novelty tricks. "Let it go. Maybe another time. Not now."

Sam sat; instead of a fifty-year-old, he looked like a scolded five-year-old. "It's a bottle of Schaefer that somehow ended up with a Schlitz cap."

"Interesting," Charles said, seeming ambivalent, with creases across his forehead. "What're the odds?"

Eva offered Virginia the cheeseboard. "It's extra sharp." She waited for Virginia to help herself, then Charles. "So, how's everything going? I hear your work commute has gotten interesting. So, the next time one of us gets pinched, you're the one to call to get us out of a jam?" Eva wanted to sound deadpan but couldn't help giggling through her nose.

"I guess Ginny told you the other day. Yeah, Dick's a real charmer." Charles took a swig of his beer and inspected the Narragansett bottle cap, which featured a rebus puzzle. "Seriously, he's fine. We've come to an understanding." He brought the beer cap closer to his eyes, studying it. "I can never figure these things out." He handed the cap to Virginia. "The good news is I figured out his tight schedule, but the bad news is it coincides with my own clocking in and out at J&L."

"Working for the man," Sam said, toasting Charles, who clinked bottles. "That's how Roy Orbison tells it like it is." Sam leaned closer to Eva. "I heard Connie playing some of his 45s."

Eva shushed him with a look and shifted the subject, choosing to keep her eyes on Sam. "Still haven't heard a peep yet out of the homeowner?"

"Actually, yes," Charles said. He shifted in his chair, glanced at Virginia as if seeking approval. "You had mentioned her to me earlier... Vera, yes... In fact, we did speak recently. She called." He looked again at his wife, who turned away, nibbling a piece of cheese on a cracker. If she intended to be stealthy, she failed.

Eva attempted to read their faces for clues, and Charles probably realized her arched eyebrows in the afternoon shadows weren't subtle enough to leave her satisfied with a phone call.

"To be honest, I'm not sure what to make of it... or her. She was friend-ly—at least at first—then she started asking if we'd be interested in breaking our lease, which is definitely not something we want to do. The lease was for a year with an option to buy."

"Did she say why?" Eva asked.

"Not in so many words."

"We know Jan Chabot. She was a classmate of Connie's." Eva knew how to plant seeds and drop hints.

"So you're asking us to call the realtor to find out what's going on, or else you will?"

"That's what she's saying, Charlie. And I agree with her. I don't want this hanging over our heads. You know from what she said on the phone that she's not likely to take no for an answer. She's gonna call back. You know it, and I know it." Virginia looked nervous, crossing and re-crossing her legs. She man-aged to pull a hair tie out of the front pocket of her shorts with some effort, and deftly redid her high ponytail—something Eva hadn't done in decades.

Sam finished his beer and asked if anyone else wanted another before heading inside. Charles responded affirmatively, while the ladies declined.

As Sam was opening the screen door, Charles asked Eva, "I think it's safe to say that you've had dealings with Vera? You said you're not broken up about her leaving, and it's none of our business, but we really don't want to get ourselves caught up in the middle of anything here."

"Nothing to be broken up about… said we weren't sorry to see her go, that's all."

Virginia seemed to relax, repeatedly pulling her hair through her fingers. "I think we're on the same page, Eva." She looked at Charles and whispered, "What she's trying politely to tell you is… good riddance."

Eva smiled inwardly. She was beginning to like this woman. Once she settled into a walking routine with Alice, who knew what worlds she might unlock?

Eva's Daily Reminder 1964: July 31, Friday

Warm. Sunny. Curse.

Got started for the Cape around 10. Stopped in Manchester to get a small cooler to go in the MG. Finally found one and filled it with beer and sandwich makings. Ate as we rode along. Lost the good weather around 1 o'clock. Misted, very windy and rainy. We were glad we put the top on. Got to Falmouth around 5:30. We both were bushed so got a motel $14 and had drinks which revived us. Found a nice place to eat with nice food and atmosphere.

No trouble with the car. Rode like a charm. Saw it turn 1,000 miles. We stopped in Sumner Falls before we left to have it inspected but we have to have seat belts!

Eva's Daily Reminder 1964: August 1, Saturday

Rain.

Misty and very windy. Got up and going around 9 - 9:30. Had breakfast a short distance from motel and then rode way down to the tip of the Cape. A lot of traffic. We noticed how scrubby the pines are. They look as though their tops were chipped off of them. Also every house it seemed had blue and rose hydrangea bushes. Very striking!

The weather was so lousy. After we got to the monument and then back to Plymouth to see the rock we decided not to stay and buzzed on to Manchester and had supper at the 88 Club around 8. We had to wait in line 3 quarters of an hour but it was worth it. Such food for $1.88.

Got home around midnight. Mom and Sybil had gone to see My Fair Lady. Connie had been down while we were gone.

21

Eva finished Connie's laundry before heading to the shoe store. It had taken her nearly a week to catch up since they returned home from California. She used the spare key, hoping to surprise them with a clean apartment and crisp, turned-down bedsheets. What she found was a sinkful of dishes, piles of clothes on the bedroom floor, apparently discarded during their rushed packing, along with an unmade bed. At least there was no spoiled food in the refrigerator, but she had helped herself to what would have spoiled before they returned, once they were staying an extra week. The first thing she did after hugging Connie and welcoming her home was to give her holy hell about the unkempt apartment.

When the phone rang, Eva guessed it might be Ruby calling to ask if there would be more clothes to iron; instead, it was Connie. "Hi, mum. Did I catch you at a bad time?" Eva sensed something wrong in the tone of Connie's voice; her cadence was slow and shallow.

"No, of course not, hon. You don't sound so hot. Are you sure you don't still have what ails you from your trip?"

"No. I don't think so. I was fine driving back, but I think I have a fever. Warren called Dr. Read before he left for work. He thinks I should go to the hospital and get checked out."

"Who thinks you should go? Warren or Dr. Read?" Eva suddenly realized it didn't matter who, as soon as the words left her mouth. "It doesn't—"

"Dr. Read," Connie interrupted. "It was Warren's idea to call him and then you for a ride. We *think* I have a fever, but I can't be sure because—"

"Let me guess, you don't have a thermometer. I'll bring one with me and leave now. You certainly timed that right." It crossed Eva's mind to ask why Warren didn't go next door and ask his mother for one. She was grateful to be their first choice. "You just wanted a ride to the hospital in the MG," she said, hoping it would keep Connie's spirits high until she got there.

• • •

Dr. Read drew some blood, ruled out appendicitis, and then delivered the news that Connie was pregnant—something Eva would have asked her about earlier over the phone if Connie had shared that she was a month late. He wasn't sure yet why she had a low fever, but he decided to keep her overnight for observation and to give her an IV for dehydration.

Holding Connie's hand while the nurse prepared her for the IV, Eva looked forward to becoming a grandmother, but her little girl wasn't quite ready to have babies yet. God willing, everything would go as planned.

"A little pinch, like a bee sting," the nurse said. Eva felt the sharp prick, mirroring Connie's pain, as the needle pierced the crook of her arm. "All set for the next couple of hours, dear. Try to get some rest... Mrs. Martin, there are no set visiting hours, but if I were in your shoes, I'd probably have some lunch and come back later this afternoon. We'll take good care of Connie. She'll most likely feel a little chilly with the IV running, but after I swaddle her, she'll be napping like a baby."

Eva almost started crying when she heard "swaddle." It was something she used to do for Connie to keep her calm when she and Sam shared the upstairs bedroom with her as an infant. The room became hers as she grew older, even though she had moved most of her belongings into the apartment. Eva kept much of Connie's baby clothes, including her blanket and little red tennis shoes, in boxes under the eaves. She'd have plenty of time over the next nine months to dig them out and sort through everything.

• • •

Sam suggested having lunch at the Riverside Cafe at Quechee Gorge when Eva asked to stop and pick up some material for two new skirts at Dewy's Mill, which they did after eating. The cafe's patio overlooked the glacially carved gorge and bridge—a popular spot for leaf-peepers and suicides—over the Ottauquechee River.

"So what do you think about all this?" Eva asked. "Are you ready to step up to the plate and be a grandfather? Things have been pretty good lately." She took a sip of Chablis, gazing down the river's whitewater breaks, eager to return for the fall foliage. "The way I see it… Our only problem for the next year is to decide if our first baby purchase is a set of plastic golf clubs, a fishing pole, or a baseball mitt."

"Don't forget the hockey stick."

"What if it's a girl?"

"It's still easier to learn on hockey skates." Sam gulped his Budweiser. "That's a beer." He held up the half-empty glass, examining it as the afternoon sunlight filtered through the golden hue and suds. "When do you think they'll tell your parents?"

"You'd better hush up and mind your own business. Keep your yap shut and don't go spilling the beans. Let her tell them in her own time." He'd be hard-pressed to keep his mouth shut. He was always the one to do the talking. Connie was only a month along, and Eva knew she wasn't out of the woods yet. She counted on her fingers and added, "It would seem her due date is probably sometime in March. I hope you're gonna like sharing your birthday." She could only pray that Connie would deliver late because she might not be able to handle another mud-season birthday. "A lot can happen between now and then," she said, aware she sounded so dour and blamed the Red Sox.

• • •

At the hospital, they peeked in on Connie, who was tucked in and still fast asleep, and stopped Dr. Read while he was making his rounds. "She should be able to go home tomorrow. I'd only encourage her to eat a healthy diet, but certainly no bed rest is needed," he said. "However, Mr. Bradford, on the other hand, Warren… if he were my patient, I'd strongly suggest that he stop altogether, or at least cut back drastically, on his smoking. The surgeon general's report issued a warning this year, linking smoking with lung cancer. Connie told me his preference is unfiltered Camels. He should seriously think about making a change."

"Well, it certainly makes for a lot of extra washing, that's for sure," Eva told him while wondering if Henry's pipe was in the same boat as cigarettes—probably not. Ruby never allowed him to smoke inside the house or in the car. Besides, he was too old to change—can't teach an old dog new tricks. "We'll try our best to encourage him."

•••

"You'd better drop me off," Eva told Sam, pointing to the curb along Main Street as they neared the shoe store. "I should catch up with Merrill and Faye." Her time off nearly stretched into a long weekend, and she had already taken an entire unexpected week off. Henry's voice in her head repeated his mantra: no one should take sick time or vacation, lest there might very well be no job waiting for you when you return. "Merrill will give me a ride home. I'm sure he won't mind. And besides, you can choose to use your time either mowing the lawn—Lord knows it needs it after all that rain—or get on the radio. At least I won't be there to have to listen." She wanted to keep that to herself, but it came out anyway. "Don't worry about supper. I took some frozen spaghetti and meatballs out of the freezer yesterday—just need to reheat it when I get home."

"Are you sure he won't mind?"

"Ayutt. Now get going while there's still light. I'll find a way either by hook or by crook." Eva watched him pull away, secure in knowing there wasn't anyone at home next door worth worrying about.

She watched Sam pull away, then stepped off the curb to cross the street. The idea of jaywalking didn't cross her mind until she took her first step and looked the other way, locking eyes through the windshield of Officer

Poole's cruiser as he braked to a stop. Eva hesitated, her momentum carrying her an extra step. She tried to appear casual, hoping that if she waved him on first, he would let it go, but he didn't—he pointed his finger at her over the steering wheel, motioning her to cross in front of him, which she did, reluctantly. She was sure he would circle to the opposite curb, make a U-turn after she'd passed, to give her a ticket based on his displeased scowl and the way his eyes tracked her. If it hadn't been for the fully loaded logging truck slowing behind him, he might've rolled down his window to scold her, but instead, he accelerated ahead of the heavy truck without so much as a wave.

Inside Merrill's store, Faye was surprised to see her. Faye was on her knees, readjusting and aligning shoeboxes stacked on the floor beneath the display racks. "Oh, Eva! We didn't expect to see you today. How's little Miss Connie? Doing okay? I hope she isn't too sick?"

"She's fine. No need to worry. Just a little dehydrated from all the cross-country driving. Dr. Read whipped her into shape. She'll go home tomorrow."

"I bet it seems odd to say that. It sure feels odd to hear it." Faye appeared to laugh it off while standing up. She brushed the knees of her slacks, then her hands, ridding herself of dust and dirt.

This time, Eva kept her thoughts to herself, not wanting to spark the conversation about becoming a grandmother. "Is Merrill around?" she asked, scanning toward the back. "I had Sam drop me off, and I figured he'd be here to give me a lift home after closing. Sam has plenty of yardwork to keep him busy. I didn't want to use any more time."

Faye waved her off. "Think nothing of it. I'll take you home. As a matter of fact, Merrill's not here. He took Carolyn out to lunch, then to a follow-up visit. I'll look the other way if you want to sign yourself in a *little* earlier." Faye flexed her index finger and thumb near her eye. "It was a good weekend for the numbers. All the rain drove folks inside the shops. And he thinks Labor Day weekend will put us over the top for the year, so that's good, not having to wait for Christmas."

Eva looked around the store, scanning for anything that needed attention before coming full circle to Faye. "Actually, it's good Merrill isn't here. I wanted to ask you something… A little bird told me…" Eva sighed heavily.

"Let's not beat around the bush. A little bird told me that you know something about Vera and Ray? At the Catholic Church?"

It was Faye's turn to take a deep breath and exhale. "Well, I should guess so… I mean, not beating around the bush… Let's see…" she said, her eyes drifting and processing. "You really want to know? I guess that's a stupid question, isn't it?" She parked her fists on her hips, and Eva braced for whatever might come next.

"They're joining the church?"

"More than that, Eva. They're engaged… and they've already made arrangements to get married."

Vera marrying Ray would bring everything to an end. It would close—slam—the door firmly shut. Sam would be angry with both of them and push them aside. Eva would be able to move on, stronger, and help raise a grandchild without looking over her shoulder or across the yard. If she had to save her marriage and her daughter's marriage by moving away from the only home she'd built, it would've broken her. *So why was that creeping itch on the back of her neck?* The same itch she scratched when she threw out the Miller High Life beer that Sam had stashed under the cellar stairs.

"Father William is officiating the ceremony in a couple of weeks. They've already put down a deposit."

"Any talk of—"

Faye interrupted, "I don't want to hazard a guess, and… if there was any scuttlebutt, I'd be the first to tell you. As far as I know, they're living at his place north of town. Whether or not they—"

"I know. Believe me, I know." Ray's house was smaller than Vera's and faced traffic, neither of which hampered Vera's house. She rubbed the back of her neck and hoped the itch would go away before it was time to take Faye up on her offer to drive her home.

· · ·

Faye dropped Eva off in front of her house, stopping at the foot of the stone steps, and waved good night after telling her she'd see her tomorrow morning.

The first thing Eva noticed was that the front lawn looked too lush and green to have been mowed, which Sam should have already finished by now. She didn't hear the drone of the riding mower or the higher pitch of the push mower. She climbed the steps and confirmed that the grass had not been freshly cut. Circling to the back of the house, the toolshed was open, and the Simplicity riding tractor was parked outside, sitting quietly. There was no sign of Sam. It seemed he hadn't started yet.

As she turned toward the door, she could clearly see across the yard and into Vera's driveway. *It was still too fresh to think of the property as belonging to the Stansteads.* A Ford F-100 was parked, looking like it had seen better days. Rust spots covered the sun-faded blue paint like eczema. Eva didn't recognize the truck, and Charles shouldn't be home, working the second shift. She hesitated, debating whether to look inside the house for Sam or cross the yard to check on Virginia under the pretense of being a nosy neighbor. She knocked on the screen door, giving Sam a chance to answer if he was in the kitchen, then moved on after a few seconds.

Eva didn't need to wait and see who was in the Stansteads' kitchen because she could hear their voices arguing inside before she reached the porch. Sam's voice was the first she recognized, followed by Virginia's, and then the owner of the truck—Ray Whittman.

"You should be speaking to my husband, not me, and I'm sorry, but he's at work now," Virginia said. "Anything you have to say will have to wait until tomorrow, preferably before lunch."

Eva ascended the steps to the covered porch, unable to ignore that they desperately needed a fresh coat of paint. The door was open, and she stepped in front of the screen, catching Virginia's eye first, then Sam's, and finally Ray's. Even with the dirty screen and everyone watching her, Eva looked past them through the kitchen and couldn't help but notice Cynthia peering around the corner from inside the bathroom. The glimpse was brief as the little girl ducked inside.

"Eva," Virginia said. "I'm so sorry about the shouting." Virginia placed a palm against her forehead. She removed a tissue from her sleeve cuff and dabbed under her eyes.

"C'mon, Ray, let's go. It's time to leave," Sam said, raising a hand toward Ray's shoulder, who flipped it away with the back of his own. "Hey, take it easy."

Sam was a few inches taller, but Ray was wiry, muscular, and younger—a physical confrontation that Eva didn't want to risk happening. She opened the door, stepped inside, and positioned herself between them. If he pushed her, he'd regret it in more ways than one. She was certain the men in her life outnumbered the men in his. Big Ben would put a stop to his meddling without saying a word. "What's this all about?" Eva shifted her stance, placing herself between Ray and Virginia. "Why the hell are you even here? You've got no business here."

"The hell I don't. We've already asked nicely over the phone. Vera just wants her house back, that's all."

"Virginia, do you have Jan Chabot's number?" Eva asked. "Let's give her a call. She'll straighten this mess out."

"It's not a mess. We beg to differ."

"You signed a contract, Ray," Sam said.

"*You* didn't sign anything, Ray," Eva told him, leaning in a little too close, emboldened with the odds three to one right now. "Vera signed the lease with Janice Chabot. It's all legal and good for a year, after which Vera can take it up with her. But until then, you need to leave these poor people alone," she scolded him.

Ray didn't appear scared or impressed. "It doesn't matter, *they*"—he pointed at Virginia—"don't own this house… Vera does… and—"

"Yeah, yeah," Eva cut him off, "we know all about it. You're getting hitched. Congratulations and good riddance. Your name still isn't on the deed, and you're still not welcome today."

Sam bristled and pushed past Ray onto the porch, where he spun in a tight circle before pushing open the screen, holding it for Ray.

"Do we still have a problem?" Eva asked.

"Let's go, Ray," Sam said, insisting.

"Do we need to call Dick Poole?" Eva threatened. "We can do it right now… Ginny, go dial the operator."

"Alright, alright," Ray said, finally looking flustered and ready to relent. "We'll be speaking to Janice… and a lawyer." He left without acknowledging or even looking at Sam.

"I'm so embarrassed," Virginia said. "I don't know what I would've done if you both hadn't shown up when you did. He wouldn't let me get a word in edgewise. And he was"—she spun around—"scaring Cindy… Cindy? Where are you? Everything's okay now, honey."

Cynthia emerged from the bathroom and ran to her mother's embrace, burying her face in Virginia's stomach.

Eva saw the little girl's clenched grip on her mother's dress, flushed with color as she tugged at the fabric. "If he or Vera comes back… or… even if they call you, hang up, and call the police. Dick will straighten him out." She reached out and stroked Cynthia's hair, letting herself remember innocent days past. "I guess you probably never got a chance to start supper. Why don't you two come outside, sit, and relax? I've got plenty of spaghetti and meatballs—more than enough to share. What do you say?"

"That would be nice, thank you," Virginia said. "Kiddo?"

Cynthia showed her face, smiling.

Eva's Daily Reminder 1964: August 15, Saturday

Sunny. Cool. Showers.

Really feel lousy after coughing all night, but got off to work anyway. The morning went by fast. Merrill went to the hotel to a reception for the new machine shop bigwigs—a business show.

Sam went down to see Prescott about repairing the washing machine that's been on the fritz and up to see Connie.

We took off with a lunch and beer around 1:30 in the MG. Went to Rutland then over to Orwell and on to Middlebury. Ate supper at the Dog Team. They have enlarged it and built a cocktail lounge. Very nice. I debated all this time in taking Sam. I have so many happy memories there. Before we got there he brought her name up about places they had been. I asked him to tell me about it but as usual he wouldn't. Whole day spoiled. Kaput! Damn her again!

More darn blue jays. Feeders were a mess when we got home.

Connie called and was down while we were gone.

22

Monday, August 17th, was a hot and muggy day in Sumner Falls. Weekend showers had left the air thick with sweaty humidity, forcing Eva to open several windows around the house to catch even a slight cross breeze. It barely helped at all. Sam had placed a fan in one of the living room windows, but it only ended up pulling more humidity into the house, making Eva's cough worse. She couldn't imagine how this was affecting poor Connie, who was resting upstairs in her old bedroom—at least trying to nap as best she could given the circumstances.

Sam convinced Warren to join him in taking the MG to the Woodstock garage for a new windshield after Sam had tailgated a dump truck overflowing with stones on his way home the night before. Warren didn't want to leave Connie's bedside, but he relented after Eva and Sam urged him to let their daughter get some rest.

The timing of Connie's miscarriage the day before deeply affected everyone. The will to live vanished along with the twin fetuses. Eva had no words or past experiences to draw from. Sam isolated himself outside the house, working like a one-man chain gang, furiously scratching at nonexistent weeds in every flowerbed to burn off energy. Warren only annoyed Connie, apparently unable to say or do anything to calm her for even a few minutes. Despite her pushing him away, she still wanted him to stay with her tonight, and Eva allowed him, viewing the gesture as humble.

Eva encouraged her parents to give Connie a few days to come around, but told Alice it was okay to stop by the house. Maybe having Alice give them a shampoo and set would lift her mood. It couldn't hurt, even if it got her out of bed.

"I'll be over shortly after I make sure I have enough permanent solution," Alice said over the phone. "I'll bring us some Drambuies."

"I wouldn't bother with that. I bet she'd be none too pleased with the smell. Let's plan on shampoos and a set… and it's too damn hot for Drambuie, we're gonna need something on ice."

"I'll bring my thermos, then! Shall I fill it enough for Ruby?"

"You can fill it, but I told my parents to hold off for a while. Too many visitors might scare her right back into her shell."

"See you in a bit then." Alice ended the call. Even talking on the phone, moving her jaw, made Eva break into a sweat. She tugged at her collar and changed into an all-cotton top, tossing the barely worn blouse into the nearly empty hamper. Hesitating for a moment, she scooped up the clothes and carried them down to the cellar to wash. She was fooling herself, thinking the dehumidifier was doing its job.

When Sam and Warren returned from the garage, Alice had finished Connie's shampoo and set, and the three women—two in curlers—were sitting in the kitchen drinking whiskey sours from highball glasses filled to the brim with ice cubes. Sam and Warren chose cold beers instead.

Eva hoped Warren wouldn't ruin the moment by saying something they didn't want to hear. Connie needed support, not words; a calm gesture and a warm, silent smile were all that was required.

An afternoon at the garage did not ease any of Sam's built-up anxiousness. "I'm not too happy with how the windshield turned out," he said, earning stern looks from the women in the room. Warren shrugged and disappeared into the living room, turning on the television. He lowered the volume before Eva had a chance to tell him.

"Why would you go and say something like that?" Eva asked him. "You aren't gonna know anything until the next time it rains." He grunted, hefted his beer as if to check how much was left, and went outside.

Eva inwardly blamed him for causing a fuss and for not answering her question. The television volume wasn't low enough, which only added to her irritation. One man gone, one to go. She stood and headed for the doorway. "Warren," she said, waiting until she had his attention. She couldn't see what he was watching, but on a Monday afternoon, it had to be either a soap opera or a game show, and she decided he should be doing something more productive. "Do you still have another small venison roast in your freezer?"

"Yes, I do."

"Could you be a honey and drive upstreet and get it? We might have time to thaw it out on the counter in this weather before suppertime." He might be in a bad way, needing a cigarette or two, and getting him out of the house on his own might kill two birds with one stone. She also had no idea if he had smoked around Sam that morning, unless he had waited until he was out in the parking lot. "And if you have another fan, might as well bring that down too," she said, making it three birds with one stone.

"I think there's one packed away somewhere. If not, I can see if my parents have an extra."

"Oh, don't bother. No need to pester them. Hurry back."

• • •

Later that afternoon, everyone enjoyed a venison roast dinner with red potatoes, heavily buttered and sprinkled with thyme sprigs. Connie was quick to insist that Henry and Ruby join them, and everyone sat outside, where the setting sun stirred breezes cooler than the buzzing window fans inside. Dessert was skipped, replaced with more cold whiskey sours. No one had the energy to fetch a cribbage board and cards, and Eva couldn't remember the last time that had happened.

Henry and Ruby were the first to head inside. He made an excuse about needing to get up early to touch up the paint around the house, mentioning the kitchen cabinets and a few patches on the south side. Eva half-expected him to remind them that when the Golden Gate Bridge painting crews finished, they turned right around and started all over again on the far side.

"I guess I'm still worn out," Connie told Warren. She shifted her look to Alice. "Thanks again for the shampoo and curls."

"Always glad to do it. I've been doing it your whole life, and I'll keep doing it until I can't anymore. Hopefully, that's a deal?"

"You got it." Connie turned to Warren. "What do you say, hon? Ready to call it a night? I promise I'll try my best not to be *too* cranky, but if I kick you in the middle of the night, don't take it personally, I'm just so angry." She looked at Eva. "I've been dreading calling Catherine."

"You know you don't have to if you don't want to. It's nobody's business."

"I know. But still…" Connie appeared on the verge of tears. "You're the only ones who even knew we were pregnant." She looked at Warren. "I'm sorry. We should've told your parents."

"It wasn't meant to be. It's nobody's fault."

Say no more, and you're a keeper. Eva watched the twenty-year-olds—still kids—stand. "Don't worry about all of this. We'll clean it up. You get some rest," she said, watching them head toward the house, where she hoped they could get a good night's sleep despite the mugginess. Warren put an extra fan in Sam's radio room to pull a cross breeze through their bedroom window, because Connie didn't want one buzzing in her ear all night.

Halfway there, Connie turned, saying, "Don't worry. Everything will turn out A-number one."

Eva smiled broadly and agreed, "Ayutt… A-number one!"

• • •

That night, sometime before 11 p.m., Ray and Vera Whittman left The Top Hat lounge south of Sumner Falls. Full of vim and vigor—and far too many cocktails—they had been dancing, drinking, and celebrating. When they left the restaurant in Vera's Karmann Ghia, neither of them knew that Charles Stanstead was clocking out of his second shift and heading home—a drive that took him roughly half an hour on any typical worknight.

As Vera, who was driving, approached the turnoff, her inhibitions were low enough that she didn't realize she had taken the turn up the hill toward her home, which she owned but was currently renting to the Stansteads. Similarly, Ray was in the same condition.

The Whittmans parked behind the house, giggling and shuffling, laughing louder even as they shushed themselves while climbing the porch steps. They entered the house through the unlocked kitchen door. No one in Sumner Falls locked their doors. (Except Eva Martin, when she forced her husband, Sam, to move out and into the Hotel Wimmer.)

Within the hour, the muffled sounds of two gunshots dissipated into the damp night air as Virginia Stanstead desperately tried to reach a Sumner Falls operator. By the time she succeeded and Officer Poole arrived on scene, both Ray and Vera Whittman were dead.

PART III

The Killings

23

Restless during the night, her kidneys stirring her again, Eva lay awake, watching the faint red and blue lights reflect off the walls. When whispering to Sam to wake him wasn't enough, she bumped his shoulder and then rocked him until he groaned.

"Get up," she said. "Something's going on next door."

Eva and Sam Martin watched from their kitchen window as men they couldn't identify in the darkness, but who probably were part of the Sumner Falls volunteer squad, milled around the town's ambulance. Only a single bare bulb lit parts of the porch, as a dewy mist hung in the air, perhaps signaling an approaching late summer thunderstorm.

"My goodness," Eva said. "Oh, I hope nothing's happened to them." The ambulance was tight to the porch steps. "It's late enough that Charlie should be home by now. I can't tell if his car is over there or not. I wish—" Sam had read her mind. She hadn't seen him grab the birdwatching binoculars from her reading console, but he nudged her now, holding them out for her to take. "Not so dumb as you look," she said, trying to ease the tension, but realized she probably sounded bossy. "I didn't mean it that way… Did you see anything? Can you make anyone out?"

"No. Dick's over there. He was inside, but now he's outside with others looking in the grass under the window."

Eva saw their flashlights sweeping across the lawn between the kitchen window and the lilac bushes. "They're definitely looking for something in the grass over there." She flinched when someone holding one of the flashlights directed their light toward their house, flashing brightly in her magnified view.

"He can't see us," Sam said. "Our lights are off. He can't see inside."

"What the hell do you suppose they're looking for?"

"Dunno," Sam answered as the grandfather clock struck quarter past the hour, and they both startled. Neither had paused to notice the time when they left the bedroom, even though the flashing lights through the living room window would have been enough to see the clock face. "It's gotta be after midnight," he said.

"I hope all this commotion hasn't woken the kids," Eva said. "Connie needs her rest—the whole reason the poor girl wanted to stay here." Eva turned away from the sink and walked into the living room, her robe silently billowing around her legs and her slippers noiseless on the hardwood floor. She stopped and listened for any sounds coming down the stairwell, pressing her ear to the thin interior door. Hearing nothing and still unsure, she gently twisted the knob and cracked the door, listening intently. Satisfied with the silence, she closed the door and returned to the kitchen. "They must not have heard anything. I think they're still asleep. All I can hear is the fan."

"Huh."

"I said I think they're still sleeping."

Sam lowered the binoculars and looked at Eva. "No, I meant…" He heaved a sigh and repositioned the binoculars to his eyes. "The ambulance left. I can see…"

"What is it?"

Sam sighed demonstratively again. "I can see Charlie's car… but also…"

"What?" Eva whispered, barely able not to shout as she rapped his ribs with her fist.

"It's her car. *Her* car's over there, too."

"Whose car?" Eva's voice was rising well above a whisper. She was growing agitated, yet still tried to keep her voice down, knowing the ceiling register vent would carry it directly upstairs.

"You know who," Sam said. "Vera's car. It's over there now."

Eva chose not to grab the binoculars. She didn't want to see anything. What she really wanted was to pick up the phone and call Virginia to find out what was happening—whether she was okay and if Cynthia was all right, too. "We can't call over there, can we?" she asked, knowing the answer was no. "It's not our business. I don't want to get involved." It was a fool's errand to think news of this wouldn't spread throughout Sumner Falls by morning. The police would definitely come knocking, asking questions, looking for witnesses who might have heard or seen something or someone. It was only a matter of time—whether within minutes or after sunrise—before the police woke up every neighbor, looking for help and answers.

"What in God's name was she doing over there at this hour?" she asked, unable to keep her voice lowered any longer. "If she and Ray have done something here..." she trailed off. She unfolded her arms and covered her face with her hands, trying not to imagine what was happening inside that house. She really wanted to pick up that phone.

"Whoever it was," Sam said. "They must be dead. Those volunteer guys didn't look to be in any hurry whatsoever. If any of them work at the shop and they aren't too shook up to stay home, I'll get the story."

"Should we get dressed and get it over with? Go over there? Why stand here like a couple of looky-loos, awake and waiting the rest of the night for someone to come and knock?"

"I hope it was him... Ray."

Eva stared at Sam while his eyes remained focused through the binoculars. *Was he still jealous of Ray, or was he even a little remorseful?* "What if it were her? Would you finally let it go?"

Sam sighed heavily, drew a deep breath, and sighed again. "Huh... they're marching Charlie out in handcuffs."

"What?" Eva shouted, her voice clearly loud enough to wake the rest of the house. "I'm getting dressed. You can either stay or come with me, but I'm going. I'm not waiting around."

When she reached the front stairwell outside her bedroom, the door was partially open. She wasn't startled to see Warren on the landing step. "What's happening?" he asked, peering around her. "Are those police or firetruck lights next door? We didn't hear anything. Did you?"

"Police. Looks like some sort of disturbance over at the Stansteads, that's all. I wouldn't worry. Go back to bed. Is Connie awake?"

"She is now, yes."

"Oh, that's a shame. She needed her rest… Tell her it's nothing to worry about, and you both should go back to sleep. I'm getting dressed and checking on Ginny. I'll see if I can find out what's going on."

Warren nodded and closed the door after lingering a moment.

Eva listened to his retreating footsteps, and God willing, he'd soothe Connie's worries before going back to sleep.

• • •

Eva and Sam crossed the yard, avoiding stepping through the lilac bushes to prevent the officer at the foot of the Stansteads' porch from becoming defensive and possibly drawing his service revolver. Only two local cruisers remained on scene. The ambulance and the state cruiser with Charles in custody had left an hour earlier.

Sam illuminated the darkness with an Eveready lantern, giving the officer plenty of warning as they neared the house. He aimed the heavy-duty beam at the ground near their feet, occasionally lighting up their faces while keeping it out of the young officer's eyes. Once they were close enough and had introduced themselves, Eva recognized the young officer as Wendell Buchanan, one of Richard Poole's deputies, who looked relaxed despite any violence he might have seen inside the house earlier that night. He raised a hand, palm out. "That's far enough, folks," he said. "This is an active crime investigation. You should return home." Wendell was in his late twenties, pale, taller than average, with an Errol Flynn look that made him appear twice his age, complete with a swashbuckling pencil mustache.

"Wendell… Sam Martin, and this is my wife Eva. We live next door." When their introduction elicited no response, Sam added, "Your father, Olie, and I are Freemasons. I've known you since you were a rambunctious little kid. Your dad would bring you to lodge meetings. You probably don't remember me."

"Sounds like something my old man would do, but I guess I was too young. I'm afraid I don't recognize you, even though I probably should." Wendell lowered his hand and shifted his eyes to Eva, who stepped out of the shadows and more into the amber glow of the porch lightbulb. "Oh, Mrs. Martin… Eva. I wasn't familiar with your first name, but now I recognize you from Merrill's—all my high school basketball sneakers."

"When you get to be our age, you'll know everyone's name in Sumner Falls," Eva said. "And now that that's all out of the way, we couldn't help but notice there's been some goings on over here. We saw Charlie taken away," she paused, giving the young man a chance to volunteer, and when he didn't, she continued, "And I was hoping I might be able to check on Ginny? And Cindy? Inside?"

Deputy Buchanan stood firm, straightened up, and seemed to regain his composure, reminding himself that he was a law enforcement officer, not a reckless child. "I'm not sure that's a possibility tonight." He seemed hesitant to share more.

Eva widened her eyes in a moment of panic, her cheeks flushing. There was no mistaking Vera's car, parked a few yards from where they stood. "That's Vera Flynn's car. Why would you be arresting Charlie Stanstead, if not…"

"You mean"—he pulled a notepad from his back pocket and flipped it open—"Vera Whittman? You recognize this vehicle as belonging to Mrs. Whittman?"

"Of course," both Eva and Sam said. "She was our neighbor for years, and we know she still owns this house, but she has no business being here," Eva said, wondering if she'd said too much, judging from the interested expression on the officer's face. In the dim light, it wasn't a stretch to see his peaked brows.

"It's a small town, Wendell," Sam said, pointing at the Karmann Ghia. "It's probably the only one around for miles. And it's the same color as Vera's."

"How do you know the two bodies removed weren't…" He referred to his notepad again.

"What *two* bodies?" Eva shouted, grabbing for Sam.

"Maybe you *should* talk with the lead detective after all. It'd be a good idea to give your statement tonight rather than wait until tomorrow."

"It *is* the morning," Eva reminded him. "And yes, I'd like to speak to Dick… Officer Poole! And inside, if you don't mind. I'll take my chances if Vera and Ray are the ones being interrogated in there."

"Wait here, then. I'll go and let him know you're out here." Before heading into the house, Deputy Buchanan jotted something in his notepad, closed it, and slipped it into his pocket. When he returned shortly after, he told Eva she could go inside, but Sam had to stay with him.

Inside, Eva was relieved to see Virginia and Cynthia. "Ginny, I'm so sorry. I wanted to—"

"Do you have something to be sorry about, Eva?" Richard Poole asked her. "I'd like to ask you some questions about Ray and Vera Whittman."

"Dick, can't it wait? For God's sake, you know where we live and where I work. It's not like we're going anywhere." Eva turned her attention to Virginia, placing a hand on her shoulder, and with the other, she brushed Cynthia's hair, noticing how thin and matted it was between her fingers. The girl had been crying, and Eva could feel her trembling, despite being held tightly against her mother. Eva knelt and asked sincerely, "What happened?"

Richard coughed and blurted, "Eva, may I remind you that this is an active investigation, and Mrs. Stanstead and Cynthia are witnesses. If I need to remove them from the home to question them at the station further, I will."

Cynthia Stanstead pushed away from her mother and whispered, "Ne dis rien!" She wiped her eyes and her face with her sleeve, thrusting her nose toward Officer Poole. *Don't say anything!*

"What did she say?" he asked, adding, "I know she speaks French. Charles said something to her in French, earlier… in the bedroom." He riffled through a few pages in his notepad. "He said he told her not to worry. But I have to admit…" he trailed off, staring hard at both of them as if gauging their truthfulness. "Your husband is French Canadian? Are you and Cynthia also Canadian? I assume you speak French as well? Your driver's license lists a home address in Springfield. To my ear, none of you has an accent."

Virginia Stanstead patted her daughter's arm and nodded subtly. "So many questions," she said, turning and looking up at him.

He looked at the spot on the kitchen floor where the state police had taken a blood sample from beneath the deceased Vera Whittman's head. Only a few rust discolorations remained in the linoleum creases. "Under the circumstances…" he said.

Eva followed his eyes to the floor. *The circumstances here were certainly not as simple as a flat tire or a speeding ticket.*

"Yes, Charlie was born in… c'mon, you're the detective… Stanstead, Quebec, but I was born here. Not in Sumner Falls… I mean, in Vermont. We met inside the Haskell Free Library, of all places. I was raised in Derby Line, born in Newport. Cynthia was born in Bellows Falls. I learned enough French to get by. Charles insisted on Cindy being fluent."

"What did you tell your mother?" he asked, looking directly at the scared young girl.

"She told me what you said before… don't worry," Virginia answered.

Richard, always suspicious of everyone and everything, looked genuinely suspicious. "It would be greatly appreciated if everyone could keep things in English." He turned to Eva and asked, "Did you hear anything tonight?" He again glanced at Virginia from his notepad. "You called the town switchboard just before midnight. You told the operator that a man and a woman had broken into your house and started a fight with your husband? I assume you already knew the Whittmans since you're renting their house."

"Hers," Eva said. "Not theirs."

"Again, Eva, I'll ask the questions." His chastising expression did little to intimidate Eva, who knew his bark was worse than his bite.

"You didn't report any gunshots. Why not?" he continued asking Virginia. He cocked his head, darting his eyes between the women. "Eva? Did you hear gunshots last night around midnight? Or at any time before then? And I'll remind you, we'll be interviewing Sam and the other neighbors."

"We were asleep. I didn't hear anything. I woke up around midnight to go to the bathroom. That's when I noticed the flashing lights streaming through the windows and woke Sam."

Eva followed his glance, and it didn't take long before she spotted what he appeared to be so interested in—a small tear in the window screen above the sink.

Richard moved across the kitchen and, using his pen, he pointed to the small rip. "How many times did you say your husband discharged the .22 rifle he was *still* holding when we arrived?"

"Twice."

"Mère…" Cynthia balked when Officer Poole glared at her. "Mother…"

"Charles said he shot Ray in the back bedroom. You both claim the Whittmans were intoxicated, and somehow, despite them claiming they'd made a mistake—a wrong turn—they then managed to turn irate, becoming aggressive, demanding you move out and give them their—her—house back? Do I have that right so far? Then Charles comes into the kitchen, sees Vera threatening you, and fires again. So twice… two gunshots." He looked at Eva again, and she could see his face was incredulous. "And you're trying to tell me that you heard nothing? Not a one?"

Eva didn't flinch. "Not a *one*… Our bedroom is on the south side of the house. And we've had window fans running all night. Can you blame us?"

Poole dismissed her question. "It's common knowledge around town that there's no love lost between you and Vera. Isn't that right?"

Apprehensive, Eva could feel him coaxing. She didn't give in and only curled the corners of her lips. She wasn't about to tell him she was tickled pink that Vera got what was coming to her. *Ray might not have deserved this outcome, but he should have made wiser choices.*

"We only found one spent casing in the bedroom. Seems there ought to be another between here and there." He gestured with his pen between the bedroom and the kitchen. "Seems *highly* plausible, wouldn't you say so?"

"Officer?" Virginia asked. "Could we please continue this later today? We're exhausted." She rubbed her daughter's back, who nuzzled her face into Virginia's armpit. "And I think we should speak with a lawyer."

Eva's face lit up as she finally heard something sensible. "That's a damn good idea, Ginny. You should talk to Carl Alderman. He's local and has an office in town on this side of the diner."

The porch door swung open, and Wendell Buchanan peeked into the kitchen, yawning. He rubbed his eyes, which only darkened the circles under them, and took off his cap. "Mr. Poole? Sir." He signaled with his fingers, motioning Richard to come hither. "Mr. Martin wants to know how things stand. He's getting antsy. Wants to know why his wife is in here taking so long?"

"Tell 'em I'll be right out. I have one question I'd like to ask him before we wrap things up here." Richard waited until Wendell stepped out and then faced the women. "Virginia… I know it's late, and I'm genuinely sorry to have kept you and Cynthia for so long. I'm sure you understand the circumstances, but I'm afraid this is still an active crime scene, which means you and your daughter can't stay here. Not until further notice. Do you have any family or friends in town that you can stay with?"

Virginia rested her chin on top of Cynthia's head, gently stroking the outside of one of her earlobes. She almost looked mournful, as if Charles had been murdered. After a brief moment, she kissed her daughter's head and turned away, appearing as if she were pondering who might take them in tonight with the fewest questions. "I could probably ask a girlfriend or a former co-worker down in Springfield. Someone who doesn't have kids… Give me a moment to think."

"Is there anyone local, Mrs. Stanstead? I'd rather you not leave town," Richard said. He rested his fists on his utility belt, which revealed a farmer's tan beneath his uniform's short sleeves.

Eva couldn't wait any longer, watching Virginia mentally struggle through the fog of exhaustion. She crouched low, bending at the knee to get Virginia's undivided attention. "Don't be silly, Ginny. You'll stay with us. There's no need to worry about driving somewhere at this ungodly hour. Besides, you're in no shape to drive, period. We've got plenty of food."

"Oh, that's so gracious of you." Virginia looked up at Richard and asked, "Can we at least pack a bag? How long will this take? School starts in another couple of weeks."

Virginia's eyes appeared glassy to Eva, and she wasn't sure if Virginia might have a spell or go into shock. She stood up, a little lightheaded, and turned to Richard. "I'll help her pack an overnight bag while you go talk to Sam. I know what you're going to ask him. And the answer is none."

"I'm afraid you cannot enter the back bedroom. I hope you can find what you need either upstairs or in the basement. I'll send Wendell inside to—"

"Really? Does he need to watch a lady pack *one* overnight bag with *ladies'* clothes?" Eva turned to Virginia. "Do you need anything at all from the bedroom?"

"No. Cindy's things are upstairs in her room, and I have clean laundry downstairs… I don't need or *want* to see the bedroom."

"Good enough?" Eva asked Richard. "I'll sit with the girl."

"Fine. But you'll wait for Wendell." Richard hesitated until he seemed satisfied that Virginia Stanstead wasn't heading toward the back bedroom. Then he quietly slipped out, closing the screen door discreetly.

Virginia looked pained. "I have to pee," she said. "I don't think I can wait."

"Then go, now!" Eva insisted.

Virginia let go of Cynthia and slipped into the bathroom.

Eva crouched low in front of Cynthia, her knees tight and her blue jeans stretched so snug that she felt something poking her backside. She knelt on the floor, easing some of the pressure, and slipped her hand into her back pocket, touching something small and metallic lodged in the seam stitching. *How on earth did that not come out in the wash?*

Eva carefully pinched the top and bottom of the tiny cylindrical object between her thumb and index finger with her right hand. With her left hand, she pulled Cynthia's face into her chest and wrapped her arm as best as she could around the girl's ears, cradling her neck in the crook of her elbow. Eva glanced at the interior doorway, then at the screen door. *If Dick needed two, then Dick would get his two.* She took the spent .22 brass casing from her pocket and rolled it under the stove. She let go of Cynthia and pressed a finger to her lips.

"J'ai rien entendu," Cynthia whispered. *I didn't hear anything.*

Wendell Buchanan pulled open the screen and stepped inside just as Virginia flushed. "Hey!" He glanced at Eva and Cynthia, then Virginia as she came out of the bathroom. "You're not supposed to be in there! Did you touch anything? Did you flush something?"

Virginia raised her hands, surrendering. "I had to pee. I was desperate!"

"Would you rather she go in her britches or on the kitchen floor?" Eva asked him.

"No. Of course not." He looked at Cynthia, shamefaced. "I'm sorry I yelled."

Virginia lowered her hands. "I'll be down in a minute after I grab a few of Cindy's things. Officer Poole said it was okay."

"I know."

Outside, everyone seemed content to call it a night, watching the gray skies to the east where the sun would soon rise over the New Hampshire hills. Richard reminded them, "I'll give you all a chance to get some rest, but we'll be back in a few hours with more questions." He took a deep breath, looked at Cynthia, then added, "Perhaps we can wait until after lunch."

"What will happen to Charlie tonight?" Virginia asked. She turned to Eva and said, "I'll need to call… Carl? His office probably doesn't open until later. I don't even know what time…" She started to cry. Cynthia hugged her low around the waist, while Eva hugged her shoulders.

"He might have an after-hours answering service," Richard said. "But I can't be sure." He looked at Wendell, who shook his head and shrugged. "Charles will stay in holding until the county offices open, then he'll be transferred and booked into custody, pending a judge's hearing. That's when you'll need to secure the services of a lawyer."

"Thanks, Dick," Sam said, motioning the women toward the Martin house. "Will you call before you come down tomorrow… well… later?"

"Sure. I'll give you a heads-up call. I can't guarantee a set time. We'll be interviewing some of the other adjacent neighbors."

"How long do you think the police will need the house?" Virginia asked. "Does anyone with the police…" She struggled with her words. "Take care of… or… clean?"

"I'm afraid not, but I'm sure someone in the department or county can help you locate someone." Richard looked at Wendell again, who seemed more positive this time, nodding once. "The state police will send a larger team sometime after daybreak. Once they sign off on the completed evidence collection, then—"

Virginia buckled at the waist, clasping her hands as if praying to the officers. "It was self-defense! That means he's innocent, right?"

Deputy Buchanan turned away, exhaling, while Officer Poole remained stoic. "I've already taken your statement, Mrs. Stanstead. All I can offer at this time is to encourage you to try and get some rest, have something to eat, and then make that call to Mr. Alderman, as Mrs. Martin has suggested. It's good advice. You should take it." Richard turned to Wendell. "I think we've done all we can tonight. Let's go."

"Wait," Sam said. "What about the car?"

Wendell answered this time, "I'll put in a call with town maintenance. Buster will come and tow it wherever the state police want it impounded. Up to them if they want to look it over."

Eva was relieved that she would never see that car, Vera, or Ray again. *Good riddance.* As she walked across the yard, she looked up at the darkening sky, praying she wouldn't learn where their bodies had been buried. It would be a shame to disturb the graves so that she could dig them up and stomp all over their—her—bones.

As they reached the steps, Smokey jumped out of the Stinking Benjamins onto the concrete footer, where he sat proudly at attention. Eva was happy to see him and relieved that he hadn't brought home any dead presents from his overnight hunting grounds. He didn't fuss when Cynthia scooped him up in her arms, purring and rubbing cheek to cheek.

24

Virginia didn't resist when Eva offered her and Sam's bed for the rest of the early morning. Mother, daughter, and cat had climbed in, and all were snoring softly before their trio of heads hit the sheets. Sam took the living room couch, and Eva settled into her reading chair, where she now sat, watching the birds sing and dance and welcoming the sunrise. She couldn't stop staring across the yard at the empty house—at the kitchen window. She wished Buster would hurry up and get rid of that hideous car—one less reminder to look at. She turned and realized the upstairs door was still closed and wondered how on earth they hadn't woken Connie and Warren. She had no idea how she would handle the upcoming sleeping arrangements. Somehow, she had to convince Connie they'd be better off going home to their apartment without revealing too many details about last night.

Smokey emerged from the front bedroom and casually made his way to Eva's chair. He sat patiently, looking up at her as if he were waiting for a divine invitation. She finally relented, rubbing her fingers together, and he jumped onto her lap, using her as a step to the windowsill. Eva didn't want to think of the birds as his breakfast, and when his tail swishing caused her crocheted doily to fall to the floor, she pulled him onto her lap and distracted him with some chin scritches.

She didn't want to wake anyone, but it was close to coffee time. "Psst," she whispered to Sam, still breathing rhythmically on the couch. She couldn't tell if he was in a deep sleep or resting his eyes. *Probably the latter.* She bent down to pick up the doily while holding Smokey in place with her other hand, and when she tossed the doily toward Sam's chest, the cat jumped down. She didn't care if the thud of Smokey's paws landing on the hardwood or the doily landing on his chin woke him. He must have been in a deeper sleep, judging by how both his legs and arms shot up like he was a dead animal on its back.

"What the…" he grunted and tried to sit up. "For God's sake," he said, dabbing at his face and finding the doily. It took him a moment to focus, and when he seemed to realize the piece of linen hadn't fallen from the ceiling, he sat up and looked around.

"Morning," Eva whispered. "Are you gonna sleep all day or what?"

Sam looked at her and sighed heavily. Their eyes locked as if they were trying to read each other's minds or decide who would speak first. Sam composed himself and said, with a gravelly voice, "I guess I'll go downstairs and make the coffee."

"That would be good. Maybe see if he'll go with you," she said, gesturing toward Smoky, who apparently took the hint and dashed toward the kitchen, making a sharp left down the stairs, his claws skidding on the floor. "I guess he understands English."

"I guess so."

After Sam left the room, Eva sat back, wondering if she'd made a mistake. *What if the other casing is under the stove or the fridge, and in her haste, she made things worse?*

She needed to talk to Virginia over coffee or tea. Earl Grey was downstairs if that's her preference. Listening to her side of the story, especially what Charles might have said, was something that had to be addressed before Richard arrived, looking for more answers. She had the idea of putting Virginia at ease when Cynthia appeared, yawning.

"Good morning, sleepyhead. How're you doing? Okay?"

"Okay, I guess. Mom's still sleeping. When can I see my dad?"

Eva was overwhelmed, not knowing the truth, and she didn't want to lie. Heck, she didn't know this young girl beyond the fact that she seemed like a good kid—at least she carried herself well, and was clearly intelligent. Maybe someday she'd teach them all a little bit of French. But for now, she focused on Cynthia's striped pajamas. "I dunno, Tiger. Hopefully, soon… Does your mom like coffee or tea?"

"They drink coffee in the afternoon at lunchtime before my dad leaves for work. He takes a thermos of coffee with him, too. Is that a fireplace? We've never lived in a house with a fireplace before."

"Yes, it most certainly is. Too hot for a fire now, though, wouldn't you agree?" Cynthia's hair looked even flatter than it did a few hours ago. Eva couldn't remember if Connie had oily hair as a youngster. There was only one person who could help with hair, Alice, and she would call her after everyone was dressed.

"Oui, très chaud." *Yes, very hot.*

"So, I take it you and your parents speak French at home? All the time?"

"No, not really." Cynthia moved to the couch and sat, facing the fireplace. "My dad taught me French. My mom speaks English. He and I will sometimes try to keep secrets from Mom in French, but… she's caught on recently."

"So last night you told your Mom something… in French."

"I said not to say anything." Cynthia looked around the living room, then got down on her hands and knees and looked under the couch. When she sat up, she asked, "Where's the kitty cat? The gray one. She slept on my pillow for a while."

"That would be Smokey, and he's a he… and I'm pretty sure he's down cellar with Mr. Martin. I suppose he's helping him make a pot of coffee… You must be getting hungry."

"Kind of. I'd better wait for Mom. I'll go wake her up."

"Wait, not quite yet… Last night, you told Mr. Poole that your Dad told you not to worry?" Eva asked, smiling warmly, trying to look disarming.

"I was scared."

"I bet you were. I'm really sorry you had to see that. I can't imagine how scared you must've been. And it's *not* your fault that you got caught in the middle of grown-ups who were arguing."

Cynthia pulled her knees to her chest and rubbed her face between her kneecaps, perhaps scratching her nose. Without making eye contact, she said, "I was scared, and he told me not to worry." Eva sensed she was bending the truth.

•••

When Eva called the shoe store and asked Merrill for a sick day, he didn't hesitate. He told her to drink plenty of water and hoped her kidneys would feel better tomorrow.

She called Alice next, catching her before she headed out to open the salon. She debated whether to tell her it would be okay to bring Impy along, ultimately deciding to do so in the hope that she'd keep Cynthia busy after letting Smokey outside. Alice agreed, eager to establish two future paying customers for the salon.

Whether it was the smell of coffee or the sound of voices rising from the floor vent, Connie and Warren eventually made their way downstairs fully dressed. Warren carried an armful of bedsheets, and Connie had her purse and a couple of skirts from her closet slung over her arm. "I think we'd better be getting along," she said. After noticing Cynthia sitting on the braided throw rug she, Eva, and Ruby had sewn together years ago, she knelt next to her and looked at Eva, confusion on her face.

Eva was equally confused. "You didn't hear all the commotion last night? Next door?"

Connie looked up at Warren, who shrugged and offered to take Connie's skirts with a free hand. "I must've been out of it… You?"

Warren shifted his gaze between Connie and Eva. The downturned corners of his lips and his doe eyes made him look like he was caught with his hand in Ruby's doughnut jar. "I came downstairs around midnight. Your mom mentioned there were a couple of police cars outside. I assumed I woke you when I got up, but you were dead to the world by the time I came upstairs."

Virginia stepped in from the kitchen, Sam close behind, both holding coffee mugs. Virginia had to steady her grip with both hands, looking startled to see Connie and her husband all dressed. She jumped, nearly spilling her coffee when the grandfather clock chimed.

Eva wished she had time to talk to Connie, but the police would arrive soon. "So you're feeling better? It doesn't feel like we had time to…" she trailed off. When Connie nodded, she tried to smile warmly. Her kidneys ached along with her heart, but she needed Connie and Warren out of the house before Officer Poole called or appeared unannounced, the latter causing her anxiety deep in her gut and kidneys. "We'll talk later, but you two should skedaddle. There's no need for you to get caught up in all of this." She reached for the bedsheets and told Warren he'd better go and bring the Corvair out front. He didn't need to be told twice.

Connie stood and hugged Eva, wrapping her arms tightly around her mother's neck and back, pressing the pile of bedsheets between their chests. When she loosened her hold, Eva felt the familiar touch of Connie's fingertip, tracing their initials on the nape of her neck.

A knock at the front door interrupted their conversation, prompting Eva to gather the sheets. She hoped like hell it was Alice, but she huffed when Henry appeared on the steps with Alice and Impy partly hidden behind him. If her mother were there too, she was sure to have a spell. "Now is not a good time, Dad. We've got company."

When Impy yipped once, and Cynthia ran into view, he said, "Well, I should say so."

The mosquitoes and black flies had burned off in the heat, but Eva never took chances, telling Henry to either come inside or get going before he let any bugs in.

"Isn't that Warren out back with his car?" He smiled at Connie and asked, "Are you comin' or goin'?"

"We're going. We just spent the night."

Henry's ears perked up like a beagle catching a scent. "Oh?"

Eva grew anxious. There were too many people inside and outside, not to mention the neighborhood's eyes on them for an early weekday. "Step aside, let Al in, she's here to do our hair."

Henry turned and pulled his pipe. "Well… should I send your mother over? She was dressed before the sun was up."

Eva grunted. It felt like someone was jabbing her lower back with her own fireplace poker. Everyone's shoes tracking in was grating. She couldn't focus on when she could vacuum again. "Nope. Al's only got time for Ginny and Cindy. We'll stop over later for a chat." Skeptical, that wasn't good enough to satisfy her father. "Why don't you see if Mom's in the mood to make supper this afternoon? Tell her to put out six place settings—no need to use the good Buffalo. We'll have plenty to talk about then, but in the meantime…" She didn't want to tell him to go away and let the women talk, so she waved him off, smiling, and hoped he wouldn't pout like a petulant child.

"Alright…" He looked skeptical. "I'll dig out the table leaf." He bit on his pipestem, then took it out of his mouth and pointed it at her. "What about Sam?"

"He's about to get on the radio."

Henry Fischer's face scrunched. He looked like a pouting, petulant little boy after all. "Fine. I'll leave ya be."

Warren pulled his Corvair along the front wall, and Connie stepped outside. She kissed Henry on the cheek. "C'mon, Gramps. Walk me down to the car." She hooked her arm around his elbow, and he seemed to transform, proudly smiling. She returned the gesture, inhaling the scent of apple tobacco on his shirt.

"So who wants to be pampered first?" Alice asked.

"Me!" shouted Cynthia, dashing toward the bathroom.

Virginia, clearly embarrassed, tried to snatch at her daughter's arm playfully. "Not in the bathtub. Today—"

"Today," Alice interrupted, "you get to be a big girl and sit in a chair and lean over the sink, and we'll pretend you're at the salon."

Eva couldn't help but chuckle, releasing nervous energy. "Almost seems like we've come full circle. I remember us giving Connie a bath in the kitchen sink." She felt a pressure building behind her eyes. To think that Connie was due in March, around Sam's birthday, which she hoped would end his stretch of grumpy episodes during mud season. Visions of raising twins were now dashed. Feeling sorry for herself would have to wait for another day. "We should probably call Carl while Cindy's busy."

• • •

Eva's gut instinct was correct; Officer Richard Poole did not call before stopping by the house. He arrived at Vera's alongside another police vehicle. He entered through the back, followed by two men. Their green uniforms identified them as state police, and each carried what looked like a metal toolbox rather than the leather medical bag Dr. Read used.

Alice finished rinsing Virginia's hair and grabbed a towel. "What in the world…" she said, looking through the window and across the yard. "Is that the police? Virginia, I think the—"

Eva took the towel from Alice and handed it to Virginia. She was relieved to see that Buster must have come not too long after they'd left and removed Vera's car. It was one less thing she had to explain to her friend. "Ginny and Cindy had to sleep here last night."

Alice Fairbanks seemed frozen, unable to tear her eyes away from the police cars. When she finally turned to look at Eva and at Virginia, who struggled to sit up without a helping hand, she said, "What…" She glanced behind, then through the window. "Where…"

Eva realized she was counting heads.

"Where's Charlie?" Alice asked. "Has he gone to work already? Isn't it too early?"

"You'd better sit down," Eva urged her, motioning toward a kitchen chair. "Something terrible happened last night." She could see that Alice's pallor had turned nearly as gray as her hair. "Vera and Ray came down last night, and things got out of hand."

Eva retold the events of the previous evening, leaving the devoutly religious Alice Fairbanks anguished. Red capillary streaks spiderwebbed across her cheeks. "Did Charlie really do it?" she asked Eva.

"Yes and no. It's complicated." It was Eva's turn to stare across the yard and through her lilacs, wondering if they'd found what she left behind. *Would it change the investigation? Would Richard be satisfied that it was self-defense?* Ultimately, she realized, it wasn't up to him. She looked at Virginia, gave her a moment to say something, then said, "We called Carl this morning, and he's gathering what he can before we drive up and talk to him a bit later. Dick told us he'd be checking in this morning."

No one heard Sam behind them, but Alice was still on edge enough to jump with her hand over her heart when he cleared his throat. He went to the kitchen window, holding up a larger pair of hunting binoculars. "I dunno what the hell they're doing over there that they didn't get last night. But I can see Dick and the two staties in the kitchen."

"What are they up to?" Eva asked.

Sam adjusted the binoculars, which had a higher magnification than the smaller set Eva kept on her console for birdwatching. "It's hard to see through the lilac bushes. Looks like they're just standing there. Dick's pointing at the window… wait… looks like they're leaving." Sam lowered the field glasses, then raised them again. "Guess Buster took the car already. I wish I'd stayed awake and seen him."

"What for?" Eva bellowed. "What do you care?"

"It would've been interesting to know where… oh, never mind."

Everyone stood looking, two faces to a window. Without the binoculars, Eva didn't know who was who, only that Dick's uniform was black and the two state troopers' were dark green.

"What are they doing now?" Alice asked.

"They seem to be poking around under the kitchen window again," Sam said. "They're pointing at the window and looking at the ground below."

"They already looked out there last night with flashlights," Eva said, huffing. She had seen the small tear in the window's mesh, and it must be what Dick was showing them.

"I think one of the staties found something," Sam announced. "Looks like he's digging at something… handing it to Dick now… oh, shit."

"Samuel," Alice said. "Not in front of Cindy."

"What is it?" Eva asked him. "What do you see?"

Sam lowered the binoculars and looked at Eva. He sighed, huffed, and sighed again. Eva knew he was stalling. "It looked like a golf ball. I dunno. It was small and had dirt on it."

"You know damn well what a golf ball looks like." Eva snatched the glasses from his hands and looked for herself. Whatever it was, it was now hidden in a bag, and one of the troopers placed it in his box. "Vera brought over a whole bagful of your practice balls… I guess she missed one." She handed him the binoculars after seeing Dick head toward their yard. He'd be at the door in about a minute. "Al, why don't you take Impy and Cindy out the front door and go for a walk? Go on, be quick about it."

•••

Sam signaled Eva to open the back door after Alice slipped out the front. "Richard… long time no see," she said, noticing his stone face devoid of humor in her greeting.

"May I come in?"

"Of course." Eva held the door while he climbed the steps into the Martins' kitchen.

"Where's my husband?" Virginia blurted out, sounding more angry than curious. "What have you done with him?"

Eva tried to shield her by stepping between them, but she was too heavy for Eva to restrain, yet she easily kept her at arm's length. Her determination grew stronger when Cynthia appeared from behind and wrapped her arms around her midsection.

"I want to know where he is."

Officer Poole removed his cap. "Mrs. Stanstead… your husband Charles is currently housed in the Woodstock county jail."

"For how long?"

Richard studied their faces, including a glance at Cynthia, whose anger and fear swept over her face in waves. "From what I've been told, as of this morning, he waived his right to counsel and signed a full confession. He'll be arraigned before a county judge in a day or two." He then looked at Eva and asked, "Have you spoken with Carl Alderman yet?"

"By phone, yes. We have an appointment today. Sam and I will take her."

He shifted to the girl, then to Eva. "I'd recommend finding a sitter for young Cindy."

"Ayutt. Will do."

Richard brushed the top of his cap, almost out of habit, since it showed no dust or dandruff. His uniform looked pressed and starched, with his badge and shoes polished. Today must be his first and only order of business. He replaced his cap and nodded once before turning, then hesitated. "I said I'd have more questions for you all, but as of now, I guess I'm satisfied until the state has run some comparison forensics on all the evidence collected last night and this morning."

"This morning?" Sam asked.

He turned and faced them all, focusing again on Eva. "We believe we've found what we needed, but it will take a day or two for the forensic lab in Montpelier to process everything." He pointed halfheartedly, as if he had forgotten something. "If you don't mind, could you stop by the station today? It doesn't matter if it's before or after your meeting with Carl. We need to cross our T's and dot our I's, and that includes collecting your fingerprints for cross-reference."

Eva forced herself to keep her breathing shallow. She didn't even want to blink until Richard released his locked stare on her. When he finally looked away, waiting for any objections, she took in a deep breath as quietly as she dared. It was clear to her they had found what she had left behind. Nonetheless, she wasn't about to start fishing. "No skin off our noses," she said.

"My prints must already be on file," Sam said, "with the National Guard."

"Army or Air?" Richard asked curiously.

"Army."

"So you've had arms training."

Eva chuckled, recalling Sam's near-miss with buck fever at point-blank range using a shotgun slug. "He can barely hit the broad side of a barn. Our friends, the Hoisingtons, will vouch for that. As a matter of fact, the only things he ever shot were pars on the golf course."

Richard pulled a notepad from his back pocket and jotted down something before putting it away. "Good to know." The binoculars on the countertop drew his attention. "Those look pretty hefty. What are you spying on?" He seemed focused across the yard. "All I see are feeders full of birds and not much else beyond the bushes."

Sam moved the field glasses out of reach. "We were just watching. That's all."

"So to be clear… You need *my* fingerprints?" Eva asked. "Did you speak to the Mootes next door? Did they hear or see anything last night?"

"I did… and they did not."

It was Eva's turn to glare and wait for an answer.

"And we decided not to ask them for prints."

"And why not?"

"Because Eva… despite Mr. Stanstead's confession, along with the on-going evidential analysis"—Richard darted his eyes between them—"you and you both have a history with the victims. And from where I'm standing, you both have motive. So, until Mr. Stanstead enters a plea with the court, I will continue to investigate their homicides to the best of my abilities. I said I wasn't asking you any questions today, but I'm changing my mind. Will we find your fingerprints inside the house? And do not ask me whose house."

Eva's heart rate soared, and she hoped any color on her face was from the rising temperature and humidity. Her thumbprint was probably on the base of the .22 casing when she pushed it into the chamber of Henry's single-shot Savage, but after all the laundry washings since she'd picked it up off the kitchen floor, she had no idea. She was about to sputter when, from behind Virginia, a whisper came: "Ne dis rien." *Don't say anything.*

"No, you won't," Sam interjected, silencing the monster inside Eva. It had always demanded an answer to the question she wanted to ask but dared not. *Had Sam ever been inside her house? In her bed?*

Sam reiterated, "Neither one of us has been inside that house." He turned to Eva, looking her in the eye. "Not once—ever."

"Would you submit yourselves to a polygraph?"

Before either answered, Virginia said, "I think we'll talk to Mr. Alderman before we say anything else. And now it looks like I need to somehow find a sitter before heading into town."

Officer Poole showed himself out, but not before letting them all know he'd be in touch within a few days once the forensic lab report came back.

"How am I gonna find a sitter on such short notice?"

"No need to worry about that. Let's walk over to my folks' place. They'll have fresh coffee and, I'm sure, my mother has already made muffins. She's on a blueberry kick. They'll watch Cindy for you. I bet my father will keep her busy, put her to work picking berries."

"What will you tell them?"

"Dunno. I guess we'll have to figure something out."

"Do they know about—"

"Sam's little affair? Ayutt."

"But last night?"

"Dunno. But leave it up to my father to be nosy. Nothing goes on around here that he doesn't know about."

Eva's Daily Reminder 1964: August 18, Tuesday

Sunny. Humid.

Ding Dong the Witch is Dead!

Ginny and Cindy staying with us until further notice. Gave them my bedroom. Smokey seems to enjoy Cindy's company.

Asked Merrill for the week off. Carolyn and their daughter off to Boston for a few days.

Mom and Dad watched Cindy when we drove upstreet to talk to lawyer.

Mom made beef stew in her biggest pot. Not much appetite. Lots of leftovers.

After supper Sam and I went upstairs. His lovemaking is on the kaput again. Just the same as before. I can't understand it. We both wanted each other but nothing could be done about it. It makes you exhausted physically.

Also I've coughed every night and guess I am bushed. Chest still hurts. We both dozed off and came down at 9:45. Watched TV and went back to bed 10:45. Coughed again!

Hope to have a talk with Cindy.

25

Carl Alderman was a curmudgeon in his mid-sixties, with a wet-straw-colored beard that hid his age. He was tall, over six feet, and used his wingspan to become an expert fly fisherman, which is where he could be found most weekends, wading in Vermont's babbling brooks and streams. With such a demanding hobby and writing for the New England Outdoor Writers Association, it wasn't too hard to understand why he was a life-long bachelor. In his younger years, he was a sports beat writer for the Rutland Herald, covering high school sports. He was an easy man to spot, always with a pen and pad, a Pentax camera around his neck, and a cigar butt in his mouth. He once bragged that he smoked them by the bushel. His signature outfit always included a cigar-brown tweed jacket, complete with suede elbow patches, which he wore when he answered the knock at his office door.

"Come in," he said.

As Eva entered, she watched him slip his cigar into a thin metal tube, which he deposited into his jacket lapel pocket. "Howdy," she said.

"Good afternoon, come on in, sit down, please." When Sam followed last, he apologized for not having enough chairs, then extended his hand to Virginia. "You must be Mrs. Stanstead?" He shook her hand. "The Martins, I'm acquainted with."

When he shook Virginia's hand, Eva hoped his fingers weren't sticky with cigar spit.

"So…" he said, rearranging some paperwork on his desk. Eva and Virginia settled into the two Hitchcock chairs opposite him. "After our call this morning, I had a chance to call the courthouse in Woodstock and speak to the clerk." He placed two legal pads in front of him; one with judicious notes and the other blank. "It seems your husband,"—he glanced at his notes—"Charles, waived his right to my counsel already and foolishly—in my opinion—signed a confession. Now, unless I can convince him to recant and plead not guilty, I'll have time to prepare a defense. Otherwise, if he decides to plead guilty, I'm afraid my services can only help temper the judge's sentence. It's up to you."

Virginia Stanstead, against her daughter's insistence that she not say a word, said, "There's something I'd like to confess." She turned to Eva. "I'm sorry."

"Don't say another word, Mrs. Stanstead. If you choose to retain my services for yourself—*or*—your husband, I'll need to ask the Martins to step outside."

Carl Alderman stood and pointed toward the door, smiling warmly. The discoloration of his teeth wasn't quite as charming as his jacket, which he buttoned as he got to his feet.

"I understand. Yes… I need your legal advice."

Eva had no idea what was happening, but she kept her mouth shut while Sam, who still seemed to be holding a grudge, led her out.

• • •

Sam wanted to linger, but Eva persuaded him to wait next door at the Sumner Falls diner over coffee instead of standing around the cramped hallway outside Carl's office.

"Did she mention anything this morning while I was upstairs?" Sam asked. "When Al was here?"

"No. Certainly nothing worth paying attention to." Eva sipped her black coffee while watching the sporadic afternoon traffic along Main Street. Sitting in a booth of the old railway car, she struggled to recall what, if anything, Virginia might have said while Alice was shampooing and doing everyone's hair. Her heart had been preoccupied with the little girl's well-being, who was clinging to her mother like glue. "She wouldn't say anything alarming in front of Cindy. The poor girl must still be in shock. Whatever happened in that house is something no child should ever have to experience." She couldn't help but think about Connie, who was so close to losing Sam over such a stupid and selfish mistake on his part. What Cynthia must be going through cannot be compared. "I hope she's making out okay with my folks."

"Henry's probably got her outside, putting her to work, painting the house, getting some fresh air. But knowing your mother…" Sam added a dollop more cream to his mug before taking a sip. "She's got her mixing dough, or showing her how to make hermit cookies."

Eva did not envision either scenario as helpful.

The diner was sparsely filled. It was after the lunch rush and before the early-bird specials, leaving Eva and Sam alone with only a few second-shift workers from the machine shop sitting at the counter. Eva didn't care to keep tabs on who they were, despite Sam's obvious nosiness as he tried to get glimpses of their faces from behind. She was about to tell him to mind his beeswax when Wendell Buchanan entered the diner, removed his officer's cap, and hung it on the coat rack attached to the end of the counter near the cash register. He was about to slide onto the first stool when he hesitated, then walked over to their booth.

"Afternoon," Wendell said, squaring up to the booth and placing his fists on his utility belt.

"Good 'n you?" Eva said.

"Can't say I blame you for wanting to get away from the house."

"Oh, merely taking a break from the lawyer," she said, realizing Wendell looked like a bad imitation of George Reeves' Superman. "Ginny's next door talking to Carl Alderman."

"Wise decision."

Eva wanted to say, "Alrighty, then…" two words that every Martin knew signaled the end of any conversation, when Sam interjected, "So, Wendell, what Masonic degree does Olie have you prepared for next?"

Wendell Buchanan shook his head, rolled his eyes, and seemed to relax as he dropped his arms to his sides. "I went along with the first, but no offense, Freemasonry is an older man's thing. I'm not really into waiting around. And it's expensive, paying for degrees of enlightenment. I don't get it… The brotherhood of police—that I get. Again, no offense, and I know you and my father are third-degree master masons, but…" He shrugged. "I'll probably bow out after this case sugars off."

Eva glanced out the booth's window up and down the sidewalk. "We didn't catch Dick following you in…"

"Yeah, he's a bit tied up at the station doing paperwork." Wendell glanced sideways. "I bet you didn't know we spend more time writing reports than we do on real crime. Every time I have to chase off loitering kids outside Stony's Market and The Block, it costs me twice as much time sitting behind a typewriter."

Eva did not challenge him; her nearly finished, cooled coffee was what she was concerned about, along with why Virginia was taking so long. "No doubt," she said.

"Speaking of reports, anything new come up this morning?" Sam asked. He always seemed to find a way to embarrass Eva with his nosiness, but this time she kept to herself and let it happen.

Wendell looked around the diner, then placed his hands on the edge of the booth table before lowering his voice. "The staties found the second shell casing in the kitchen this morning, so it would seem Mr. Stanstead's story lines up."

Eva figured the young man's inexperience would loosen his lips, something the much wiser Officer Poole wouldn't do.

"It looked like they also found a—" Sam started, when Eva nudged his foot under the booth with her toe.

"They dug up something out of the grass," she interrupted.

"Yeah," Wendell smirked nonchalantly. "Just an old golf ball. Seems to match a dimple tear in the window screen. All that does is add yet more paperwork."

"Was it a—"

Again, Eva nudged Sam's foot a little harder this time, hoping he'd shut his trap. When he glanced at her, she made sure the whites of her eyes were fully visible. Over his shoulder, she spotted Virginia pacing along the sidewalk, looking up and down the street. "I see Ginny. She's waiting outside. We need to go." She took a $5 bill from her wallet and placed it on the table for their two coffees. "Why don't you go and start the truck while I pay the tab?" When Sam slid out of the booth, forcing Wendell to lean off, which he did politely, she said, "Thank you. It was nice running into you, Wendell. We appreciate the update. Tell your father thanks again for helping my dad shingle his roof."

"Will do. Enjoy the rest of your day."

After Wendell returned to the counter and the waitress handed her change, Eva made her way outside. Once on the curb, she opened and held the passenger door of Sam's truck for Virginia and said, "We best be getting you back to Cindy. I imagine she's missing you by now."

The ride to the house was short and quiet.

• • •

Sam parallel-parked his Chevy truck in front of the retaining wall and said he was about to give it a quick rinse before parking it behind the house. "When I'm done, I'll put on some hamburgs and hot dogs."

Eva cocked an ear after he disappeared inside the garage to grab his bucket and chamois. A child's laugh echoed from somewhere out back, the shrill of giggles bouncing between the houses. She turned to Virginia with a hint of a smile and asked, "Did you catch that? I think someone's really having a good time."

"I'll take your word for it," Virginia replied, rubbing her ears as if massaging them instead of reaming. "My ears still seem to be ringing after…" she said, trailing off. "Shall we go find out?"

Eva led the way up the front steps, but before passing by the decorative slate flower beds, Virginia said, "Your flowers are so beautiful—so imaginative. I love the colors of these petunias and tea roses." She pointed and counted. "I'm seeing at least five different shades."

Eva gently touched Virginia's elbow. "Come see the irises along the south side." Continuing to lead Virginia around the south side of the house, Eva pointed to several clusters of blue boys, each growing as high as her waist. "Can you believe that before any of these were here, Sam planted a single bulb with nothing more than the slimmest of green stalks? And once it took root… oh my gosh, did it ever take off. He'd dig up a few bulbs and keep transplanting along the walkway." As Eva scanned the full length, it occurred to her that it might be time to start thinning them out. "It sure looks like there's plenty to spare. I'll have him pull up a bunch, even things out, and send him over to transplant some around your place."

An awkward silence lingered between them for a moment as Eva realized the full implications of *your* place. *Would the house stay with Ginny and Charlie? Or would it revert to the state? Oh, goodness gracious, would they even want to stay?* Finally, she said, "I know it's none of our business what you discussed with Carl Alderman. Whatever it was, you had your reasons. You should talk to him some more about what happens to the house. Just make sure he knows Janice has all the paperwork." Eva started to well up and was drawn to hug Virginia, but thoughts of Vera's relatives who might swoop in kept her tears at bay as she embraced her friend.

It was Cynthia's laughter that loosened their embrace. She was running around Henry's berry bushes along the property line. Eva couldn't tell if her hands and face were smeared with dirt or juice. Henry held a pail while leaning on a long-handled weeding hoe. As she and Virginia moved closer, she noticed to her left that Ruby was sitting resolute in a lawn chair, furiously knitting while keeping an eye on the young and old. When Eva came into her view, she startled, jumping nearly out of the chair.

"Jeezum Crow!" Ruby yelped, abruptly lifting and dropping her knitting into her lap. "Chrissakes! Tryin' to scare an old lady to death?"

"Mommy!" Cynthia yelled. She made a beeline for her mother, running into Virginia with enough force to stagger her. "We picked *so* many blackberries!"

"I can see that," Virginia said, gently cupping her daughter's smeared face and holding it away from her blouse. "Careful. I'll never get the stain out."

Henry slowly made his way toward them, using the hoe as a walking stick. Sweat stains showed through, seeping out from under his suspenders and across the long-sleeve, faded blue work shirt he wore almost every day—weather be damned. When he reached the group, he set the pail down at Ruby's feet and used a handkerchief from his pocket to wipe his brow.

"Aren't you hot as hell in that shirt and hat?" Eva asked. His excuse would be that the long sleeves kept the berry bushes and pucker brush from scratching his arms, and the hat and pipe only came off at bedtime. He smiled and ignored her, unwilling, it seemed, to take the bait.

"Looks like you'll be busy tonight," he told Ruby, pointing down at the offering.

Ruby bent over, peered into the pail, and huffed. "What am I supposed to do with that?" she asked. She looked at Henry, then Cynthia. "By the looks of you… I guess you ate more than you put in the pail!"

Henry winked and clucked his tongue at Cynthia, who giggled and wiped her mouth with the back of her hand. When she licked the back of her hand like Smokey and whispered, "Tabarnouche," his expression switched to mock horror. His corncob pipe dropped from his lips, which only made her giggle louder.

"Did she say somethin'?" Ruby asked.

Henry took off his hat and waved it at the young girl. Nervously, he told Ruby that the youngster had called her funny. "I think she likes you," he added.

"Alright, crazy girl, let's get you home." Virginia scanned their faces, her flushed cheeks suddenly noticeable against her white blouse. "I meant to say…"

Eva discreetly caught Henry's eye as he stooped to retrieve his pipe. She didn't like keeping secrets from him and hadn't had a chance to get on the same page. His searching for answers alone wouldn't help anyone. "Let's not get into that," she said. "We've got plenty of time to clean up before supper. I've got a basket of clothes ready to toss into the wash—no problem making room for one more." Seeing a small handful of berries at the bottom of the pail meant there wouldn't be any pie-making tonight. "Sam's making hot dogs and hamburgs, so you might as well come over and have supper with us. Two more won't matter. And those"—she pointed at the pail—"will go nicely poured over vanilla ice cream for dessert."

Ruby sighed again, looking down at the poor harvest, and this time Eva suspected she might be a little melodramatic. Ruby leaned back in her chair and resumed her knitting. "Holler when it's ready," she said, glancing at Cynthia's dark, fruit-stained face, and exhaled again. "What goes in… must come out," she muttered.

"Mom… for heaven's sake," Eva said, much to her chagrin. Whispering, she added, "Don't spoil her fun. She's been through enough."

"C'mon, sweetie. Let's go and get you cleaned up," Virginia said, tugging gently on Cynthia's elbow. "You can have a bath while I help Mrs. Martin with supper."

• • •

Virginia Stanstead wiped her mouth with a napkin after taking a second bite of hamburger. "Wow, these are so good," she said as she dabbed her bun in the dripping grease. She seemed to ogle it too long. "And cooked perfectly, too… Excuse me, but I think I'd better use a second plate."

When she started to rise from the dining room table, Sam stopped her. "By all means, sit down, please. I'll grab you another." He darted nimbly out into the kitchen and returned with a paper plate, which she slid under the one in front of her. It was heaped with a half-eaten burger, a plain hot dog, green beans, and potato salad. "Thank you so much. What's your secret?"

"Butter," Sam said. "Never be stingy with the butter when frying hamburg and hot dogs in a cast-iron pan."

"Oh dear." Virginia watched as Cynthia chonked down her second dog.

"And toast the buns in the pan—"

"In the butter," she said, smiling.

Eva stared at her mother, willing her to remain quiet.

"Of course," Sam said. "Can never have too much."

Eva's stern glare only shifted Ruby's focus toward Sam, saying, "You've got so much food on your plate that it ought to have sideboards." She stabbed at a forkful of beans and nudged her salad. She'd only taken half a hot dog, giving the other half to Henry. "You still eatin' those peanut butter sandwiches damn near every day?"

"Half Skippy and half butter, folded once over. Can't beat it."

Ruby speared a chunk of potato. "I think you've got a damn tapeworm."

Eva's shoulders tensed at the cringeworthy conversation. She tuned everyone out by glancing around the room at the curtains, reminding herself to take them down, wash, and iron them tomorrow. Ironing would be a good job for Ruby to stay busy and keep her nose clean.

Henry, always the quietest eater, finished first and patted his empty pipe that he had tucked into his shirt pocket. He took it out and turned to Cynthia. "After I go outside and have a smoke, would you like to play a game or two of cribbage?" he asked her. "Did your folks ever teach you?"

Cynthia swiveled toward her mother, who shrugged and apologized for being such a disappointment, eliciting an eye roll. "Do we have to go outside and throw something? Like those lawn darts? That was fun!"

Virginia ruffled her daughter's freshly shampooed hair. "No, silly, it's a card game. Your father and I know how to play, but we certainly don't play very well. Maybe Mr. Fischer can whip your skills into shape."

Henry puffed on his empty pipe, waiting patiently for an answer.

Cynthia stared and finally laughed. "You look like Popeye," she said.

Henry flexed his arm. His spoken impression was terrible, which was Eva's cue to leave and clear away any empty plates.

"Do you need any help?" Ruby asked.

"That's alright. Sam will do it."

"Any washing downstairs? At least let me make myself useful."

Eva gave in to Ruby's relentless persistence but couldn't honestly begrudge her, knowing the apple didn't fall far from the crabapple tree. "Sure. But be careful going down the stairs. Sam? Can you see that my mother makes it down okay?" She regretted it when the corners of his lips turned up. Fortunately, her disarming stare worked again—his mischievous expression melted away. She turned her attention to Cynthia. "Let's go, Tiger. I'll get the cards and board and set things up on the kitchen table while Mr. Fischer goes outside and smokes his pipe."

"Does it taste like spinach?" Cynthia asked, which garnered a hearty laugh from everyone, including Ruby, who uttered, "God, no."

• • •

Ruby sat in Eva's reading chair, snoring softly. Her legs were outstretched, and her hands were neatly folded in a steeple on her apron. Even in pantyhose, Eva could see her mother's swollen ankles in the dim light. She had no idea how this woman had come so far and done so much—day in and day out—on her feet, keeping house, and never once complaining. It wasn't fair to have to deal with this mess at their age. Nothing's worse than a rolling thunderstorm ruining a sunset.

"I told Mr. Alderman that I'd give him a day or two to prepare," Virginia whispered. She turned to Eva, sitting next to her on the couch. "I'd like to go see Charlie tomorrow if possible. I can drive myself if you'd—"

"Say no more. We'll watch her."

"But your work?"

"Merrill was fine with me taking the week off."

"Thank you. So kind." Virginia stared out the living room window into the dimness of early evening. "Seems so strange to look over there with it being all dark and no lights on. Home, but not really home."

Eva reached out and placed her hand on Virginia's wrist. The last time she consoled another woman was when Alice's husband, Reginald, passed unexpectedly. "Charlie will be home as soon as a judge clears this up. There's no need for him to come out on the wrong end of the stick."

When they faced each other, the glow of Eva's reading lamp reflected in Virginia's swollen eyes, and Eva sensed something painful hammering behind them. "What is it, Ginny? Charlie will be home any day now. You gotta think positive. What happened wasn't his fault."

Virginia Stanstead covered her face and whimpered into her hands. When she looked up again, she said, "It… wasn't," and covered her face once more.

"I heard Cindy say something to you the other night, and I asked her this morning. She said that she told you not to say anything. Say anything about what? Does this have anything to do with what you needed to talk to Carl about?" Eva knew she was crossing a line and backed off, holding up a hand. "I'm sorry." She stole a glance at Ruby, whose snoring had stopped, but her eyes were still closed. "We should keep our voices down."

Henry and Sam's voices could still be heard in the kitchen, helping Cynthia count fifteens.

Eva wanted to retract what she'd said, desperately eager to get up and see if Smokey was waiting anxiously at the door to be let in. Her fidgeting probably didn't go unnoticed.

"I don't know when Charles will be home," Virginia said. "We'll just have to sacrifice."

Eva's Daily Reminder 1964: August 19, Wednesday

Sunny. Less humid. Still too warm to light a fire.

Good day for Dad picking blackberries with Cindy. Said he had fun teaching her to play cribbage. Hopefully she will make a good rubber match for Mom and Dad in the future.

Ginny drove over to Woodstock to check on Charlie. I should call Dick Poole and give him the business.

Took down all the dining room curtains after Sam left for work. Washed them and mopped the bathroom floor before making breakfast. I showed Cindy how to iron after Ginny had gone.

Debated whether to call Al over for a drink to discuss this mess. She stopped in after work while Connie was here. So glad to see her again. She's interviewing at the machine shop for a secretary job. Warren working shifts at Super Duper in Wilder. Says he wants to start learning taxes with H&R Block.

No Smokey last night or this morning. Cindy helped me call for him. Hope he's ok and hasn't tangled with a darn fisher cat up back.

26

Eva carried the ironing board up from the cellar and set it in the middle of the kitchen floor, where there was plenty of natural light. She went upstairs and found the bathroom stool at the back of Connie's closet. Sam had built it, along with a matching rocking horse, both painted in red and blue with hearts and yellow-leafed vines along the curved rockers. The paint, once bright, was now chipped and faded into more brick red and Confederate blue.

Ironing came naturally to Cynthia Stanstead. The stool was the right height, allowing her to lean over the board with enough leverage to press down on the linen curtains. "Are Henry and Ruby coming over to visit this morning?" she asked. "Or we could go over there."

"I dunno. I think you tuckered them all out last night." Eva wasn't being overly hands-on, letting Cynthia linger over the heavy material without worrying it would scorch. Once she was satisfied not to redo it herself, she pulled a new section across the board. "There you go. Have at it some more."

While her apprentice continued earning her keep, Eva enjoyed her coffee. The feeders were full of chickadees, pecking away at the suet, while goldfinches nibbled at the thistle. A tufted titmouse preened its wings in the birdbath until a robin chased it away. On the ground beneath the feeders, a couple of blue jays lurked, gobbling up the fallen seeds. She wanted to scold them, but chose not to startle Cynthia and risk her falling off the stool. Instead, she checked whether the iron needed more distilled water. "Looking good, Tiger. Don't be afraid to give it the steam. Keep going. I'm gonna call Connie."

"Who's Connie?"

"She's my daughter. You met her the other morning."

Cynthia looked confused.

Eva laughed. "And you met her at the wedding, silly." She wanted to ask her again if she remembered playing lawn darts, but decided to give her the benefit of the doubt. "She left early with her husband. They were sleeping upstairs when—"

"Like a sleepover?"

Eva laughed again. "Yeah. They were here on a sleepover." Memories of young Connie staying overnight at Alice's flashed behind her eyes. Her childhood on the farm lacked friends, except her brothers. There were no sleepovers. She jutted her nose toward the ironing board. "Keep the iron moving or else it'll burn… that's right, you're doing good," she said, lifting the phone receiver and dialing.

After a few rings, Connie answered. "Good 'n you? What're you up to today? Any plans?" Eva asked. "Glad to hear… you wanna stop by the house and meet my little helper? I was about to give Al a jingle… I think it's warranted, don't you?… Sure, can't wait to hear all about it. Okee dokee… yep."

Cynthia stretched her arms over her head, arched her back, and said, "Je suis fatigué."

"Let me guess… you're getting tired. I don't blame you. You did a great job. Even I was getting winded watching you." Eva examined the curtain and, satisfied, folded it neatly. She almost dropped it onto the table, changed her mind about the possibility of crumbs, and carried it into the dining room. She made quick work of the second curtain while Cynthia caught her breath. Connie wouldn't mind helping her hang them up.

"How about a glass of iced tea? I think you deserve it."

"Okay."

Eva poured a couple of glasses from the pitcher.

Cynthia made a skeptical face after the first sip. "This tastes funny."

"It's sweetened with maple syrup."

"Oh…" Cynthia took a tentative second sip, swished it around, swallowed, and pronounced it not so bad.

"So, did you have fun yesterday with my father? He kept you pretty busy?"

"I did. He gave me the choice of either painting or picking."

"Wise choice." Eva studied her face, wondering what lurked beneath the surface, what she had gone through, knowing that Vera had stolen from both of them. "Would you like to talk about what happened?"

"I didn't know Mr. Fischer spoke French."

Eva couldn't remember the last time, or ever, when Henry had spoken something in French. Even as a child, during visits to her grandparents in Nova Scotia, she couldn't recall hearing anyone speak the language. "To be honest, I don't know much about it. He was born in Canada, but went to school across the river in New Hampshire."

"I guess that explains why he wasn't so good."

"Why were you trying to talk to each other in French?"

"We weren't. He asked me if I wanted to talk about what happened. I told him what my dad had told me in French. And he asked why I wasn't supposed to say anything. I don't know who was more surprised—me or him."

Eva moved herself to the top of the list of surprises. She was battling guilt, and now Henry's the one withholding. "So I'll ask again, would you like to talk about what happened?"

"He said he'd take care of everything and not to worry." Cynthia finished half of her glass and pushed it away. "Can we go out and try to find Smokey?"

Eva closed her eyes and wished that they would find him in the pump house. "I know a good place to start. Wanna go for a little hike?"

"Hike?" The previous skeptical expression fell across Cynthia's face. "Really?"

"It's close to a *secret* flower garden."

"Is it far?"

"Not too far at all."

"Will we be back by dark?"

"Ayutt."

Cynthia tied her hair back, looping and knotting it once, then lifted her shoes and pointed.

Eva pointed to her own tennis shoes. "You'll be fine. We're both wearing our A-number ones." She stood and peeked around the doorway at the grandfather clock. "Let me write a note for Connie telling her where we'll be."

"And my mom."

"Good idea… But let's hope we're back before they get here."

• • •

There was no luck, and no wishes came true, despite their ambitious efforts to find Smokey. Eva, downcast, was still glad she had shown Cynthia the Lady Slipper patch first before heading home. A few wilted blooms, with their once-bright pink hoods, were hard to spot on the forest floor. It took all of Eva's patience to keep Cynthia from picking one for Virginia. Eva promised Cynthia they could come back tomorrow to show it to her mother.

They heard voices in the yard before stepping out of the woods. It seemed like happy hour was in full swing with Eva's parents, Sam and Connie, Virginia, and Alice, who hopefully brought enough to share with everyone. Eva was in the mood for an apricot brandy over ice, but even a beer would help quench her thirst after their romp through the forest.

"Mom!" Cynthia bolted down the embankment and climbed into Virginia's lap. She loosened her daughter's hair knot and massaged her scalp before tilting her face up closer to hers.

"What's the matter, kiddo?"

"He's gone."

As if to confirm she understood Eva's note, Virginia looked up at her before telling Cynthia, "I'm sure he's got a lot of territory to roam. He's probably hiding somewhere, and he'll come out when he's good and ready. Isn't that right, Mrs. Martin?"

Eva was happy when Sam interjected that he'd take a flashlight after supper and look for him. He gave up his seat next to Connie and went into the toolshed. He emerged with a large pail and flipped it upside down. "I'll use this."

"I've got brandy and whiskey sour," Alice said. "I hope you're in the mood for brandy because Ruby and Connie have polished off most of the sour mix."

"Sounds good. You read my mind," Eva assured her, taking the seat next to Connie. "I dunno what the little bugger's troubles are, but we sure called and called." She didn't want to mention the possibility of him meeting his maker, running into a fisher cat or a coyote, which was a death sentence for a house cat. "He'll show up when he's good and ready, I suppose."

Henry made an exaggerated face, removed his pipe, and took a swig of Narragansett. He straightened up when Eva shot him daggers to keep his mouth shut.

"Warren inside?" she asked Connie.

Connie leaned over and kissed Eva on the cheek. "Nope, just me. He's working late."

Turning her attention to the group, Eva asked, "So who all got here first?"

Virginia pulled Cynthia's legs up, curling her into a ball on her lap, where she looked like a napping hamster. "I brought up the rear. Everyone had already started without me."

Eva glanced across the yard and saw the Stansteads' station wagon. It was a good thing it was beige and didn't show the dirt since it probably hadn't been washed in who knows how long. "Everything go okay?" she asked Virginia. She accepted a drink from Alice and took a sip, letting the aroma of apricot and alcohol coat her tongue. "I won't make you repeat yourself if you've already gotten things off your chest."

"No, that's alright. Everything went as well as could be expected. I met Carl Alderman in Woodstock, and we spent all of the allowed visiting hours going over the plan. Charlie's been charged with both..." Virginia hesitated and kissed the top of Cynthia's head, stroking her hair, before pulling it away from her neck. She appeared to struggle and eventually continued, "killings."

Eva couldn't help but notice Cynthia stiffen and curl tighter in her mother's lap.

"He will plead guilty to the judge... sometime this week."

Eva tensed, gripping the lawn chair's armrest to keep from jumping up. "What?" She let go and sipped. "Why aren't they releasing him? I thought this whole thing was some kind of mix-up? It was all Vera and Ray's fault! They barged in on you in the middle of the night! Heck, if it'd been me, I'd have done the same damn thing!" She raised her brandy only to realize it was empty. She couldn't recall finishing it. Her breathing slowed when she felt Connie's fingers tracing lightly on her neck and shoulders.

Virginia appeared to try to shift Cynthia's weight. "Charlie doesn't want to put everyone through a lengthy trial with absolutely no guarantee that he wouldn't be sentenced to prison for the rest of his life." She hugged Cynthia tighter. "That would ruin us!"

Eva scanned everyone's faces. Silence hung in the air. Her mother's hands, deft and skillful, knitted a toque from muscle memory despite her arthritis. Henry stared into the woods, lost in thought. The way they seemed to detach themselves frightened Eva. Alice held her drink with both hands, fidgeting as if she'd rather be anywhere else. Eva half-expected her to make an excuse to leave for Impy. And Sam, who was ultimately responsible for this predicament, sat in his chair with a Narragansett bottle resting against his crotch. At first, he appeared carefree, but after a moment, he looked more stunned and speechless.

"Carl thinks if he pleads guilty by reason of insanity, the court will be far more lenient. He said if the judge didn't accept that, then he might be able to defend it as a crime of passion."

A crime of passion was something Eva understood—something she might have gotten away with. When she regained her focus, she noticed Henry was no longer staring into the darkening woods. He was looking at her—his pipe firmly clenched in his fingers. She couldn't read his mind, and it wasn't the right time to be flippant and offer him a penny.

27

Cynthia was still sleeping when a knock at the front door startled Eva and Virginia, interrupting their coffee. "It's too early for Al to be out and about, and my dad would've come to the back door, so… I have no idea who that could be." Eva jumped up and hit the edge of the kitchen table, partially spilling her mug. "I'd better get that before they knock louder next time." She retied her robe on the way through the living room, checked that the upstairs was closed, then unlocked and opened the front door, keeping the screen shut.

Officer Richard Poole and Deputy Wendell Buchanan stood outside.

Eva noticed that Richard was holding a folded piece of paper.

"Mrs. Martin, good morning," Richard said flatly without the Bing Crosby smile.

Neither officer removed their cap.

When Eva chose not to respond in kind, he said, "I have a search warrant for the premises." He unfolded the paper and stepped onto the middle step, holding it close enough to the screen for Eva to see that something was typed beneath the Vermont coat of arms, which she couldn't decipher without her reading glasses. "What's this about? Do you need to speak with Virginia to sign off on that so she and Cindy are free to return?"

Richard looked at Wendell and shook his head. "No ma'am. This is a judge's warrant, authorizing Wendell and me to search inside your home today. This has nothing to do with the Stanstead's premises. May we come inside?"

"I think I need to call Sam first."

"Whether he's here or not doesn't matter to us. I only asked politely as a courtesy. And if you're about to say that you want to call Carl Alderman, I'll save you the trouble, knowing he's already representing Mr. Stanstead. He won't be able to help you… unless you've already hired another attorney?"

Virginia appeared behind Eva. "What's happening, Eva?"

"The police want to search my house."

Eva called Sam at work, told him to get his britches home right away, then called Henry. Knowing him, he'd see the town cruiser parked out front soon enough.

"I can get dressed and go get your father," Virginia said.

"No, you can't leave Cindy. She'll be scared that you're gone, even if it's for a second." Eva turned to Virginia and took her mug. "You'd better go upstairs and wake her up. Get her dressed." She whispered, "I'll handle Richard."

After Virginia went upstairs, Eva closed the door behind her and then faced the officers. She glanced to see if Henry was making his way over. He wasn't. The road was clear. "Why don't you tell me what you're looking for?"

Richard folded the warrant and slipped it into his back pocket. "Eva, I'm afraid I can't—"

"You're looking for a gun, aren't you? Are you asking *all* of the other neighbors, too? Rounding up everyone's guns, looking for—"

"Mrs. Martin… Eva… I'd suggest that you stop talking unless you wish to incriminate yourself."

She wanted them to stay outside as long as possible so Cynthia wouldn't see police officers when Virginia brought her downstairs. It would be smart to send them to her parents, and if Henry hadn't seen Richard and Wendell outside by now, he would realize it as soon as the girls knocked on his door. She pushed open the screen. "Come inside," she told them. At the sound of footsteps, she hurriedly handed the two mugs to the officers and asked if they'd sit on the couch and wait until the girl and her mother slipped out the back, hopefully without attracting attention.

Luckily, Virginia managed to shield Cynthia with her hips as she turned the corner off the stairs and gently guided the still yawning girl into the kitchen. Eva heard Virginia say they were heading over to the Fischers to enjoy Ruby's famous blackberry flapjacks and syrup, then listened as the back door opened and closed.

"Would you like a refill on those coffees?"

Wendell looked appreciative, but Richard declined.

Eva cinched the sash around her robe, tying it into a firm knot. She wanted them gone before Henry showed up.

Richard offered the mug to Eva. "The forensics report determined that only one of the recovered .22 rimfire casings matched Charlie's rifle. The other was not a match—different firing pins. And no other .22 weapon was found inside the home or vehicles. The warrant I have today authorizes me to search and seize any .22 caliber weapon." He waited for Eva to finish her coffee. "I'm sorry, Eva, but it's my job to investigate and follow the facts."

Defeated, she opened the stairwell door. "The gun cabinet is upstairs, in the north bedroom. There is nothing else in the house, hidden or otherwise, that would concern you."

She followed them upstairs. Virginia had done a good job making the bed. One of Connie's old stuffed animals—a worn teddy bear missing a button eye—was propped up between the two queen pillows. She moved to the near side of the bed and used the side of her hand to karate chop the bed cover under the pillows, smoothing the rest of it tight and square. Standing tall and pulling the already tight sash, she watched as Richard stepped closer to the oak gun cabinet and reached for the glass door handle.

He tugged. It was locked.

Wendell looked at her, and she nodded upward. "The key's on top. It's always locked."

Richard reached above his head, blindly searching for the keys behind the cabinet's crown molding. When he finally found them, he opened the door.

Eva moved closer to Wendell, positioning herself so she could look directly into the open gun cabinet. There were her and Sam's matching lever-action Marlin deer rifles, her and Sam's shotguns—a bolt-action, three-shot Mossberg .20 gauge, and his single-shot break-action .16 gauge, the same one he'd used to drop an out-of-season buck. What was missing was her father's Savage single-shot bolt-action .22 rifle, the one that Sam had dropped on the stone wall and bent its front sight.

Richard examined each of the four guns, then knelt and opened the cabinet's two lower doors. He pulled everything out: cleaning kits, a bottle of Hoppe's No. 9, and a bottle of Remington gun oil from one side, and then all the ammunition boxes from the other side: Winchester .30-30 and Remington .20- and .16-gauge plastic shells that still looked brand new.

Eva stepped closer to Richard and peered over his shoulder. The box of Winchester .22s was not there.

Richard stood and examined the cabinet's interior more closely. He pulled out two long cleaning rods tucked on one side. He rolled their shafts between his fingers, appearing to judge their size. Looking at Wendell, he shook his head and said, "These are too big."

"Are you sure?" Wendell asked.

"Definitely, bigger than .22." He returned them to their previous place. "I'll assume they fit the guns in here."

Wendell stepped past Eva and looked for himself. "Yeah, my .22 rods are way slimmer than these." He removed each Marlin and opened the action, using the light from the bedroom window to look down each barrel. "These are nice waffle-tops from the early '50s, right? My dad has a similar model." He didn't pay much attention to the scatter guns. "Nothing special with those."

"The ammunition matches the guns here," Richard said, putting everything back haphazardly.

Eva scratched her hands, aware that once they were gone, she'd have to put everything back as it was. She watched Richard reach into the closet and move the hanging clothes aside, digging deeper, as he pawed through whatever remained of Connie's things.

When Richard seemed satisfied that he wouldn't find what he was looking for, he glanced at Eva, perhaps prejudging her as if he expected her to lie, before asking, "Are these all the weapons in the house?"

She tensed, barely able to utter, "Ayutt. If you feel like you need to check under all the beds and"—she pointed toward the knee walls—"under the eaves, then by all means, have at it. Nothing under there except storm windows, Christmas decorations, and a couple of old Lionel train sets." She yanked on her sash again, and this time it hurt her kidneys. "You know good and goddamn well that we didn't get along with Vera—"

Wendell snickered.

"But that witch wasn't worth being locked up over."

A voice at the foot of the stairs asked, "Everythin' all right up there?"

Eva recognized it was Henry.

"Are we done here?" Eva asked.

Richard looked at Wendell and nodded. "I think so."

"Be right down, Dad. Just finishing up here."

Richard tossed the cabinet keys in the palm of his hand, then locked the door and dropped them on top before leading the way down.

Henry was waiting for them in the living room, checking his pocket watch against the grandfather clock. "Dick… Wendell… What's goin' on?"

Eva needed to feel confident, despite the dread rumbling in her guts. "Oh, dontcha know, they're just here poking around, looking at everyone's rifles. Trying to cross their T's and dot their I's." A flash of cockiness overtook her. "Maybe what you found came from Vera's first husband. Maybe he tried to kill himself once before… inside the house. Can't say as if I blame him." She looked at Henry. "Can you?"

"Nope, can't say as if I do either." Henry chewed on the end of his pipe stem, watching the two officers for a moment, then said, "That Cindy sure can eat. She damn near polished off my last pint of fancy grade. I think she's got a hollow leg!"

It was obvious Richard was ignoring their banter. He stood with his hands on his hips, looking around and squinting as if trying to see what might be hidden inside the walls. "And what would we find in the cellar?" he asked Eva.

She huffed, totalling everything up in her head, exhaled again, then answered him truthfully, "A God awful mess of tools in Sam's workshop, a washroom, two freezers full of meat and greens, who knows how many cases of beer, a pantry full of crackers and peanut butter, ball game snacks and whatnot, which isn't any comfort, seeing as the Sox are losing again this year—expected a lot more outta Pesky… and the rest is filled with firewood."

Richard pursed his lips, and Eva hit him again, adding, "And a barrel of birdseed, that I hope to Christ is free of mice, which reminds me I need more suet."

· · ·

After the two officers left, Eva confronted Henry as he was about to go out the back door. "You got something to say?"

He paused, turned, and faced her, removing his pipe from his lips. "Nope… Can't say as I do."

She did not believe him.

"How about I send the girls over now?"

"Good idea… You do that."

Eva's Daily Reminder 1964: August 30, Sunday

Hot. Sunny. Humid.

Got going early. Cleaned all through and mopped.

Connie came down. She and Warren took the MG for a ride. Fingerprints all over it!

Sam put the seat belt retractors in.

Al stopped and shampooed me and ate with us outdoors—charcoal steaks, potatoes and corn. The steak was super.

Sure was bushed after Al left. Collapsed on the bed and slept right through. Restless all night. Hot and humid sleeping.

Mom and Dad off to Sybil and Clark's cabin.

Not looking forward to Charlie's court date this week.

28

The mornings the week before Labor Day were much cooler and less humid than the evenings, with the eastern sky glowing in shades of coral and sea-glass blue at sunrise. It was a facade of tranquility, hiding the small-town secrets that would be buried and erased from the Sumner Falls oral history.

Eva had Sam open the toolshed and set out a couple of lawn chairs, facing the river toward the New Hampshire skyline. He kissed her goodbye and wished her and Virginia the best of luck before heading to work. He wouldn't be able to leave early enough to make it to the Woodstock County courthouse in time for Charlie's sentencing.

"Will your parents be back in time to watch Cindy?" Virginia asked, cradling a hot coffee mug with both hands.

It was one of Eva's favorites, decorated with colorful cat images. The air was cold enough for her to cover her head with the hood from one of Sam's pullovers.

Eva sipped her own Hall mug while watching Ruby and Henry's house, its windows dark with the curtains drawn. There was no way Ruby was eating a pan-fried trout breakfast. Hopefully, the Hoisingtons were feeding them bacon and eggs. God only knows how long Ruby would keep complaining about the bread toast not being homemade—Sybil wasn't much of a homemaker. "They'll be along before lunch," she said confidently. Eva tugged at her cowl-neck sweater after another sip of coffee. "What time are you supposed to meet Carl?"

"One. Do you think that's cutting it close? I can't bring Cindy... I just can't."

Eva heard Virginia close to tears, even though her profile was hidden under the hood. She wanted to tell Virginia that everything would be okay, but empathy wasn't her strong suit. Give her an apron and turn her hair gray, and she'd see, in a mirror, that it was her mother. "I can't imagine what you're going through. I can't even begin to..." She set her mug on the grass and moved her chair closer, covering Virginia's hand with her own. "I hated that woman so much. She damn near broke up my marriage—Connie's marriage, too. She was ready to call off the wedding. I thank God for whatever she wrote in that letter to Sam that it brought him to his senses."

Virginia turned away and looked at the still-empty house that was supposed to be her home. When she faced Eva again, her eyes were filled with tears, streaming freely down her cheeks. "He told me not to tell anyone— not to say a thing. Cynthia... all he wanted to do was protect our daughter."

"He did. He most certainly did, Ginny. He protected both of you. And the judge will see that. Mark my words, he'll recommend probation."

Virginia scoffed, her eyes flickered, and the internal battle she was fighting was something Eva could neither see nor understand, until Virginia said, "We told the police that Charlie came home from work and shot Ray, but..."

Eva positioned herself, half-turning, and forced Virginia to look her in the eye. "Ginny?"

Virginia Stanstead covered her mouth with her hand and broke down as the dam holding her tears burst. Her voice muffled, she said, "Cindy..." She darted her eyes around wildly, as if the police had crept close and were listening to her confession. "It was Cindy who shot Ray *before* Charlie came home! When those two barged into the house and found me, they just started screaming at me to get out! Vera was pulling my hair!" She rubbed her head as if the smell of them still clung to her. "I didn't know what was happening! All I remember was their hands all over me... and then Ray was gone... and then a gunshot echoed. Vera fell on the floor, twisting and kicking. And then Cindy came out of our bedroom… she must've come downstairs and gone into our room, and Ray chased her. She knew Charlie's squirrel gun was in the corner. When I ran into the bedroom, Ray was lying on the bed." She began to dry heave, and Eva thought she might retch. After a brief moment, she continued, "His face was stove in!"

"Cindy found the gun?"

"Yes. She shot him."

"And Cindy shot Vera?"

Virginia's face hardened with anger. She shook her head violently. "No. How could she? She was in the back bedroom. By the time Charlie came home, they were both dead. He took the gun from Cindy and told us not to say anything—not a word, and that he would protect us. Once we got our story straight, that's when I called the operator."

"Then *how* was Vera killed?"

Virginia took several deep breaths and composed herself. "I don't know… and I *don't* care. After what they did, I hope she had a brain aneurysm. We've both told Mr. Alderman the truth. We cannot and *will not* put Cynthia through any more of this." She put her fingers to her lips and began biting her nails.

• • •

The bailiff, a burly ginger-haired and mustached fellow, who looked like an alumnus of the Vermont vs New Hampshire Shriners football game, said, "All rise. The Honorable Judge Stephens presiding. This court is now in session."

Eva sat between Virginia and Sam, who was spared the late arrival caused by the previous session's 30-minute delay. They sat on the first-row bench directly behind Carl Alderman and Charles Stanstead, who was dressed in a suit and the loafers Virginia had given Carl. The paisley jacket had blue and red threads that matched his navy-blue linen pants, and his white Oxford was unbuttoned at the collar and tieless. At least the county lockup had given him a clean shave and a toothbrush, which only made his face and smile look clean—and still scared.

Eva hoped Carl had tucked his cigar tube into his briefcase, not into his lapel pocket, for the judge to see.

"You may be seated." Judge Stephens didn't need his bench to loom over his courtroom. Standing six-foot-six, he only needed a school desk to command the room. His nose was slender and as steep as the suicidal slope at the nearby ski area. His snow-white hair, combed straight back, would look regal and presidential if he were to pose for a portrait. Removing his wireframe spectacles, he glanced at the state's prosecutor and then at Carl, nodding once to both. "Mr. Alderman, it's my understanding that you've already spoken to the state's attorney and the two of you have come to a plea agreement?"

"We have, your Honor."

"Alright, and Mr. Perkins... you and your office have agreed to this sentence, and that I should be so inclined to accept?"

Eva Martin didn't know what the Stansteads had agreed to, and she hadn't pressed Virginia earlier. She only knew that two wrongs don't make a right. She didn't want to see her friend's family destroyed by someone who was truly at fault. None of Cynthia, Charles, or Virginia deserved to be in this situation. She didn't want to see any of them punished. People aren't inherently bad—they're messy, that's all.

She leaned forward and caught Richard Poole's eye. He was probably there to testify if called, and if he harbored any doubts about her, his expression was as stony and flat as the fieldstones in her property walls.

Mr. Perkins stood and said, "We have, your Honor."

Eva held Virginia's hand tightly. If asked, she wouldn't know whether she was squeezing to show support or out of fear of the unknown. She added to their grip with her other hand.

"Would the defendant please rise?" Judge Stephens asked. After waiting, he slipped his glasses on and read aloud, "In the State of Vermont versus Charles Stanstead of Sumner Falls, how do you plead to the charge of involuntary manslaughter?"

Even in death, Eva gritted her teeth that Vera wasn't mentioned.

Charles Stanstead looked again at Carl, then briefly glanced over his shoulder at Virginia before turning to face the judge. "Guilty, your honor... by reason of insanity."

Judge Stephens straightened the papers on his desk, arranging everything into a tidy square. He took off his glasses again and looked toward the prosecutor's table, including Officer Poole, who Eva noticed bit his lips and lowered his head, remaining silent. Finally, he said, "I've reviewed the casework, including the forensic and autopsy reports, along with the witness sworn statements… Mr. Perkins, it's my understanding that the state has signed off on the forensics of this case as being inconsistent and overall inconclusive?"

Carl Alderman stood, his corduroy pants catching on the edge of the defense table and squeaking on the stone tile courtroom floor. "Objection!" he yelled. "Both parties have already reached a signed agreement."

The judge stared him down. "Overruled. It's only due diligence, counselor. The court is well aware of the signed sentencing agreement." Glancing over to the prosecution table, Judge Stephens asked again, "Mr. Perkins?"

"That is correct, your Honor… inconclusive."

"Detective Poole?"

Eva saw everyone on the defensive side turn their heads in unison.

Richard Poole, still stone-faced and not looking warm-hearted, answered sheepishly, "Correct, your Honor. All gathered forensics from the crime scene, and victim autopsies are inconclusive."

"Very well. I see no further reason to delay or disregard the state's evidence that the defendant should not stand trial. Will the defendant please rise… Mr. Stanstead, I hereby sentence you to two years of supervised incarceration, one year for each victim, to be served under the care of the State of Vermont's mental health facilities in Burlington. Case closed."

Judge Stephens gaveled the hearing.

29

Sometime before sunrise, the morning after Charles Stanstead was taken to the state hospital, Smokey appeared on the back steps, looking worse for wear. His tail was broken in the middle, and he was missing a triangular chunk from the tip of one ear. The bone spurs along his spine were clearly visible, along with his ribs. Eva noticed the bite on his tail was infected, so she shouted for Sam. After wrapping the cat in a towel, they headed uptown to the vet.

They left the poor fellow overnight, where he was treated for dehydration, and unfortunately, his tail couldn't be saved. The vet amputated it below the infection, leaving him with a bobtail. He looked funny with his shaved stub, but the vet assured her his fur would grow back and cover the stump. After hearing she fed him chicken livers, she was promised his weight would return forthwith, which it did over the course of a few weeks.

Eva waited a week before telling Cynthia, allowing the fur to sprout enough to hide the bare skin, and for Smokey to stop licking his stitches.

He was still hiding somewhere in the cellar when Cynthia first searched for him, with Eva and Connie's help. It seems whatever nearly killed him still had him terrified. He refused to sleep on Eva's bed. Sam left a litter box at the bottom of the cellar stairs, and Eva would place a dish of diced liver and tuna there twice a day. Seeing it cleaned meant he was still alive and recovering.

When Cynthia saw him nestled on a woodpile, stretched between two chunks intended for the Jøtul this winter, his dark fur blended into the shadows. Only the green of his eyes revealed his hiding spot. He purred when she picked him up and didn't resist as she carried him upstairs. Eva hoped that was a good sign for his recovery.

"I can't believe he came back!" Cynthia said, petting Smokey's head. She curiously fingered his tattered ear, rubbing it between her fingers.

Eva tensed, inhaling through her teeth. "Just be careful. Not too rough. I'd hate to have to take *you* to the vet if he bit you."

"Oh, he would never do that." Cynthia mauled the cat in a good way, and clearly, he seemed happy with all the attention. "Are we gonna play cribbage tonight? Here or with Henry and Ruby? Tonight's the night I'm gonna score my first twenty-nine!"

"Is that so?" Eva asked.

"Oui!"

Eva smiled at Connie and winked. "Someday? What do you think? A little apple that might not fall too far away from the tree?"

"Ha! Someday. We're trying." Connie winked back. "Don't worry. Everything will turn out A-number one."

"Good to know!"

"Connie, let's bring him upstairs. I want to see if he'll stay and nap on your bed," Cynthia said.

"Well, it's not really my bed anymore. I heard *you* took pretty good care of it for a while. It's like you have two homes now."

"Three! Don't forget about Henry and Ruby! What's for supper?"

"My oh my," Eva pretended to scold her. "Aren't you getting a little spoiled these days?"

Cynthia winked, pushed her tongue out through a smile, and dashed upstairs with Smokey holding on for dear life.

"To think of what might have happened to that little girl," Eva said, wondering what Charles was going through at that moment.

A knock at the door interrupted her reverie, and Eva guessed it was Alice bringing a liquid gift. But instead, only the top of Henry's hat was visible through the screen door. It was clear he was carrying something slender wrapped in a white bedsheet. He stepped into the kitchen, awkwardly trying to hide whatever it was behind his hip.

"Is the kid around? I wasn't sure if I saw her sneaking in. I didn't want her to see me."

Eva looked at the sheet and realized he had been lying all along. "What did you do?"

"Me?" He looked genuinely shocked, his pipe dangling from his lips by an invisible thread. He looked at her and Connie.

"Your mother doesn't know about this. She doesn't need to know."

"And Dad doesn't need to know either," Connie said.

Eva wanted to scream, but it came out as a whisper: "What?"

Henry held out the slender object and unwrapped it, bunching the bedsheet into a ball. He appeared to toy with the idea of stuffing it under his hat when Eva snatched it from him and threw it down the cellar stairs.

"You took it when we were at the lawyers, didn't you?" she asked him. "Why?"

"I ran into Olie Buchanan. Interesting chat," he said, his eyes flickering between them. "It's still my job to protect you… You're my girls, now and always," He extended his old Savage rifle. "You were always a good shot, Evie, sniping those pheasants, and now of all things… blue jays? I guess the apple doesn't fall far from the tree, does it?" He handed the gun to his granddaughter. "I think it's safe to put this back, don't you think?" Henry paused, then removed his pipe and pointed the stem at her, adding, "And I assume you *trust* Warren to keep his vows?"

"Constance? What did you—"

Connie turned to Eva, her breath hitching and her face flushing. "She was *never* going to leave us alone," she sobbed, reaching for Eva. "None of what we lost would've…"

Eva accepted her daughter's embrace and whispered in her ear, "Don't worry… everything will turn out A-number one," while gently tracing their initials with her fingertip on the nape of her daughter's neck.

"Pour les jumeaux," Henry whispered.

A young girl's voice agreed, "For the twins."

Epilogue

Charles Stanstead was released from the Vermont State Mental Hospital in the summer of 1966. Despite Cynthia Stanstead's pleas, Charles and Virginia decided it was best to relocate back to Derby Line by the end of summer, where they initially stayed with one of Virginia's relatives before eventually crossing into Quebec.

Eva Martin was heartbroken to say goodbye. It was worse than losing a sibling and a daughter. She left Merrill's shoe store, took a job in the blueprint department at the machine shop, working alongside Sam, and retired early, a few years before him. They spent the rest of their lives camping, fishing, and driving Little Red Riding Hood all over New England and parts north, until the wheels fell off. They met the Stansteads one more time for a lunch rendezvous in Magog, Quebec. Cynthia had grown into a tall, beautiful young woman, and Charles assured them she would be breaking hearts until the right, worthy young man swept her off her feet. Eva never asked what she and Charles laughed about while speaking French, which, by then, even Virginia was fluent in.

Henry died peacefully the following year, and Ruby stayed in the house until dementia eventually took her life sixteen years later, by then having forgotten Eva, Sam, and her sons' names. Alzheimer's was a silent killer.

Smokey and Impy crossed the rainbow bridge before Alice Fairbanks reunited with her beloved Reginald after battling a brief but fierce fight with breast cancer. Since she had no heirs, she bequeathed all her remaining assets, including her home, to Eva and Sam.

Constance Isabel and Warren considered moving to Shasta, California, but Eva begged Connie not to go. *What's done is done.* Connie was pregnant again, and Eva was determined to help her grandchild spread its wings and venture far from the family crabapple tree.

And Richard Poole? He's now the Police Chief in Sumner Falls. He continues to park and wait patiently, hidden partway up the McSwains' driveway, but sometimes he doesn't catch 'em.

Acknowledgements

First and foremost, I wish to thank my wife, Laura, and our wonderful children, Taylor, Connor, and Samuel (yes, he's named after our family's accused and hanged Salem witch, Samuel Wardwell, September 22, 1692).

Secondly, for the record, no blue jays were harmed in the research and crafting of this contemporary fictional tale.

As you may have guessed, my grandmother kept a daily journal from 1963 to 2009. An affair was real… a murder not so much. It was a deliberate stylistic choice to make Eva's epistolary entries raw, including grammatical and punctuation errors.

In case anyone doubts, yes, we native New Englanders, especially those from rural areas, occasionally speak oddly, bending the rules of traditional North American English. For example, while there's no fixed definition of what constitutes cold, temperatures below zero—approaching minus 20 degrees Fahrenheit—are known to inspire phrases like, "Colder than a witch's tit in a cast iron bra" or "Colder than a well digger's ass." I'm not exactly sure which temperature ranges each phrase refers to, but rest assured, children definitely say these on the school playground at recess without getting sent to the principal's office.

And, of course, the ubiquitous Vermont go-to curse, "Jeezum Crow." Along with another crowd favorite, which is: Garage might be spelled with one *r*, but we say it with two—ga-rar-ge. Try it; it's addictive. You've been warned.

There's another, and it's one of my favorites: Hamburg. There is no 'er'. In fact, my early childhood CB Radio handle (that's another story for another time and place) was "The Hamburg Kid." And that's because my favorite meal back in the day at the local A&W consisted of five hamburgs (no cheese) and a quart of milk. How often, you ask? No comment.

And finally, one might wonder where the phrase "A-Number One" comes from. Well, there was once a kind New Hampshire lumberjack, who was wise and along in years, who shared his jug of maple syrup sweetened iced tea on a hot summer day and proclaimed its refreshing taste as: "Ayutt, that's A-Number One!" Rest in peace, Charlie. It became one of my grandmother's daily expressions for anything that pleased her.

And for those who are still flummoxed by the Vermont accent on the pronunciation of "ayutt," it's all in the short, sharp glottal stop.

I want to thank all my beta readers for catching my mistakes! Vanessa Brown, Tim Faust, Mary Koeppel, and Carrie Teffner, for reading multiple drafts and finding all of my mistakes. Any remaining mistakes are all mine to own.

Once again, a special thanks to Max Fonseca for his tongue-twisting and catchy colloquialisms, "The situation of it being" and "The thing about it of it is."

And finally, yes, I was an unscathed GenX survivor of Lawn Darts.